DARK
MATTERS

DARK MATTERS

First in the Dark Matters Trilogy

MICHAEL DOW

ISBN 978-0-996937-5-11

Published and Distributed by
128 Publishing
PO Box 721 • Traverse City MI 49685
www.darkmattersbook.com

For Melissa, Amanda, and Rachel
My inspiration.

Mike Dow

ONE

Man holds in his mortal hands the power to abolish all forms
of human poverty. And all forms of human life.

– John F. Kennedy

At one hundred twenty-eight miles per hour, it was no small feat to look away from the road, even for an instant. But Carl stole a quick glance, catching sight of his wife and daughter, asleep in the seats behind him. He still wasn't sure why they had changed their mind and joined him, but he was glad for the company, nonetheless.

He had chewed through the Long Island Expressway, seventy miles from Manhattan to the Manorville exit, in barely half an hour. Leaving Manhattan at three in the morning certainly helped–as did his regular donations to each of the myriad police departments along the way. The darkness didn't deter him either–Carl had been driving this route for thirty-plus years. He knew the road like he knew every crease and crevice in his favorite Italian leather jacket, now folded neatly on the seat beside him.

Carl Wilson, for over fifteen years the CEO of General Resources, Incorporated, didn't consider himself reckless. And though some of his colleagues might have disagreed, he saw the drive just as he saw his time at GRI; as a series of well-calculated and manageable risks. Even now, as he left Route 111 and accelerated up the ramp to Route 27 for the final leg to their weekend home, he reflected on the vehicle at his command. At a time when even the common man could nearly afford an autocar, Carl still preferred to have his own hands on the wheel–in this case, a sophisticated array of controls that put nearly every function directly at his fingertips. It was a degree of control that suited him well, and befitted the CEO of the world's first multi-trillion dollar conglomerate.

To be sure, it was no ordinary autocar. The custom-designed machine had set him back over eight million dollars. It included a multitude of performance and safety features–from polymer resin and carbon fiber body panels that stored the electric power, to an onboard control system that monitored and even anticipated his every move and command. But the real cost had been in a handful of extravagant extras, like the claytronic seating; his shape-changing seats could be configured in an infinite number of positions. Even now, his wife and daughter were ensconced in a pair of perfectly contoured, lie-flat beds; they would sleep, safe and sound, until they reached their destination.

He continued his acceleration up the ramp, and merged onto the empty highway. Before long, the open fields on either side would give way to more populated towns, forcing him to slow down. So he pushed the accelerator further, enjoying a final few minutes of exhilaration. He'd had more than his share of adrenaline over the past twenty-four hours, but another small dose was always welcome.

As the car barreled down the last stretch of open highway, Carl's mind wandered to the events of the previous day. In all his years as CEO, he could count on one hand the number of arguments he had lost. And he didn't intend to lose this one–even if it was with the Chairman. The two of them didn't argue often, but when they did, the sparks flew. This so-called *end game* that the Chairman had proposed was a non-starter, as far as Carl was concerned. And he had no intention of backing down; he could only hope they would reconsider the request. In the meantime, he had made his position clear.

All he could do now was wait–and take some much-needed time off. A long weekend would do him wonders, especially when it included Barbara and Lilly. With Lilly's college graduation less than a year away, there were precious few of these opportunities still remaining. He was determined to take advantage of them.

They were just passing over the Route 24 interchange, Carl's landmark to begin a gradual deceleration. Beyond that was Shinnecock Canal, the unofficial gateway to the Hamptons. His house was a secluded retreat in Montauk, at the eastern end of Long Island. Over the years, he had seen more than his share of drunken fools on this final stretch of road–even at this hour. So he released the accelerator, allowing the car to reduce speed over the mile-long span leading up to the bridge.

Strangely, the car didn't slow. Carl put his foot on the brake, applying light pressure with the ball of his foot. There was no response. He pressed harder, feeling another surge of adrenaline through his veins. If anything, the car was now going faster. He looked out the window as they gained speed–the tall pine trees were a blur, flashing past in a rush. He pumped the brakes again, using all of his weight. Still nothing. He disabled the autocar system, punched the ignition button, and even tried the windows. It was all for naught.

On both sides of the road, guardrails appeared; the bridge over the canal was rapidly approaching. In an act of desperation, he wrenched the wheel to the right, hoping to slow the vehicle by grinding it against the guardrail. But the wheel wouldn't budge. All his effort didn't cause the car to veer an inch from its course.

Time slowed; Carl turned to look once more at his wife and daughter. They were serene and beautiful as they slept in the seats behind him, headphones in place, blissfully unaware. He couldn't bring himself to wake them. White noise crashed through his head; the rush of blood was becoming more than he could stand.

He turned to the front, just as the car swerved sharply toward the guardrail on his right. With a dull thud and a jolt, the guardrail gave way, offering oddly little resistance.

The car careened through the opening, plunging toward the trees below. Carl's last thought formed around a single, ineloquent word.

Bastards.

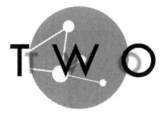

The snake which cannot cast its skin has to die.

– Friedrich Nietzsche

Rudy paced the length of the foyer, searching hopelessly for that elusive link between patience and virtue. Across the room, a wide, marble staircase curved to the second floor of their Manhattan penthouse, and to their master suite. His wife, Victoria, was still up there, and he knew better than to yell up those stairs. Instead, he paused his pacing, and took another deep breath.

From where he stood, a large picture window overlooked Central Park, and the city skyline to the east. It was a view that precious few residents enjoyed–and yet, it did little to improve his mood. Instead of the brilliant fall colors, he saw grays and browns, as cement and dirt continued its inexorable march across formerly grass-covered fields. The irony wasn't lost on him–no money to water the grass in Central Park, but billions for floodwalls to keep water away. Only a fool could avoid connecting the dots.

New York politics at its best.

His gaze returned to the street far below, and the traffic running along Central Park West. As far as he could tell, there was still no sign of his car. He triple-blinked, activating the Net overlay built into his contact lenses. It was past four o'clock; they would be cutting it close. His eyes darted left, opening a local map display. He saw his car, just a few blocks away. The thinnest of smiles crossed his lips. *Small victories.* A quick stare at the *close* icon, and the display disappeared.

Rudy turned and stole a look in the foyer mirror, running a hand through his gray-flecked hair. He was ready, at least. As he resumed his solitary march, a familiar chirp came through his earpiece. Reflexively, he reached up and touched the device. Though most of his colleagues now had a communications implant, Rudy still wore his earpiece tucked neatly against the bone, just behind his right ear. He liked the feel of it– the physical presence of the technology. And after thirty-plus years in the business, he wasn't about to embed another company's product into his own body.

"I'm here, sir."

The car had arrived, though more than ten minutes after he had sent the signal. They were going to need extra time to get across town. He took one more look up the stairs, shook his head, and turned toward his study. He could buy Victoria a few extra minutes if he said goodbye to the kids while he waited.

The study doors were closed; he pressed his ear against the small crack between them, listening for signs of activity. He strained to decipher the muffled sounds–hushed whispers, a rustling of paper, perhaps even a giggle. The girls had claimed to be doing homework, but he'd bet money they were messing with the nano-replicator he'd just brought home from the office. He pushed the doors wide, to a scene of flailing arms, wide eyes, and two teenage girls, brandishing looks of unadulterated innocence.

"How's the homework coming, ladies?"

"Hey Dad, are you and mom leaving now?" His younger daughter, Shae, was a master of the deft subject change. The slight tilt of the head, the disarming smile, and the gleam in her dark brown eyes only added to the effect.

"We are," Rudy replied.

"I wish we could go to the funeral," Rudy's older daughter, Sonja, chimed in. "Lilly was our friend, too."

Rudy considered the question again, though he and Victoria had already discussed the topic at length. Lilly had been the girl's favorite babysitter, but she was also the only daughter of Rudy's long-time boss and mentor, Carl Wilson. The tragedy of the accident was still sinking in.

"I know you'd both like to go," Rudy said. "But it's going to be mostly adults, and crowded. It's better that you stay here." Truth be told, Victoria wanted the kids to join them, but Rudy had put his foot down. Given yesterday's announcement of his promotion, and the inevitable awkwardness that might come as a result, he wanted to be able to control the environment. And his girls, as much as he loved them, were about as easy to control as New York City weather.

"We'll vid you on the way back, so you can pretend to be doing homework when we walk in." Humor was Rudy's way of changing the topic; he knew full well where Shae had gotten her subject-shifting talents.

"Very funny, Dad," Sonja said. "We'll be done before you get back, don't worry." Sonja was the diligent one; Rudy knew she'd at least make the effort.

"Rosie!" Rudy directed his shout toward the kitchen. Rosie was the family's primary home-bot, and another perk of Rudy's position at GRI. He had a soft spot for Rosie, having led the efforts to develop key aspects of her learning algorithms, many years ago. So although Rosie's torso and limbs were regularly upgraded with the latest technologies, her knowledge—and personality—had been with them for years. Rosie also managed the rest of the Dersch household home-bots; Rudy couldn't imagine life without her.

Rosie soon appeared at the study doors, striding into the room with an ease that spoke to her state-of-the-art kinematics, and the sophistication of her artificial muscles and joints. Her degrees of motion, in fact, now far surpassed that of any human. As did the capacity of her artificial-intelligence brain. She stopped next to Rudy, awaiting further instruction.

"Rosie, make sure the homework gets done. You can help, just don't do it for them. You know the rules."

Rudy pointed to the machine on his desk.

"And be sure they leave the nano-replicator alone," he added. "No new puppies while we're gone."

"Dad," Shae said. She was rolling her eyes, though a small smile also escaped her lips.

"Love you, ladies," Rudy said as he blew them each a kiss, and pulled the study doors closed. They would be in good hands with Rosie.

Rudy returned to the foyer just as Victoria was descending the stairs. She looked as radiant today as she did on their wedding day, almost twenty years ago. Tall, lithe, and classically elegant, her knee-length black dress included a modest V at the neck, sleeves to the elbow, and a stylish pattern of crisscrossed straps across her upper back. Accented with thin black gloves and a simple pearl-and-diamond-pendant necklace, she looked every part the wife of a newly-minted CEO.

Rudy soaked in the view. *No way a guy from South Jersey deserves that.* He had worked hard to get to where he was, but he knew that luck had played just as big a role. Like the night some friends had dragged him to a charity event hosted by Victoria's parents. He had been lucky that day–in both love *and* life, he recalled with a grin.

"The car is here. We should get going." Rudy grabbed two coats from the closet.

"Have you spoken to the girls?" she replied, looking down the hallway.

"I did. They're fine. Doing homework with Rosie." Rudy knew it was a partial truth, but they'd been over this topic before. No harm, no foul, he liked to say.

"Bye girls! Love you!" Victoria shouted toward the study as she pulled on her coat. Rudy was already out the door, waiting for the elevator.

●●●●●

At the street, the doorman rushed to hold the car door for them. He was the third or fourth doorman this year–Rudy had lost track. It didn't help that they seemed to come and go like the wind, and at the whim of the building residents. Rudy tried his best to remember the names, but it was no easy task.

"Thank you, Cedric." Victoria, of course, had always been good with names. Rudy smiled and slid into the seat next to her.

"Eighteen minutes to destination, sir." Rudy had already provided the destination, but he liked to re-confirm once in the car. His was pure autocar–without a steering wheel or even a front seat. Technically, he and his wife were in the front seat, with another row for the kids behind them. It wasn't his first fully-automated model; he hadn't wrapped his hands around a steering wheel in years. He just didn't see the point.

Rudy leaned forward. "Bond, confirm destination, 460 Madison Avenue." The car's command word didn't have to be customized, but Rudy found it amusing to be chauffeured around the city by a twentieth century British spy. He had even watched a few of the movies. Rudy had an affinity for twentieth century culture; he had named his home-bot as well as his assistant, Grace, after obscure television and movie characters from that era.

"Confirmed. Eighteen minutes to destination, sir." Bond accelerated into the heavy traffic on Central Park West–a move aided by his real-time link to the other autocars on the street. It was only the few idiots still driving their own cars that caused problems these days; Rudy wished they would ban them from the city, once and for all.

The trip to the church was relatively short. Rudy watched the city flow by, listening to the hum of the streets, and the cacophony of sounds that made the city so unique. He couldn't imagine living or working anywhere else. Of course, his version of living was a bit out of touch with the vast majority of city residents–all twenty-five million of them. He felt no guilt about it; he had clawed his way to the top from almost nothing. Though admittedly, he had a hand-up from a few others–like Victoria's family, and Carl. But that was how it worked. The fact that the same feat was all but impossible today wasn't Rudy's problem. If it was his to do over again, he'd find a way. He was sure of it.

"This whole thing feels so surreal." Victoria's comment brought him back from his musings. "Are you ready for the funeral? And all the rest of it?" He could see the concern at the corners of her eyes, and in the turn of her lips. But he could also hear a touch of pride in her tone.

"Ready as I'll ever be. I know Carl wanted me to have the job. I just wish it could have come some other way."

The circumstances behind Carl's accident continued to baffle him. No one had seen it; no one had heard it. And no one could understand it. Carl had been driving that stretch of road for years–decades, in fact. The investigation had discovered a malfunction in the controls of his multi-million dollar, custom autocar. It wasn't merely tragic; it just didn't make sense. Some of the best engineers in the world maintained that car.

And that was only the beginning of the whirlwind. The past week had been the most intense of Rudy's life, as the tragedy was quickly supplanted by the inevitable office politics amongst the remaining GRI senior executives. It had all come to a head yesterday, less than a week later, with the formal announcement of Rudolph Dersch as Carl's successor, and GRI's new CEO.

They arrived at St. Patrick's Cathedral twenty minutes early, just as he had planned. The autocar stopped on 50th before reaching Madison, dropping them at a side entrance. Rudy helped Victoria out of the vehicle, which then disappeared to find parking. It would stay close, thanks to the price-is-no-object setting he used in the parking parameters. Turning away from the curb, the two of them quietly slipped through the 50th street entrance.

Inside, the grandeur of the church took hold of him. Rudy wasn't Catholic–or even particularly religious, for that matter–but Carl had been a long-time fixture in New York's Catholic community. That, along with a sizable donation to the latest restoration efforts, was enough to secure St. Patrick's on short notice–though they had to settle for a Thursday afternoon. The sanctuary was massive, and yet it was already close to full.

Rudy took a deep breath, as the significance of the moment began to set in.

"We should find a place to sit," Victoria said.

Rudy watched her scan the crowd as she escorted them toward the center of the church. His eyes caught sight of the caskets–all three of them–dominating the broad expanse of the altar. Even the vibrant colors of the stained glass windows, flashing vivid hues in the afternoon sun, couldn't distract from the somber scene. They worked their way through the crowd to join the rest of the GRI executives.

Rudy did his best to engage in small talk as they walked, accepting a mixture of congratulations and condolences–though the sincerity was occasionally lacking for the former. Of course, a few of them had thrown all their chips on the table and openly lobbied for the CEO position; they knew the likely consequences. Rudy did little to hide it, holding their handshake just an awkward moment too long, and giving them his best see-you-next-week greeting and big, phony smile.

But all the while, it was hard for Rudy to ignore Carl's presence. The sooner the funeral got started, the better. Victoria led the way to the front of the church, where they found seats next to GRI's Chief Operating Officer. The woman only hesitated a moment before sliding over, giving them the aisle. Victoria gave her an appreciative smile before turning back to wink at Rudy.

The funeral service was about to begin.

● ● ● ● ●

After the service, Rudy exited to 5th Avenue, where they joined the rest of the attendees. The funeral had been poignant–most notably one of the eulogies, delivered by Lilly's childhood friend. It had been a good decision to leave the kids at home, he was sure.

Rudy was still shaking hands and talking with a few colleagues when a long, black sedan fought its way through the traffic and pulled to the curb. A door opened, and a portly, older man with a cane struggled out of the car. He ambled directly to where Rudy was standing.

"Good to see you, Rudy. Sorry we aren't meeting under better circumstances." Arthur Knowles was a member of the GRI Board of Directors, a position he had held for several years. Rudy had met him on numerous occasions, but had gotten to know him significantly better over the past few days. He had the slightest of British accents; Arthur had been raised in London, but spent the vast majority of his career in the United States.

"Hello, Arthur. Good to see you," Rudy said.

"Might I have a word with you?" Arthur said. "I'm sorry to bother you on a day like this, but it is a pressing matter. If it could wait, it would."

Rudy looked at Victoria, then back to Arthur. "Let me first send Victoria on her way."

Arthur shook his head. "Actually, Victoria can stay if you'd like. She's family, right?"

Rudy shot Victoria another glance; she remained in place, waiting impassively.

"Of course," Rudy replied.

Arthur leaned in, close to Rudy's ear, lowering his voice below the din of the crowd.

"We have a bit of a crisis," he began, "In part due to the recent change in leadership. Without boring you over the details, there are some activities underway that need immediate attention. Things that Carl was personally overseeing. I'm pulling the details together now, but I'm afraid we won't be ready until tomorrow evening. I do apologize; I know it's a Friday. The whole thing shouldn't take more than a few hours."

To her credit, Victoria didn't react. Rudy could guess what she was thinking, but she would let him handle it. And most likely, she'd handle him later.

He took a quick moment to consider the invitation; he knew it wasn't really a request. Someday, he'd learn when he could say no—but one day into his tenure as CEO wasn't that day.

"Arthur, I'm happy to help. How about tomorrow evening, say six o'clock?"

"Six o'clock it is. And I promise not to keep him out too late." He gave Victoria a grin, though it appeared a bit forced.

"That would be great," Rudy said. "I have a nine o'clock virtual reality date with the girls. Big trouble if I miss it."

"Excellent," Arthur replied. "I'll see you then." Arthur shuffled back to the sedan. A moment later, it pulled away from the curb and disappeared.

Rudy turned back to Victoria. They began to thread their way through the dwindling crowd, and toward their car.

"Nice move with the nine o'clock thing," Victoria said. "The girls will be thrilled to hear about the date." She gave Rudy the smallest of smirks.

"Just trying to establish some ground rules," Rudy said. "Are you complaining?"

"No, as long as you're actually back by nine."

"I'll do the best I can, but you know how that goes." Rudy paused for a moment. "Maybe you'd better not tell the girls I said nine o'clock. I'll surprise them."

"Well, you're right about one thing. If you're home by nine o'clock, you'll certainly surprise them."

Rudy knew where this conversation was going; better to shift gears now.

"Look, the car is already here," he said. Bond was waiting at the curb, having returned to the precise spot where it had left them.

Rudy opened the door; Victoria slid inside. He climbed in behind her as she continued to look at him.

"Thanks for the help today," he said. "You were fantastic." He took her hand and gave it a squeeze. Just to be safe, he leaned in and gave her a kiss. She gave him her patented, lucky-I-put-up-with-you face. He wasn't fooling her, he knew. But apparently, she was going to let him get away with one. This time, at least.

Rudy turned to face the front of the autocar. "Bond, take us home." Bond signaled his acceptance, and pulled away from the curb.

Giving directions to his British-spy-turned-driver never failed to put a smile on Rudy's face.

THREE

Art washes away from the soul the dirt of everyday life.

– Picasso

"Don't give me that look," Monique said, stepping back from the nineteenth century Degas self-portrait she had been wiping down with a soft cloth. Despite her warning, Degas did nothing to avert his stare.

"I know where you live," she added, pointing a finger.

Degas remained unimpressed.

Monique smiled as she continued to wipe down the painting. She enjoyed her time alone in the gallery; as both manager and curator, she had plenty of it. Her back-and-forth with Degas helped pass the time–and occasionally, even led to small moments of self-discovery. Today, however, her debate with Degas was interrupted by a customer–a tall, slim man who pushed his way through the front door. He strode purposefully to the center of the room, glancing about as he walked. He wasn't someone she had seen in the gallery before.

Monique remained where she stood, covertly watching the man as he took in his surroundings. She gave him a minute to browse, and approached only after his third or fourth furtive glance in her direction. Monique was hard to miss–a tall, exotic beauty with long dark hair and an athletic build. Her olive complexion and pale blue eyes, flecked with hints of gold, made her mixed heritage difficult to decipher. She was in her mid-thirties, but guesses at her age were often wildly off-base.

She gave the man a warm smile, crossing the room and extending her hand.

"Welcome to Art and Soul," she said. "My name is Monique Durand. Are you looking for something in particular?"

He shook her hand, offering a curt smile. He was clearly a man of wealth–a custom-tailored charcoal suit, expensive watch, shoes polished to a mirror shine–all the clues were there, even for someone without Monique's keen eye. But most of all, it was in his stare; the practiced look of seeing right through people he deemed beneath him. Monique recognized that sign almost immediately.

"Actually, I need something for a party. My name is Charles. Charles Jones."

Monique nodded. "Is this a gift?" she asked. "Can you tell me a little about the recipient?"

"No, sorry. It's our dinner party. A fundraiser for a friend. My wife wants something new for over the mantel. Says it will help raise money." Charles glanced around the room, settling on a portrait that hung on the far wall.

"How about that one?" he said. "She looks a bit like my mother." He pointed to the painting.

They crossed the room together, stopping a few feet from the painting.

"This is a work by Robert Henri," she said. "He's a well-known nineteenth century American artist. His work is still on display in a number of galleries, including one here in Washington DC. This one has an interesting story–"

"Yes, yes, perfect. How much?"

Monique was beginning to wonder whether the man even cared about art. Most likely, he cared to the extent that it matched the window treatments and didn't clash with their latest taste in furniture. She did some quick calculations.

"It's a unique piece," she said. "I'd need to go check, but I'm sure it's north of four million. Is that in the range you were looking to spend?"

"How about we say four point five and call it done?"

Monique paused, considering the offer. She was sure he'd pay more, if she pushed him. But that meant she'd have to spend more time talking to him.

"Are you able to purchase it right now?" she said.

Charles walked to the small counter and pointed to the scanner. "Fire away."

Monique followed behind, punching her code into the terminal as she turned to face him. She touched the screen and retrieved the Henri painting. Her quote had been right on the mark.

"With all the taxes, the total is–," she began. But before she could complete the sentence, Charles interrupted her again.

"Oh, and I do need that delivered. The party is tonight. Did I mention that?" He pulled a card from his pocket and handed it to her. "This is the address."

Monique looked up as she took the card. "I'm sorry, but I'm the only one here. We could most likely deliver it sometime tomorrow, but I won't know until the morning. Sorry about that."

Charles' voice took on a more formal tone. "I really need it there tonight. I'm happy to pay you for your time, why don't you add five thousand to the bill?"

Unbelievable. She did her best to hide her growing ire.

"Mister Jones, I appreciate that you're in a rush. But I can't do a delivery. The painting is large, it's heavy, it needs to be properly packaged for transport, and I don't have an autocar–I'd have to drive it myself. So it's just not practical. If it's that urgent, perhaps you could wait while I pack it? Then you could take it with you."

Charles shifted his feet and leaned in a bit closer, making a point to look down at her.

"I'm not trying to be difficult," he said. "I stopped in from the office and I'm not heading home. I can't wait, I can't take it with me, and I really do need the painting tonight. How about we say ten thousand dollars for your trouble?"

It was all Monique could do to remain calm. *Does he really think I'm for sale?* She considered telling him what he could do with his cash. Just for an instant, she even considered telling the pompous fool that his net worth was probably a fraction of hers. But she bit her tongue; she knew that Gloria, the gallery owner, really needed this sale. The profit from this single painting would pay the bills for months. So she swallowed her pride.

"I'd be happy to deliver the painting. It's just going to be this evening before I can get it to the house. Is that all right?"

Charles straightened and gave her a smug look—it sent a chill down her spine.

"You know," he said, "I have another idea. Since you'll be coming to the house anyway, why don't you stay? We could use an extra hand. Serving drinks, that kind of thing. We'd pay you, of course. And who knows? You might meet a few other people worth knowing."

Breathe, Monique thought. She made a face to imply she was considering the offer, just to buy a few extra seconds to regain her composure.

"Thank you, Mister Jones," she said at last. "But I have plans tonight."

"Of course you do," he said. "But you have my card—call me if you change your mind."

"And I don't just mean tonight."

Monique clenched both hands, willing herself to control the tempest that was swelling inside her. An icy stare was all that escaped.

"How about we settle the bill?" she said. "I gave you a discount to make the total an even five million."

Kill him with kindness. She set aside some other options that had crossed her mind.

Charles nodded, pressing his thumb to the scanner. Monique heard the familiar *beep,* and shifted her gaze to watch the transaction's progress. It felt like an hour, though she knew it took just a few seconds. The *double-beep* confirmed that the funds had been transferred.

"All set. Thanks for your purchase." Monique looked up as she extended her hand.

Charles was already halfway out the door.

FOUR

*I have a theory that the truth is never told
during the nine-to-five hours.*

– Hunter S Thompson

Rudy had his feet on the desk, enjoying the welcome respite of his home office. Friday morning had been a blur of meetings and calls, so he had come home to spend the afternoon buried in the details of GRI's divisions and subsidiaries. Some were well known and part of the public portfolio. But others, through a byzantine network of shell companies and foreign interests, were not. He was familiar with most of the technology-related businesses; he had grown up in that world. But the media divisions, the various manufacturing businesses, their space-based operations, consumer products, finance, and security solutions–they were far less familiar. He spent time on the phone with old and new colleagues, and by the end of the day, he feared he had already forgotten as much as he had learned. It would have been far easier if Carl had been here to ease the transition.

Victoria and the kids returned home around five. As Rosie served dinner, Sonja regaled them with the latest gossip from school. Shae took notes, Rudy was sure. The discussion revolved around boys, virtual vacations, and whether Sonja could go to Rio de Janeiro with a boy named Carlos–

virtually, of course. Rudy could barely keep up with the machine-gun pace of the discussion. But Victoria seemed to be saying *no* about four times as often as she was saying *yes*, so he was fairly certain that no permanent damage was being done. Still, Sonja wasn't quite ready to let it go.

"I know Carlos, Mom," she said. "He's really nice."

"No you don't," Victoria replied. "You don't *know* Carlos–you *know of* Carlos. You've only met him in virtual reality."

"What's the difference? I know some of my virtual reality friends better than I know most of the kids in school. Who cares where they live?"

"I care," Victoria said. "When you join us here in the real world, face-to-face relationships matter."

"Carlos *is* a real-world friend. He just happens to live in Brazil."

Victoria gave Rudy a look; he was trying his best not to laugh. But Victoria was having none of it.

"I think our generations have a different definition of the word *friend*, sweetheart," she said. "My friends are people who are a part of my real life. The short list of people who are willing to walk in, when everyone else is walking out. The rest are just acquaintances. I'm not sure your generation has discovered the difference yet."

"What I want to know is–when are we going to discover dessert?" Shae stood up from the table, spoon in hand. Of course, Rosie wasn't going to serve anything until an adult gave the approval. But Victoria nodded, and the argument quickly turned to a battle over dessert choices. Rudy remained on the sidelines for that debate, as well.

At least some topics span generations.

Shortly before six, he excused himself, giving Victoria and the girls a kiss goodbye. He rode the elevator down to the building lobby, where Arthur was already waiting with a car. Rudy climbed in.

It was a quiet ride to GRI headquarters. Arthur seemed preoccupied, and Rudy was still processing the day's research. As they pulled to the entrance, Rudy hopped from the car, circling to Arthur's side and offering him a hand. Arthur waived him off, using his cane and the doorframe to extract himself from the vehicle. They walked together to the main door; the security system recognized both of them as they approached, and de-activated the door lock. Rudy held the door for Arthur, and followed him inside.

"The boardroom, I assume?" Rudy strode past the guard station and toward a door against the far wall. He had always found it strange that the GRI boardroom was on the first floor, and had said as much to Carl. Carl called it a concession to the older Board members—a fact Rudy could better appreciate as he waited for Arthur to join him. A few times, though, he had heard Carl tell others that GRI preferred a room for getting things done—not for daydreaming over dazzling views of the city. That was the version that Rudy would repeat, if asked.

"Yes and no." Arthur's words brought Rudy back to the present.

"Sorry, what?" Rudy said.

"You asked if we were going to the boardroom. And my answer was yes, and no."

Rudy smiled. "Well, I hope the meeting itself is a bit less ambiguous."

"It will be," Arthur said. He pushed open the boardroom door, and Rudy followed him inside.

The room was empty. In fact, it didn't appear to be ready for any type of meeting, let alone a GRI board meeting. No food, no drinks, no headsets or e-pads. Nothing. Rudy heard the door lock behind them; in fact, he would have sworn he heard the faint hiss of sliding metal-on-metal.

"Okay, Arthur. Can you clue me in?"

Arthur waved his hand, gesturing for Rudy to follow him. Rudy trailed behind as Arthur walked toward a small closet in the corner of the room. Arthur turned as he reached the door, speaking in a subdued tone.

"Rudy, what I'm about to show you is known to just a handful of people on the planet. I'd ask that you bear with me for a few minutes. You are going to have questions; I promise they'll all be answered in due course."

Arthur disappeared into the closet. Rudy was still processing his last words when a faint, low-pitched hum broke the silence. Rudy turned to see all of the window blinds lowering to cover the windows. The room darkened as the blinds fully obscured their street-level view. From the corner of his eye, Rudy caught another motion, and turned to see the wood-paneled back wall of the room split and slide apart at the center. The two pieces slid aside in near-silent harmony; Rudy could see no tracks or moving parts in the floor or ceiling. Until this moment, Rudy would have bet a month's salary that the massive wooden wall was immobile, as it held dozens of monitors, cameras, holographic projectors, and untold other electronic gadgetry. In fact, some of the monitors now hung precariously over the edge of the split, serving to hide most of the middle seam. When the walls came to a halt, a six-foot gap had been created, exposing a polished silver section of floor that didn't match the rest of the room. Rudy looked back at Arthur, who was closing the closet door.

"Come with me," Arthur said.

He walked across the room and stood in the space between the two walls. He motioned for Rudy to join him. Rudy hesitated–more from annoyance than fear. *What the hell was going on?*

He crossed the room to join Arthur. "Neat trick. Care to explain?"

Arthur put a finger in the air, while waving his other hand near the wall. "Best if you stand in the middle."

Rudy took a step toward the center. Silent as a whisper, the floor dropped out from under him.

● ● ● ● ●

The metal platform descended at a quick but not break-neck pace. Rudy's body had reflexively stiffened when the floor fell away; it had taken him a moment to catch his balance. It was an elevator without walls–in fact, he could still see the ceiling of the boardroom when he craned his neck upward. Doing so, however, caused a near-vertigo sensation, so he quickly returned his gaze to the floor. Through his peripheral vision, he could see a seamless, silver-metallic wall sliding by on all sides. The lack of markings or seams made it difficult to judge their speed or distance travelled, but he was sure they had descended at least two or three floors. *Into the rock under Manhattan.*

Rudy tried to regain his composure, glancing over at Arthur. He stood there, impassively, running one hand lightly along the wall as it passed them by. Rudy opened his mouth to speak, just as the platform slowed its pace, and then stopped its descent. Arthur again waved his hand; Rudy heard another hiss, and turned to see a set of doors swing open. They revealed a short hallway, barren except for a few overhead lights, and ending ten feet away at another set of doors.

"Follow me."

The two men stepped off the platform, with Rudy following behind. The only sound was the thumping of Arthur's cane as he ambled down the hallway. They reached the doors, where Rudy counted a keypad, at least two cameras, and several other small openings of unknown intent scattered around the space. *Tight security, even for GRI standards.*

"Stand still," Arthur directed. A green light flashed on the keypad. Arthur punched in a long key code sequence, and the doors in front of them responded with a metallic click.

Old school. He hadn't seen a security keypad in decades. He couldn't imagine having to remember all those codes.

Arthur pulled one door open, and gestured for Rudy to precede him into the room.

There was nothing *old school* about the room; Rudy did his best to absorb what he saw. The room wasn't large, and there were two other people working inside. But it wasn't the size or the people that drew most of Rudy's attention; rather, it was the technology. Displays of all types and sizes filled the walls; a holographic video-conferencing system sat in one corner. But the real attention-grabber was the array of pure processing power he could see through a line of glass windows, in a separate room to his left. Rudy understood the implication, especially in a world where one computer processor contained more processing power than the human brain. He could not begin to fathom the power, and the cost, of the equipment in that room—it dwarfed even the best of GRI's impressive processing centers.

It's a command center. But where were the commanders?

Rudy looked at Arthur, who was clearly allowing him a moment to take in his surroundings. He shifted his stance, feeling an odd rush in his veins as he alternated between bewilderment and annoyance.

Rudy made a conscious effort to relax, and speak in a level voice.

"I suppose I should say thank you," he began. "For showing me what's under my own company. Now how about filling me in?"

"Of course. But first, some introductions."

Arthur pointed to his right, where a thin, older man sat hunched over a small desk.

"This is Gunnar Gerst, a world-class mathematician and economist whom I'm sure you've never heard of." Gunnar raised his eyes and gave a perfunctory wave before returning to his work. "And that," Arthur pointed to a man in the computing room, "is our Technology Director, Liu Xhang. He helps keep the lights on." Liu had his back to them and didn't turn to acknowledge the introduction; Rudy wasn't even sure if Liu could hear them.

"Rudy, come have a seat at the conference table. What I need to tell you is going to take some time. Can I get you a drink?"

Rudy shook his head. He took a seat, and Arthur joined him, leaning his cane against the corner of the table.

"First, let me ease one of your concerns. Aside from the access point, this facility is entirely unrelated to your company. Though of course," Arthur paused for a moment and smiled, "I'd prefer to call it *our* company. In any case, I should also tell you that this facility has been here for nearly twenty years."

Arthur pulled a piece of paper from his pocket, glancing at it briefly before looking back at Rudy. "I don't give this speech often, so forgive me if I use some notes. Let me start at the beginning and provide some context. Then, you can ask your questions."

"Sounds good," Rudy said.

"The story goes back more than a hundred years. In 1970, the wealthiest one percent owned less than ten percent of the world's assets. Barely forty years later, they owned over half. In fact, there was a decade in the early twenty-first century when over ninety percent of all new wealth went to the richest one percent. The media noticed, of course. And the attitudes of the *nouveau-riche* didn't help, either—they were too stupid to realize the impact that their lavish and public lifestyles were having on the masses."

"I'm one of the *nouveau-riche*, you know," Rudy interjected.

"Maybe," Arthur said. "But Victoria isn't. And you're a lot smarter than most." Arthur gave him a wry smile.

"In any case," Arthur continued, "the California riots were a tipping point. Hard to believe that was forty years ago. The history books say the riots were a result of the 2034 mid-term elections, but that's an oversimplification. The masses were fed up with the blatant disregard for equality—on many fronts. The rigging of a California senate seat by a multi-billionaire was just the final straw."

"I'm familiar with U.S. history," Rudy said. He didn't want Arthur to give him a lecture.

"Perhaps," Arthur said. "But here is what you don't know. Not long afterward, a handful of the world's wealthiest citizens got together to discuss the implications. The group represented individual and family fortunes that were a measurable percentage of the world's total wealth. It was quite a group. At the meeting, they agreed to stop talking about the issues, and to start doing something about them. To divert humanity from its path toward imminent self-destruction. What you see around you was born on that day. We call it the Consortium."

"Why–" Rudy began. But Arthur cut him off.

"I know you have questions. Let me finish giving you the background. Then I'll answer them."

Rudy nodded.

"Since then," Arthur continued, "the Consortium has done its best to help guide the course of human events–intervening only when there is clear evidence of a crisis, or a threat to what we call the *status quo*. Our mission is to maintain stability, and to help get things done–great ideas that politicians or business leaders wouldn't otherwise be able to accomplish on their own."

Arthur looked up, sweeping his arm across the room.

"Over the years, facilities like this one have been built to support the cause, and new members have been added. And when a member passes away, we look to find a suitable replacement.

"Which brings us to where we are today," Arthur finished.

Rudy took a moment to process Arthur's words. The pieces were beginning to slide into place.

"So I'm your replacement for Carl," Rudy said.

"In a way. Assuming you agree to join us." Arthur leaned in across the table. "You've been on our radar for quite a while. And Carl advocated for you. We were devastated to lose him."

Arthur stood up; he no longer appeared to need his written notes.

"All of this," he waved his hand around the room again, "would be at your disposal. And much more. Believe me when I say, the resources of the Consortium are immense. We have fewer than a hundred members, and yet those members control the majority of the world's wealth–through family assets, the positions of power that they hold, and their vast network of personal influence. Everything from media outlets, banking interests, and government leaders to educational institutions and emerging technologies."

Arthur sat back down again.

"It's the technology aspect that eventually convinced us to bring you in. We know how much you love technology, and I think you'll find that the Consortium has access to some things that are–let's say–not yet available to the general public. Over your career, you've shown a remarkable ability to find innovative uses for new technologies, and we'd like you to bring that talent to bear for us."

Arthur paused again, and appeared to be shifting gears. Rudy let him continue.

"At the same time, we want to be clear, and fair to you. This is no small thing we ask. What we do—the decisions we make—can be difficult at times. Extremely difficult. We are an organization of action—not talk. We are sometimes forced to sacrifice a few for the good of many, when the end clearly justifies the means. And I'll be the first to admit, these decisions can weigh on you."

Arthur took a breath. "One last thing. I should also mention that this is a paid position. And since I happen to know what you earn, let me just say that your GRI salary pales in comparison to what the Consortium would pay for your time and talent." Arthur folded his piece of paper and returned it to his pocket.

Rudy took a moment to reflect on Arthur's speech. It would be a colossal understatement to say it wasn't what he was expecting when he left his home barely an hour ago. But he hadn't become the CEO of GRI without an ability to think on his feet.

"Tell me about the other members." Rudy was sure he would know some of them; he could learn a lot just from the names.

"I'm sorry, Rudy, but for now the three of us in this room are the only members you'll meet. We keep it that way for a number of reasons, not the least of which is security. It's no small task to operate for forty-plus years without the world knowing you exist.

"I can tell you this, though," Arthur continued. "Collectively, Consortium members have over fifty *trillion* dollars in personal wealth. And that doesn't include the broader family fortunes—built over generations—that some of them effectively control. Or the assets they manage through business interests—global banking executives, technology executives, and the heads of large conglomerates. Like you. Plus we have a few members whose influence can't be measured merely in dollars."

"Politicians?" Rudy asked.

"No," Arthur said. "Too much ego; too little talent. A common thread amongst our membership is *decisiveness*—the ability to make tough decisions. Today's politicians are bred to *avoid* tough decisions."

Rudy considered Arthur's response; it did make sense. He decided to pursue a different line of questioning.

"Okay, put the names aside," Rudy said. "How about these decisions you mentioned? Who actually makes them? And how are they coordinated without knowing who else is involved?" Rudy paused for just a moment to frame his last question. "I'd also like to hear some examples of tough decisions, if you don't mind."

"Fair enough," Arthur said. "The short answer is that we have a simple chain of command, and we do have a well-developed and proven means for secure communication. You'll do most of your Consortium work from here, but you can also do it elsewhere–like on our private island." Arthur flashed a brief smile.

"As to your last question, what we do runs the gamut–from helping to get legislation passed, to steadying world financial markets, to developing new technologies. Anything we feel is crucial to maintaining the *status quo*. And that the world's elected leaders seem unable or unwilling to accomplish.

"But let me be even more blunt," Arthur continued. "We have, on occasion, made the decision to end a life. It's not something we do lightly, but as I said, the needs of the many can sometimes outweigh the needs of a few. And we are a group of action. So if you decide to join us, you should be comfortable with that possibility. Ask yourself–would you be willing to end one life, if it was absolutely guaranteed to save one hundred? These are the kind of decisions that a public figure cannot possibly make. So we fill that gap."

Arthur paused, but Rudy didn't speak. He was still digesting the full implication of Arthur's words. *I came to a business meeting, and instead, we're talking about killing people.* But Arthur's gaze never wavered.

"Please understand, Rudy. The Consortium is no small-time cabal. And we're not here to cater to the wealthy. For forty years, our mission has been to improve the lives of all ten billion people on this planet. And we've done that; trust me when I say, the data speaks for itself. But to do so requires a *hidden hand*. A handful of the ultra-powerful–and ultra-discrete–to make the decisions others can't. Or won't."

"To what end?" Rudy asked. "What's the end game?"

"The end game is long-term stability, in a world of rapidly dwindling resources. To find a more permanent and resource-efficient way to keep people happy."

"And under control," Rudy added.

"On the contrary," Arthur said. "No one can control ten billion people. In fact, our long-term goal is to put the Consortium out of business. A world order that no longer needs us at the controls."

"What does *that* look like?" Suddenly, Rudy had a hard time imagining humanity back at the helm.

"We're not sure yet," Arthur said. "But the clock is ticking. Humanity took a leisurely stroll through the Industrial Age–two hundred years, give or take. Then, we ran through the Information Age in barely one hundred. Now, here we are at the dawn of the Space Age. But we're over-populated, our natural resources are dwindling, and we've screwed up the planet. Most would say we were lucky to commercialize fusion power in time to replace fossil fuels–though the final verdict on the impact of climate change has yet to be written. Our window for a long-term solution is decades, or maybe even years–but certainly not centuries."

"I don't think my kids would be happy to hear that."

"Nor are we," Arthur said. "That's why Gunnar is here. In fact, it drives most of our research. And it's why we need you–to help get us across the finish line."

Arthur stood up again, grabbing his cane and pushing away from the table.

"I know this is a lot to digest," he said. "And I have a few things to discuss with Liu. So I'm going to give you a few minutes. Then I'll answer the rest of your questions."

Arthur was walking away, but Rudy wasn't quite finished. He stood up and crossed the room, catching Arthur just before he reached the processing room door.

"Arthur, one more question," Rudy said. He took a moment to gather his thoughts.

"You've described a secret organization, with members unknown even to each other, making decisions and taking action to preserve the *status quo*, I believe are the words you used."

"You could describe it that way," Arthur said.

"So in that scenario, where is the accountability?"

Arthur gave him a knowing look. "Well Rudy, I suppose you could say we're accountable to each other. But to be honest–your gut is right. There is none."

FIVE

By three methods we may learn wisdom: first, by reflection...

– Confucius

Monique didn't get to bed until nearly midnight, and when sleep finally did come, it only blackened her mood. In her dreams, she couldn't speak–which was often the case–so she ran in eerie silence, chased by a faceless horde. They gained ground, in relentless pursuit, until one reached out and touched her arm. She awoke all at once, covered in a thin film of sweat. She slept in fits and starts for the remainder of the night.

Even later, in the glow of the early morning sun, she remained in bed, fuming over the events of the previous evening. She understood the dichotomy of her world view–being wealthy, yet largely disaffected by those with a similar fortune. Or more precisely, those who abused that fortune. But understanding the source didn't help overcome her frustration.

She had spent the last several years trying to give back–to spread the wealth. And her efforts had made a difference, on a smaller scale. But her lack of impact on the broader issues had left her with an empty feeling, and ultimately caused her to question her own motivation. Where was humanity's concern for the common man? Where was the hope for the ten billion who were trying to get ahead? Or even just trying to get by? And those questions, in turn, had brought her to where she was today.

Enough with the brooding. But still she remained strewn across the bed, sheets askew, resisting the inevitability of the coming day.

At last, she mustered the energy to roll out of bed. She walked into her dressing room, pulling on a simple gym outfit. As she twisted her hair into a tight ponytail, she tried her best to forget Charles Jones, and the events of the previous evening. But it was not to be; as if on cue, a short chirping sound announced an incoming call.

Monique grabbed her earpiece, slipping it over and behind her ear. Her net lens had already popped an alert into her field of vision, telling her the call was from Gloria–technically her boss, but also a good friend. Doubtless she had seen last night's sale, and was calling for the juicy details. Monique briefly stared at the icon to accept the call.

"Hello, Gloria."

"Monique, how are you?" Gloria didn't pause for an answer. "I saw the numbers from yesterday. Thank you so much, I wasn't sure we'd ever sell that Henri!"

"I doubt the buyer knows you sold one, either," Monique said. "But a sale is a sale, right?" Monique didn't want to revisit the rest of the details, though she knew they would eventually share the story, and a few good laughs.

"And then some," Gloria said. "Can't wait to hear more. Are you coming to the gallery today?"

"I'm not sure. I'm going to my studio now; I could use a workout. And I think I may do my meditation."

There was a moment of silence; Gloria's voice took on a lower, almost conspiratorial tone. "Are you sure about that? Last time you told me you were done with it–that it was too much."

Monique remembered the conversation. The smallest of shivers ran down her spine as she recalled the potency of her last experience. But on the drive home from the Jones' residence last night, she had resolved to go back. To stop hiding from it.

"I know, Gloria. But the longer I stay away, the more I feel disconnected, like something's missing inside of me. If anything, the feelings are getting stronger."

"Well, at least call me later today. Let me know what happens. Plus, it's going to be a beautiful fall day. I don't expect much traffic in the gallery. You need to keep me company. And Coco too!"

Monique laughed; Gloria may have needed some company, but Coco–her robotic pet dog–certainly did not. Gloria would undoubtedly lavish a measurable portion of yesterday's profits on gifts for the furry little k-bot.

Nevertheless, Monique did appreciate Gloria's concern. She was the only one that knew about Monique's meditations, and the visions she'd been having. And even Gloria didn't know all of it.

"Okay, I'll see what I can do. Maybe after lunch."

"Great! Talk to you soon," Gloria said before ending the call.

Feeling a newfound resolve, Monique left the bedroom and headed downstairs to her studio.

When she moved into the house, almost five years ago, Monique had fashioned a personal studio in the basement. It was an all-purpose setup, including free weights, various cardio and weightlifting machines, video screens, mirrors, and the latest monitoring technology. She glanced briefly at the door to the small room next door, but stayed primarily focused on the task at hand. For more than an hour, she worked her way through one of her favorite routines, starting with stretching and yoga, moving into light cardio, then weights, and finishing with a more intense jiu-jitsu routine. She didn't often string all of them together, but the sweat and exhaustion had a cleansing effect–and truth be told, she was also stalling. *Normal people procrastinate to avoid exercise–I exercise to procrastinate.*

She smiled and shook her head, while turning off her music–the rhythmic thumping she enjoyed as part of her routine. Then she took her earpiece off, and set it on the table. *No distractions.*

Monique crossed the room and opened the door to her private sanctuary, a small, simple room connected to her fitness studio. She had separated this space from the rest of the studio a few years ago, when she had become more serious about her meditation practice. She liked the simple, spartan feel of it.

She stood in the center of the room, and closed her eyes. Years ago, she had begun meditation on the advice of a friend. She had even joined a group and learned some of the basic techniques. But her experiences had been far different than most others. As just one example, she had felt constricted–like a ball of twine–when she sat cross-legged on the floor. So, she had learned to meditate in a standing position. It seemed to open her senses, giving her a fuller experience.

She stood now, and began taking slow, steady breaths. Fresh from her workout, she could still feel her heart beat—her own rhythmic thumping. She let the breathing exercises slow her body, as well as her mind.

This first phase was always the most difficult, as her mind tried its best to intervene. It was no easy task to let go of her thinking self. Thoughts of her parents—her mother—pressed at her conscience; they were difficult to quell. Finding a way past the limitations of the mind had been her first real breakthrough. She let go of time—last week, last night, tomorrow—and put her focus on the Now. She was present here, in this instant, and nothing else was relevant. The moment washed over her, cleansing her of all thought.

She sank deeper, deeper inside herself. Her breathing was slow and even. She left the room she was in, and passed to an inner place—a place she knew well. It was joy, it was security, it was energy. But most of all, it was a place of simple *connectedness*. Of *Being*. She felt connected to her true self; she felt complete. The release of her mind—of thought and time—allowed her to connect with a part of herself that yearned for release. This was the place she had found for herself; a place from which she drew energy and enlightenment. She could spend an hour here, in the blink of an eye. She enjoyed an almost-perfect stillness, like the faintest of ripples on the smoothest of seas.

But this place, it had turned out, was merely a way station on her inward journey.

What came next was harder to explain. She had first seen a faint point of light—a will-o'-the-wisp at the farthest reaches of her consciousness. Early on, she ignored it, focusing instead on the pureness of the Now and the joy that came from it. But the light became more prevalent, until it almost seemed to beckon her to follow. It gave her an intense feeling of *oneness*—of connection not just within but with the light itself. It was as if the light was saying, "Yes, yes, follow me!" or perhaps more accurately, "Join us!" It was both exhilarating and terrifying.

It had taken her several more visits to find the courage for the next step. She wanted to follow, but she also wanted to keep the connection to her inner place. On that fateful day when she finally did let go, it was less a conscious acceptance than it was an end to her resistance. That was the first time, almost a year ago, that she had made The Leap, as she now called it. A leap that had changed everything.

She was at that moment now, and once again the dancing light beckoned. The Leap had become easier, and quicker, over the previous several months. Today, there was almost no transition. There was a physical perception of movement, a long stretch across both everything and nothing, where time seemed irrelevant. Her senses opened to a multitude of sights, sounds, and smells. She called them visions, though the word fell far short of describing her intense sensations. Having arrived once more, she steeled herself for the onslaught.

Her senses were awash in the now-familiar vision: the sound of an airplane, the sight of a soaring, triple-towered, glass-framed building, and the strong scent of coriander, mixed with the faint stench of durian, like sweet, rotten onions. But most of all, there was the marketplace, and the face of a young Asian man, with short black hair, thin nose, a long scar on his chin, and dark eyes that bored into hers with a fierce sense of urgency.

The intensity of the moment was etched in the young man's stare. Monique held his gaze, resisting the urge to flee, as well as her mind's attempted intrusions—its need to apply structure and logic. Until today, her mind had always won this battle, escaping from the vision and returning to the world it knew and could control. But not today. Charles Jones had made sure of that.

I'm ready. Tell me.

Monique released her fear and confusion, matching the power of the moment with her own newfound resolve. And with that release, her vision further crystallized. No one moved, nothing changed—except perhaps for a fleeting spark of recognition that passed between them. In an instant, the sense of *oneness* she had felt for months had become something more.

Her eyes opened, and she was back in her meditation room, drained and breathless. And at last, she knew exactly what she needed to do.

She still didn't understand where the visions came from, how they found her, or their ultimate purpose. What she did know was that it was time to stop sitting on the sidelines. It was time to find this man. Time to make a difference.

She was going to Singapore.

S I X

*Two things are infinite: the universe and human stupidity.
And I'm not sure about the universe.*

– Albert Einstein

Professor Jonas Hanssen stood behind his array of electronics, arms casually folded across his chest. After years of hard work, the technology in his downtown Honolulu office was all but complete, and he couldn't help but admire the results. Truth be told, the journey had been much longer than that. But in this current phase of waiting and watching, it was hard for him to stay focused. The cluster of telescopes was perfectly aligned in low Earth orbit; all of the transmitters were functioning properly. *Here we go*, Jonas thought. *Time to bag an asteroid.*

Jonas glanced over at the rest of his science team–all one of them. Brent, as usual, was hunched over his own computer station, doubtless triple-checking the real-time data from each of the orbiting telescopes. *Hanssen Scientific* was small, but talented; he and Brent had been together for more than three years. And before that, they had worked together at the University of Hawaii research facility.

"This run has been a big zero," Brent said, leaning back in his chair.

Jonas glanced at his friend. "Relax, it's still early. I've got a good feeling about this one."

He hoped he had reason for his optimism. Until recently, the team had been on a roll. But with the mining of near-Earth asteroids all but complete, companies like Hanssen Scientific had turned to the asteroid belt itself. And this, they had soon discovered, was another animal entirely.

As he studied the most recent data, a noise from behind him caused Jonas to turn. It was their project administrator, Kahli, joined by a young woman with an eager smile, peeking out from behind the hallway door.

"Professor Hanssen, your visitor is here. Can she come in?" Kahli was already in, of course.

Jonas nodded and waved as he stepped back from his console, watching them as they crossed the room. He remembered now—she was a newly enrolled graduate student at the University of Hawaii. She had fair skin, inquisitive eyes, and long, blonde curls—similar in color to Jonas's own short-cropped hair. She wore a mid-length skirt and sleeveless blouse, but it was her casual, confident walk that caught his attention. He guessed she was in her late twenties, maybe thirty. She undoubtedly drew attention in most rooms, but in a graduate physics program, Jonas guessed she stuck out like an orchid amidst the volcanic rocks of Mauna Kea.

Her visit wasn't unusual; Jonas had a standing agreement with the University—or more specifically, with his friend and mentor, Kaito Matsui, the physics program chair—to give tours to interested students. Kaito, of course, provided Jonas with a significant favor in return. Jonas had simply forgotten that a student was coming today. It wasn't the first time he had forgotten, as Kahli would be sure to remind him.

"You must be Katherine." Jonas offered his hand.

"Call me Kat," she said. "And thank you so much for letting me tour the lab. I've heard so much about you. And your work," she added with a smile.

Jonas could guess the kind of stories she had heard from his former colleagues at the University; he saw Kahli shake her head as she disappeared through the door.

"No bother at all," he said. "Kaito knows I'm happy to oblige—as long as he doesn't mind me poaching a few of his best students."

Jonas was still holding Kat's hand; he let go, putting his hand to his mouth and clearing his throat as a cover for his momentary embarrassment. Kat didn't seem to notice; she shifted her gaze to scan the room.

"So have you met Kaito yet?" Jonas asked.

"You mean Professor Matsui? Yes, when I first arrived. He was the one that suggested I come see you."

"I bet he did." Jonas and Kaito had worked together for nearly ten years. And although Jonas's career had taken him on a different path, they remained close. Jonas often told friends that Kaito had helped keep him off the streets; he smiled at the thought.

"What's so funny?" Kat asked. Her question brought him back from his reflections.

"Sorry, just thinking about Kaito. He's the main reason I'm here. Or in this case, the reason we're both here."

Kat was still scanning the room. "So this is where it all happens?" she said.

Jonas gestured with his hand, pointing to the ceiling. "Well, I'd argue that most of what happens is out there. But follow me."

He led her toward the center of the lab. "First, let me introduce you to the real genius in the room. This is Brent, who runs all the data analysis and our spectroscopy technology." Brent looked up just long enough to nod in Kat's direction.

"Professor Matsui mentioned the spectroscopy," Kat said. "I'd love to hear more about it."

Jonas shook his head. "I'm sure you would. Unfortunately, I can't give you all that much in the way of details. Welcome to the world of big business. It would be great if we could share all of our discoveries, but I doubt the underwriter of our grant would appreciate that. They might just have to shoot us." His half-hearted attempt at humor did little to diminish her obvious disappointment; Kat's smile had gone from radiant to the dimmest of red dwarfs–at best. Jonas felt a sudden urge to placate her.

"I'll tell you what," he said. "Let me give you a quick overview. Then, you can ask me all the questions you want. I'll answer as best I can. Okay?"

Kat nodded; a small spark had rekindled in her eyes. Jonas plowed ahead.

"I'll assume you're familiar with the battle for ownership of NEO's–near-Earth orbit asteroids," Jonas began. "At the end of the day, when the auctions finally happened, all of those asteroids were effectively spoken for. We still occasionally find a new one, but nothing significant. The best ones are long gone.

"So, the next frontier was the asteroid belt itself. But the distance to the belt posed two major problems. First, it's too far for humans to be part of the mining mission. And second, it fundamentally alters our formulas for the optimal asteroid composition, in order to achieve the best possible return on investment. In general, we're looking for M-type asteroids. They have a higher mineral concentration than the C-type or S-type. Though in a perfect world, we need an M-type that also contains ice–or more precisely, the water we need to power mining operations. Unfortunately, M-type asteroids with water content are exceedingly rare."

He paused to see if Kat was keeping up. She was nodding her head, so Jonas continued.

"For a near-Earth asteroid, we could be off by a bit in the amount of platinum or other rare elements; it wasn't the end of the world. At a certain threshold, the value more than covered the cost to mine it. And the margin of error was wider.

"But all of that changes when you start talking about travel to the asteroid belt. No one wants to send equipment all the way out there, only to find that the asteroid has one-third the amount of the rare metals we had projected. So we needed a better way to determine the internal composition."

Kat jumped into the conversation.

"So you found a way to look inside an asteroid from two hundred million miles away?"

"Sort of," he replied. "Our technology is state-of-the-art spectroscopy, combined with some really sophisticated number-crunching that Brent over there came up with in his spare time."

For most visitors, that answer had been enough. But for Kat, apparently, it was not.

"So let me guess," Kat said. "You combine physical readings with known data from previously mined asteroids and historical mineral dispersion patterns? And that improves the accuracy?"

Jonas arched an eyebrow as he weighed her response. She seemed genuinely interested in the research, which was unusual; most of the students just wanted to check out the telescope.

"Insightful analysis," he said. "And not too far off base. But I can't get much more specific. Sorry."

Kat gave him another look of disappointment; she tilted her head slightly, as if mulling over her next line of questioning. Jonas found it strangely charming.

"I understand, I suppose," she said. "But it seems a bit obvious. Why don't others just do the same thing?"

Suddenly, Jonas was on the defensive–though there was little need to defend his work to a grad student. But the words spilled out almost before he realized it.

"I'll tell you this much," he said. "The secret is really in both dimensions. It's in the number of factors we include in the calculations, as well as the technology we use to get the data. For example, how many companies have access to precise composition data for thousands of actual asteroids?" He paused to let that sink in.

"Ah," Kat said. "I see."

Jonas pressed on. "And that's just one example. Here's one more–how many physicists include the standard deviation in market price fluctuations as part of their profitability models? There is a huge difference in being off by one percent in your estimate of iron deposits, versus being off by one percent in something like rhodium.

"Plus, there are all sorts of other factors–its spin, the trajectory, its shape–all of them have an impact on cost."

Jonas saw Brent glance in his direction, a frown on his face. *Okay, that was probably too much detail.* But he could see that he had re-established himself on the upper rungs of Kat's intelligence meter; she was nodding again, digesting his words like a handful of chocolate-covered macadamias.

"So how long until you know whether your estimates and extrapolations are accurate?" she said.

Jonas couldn't help himself. He leaned in closer, and his voice took on a conspiratorial tone.

"Here's the punch line," he said. "We actually developed our original models a couple of years ago. They were the foundation of this company, and the primary focus of our first research grant. Since then, the company behind our grant has sent a probe to one of our highest-value targets." He could feel his pulse quicken as he recalled the events.

"And?" Kat said.

"And the tested asteroid composition was within one half of one percent of our projections–for every one of the top ten mineral deposits. As well as for the water content.

"And," he paused for effect, "we've made over a year's worth of improvements since then."

Kat nodded. "Well, I can see why they pay you the big bucks," she said.

Jonas pinched his lips together, resisting the urge to respond. *If she only knew.* Best to change the subject.

"Don't be fooled," he said. "Brent is the true genius. I'm just a pretty face."

Kat laughed. "Or so you'd like to think," she said. "What about the equipment? Can you show me the telescope? I heard you had a prototype here."

Now he couldn't help himself–he looked to the ceiling and rolled his eyes. *Always the telescope.*

"Sure," he said, pointing across the lab. But before he could take a step in that direction, Kat grabbed his elbow. He turned back to face her.

"Sorry," she said. "Did I say something wrong? Kaito told me to ask about the telescope–he said you'd be disappointed if I didn't."

Jonas laughed. "Did he? Sorry about that, it's a bit of a private joke. Not your fault."

"In that case," Kat said, "Can we skip the telescope? To be honest, I'm more of a theories-and-speculation kind of girl. The hardware isn't all that interesting. I'd rather keep asking you questions; you can keep saying 'no'. It's not a word I get to hear very often."

Kat released his arm, flashing an enthusiastic smile across the short distance between them.

He laughed again; she had certainly captured his attention. "Sure, fire away," he said.

They spent another hour in thrust-and-parry discussions; he undoubtedly told her more than he should have, but far less than she wanted. Occasionally, Jonas caught sight of Brent–shaking his head, or just strumming his fingers on the desk as he stared in Jonas's direction. Granted, the tours didn't usually take this long. But Brent had things well in hand, he was sure.

"Seriously, I really do have to get back to work," Jonas said. It was the third or fourth time he had said it.

"I know, sorry," Kat said. "I think Brent is ready to strangle me."

"He's harmless," Jonas said. "And don't be sorry. It was fun. You've got some serious talent in that head of yours."

"Thank you. I wish that was always the first compliment I got from a guy."

Jonas gave her another smile. "Let me walk you out."

But as he walked her to the door, he had a sudden burst of inspiration.

"Kat, I had a thought. I'm as frustrated as you are that I can't tell you more about our work here." She stopped beside him as he held open the door, an expectant look on her face.

"Any chance you might like to see an entirely different set of research? One where I can actually tell you what I'm doing? It includes plenty of crazy speculation, I promise."

Kat looked like she had won the lottery. "Absolutely! Right now?"

"No, unfortunately I've got a full schedule today. How about tomorrow? I'll be at the Watanabe Hall physics lab on campus. I assume you know where that is?"

"Sure, it's close to my apartment. I can walk there."

"In the morning? Nine o'clock?"

"Deal. See you then. Thanks so much. Oh, and by the way, Kaito was right about you."

"Oh really? What did he say?"

She flashed him a look he couldn't decipher.

"I'll tell you tomorrow," she said on her way out the door.

●●●●●

Jonas remained in the doorway for several seconds, watching her go, before returning to his desk in the lab. Brent was waiting for him–still sitting in his chair, but now turned toward Jonas, hunched forward, elbows on his knees. Jonas knew what was coming.

"She sure enjoyed the tour," Brent said.

"I'm quite the tour guide," Jonas replied. He hoped to diffuse the moment with some humor, but it wasn't to be.

"Did you really just invite her to see your research?"

"I did. You heard her–she's sharp. And interesting." Jonas could hear the defensiveness in his own voice; he tried his best to cover it with an easy smile. Brent shook his head.

"And how many other students have you taken over there?"

Jonas didn't respond; Brent knew the answer to that question as well as Jonas did. Until recently, there hadn't been much to see. But that had changed. *I finally have something to show off.* But he knew it wasn't that simple; there was more to it than that. Something about her intrigued him.

Brent continued to press the issue. "You do have a day job, you know."

"No kidding. Has my other research ever gotten in the way of our work here?"

"No, of course not." Now Brent sounded a bit defensive. "You know I trust you. I was just surprised that you shared so much with her. And then you invited her to Watanabe Hall. It's not like you."

He's right, Jonas had to admit. For years now, his life had been Hanssen Scientific, and his research. There hadn't been time–or money–for much of anything else. But the morning with Kat had *felt* right–new and exciting, but also familiar, like re-discovering a favorite T-shirt that had been buried in the back of a dresser drawer. His gut had told him to invite her to Watanabe Hall, and he had learned long ago to trust his gut. Just the thought of her, and the moment when she had accepted his invitation, brought a brief smile to his face. There was no harm in showing her his true passion–his real life's work. Brent would have to understand that.

"I'll admit, she intrigues me," Jonas finally said. "But it won't impact our work. Hanssen Scientific comes first."

Brent nodded. "I know. But I also know how you can get obsessed with things. Call me selfish, but I'd rather see you obsessed with our work here. With finding asteroids."

Ouch. It wasn't the first time Jonas had heard someone use the word *obsessed* to describe the way he operated. He preferred to call it *devotion*–a commitment to something important. Something bigger than himself. And he would never make apologies for that.

"I hear you," Jonas said. "But that's why you're here. To straighten me out when I stray from the one true path."

"You're not so easy to straighten out," Brent replied. But he said it with a smile, and came out of his chair to give Jonas a friendly shove.

"Funny," Jonas said, feinting as if to shove him back. Brent flinched, of course.

"Enough distractions," Jonas added. "Let's go bag us an asteroid."

SEVEN

*Nearly all men can stand adversity, but if you want to test
a man's character, give him power.*

– Abraham Lincoln

Rudy sat alone at the conference table, reflecting on the tumult
of the past several days. In barely a week, he had seen the death
of a long-time friend and mentor, his rise to CEO, and now an
offer to join a secret, world-straddling organization called the Consortium.
It was a lot to digest.

As he waited for Arthur to return, he glanced over at Gunnar, who
was tapping away at a computer screen. He leaned over to get his attention.

"Gunnar, right? I assume you heard my conversation with Arthur. Can
you tell me more about your role?"

Gunnar looked up. "Sure. I've been here about three years. Actually,
I met Carl at a conference in Boston; I was working on a research grant.
Sorry about Carl, by the way. He was a really great guy."

Rudy nodded. "He was," he said. "Thanks."

"Anyway, Carl said it was my research that brought him to the
conference. We spoke, and eventually he convinced me to join him here.
Most of what I do is a continuation of that work."

"And what is that?"

"Basically, it's a mathematical model that uses economic and sociologic data to weigh risk and rank the likelihood of future events."

Rudy took a moment to consider Gunnar's statement. "So, you are using math to predict the future?"

"Not exactly." Gunnar spun in his chair to face Rudy. "That's still science fiction. We're just applying probabilities to specific, possible near-term events. We can't predict for certain when any one of them might occur."

Rudy mulled over Gunnar's words. "So all this processing power," he said, pointing to the room behind them, "provides the information. You run it through your models. And then the Consortium takes action."

Gunnar gave him a begrudging smile. "Almost. At this point, we are still fine tuning. We aren't yet taking any actions based on the model alone. We compare predictions to actual events when they happen, and then tweak the model to improve future forecasts."

Rudy nodded. So the model was still in beta. It was a small bit of relief to know that the Consortium wasn't making life-and-death decisions based on mathematical models.

Rudy heard a click at the far door, as Arthur returned from the processing room. He leaned his cane against the edge of the conference table, and took his seat.

"I know I promised your wife that we'd have you home by nine," Arthur said. "What other questions can I answer?" Arthur gave him an expectant look; Rudy could see he wanted to wrap this up.

"Arthur, first let me thank you for the opportunity. I'm flattered by the offer. But as I'm sure you know, it's no small decision. So I do have a few more questions, if you don't mind."

Arthur nodded, so Rudy continued.

"Let me get straight to the point. First, it would help to understand a bit more detail as to what I would be doing. Some examples of the day-to-day work. I assume it doesn't involve killing anyone." Rudy hoped his last comment would elicit a reaction, but Arthur remained silent. So Rudy pressed ahead.

"Second, how does this relate to my job as CEO? I'm sure you don't want my day job to suffer, and obviously my public role is important to me. GRI should come first."

Arthur seemed to weigh both questions for a moment before responding.

"OK, let me attack those in reverse order," Arthur said. "First, I think you'll find that the roles are complementary. Ninety-nine percent of the time, our interests are aligned. Keep in mind that Carl did it successfully for many years, and I think his track record at GRI speaks for itself. And then there is me. I also serve both interests. I'm sure it's why I was chosen to make the offer to you. I have one hundred percent confidence that you can do both jobs. And not just do them, but excel at both. It's one of the reasons I lobbied for you to be GRI's next CEO."

The last comment took Rudy by surprise. He didn't know Arthur that well, and when he had done his own math, Arthur's vote wasn't one he had counted on. Arthur's comment helped him fill in a few blanks.

"As far as your specific duties go," Arthur said, "I think you'll find that they fit well with your job as CEO. But it also fits with your own unique talents, like your background in technology. For instance, the Consortium spends an enormous amount of money on research. Some of that work is for specific applications, but other work is longer term and more speculative. When a discovery is made, we think you can help us decide how to best take advantage of the new technology."

Rudy nodded. That was certainly something he could do, and would probably enjoy. His track record in successfully monetizing new technology was well established.

Arthur continued. "But beyond technology, several other GRI divisions also help us to maintain the *status quo*. The media divisions, security services, finance, robotics–it doesn't take much imagination to see how each applies. But we would never ask you to do something that would compromise GRI's business. That would hurt all of us."

"And Carl went along with all of this?" Rudy asked.

"He didn't just *go along*, Rudy. He led. For more than a decade."

Rudy tried to recall some of the major decisions Carl had made over the past few years. He couldn't think of any that seemed the least bit unusual or out of character. In fact, he had considered most of them to be brilliant.

Arthur leaned in, and again lowered his voice. "As far as killing goes. Of course, we wouldn't ask you to do that. Each member of the Consortium works in their own field of expertise, and we have experts in that field as well." Arthur lowered his voice even further. "But the time may come for you to make a decision with that kind of implication. Let me ask you this—when you made the decision a few years ago to continue trials of your embedded health monitor, even though it had shown serious potential risks for individuals with heart conditions, weren't you in a way deciding to kill some people? Sacrificing a few for the good of many?"

Rudy was taken aback. His award-winning *myHealthScan* device had been a huge success; the early issues had been corrected. Well, mostly corrected.

"Arthur, I don't think—"

Arthur cut him off. "Rudy, let's not mince words. The data was clear about the risks. Maybe a few more years of research would have solved all the problems. Or maybe not. But you made the decision—which I agreed with, by the way—to move forward with production. And it's probably saved thousands of lives since then. Who can say for sure whether those heart attacks would have occurred even without the device? You decided that the needs of many outweighed the dangers for a few."

Rudy considered Arthur's words. Certainly, that was one way to look at it. Of course, GRI had spent a small fortune to defend the device, and to argue that deaths were to be expected in a sufficiently large sample size. Who was to know if the device was the cause? In the end—and thanks to significant media support, Rudy knew—the public got access to the device. And no one was forced to have one implanted—it was a choice.

Rudy broke away from his reflections. "Okay. I won't say I'm one hundred percent in agreement, but I see your point. So let me switch topics. You also mentioned a hierarchy, a chain of command. Who's my boss?"

Arthur grinned. "Now that is some good news. Thanks to the work of your predecessor, and also as a sign of our faith in you, the position you are taking will eventually report directly to the top—to the Chairman."

"Do I get to meet this Chairman?" Rudy asked.

"Not directly, no. But you'll communicate with him on a regular basis, through our secure system." Arthur leaned in even closer. "This is a big deal, Rudy. Truth is, only a few of us communicate directly with the Chairman. You'll have enormous influence; you'll get things done—just as you like it."

Arthur was right. Rudy despised bureaucracy, and had no use for layers of middle management. His organizations had always been flat, with a huge emphasis on leaders who could process lots of data, and be decisive. He had to admit, this aspect of the offer also appealed to him.

"Okay, that helps. But it might help more if you could give me specific examples of Consortium work. Something significant–maybe something Carl accomplished–that would help me see the breadth and depth of the organization in action."

Arthur responded immediately. "Sure. You remember the Child Affordability Relief Act, right?"

"CARE? Of course. It's not every day we pass a law to limit the reproductive rights of U.S. citizens."

Arthur frowned. "Well, as I'm sure you know, it didn't actually limit anyone's rights. It just eliminated government assistance for families with more than two children."

"So the Consortium was behind that legislation?"

"Do you remember how the bill got passed?"

"Sure. A handful of *Realist* party candidates rode the issue into office; some would say it was how we finally got a third political party into Congress. Are you saying the Consortium was behind all that?"

"It's not nearly that simple. But yes, that bill never gets passed without the Consortium."

"So you work directly through politicians."

"No," Arthur replied. "Early on, we paid for elections and bought votes. Like everyone else. But involving politicians directly was too much of a risk; they just can't be trusted. Today, we are infinitely more sophisticated. And much more successful."

"Another example where the interests of many can outweigh the needs of a few?" Rudy asked.

"Exactly. The CARE Act, campaign finance reform, tax reform, gun control, all untouchable without our help. Someone who can free the silent majority from a very vocal minority."

"Why tax reform?" Rudy asked. "That bill hammered the wealthy. Believe me, I remember."

"Like I said, this isn't about the haves versus the have-nots. It's about the bigger picture–preserving the *status quo*. After the riots, we needed to make peace with the masses. And let's face it–the rich *were* keeping too much for themselves. So we pushed through the new, high-wealth tax tiers at fifty percent and more. But with one important caveat. The tax cap."

Rudy nodded. "The limit of two hundred million per year, per individual," he said.

"Exactly. It's a meaningless number to the average citizen. Two hundred million. Five hundred million. A billion. Abstract concepts. But by slipping that in, the net effect was enormous. Not only did we fill the tax coffers with dollars from the rich–but we effectively did to the one percent, what they had been doing to the ninety-nine percent."

"Still, I was surprised the one percent weren't able to get that bill killed," Rudy said.

"That's because even back then, there was a small group of us with even more money–and more power–than all the rest of the one percent combined. It was well reported that the tax bill for the top one percent went up by over 10% that first year. More than *sixty billion* in new taxes. What *wasn't* reported was that a few hundred of us, thanks to the cap, paid ten billion dollars *less*. And we've been reaping that benefit for decades. You do the math."

Rudy remembered the cap debate, but he had been relatively young at the time. Arthur was right; to him it had been an abstract concept. In fact, what he remembered most was the catchy slogan–*the max tax*. Even then, he had understood the concept of a limit to any one person's tax bill. Coupled with tens of billions in new tax revenue–from seemingly the same set of people–it had been an easy sell.

Rudy pondered the broader implications. The new tax revenues had led to expanded government services, which had led to other reforms–like public education. That was where Rudy had first cut his teeth at GRI–in the education technology division. And where he had first met Carl. It was a curious coincidence, to say the least.

He decided to change tacks.

"Give me some examples outside of politics," he said.

"Certainly," Arthur replied. "How about technology research? That's more up your alley. Here's a good one–you could argue that the Consortium holds the world record in the one-hundred-meter dash."

"Delford Lee? I knew he was too good to be true."

"He's a good man. He just happens to also be part of our biotech and human performance research. The sub nine-second, one-hundred-meter dash was just a by-product. He's all human, but enhanced in ways that aren't yet on the testing radar. You could say we are three steps ahead, in that regard. No pun intended." Arthur gave him a half-smile.

"What about other sports? The robotic tennis champ? Or the robot that just broke fifty at Augusta? They're ruining sports, you know."

"Relax, Rudy. That's not us. It's just humanity, desperate for the next big thing. The next circus. Not that we mind. Harmless distractions are an important staple of our business."

"Interesting," Rudy said.

"That's just the tip of the iceberg. Picotechnology, fusion power, claytronics, space exploration, artificial intelligence—we have our hands in all of them. In a few cases, we even have our own research facilities. But most often, we simply fund and direct work at some of the world's leading research institutions."

Rudy weighed Arthur's words. Without question, the technology opportunities intrigued him. The chance to fast-track or even circumvent the new-technology-approval bureaucracy was enticing—a few possibilities came to mind almost immediately.

But for now, he had heard enough.

"Okay, Arthur. You've piqued my interest. Let me go home and think about it. I can give you an answer soon. And just to be clear, I assume the position lasts only as long as I'm CEO? Once I retire, I leave the Consortium, right?"

"No, Rudy, the position is for life. Your role will change, of course, and in retirement, frankly, your ability to help our cause will be greatly diminished. But you'll always be part of the organization.

"Also, I'm afraid I need an answer today. Right now. We need you to be in, or to tell us you're out."

Rudy was surprised for a second time that day—something that didn't happen often. Arthur was still sitting in his chair, but Rudy could see from his posture that this wasn't a subject for debate.

There was an awkward silence. Finally, Arthur pushed back from the table and stood.

"Rudy, let me do one more thing for you. Follow me, would you?" Arthur grabbed his cane and hobbled across the room, stopping at the desk where Gunnar was still working.

"Gunnar, would you mind giving us a moment?" Arthur looked down at Gunnar expectantly.

"Sure, no problem." Gunnar tapped on the screen a few times, and got up from his chair. "I'm just about done for the day, anyway. Good to see you, Arthur. And good to meet you, Rudy. Looking forward to working together." He turned and walked to the exit.

Arthur was already sitting at the desk, tapping a few quick commands on the screen.

"Rudy, if you don't mind, watch the main display."

Rudy looked up, where a large monitor flickered to life. He recognized the image—it was the main conference room from his GRI Technologies division. His key lieutenants at the time—maybe ten years ago—sat around the table. He was in the midst of a speech.

"Listen, folks, you can bitch and moan all you want, but the decision's been made. This isn't about privacy—it's about the long-term benefits to society. The potential here is enormous, and I don't just mean for GRI. This is the next big step in connecting the human race, and we're going to be on the forefront. And remember, we're not transmitting the videos themselves—just the underlying data. If someone finds that intrusive, they can refuse to buy the damn thing."

Rudy remembered the moment well—they were launching GRI's now near-ubiquitous home-bot line—still one of the most successful product launches in history. They had priced the base unit below cost, in large part due to the advanced video recognition software that would transmit enormous amounts of consumer data back to GRI. Over the past ten years, that data had launched a host of new products—and profit centers—for the company. Many had argued that it went too far from a personal privacy standpoint, but Rudy had held fast to his decision. The results spoke for themselves; it was a crucial turning point in his career at GRI.

The video continued for a few more minutes. Several more video clips followed, one after the other, spanning nearly half of his GRI career. Rudy couldn't help but watch, transfixed, as he re-lived some of his best moments of decision making and leadership. It was an episode of *Rudy's Greatest Hits*, and he was proud of them all.

At the same time, he wasn't so naïve not to understand the broader implications. Someone had spent an enormous amount of time and energy collecting these clips—ignoring the fact that they even existed. Clearly, it was a play to his ego—visual proof that he was more than capable to do the job. *It's a hell of a sales pitch*, he realized.

The scene shifted, and switched to another venue. This time he was in his own kitchen, speaking to Victoria. He recognized the moment immediately—it had been barely a week ago. Now the implications hit him like a sledgehammer to the chest, even as he listened again to the words they had so recently spoken.

"Rudy, I understand all the points you've made," Victoria was saying. "I'm just telling you, this job is going to change us. Change the family. And I like this family. I like who we are now. I'm just worried about what it will do to us."

"I understand," Rudy had replied. "But you know that Carl's been grooming me for years. He wanted me to have this job. Not today, obviously, but we can't control that. It's now or never. I'll be out of GRI if I don't win this job. Trust me to go after it, and I promise the family won't regret it."

There was a long moment of silence on the video, just as there had been that day. Rudy's muscles tightened as he waited for the response he knew was coming.

"It's your decision. You know how I feel," Victoria had said at last. "But also know—I'm one hundred percent behind you, either way. And always."

The video screen went blank. Rudy blinked, at a rare loss for words. He should have been furious, but strangely, the anger didn't come. The video had come full circle—from his decision to deploy the data-collecting home-bots, to a video that had likely come from his own home-bot, Rosie. GRI didn't reconstruct the original video from home-bot data feeds. Apparently, the Consortium did. Or worse, they had other sources. *Why am I more impressed than I am incensed?*

He barely heard Arthur's voice as it cut through the noise in his head. "Rudy, don't take this the wrong way. But I thought it might help you understand that we don't make these decisions lightly. We aren't just rolling the dice with you. We've been planning, watching, and working toward this day, for over a decade."

Arthur turned to look directly at him. "We're not just asking some guy in the CEO seat to join our organization. You've been chosen."

Now Rudy understood. There was a choice—but it wasn't his. And the choice had already been made.

He thought about the ramifications of saying no—and the possible repercussions. Arthur had already hinted at his role in Rudy's promotion to CEO; could the Consortium just as easily take it away? And more importantly, what would that mean for his family? He couldn't bear the thought of disappointing Victoria—or the girls. Everything he did was to build a better life for them, so they didn't have to claw their way up the mountain, like he had done. Especially today, in a world where the mountain was all but impassable.

Rudy watched as his hand reach out, seemingly of its own volition. Arthur smiled, clapping him on the shoulder as he returned his firm handshake. The job was his.

E I G H T

Not all those who wander are lost.

– J.R.R. Tolkien

Monique relaxed in a seat by the window, adrift in her own thoughts, as the Silver Line train sped toward Dulles airport. She gazed absently at the gleaming, gray and white skyscrapers that dominated the poorly-planned suburb-cities of Washington DC. Arlington, Falls Church, McLean, Tysons Corner, Fairfax–they blended together as a single, sprawling metroplex, with no clear beginning or end. Except for the less fortunate, Monique reminded herself. For them, the suburbs ended many miles further west–where they might finally afford to live.

The train was nearly full, but nothing like it would have been on a weekday, when one million-plus daily commuters vied for their sliver of space. The ever-increasing city population, combined with decreases in car usage and rural living, had made the DC metro more and more the central nervous system for the entire region. Luckily, there was a station near her home. She enjoyed the ride, and the irony of solitude in a crowd of fellow travelers.

The train approached another station; again, she felt the smallest of urges to disembark, cross the platform, and jump on a train headed east–

and back to the safety of her home. The sudden resolve to follow her vision still put a knot in her stomach, even two days later. But so far, she hadn't wavered. On the outside, at least.

She had known immediately that her vision would take her to Singapore—the glass building was the Marina Bay Grand Hotel, where she had stayed once before. It was an older but newly renovated three-tower complex, overlooking a shallow bay on one side, and the Singapore Straight on the other. The three smoky-glass towers were topped by an expansive, low-slung rooftop oasis, as if the deck of an enormous ocean liner had been set precariously atop a giant, three-pronged fork. One of the first things she had done was to book a small suite at the hotel.

The preparations had been straightforward, beginning with the airline ticket. The next available direct flight had been for Saturday evening, which gave her almost two days to prepare. As usual, Gloria had been understanding. In fact, she seemed relieved that Monique was ready to confront the visions, and was happy to handle the gallery until Monique returned.

There was nothing to do with her home, either—it would notify her if anything was amiss, right down to the fresh food in her fridge, which her kitchen-bot would keep replenished. Normally, she would have suspended the deliveries, but she had no idea when she'd be home. And she didn't want to worry about returning home to a fridge devoid of fresh produce.

Monique enjoyed the simplicity of her life, and the ease with which she was able to come and go. She was an only child, whose parents divorced at an early age. And since her mother's death, she really had no family to speak of; the money was all that was left of those days. And the memories—though many of those were better off forgotten.

Monique retrieved her purse from the floor beneath her seat as the train arrived at the Dulles airport stop. She didn't have any luggage; the Marina Bay was a full service hotel, to include a wardrobe of instantly-customized, perfect-fit nanotech clothing that would be available to her throughout her stay. She was a short walk from the airport terminal; Monique crossed the distance at a brisk pace, as the air was a bit cooler than usual for this time of year. She had dressed in preparation for the heat and humidity of Singapore, without even a light jacket. But the short bit of exercise was a welcome distraction, especially prior to a long flight.

Once inside, she weaved her way through a handful of other travelers to reach the Elite Airlines check-in counter. She glanced down the broad expanse of the Dulles departures hall, briefly observing the mayhem in the rest of the terminal. Long lines, over-stimulated children, and under-appreciated airport staff dominated her view.

She shook her head. Once again, the disparity between her current lifestyle and that of the world at large was on full display, and she struggled to put a label on her feelings about it. Like everything else, she found it easiest to blame her father—but it was more complicated than that. She would never be able to separate her feelings for money from her feelings for him. Society provided her with too many reminders.

There was an actual human at the Elite ticket counter. She did her best to smile as she approached him.

"Hello, I just made a reservation. Last name Durand?"

The man behind the desk repeated her name in a slow, monotone voice.

"Durand, Durand, Durand," he said as his fingers danced across the monitor.

"Monique? Traveling to Singapore?"

"Yes," she said.

"I'll need to see your identification card, and do a retinal scan as well, if you don't mind."

"Sure." Monique was familiar with the procedure. It was one thing to buy groceries, or even an expensive work of art, with a simple thumb scan; it was quite another to grant access to an airplane full of the über-elite. The triple-verification process was just one of many ways that the privileged preserved their safety. And there would be another scan at the gate, of course. Monique pulled her smart-ID card from her purse.

The agent studied the photo, glancing again at her face. Satisfied, he reached behind the monitor to retrieve the retinal scanner. Monique held still while he placed it to her right eye. The familiar beep took just a second.

"Thank you, Ms. Durand. May I charge your account?"

"Please."

"The total today will be eighty-nine thousand, six hundred eleven dollars. Would you like to book a return flight?"

"No, thanks. Not sure when I'll be returning." Monique held her thumb to the payment scanner while she silently cringed at the one-way ticket price. In all fairness, it was probably reasonable for a hypersonic flight to Singapore–especially one that took barely four hours. But with sixty seats on the airplane, she didn't need a math degree to know that Elite Airlines would be doing just as well. Their business model was a good one, running high altitude, hypersonic-only for long-haul, point-to-point flights all over the world, catering to wealthy business and leisure travelers. She was fortunate that Washington DC to Singapore was one of those routes, and that it ran on Saturdays.

"You're all set; our private security line is just around the corner. Thanks for flying with Elite." Her net lenses flashed a ticket confirmation across her vision, indicating that the flight documents had been transferred to her account. The agent smiled, and pointed to Monique's left. She nodded; she had been through the line before. She grabbed her purse and headed toward security.

● ● ● ● ●

Monique arrived at the departure gate to see that her flight was already boarding. She breathed an inward sigh of relief; there were few things she despised more than waiting in the gate area. *If you've never missed a flight, you spend too much time in airports.* Monique smiled; she had missed her share of flights.

She approached the gate. When the proximity technology sensed the smart-ID card in her purse, it matched the ID with her ticket, and the thumbscan lit up. She placed her thumb on the glowing screen. There was a familiar *beep*, the glass doors slid open, and she walked onto the jetway.

Once inside the plane, she turned down the center aisle. Each row had one seat on her right, and two on her left. Twenty rows in all. It felt a little claustrophobic as she looked down the length of the plane–it was a large metal tube, without windows. Glass was too heavy, and the seams too weak, to permit windows on these flights. But the in-wall, real-time video system that simulated the outside view, once they were aloft, was a more than adequate replacement.

Monique found her seat, a single on the right with plenty of room to stretch and relax. Once airborne, she could gaze at the simulated view, enclose herself and take a nap, or mingle at the café with her fellow passengers. She could even take a turn in one of the virtual reality booths. But she would likely just stay in her seat; she preferred the time to herself. She had plenty to think about.

As she sank into her seat, she reflected again on the visions, and her decision to see where they led. Here, on the plane, the implications began to weigh on her. She was a boulder on a cliff's edge, teetering over the rim. No movement was yet discernible to the outside observer, but she could feel the shift–the approaching moment where an inexorable downhill roll would begin. Right now, here in her seat, suddenly felt like a point of no return. But instead of trepidation, she was strangely at ease; a sense of calm had washed over her.

She pondered the questions still floating at the edge of her consciousness. Who was the man in her vision? Why did she feel so compelled to find him? And even if she did find him, what in the world was she going to say? How would she capture his attention? She had the barest outline of a plan, but it was based on a thousand assumptions–and she had a four hour flight to second-guess those assumptions.

But there was one assumption she held as truth–one she had leaned on since her decision to get on the plane. There was another aspect to her visions–one she had shared with no one.

She had more than just a story to tell the man in Singapore; she had something to show him. And she was confident that *showing*, rather than *telling*, would more than capture his attention.

N I N E

*The universe is full of magical things, patiently waiting
for our wits to grow sharper.*

– Eden Philpotts

The autocab sped through the streets of Honolulu, set to best
time mode and using a combination of the H-1 highway and local
roads. In typical fashion, Jonas was running late–so he was forced
to pay for a taxi, as opposed to his usual bus ride or bike share.

So much for eating out tonight.

To help pass the time, he spent most of the trip arguing with the car;
he had lived in Honolulu long enough to think he could outwit the routing
technology. He couldn't help himself; it was ingrained in his DNA. Plus,
he knew the wealthier residential streets that the autocar wasn't allowed
to use on its own.

In a few more minutes he was on University Avenue and the outskirts
of the University of Hawaii, his true home away from home. They looped
through campus, past the baseball field where he still played occasional
pickup games, past the theater and Japanese garden, before finally stopping
at Watanabe Hall. Jonas jumped out of the car and jogged past the meager
landscaping, across a wide sidewalk, down an outdoor hallway, and to the
laboratory door.

As he feared, Kat was already there. She stood just inside the door, arms folded.

"Are you always this prompt?" he said.

"Early is on time. On time is late."

He looked at his watch. "So what does that make me?"

"Lucky," she said.

"Lucky?"

"Lucky I'm still here."

Her tone was more joke than rebuke, but there was a message behind the banter; it was in her eyes. He made a mental note: *no more running late with Kat.* That would be a challenge–and there were more than a few who would attest to that. Still, her words had a strangely potent impact; he had been anticipating this moment, more than he cared to admit.

Today, Kat was wearing a thin, silk blouse, skirt, and heels–showing off the kind of symmetrical curves that would make any mathematician proud.

Not fair, Jonas thought.

He performed an exaggerated bow. "Consider me properly chastised," he said. "Can you ever forgive me?"

"Maybe. Depends on what you've got to show me."

"You're on." He led her to a bank of computers in a quiet corner of the room. They stopped at a desk with a single monitor and chair; he pulled over a second chair from a nearby desk. As they both sat down, he spoke.

"So first, a question. How much do you know about dark matter?"

"Well, it's not really my field of study. So probably less than anyone else here." Kat glanced around the room, as if to confirm her suspicion.

Jonas appreciated her modesty, though he wondered whether it was true. If so, it would likely be a first for her. Nevertheless, he launched into his speech.

"To me, it's the greatest of all mysteries. What's more compelling than the origin of our universe, and why we're here? Since I was a kid, I've had a sense of–" he paused to search for the right word, one that would describe his feelings without going too overboard, "–of incompleteness. Like there was something missing. It's hard to explain."

He paused to collect his thoughts.

"Anyway, in high school I stumbled onto the search for dark matter. All the known mass of the universe isn't nearly enough to hold galaxies together–they spin at a rate that should throw everything apart. Turns out that the ordinary matter we see every day is only about five percent of what must exist. So where is the other ninety-five percent? And what is it? I was hooked."

"So you've been studying dark matter since high school?" Kat asked.

"Sort of. I went to college to study physics, got in debt up to my eyeballs, and eventually found some creative ways to earn my PhD. Then I worked at the observatory here on Maui."

"And that's where you met Kaito. And probably Brent as well."

"Exactly. And in all those years, still no answer to the dark matter mystery. In fact, it's stumped humanity now for over a century. We've done all sorts of tests—smashing particles together in huge accelerators, running all sorts of direct and indirect experiments in the bowels of the earth, and nothing. We kept hoping for some kind of particle to magically appear, and it never happened. Eventually, most scientists came to the conclusion that we would never detect dark matter here on Earth."

Kat broke in. "Maybe I shouldn't have told you I know less than anyone else in the building. This is a physics research lab, you know."

Jonas laughed. "Okay, miss know-it-all. But here's something you may not know. Coincidentally, about the same time we decided that we weren't going to find dark matter here on Earth, some other big research efforts were bearing fruit. We established a permanent station on the moon, we started bringing asteroids into orbit for mining, the first low-earth orbit hotel opened, and we built a space elevator. The demand for capital investment was enormous. Suddenly, funding for things like dark matter research, with no obvious financial benefit, took a back seat to all these other space-based initiatives that had a clear path to earning revenue and profits."

"So no more funding for dark matter," Kat said.

"Pretty much. So now guys like me are stuck building algorithms to exploit distant asteroids, so that other people can get rich." Jonas sat back in his chair, trying to avoid the exasperated tone that was undoubtedly creeping into his voice.

"Don't get me wrong," he continued. "The stuff I do at my company is interesting, and it pays the bills. Mostly. But here's the best part. Thanks to my team and the time they afford me, and thanks to Kaito, I still get to do my dark matter research."

Kat leaned forward in her chair. Jonas could see he had piqued her interest.

"So are you going to tell me now?" she asked.

Jonas nodded. "You're familiar with the Planck III satellite, yes?"

Kat nodded. "It's about half way to the Oort cloud, I think."

"Correct. It was launched from Earth orbit over fifty years ago, and left our solar system about ten years later. It's the fastest-moving man-made object ever built, and still moving at over 40 kilometers per second. Commissioned to study the outer reaches of our sun's influence." Jonas took a breath. *Here comes the good part.* Kat was listening intently.

"What most people don't know is that a portion of the satellite's processing time is managed right here—in this research lab," Jonas said. "We get all of the data streamed to us. And it's collecting some fascinating data."

Jonas turned to the monitor in front of him, and tapped on the screen.

"Call it a confluence of ideas and opportunity," Jonas said. "For decades, all of our experiments here on Earth were done in a way that minimized background noise—like shielding the test from radiation. Cosmic rays and the like. But the faster we smashed together particles, and the deeper we hid these tests from the Earth's radiation field, the more surprised we were by the complete absence of results. Sure, we found Higgs, and Axions, and other fascinating stuff. But where was dark matter?

"So a thought struck me. What if we were going in the wrong direction? What if you *needed* radiation in order to find dark matter? What if they were somehow intertwined? Radiation is everywhere. Theoretically, so is dark matter. Maybe eliminating one causes the other to also disappear."

"Interesting," Kat said. She paused a moment more. "My knee-jerk reaction is to say it's a bit counter-intuitive. But like you said, the intuitive search has been a failure."

"Right. But now it gets a bit complicated." He did his best to suppress a grin.

"Over the years, we've also theorized that our universe contains more than just the four dimensions we experience in our daily lives. I won't bore you with the details, but this always *felt* right to me. And the math fits nicely with my next hypothesis." Jonas took another deep breath. This is where he usually started to lose people.

"So we have an enormous amount of missing matter. And we have a bunch of dimensions we can't see. So that leads to an obvious question—what if the dark matter hides in these other dimensions?"

"Well, that would be an inconvenient truth, since we can't test for it."

"Maybe. We'll get to that. And others have put forward this same hypothesis; it's not really my idea."

Jonas watched as Kat processed the information. Once again, he was probably crazy to be divulging so much of his research, but it had been months since he had spoken to anyone else about his dark matter work. For some reason, it felt right to him.

Kat spoke up. "It's an interesting idea. But plenty of past experiments had some radiation present. It seems like we should have stumbled onto it, even if just through a botched test."

"Good, exactly," Jonas said. "So now comes the final piece to the puzzle. And that has to do with speed."

Kat gave him a look. "Okay, now you've got me. The speed of what?"

"The speed of dark matter. What if dark matter travels at or near the speed of light? And what if it spends the vast majority of its time in these other dimensions, only visiting our space-time as it jumps between them? Maybe even to use radiation as a means of travel? According to most theories, the distance between these other dimensions is very small; they nearly overlap. So in other words, the time that dark matter spends in our dimensions of space would be so short that we would never see it. Especially when we're looking in the wrong place, and under the wrong conditions."

Jonas let Kat process the information. It didn't take her long.

"But what about the effects of dark matter in our own space-time? You're trying to say that dark matter spends almost all its time in other than our four dimensions. Then how does it provide so much of the mass to our universe? The mass that keeps galaxies from flying apart?"

Damn, she's quick.

"It's a good question," he replied. "My best answer is that the other dimensions must share some properties with our own space time. Being in these other dimensions doesn't alter the impact of dark matter, any more than movement in our known four dimensions does. Does that make sense?"

Kat was silent as she pondered his response, but only for a moment.

"Maybe," she said. "Let me try to paraphrase. What you are saying, I think, is that we have all this dark matter, flying around at near the speed of light, using radiation like an intergalactic superhighway. And these other dimensions are like rest stops on the superhighway. Separate, but still part of our universe."

Jonas laughed out loud. "Well, I've never thought about it quite that way. But I suppose your analogy is as good as any. Except that these other dimensions probably aren't rest stops. Really, we have no idea what goes on in those dimensions."

Jonas leaned back in his chair, studying Kat intently. *So now she knows the theory. But do I show her the data?* No one had seen it yet, not even Kaito. He couldn't put his finger on it, but Kat felt like someone he could trust, and he had rarely regretted following his gut. It was why they were here in the first place. She intrigued him–no question about that.

Kat waited. Her look said she was enjoying the moment–though it was also the look of someone well accustomed to getting what she wants. He made his decision.

"So. Can I show you the data?"

"Thought you'd never ask," she said.

● ● ● ● ●

They had moved to another console, where Jonas scrolled through the satellite data, while Kat leaned over his shoulder. Her inquisitiveness was infectious, and Jonas found himself admiring her ability to absorb so much new information. She split her attention between him and the screen as Jonas continued to explain.

"So like I said, most of the Planck III satellite is heavily shielded from cosmic rays, which would otherwise wreak havoc on the instrumentation. But there is one set of instrumentation that was set up to study the radiation fields. And they include one additional feature that's critical to my research."

"And what's that?" Kat asked.

"In my hypothesis, dark matter travels at close to the speed of light, and is only visible to us as it jumps between these other dimensions. If you do the math, the length of time it would be visible to us is ridiculously short."

"How short? Like Planck time short?" Kat said.

"Not quite, but close. Until recently, the shortest length of time that we could measure was an *attosecond,* which is a billionth of a nanosecond– or a billionth of a billionth of a second. According to my calculations, dark matter stays in our physical space-time for less than an attosecond.

So not close to Planck time, but too short for us to be able to detect–until now."

"Why now?" Kat asked.

"Well, lucky for me, some new, experimental instrumentation was added to the Planck III platform just before its launch. Basically, a laser with stabilized light pulses down to a fraction of an attosecond. Even today, we can't do much better than that. So this laser can see things that happen at incredible speed and in miniscule spaces, like between atoms."

Jonas pointed to readings on his computer screen.

"Like this," he said.

He could see Kat frowning as she studied the numbers and graphs on the screen. He had to admit, he enjoyed her intensity.

"OK, you got me," she said at last. "What is it?"

"Don't feel bad. Truth is, I don't know either. Welcome to the current state of my research. But, the point is–there is something. At this speed and scale, we shouldn't be seeing this. Something is there. I just don't know what it is yet."

"That's amazing," Kat said. "Amazing. Have you shown this to Kaito? Or anyone else?"

"No. Not yet. I did some re-calibrations a few weeks ago, and this data just appeared. You're the first to see it. Besides me."

"Kaito told me I'd be impressed," Kat said. "But how did he know you'd show me the dark matter research?"

Jonas could already imagine half-a-dozen reasons why Kaito might have come to that conclusion.

"Well, he's known me for a long time. You must have impressed him–he doesn't just send anyone over to my office."

There was a brief silence between them. Kat appeared to be measuring her next words.

"Professor Hanssen. I know we've just met, but I'd love to help you with this project. My apartment is less than a mile away, so I'd have no trouble being here on your schedule. And I'd do it for free–well, for the experience, I mean."

Jonas weighed her offer. Could she help with his research? He wasn't sure. But he *was* sure about the momentary jolt of electricity he had felt when she asked the question.

What the hell.

"How about this," he said. "I realize that it's last minute on a Saturday, but what if you let me buy you a cup of coffee tonight, and we can discuss it further?" The words tumbled out; he prayed they didn't sound too desperate.

"Yes," she said immediately. "Perfect. Where?"

"Have you found the coffee shop a few blocks from here? Next to Hamilton library? Best coffee in Manoa. Seven o'clock?"

"That works."

"Just one other thing," Jonas said.

The smallest of clouds formed in Kat's features; once again, Jonas found the look charming.

"Yes?"

"Promise you'll call me Jonas," he said.

A warm smile returned to her face. Jonas stood and extended his hand; Kat ignored it and gave him a hug.

"Thank you! I promise you won't regret it. But, I should let you get back to work. And I've got some errands to run. See you tonight!" Kat walked backwards a few steps before turning to leave.

Jonas watched her walk across the lab and out the door. He shook his head. *Did I just do that? The data must be making me giddy.* But his gut had spoken.

He turned his attention back to the computer screen.

He needed confirmation that the dark matter data wasn't an anomaly–which meant a second set of readings. The same data in a different region of space–that would tell him a lot. But at this point, new data of almost any type would help him to solve the puzzle.

He spent a few hours finishing the instructions, double- and triple-checking his calculations before making a show of punching the TRANSMIT button. Even at the speed of light, it would take the signal more than two days to reach the Planck III satellite. Then, after the readings were complete, it would take another two-plus days for the signal to return.

Jonas stood up from his seat and glanced at his watch. There was nothing more to do at this point.

He had almost seven hours to kill until his coffee with Kat. He could run home and clean up, maybe even go surfing for a few hours. And relax at the beach. Time always seemed to go faster there. Between the beach and a couple of bus rides, seven o'clock would be here before he knew it.

And he could eat early at the community center—that would save a few bucks. With any luck, Kat would have eaten as well, and they could just hang out. And talk.

"Thank you, Kaito Matsui," he said, only half to himself. A nearby student glanced in his direction, nodding in agreement. Jonas smiled in return, giving the young man a wink as he walked out the door.

TEN

*You see things, and you say "Why?" But I dream things
that never were, and I say "Why not?"*

– George Bernard Shaw

As far as Monique was concerned, the value of an Elite Airlines
ticket wasn't so much the in-flight café, the bar, the claytronic
seats, or even the spectacular floor-to-ceiling simulated window
views. Instead, it was moments like this–as they walked through Singapore
immigration, bags in hand, with nothing but a wave and a smile from
the woman at the immigration desk. They were led by an Elite Airlines
representative, directly from the plane and out into the main concourse.
The traditional immigration lines stretched as far as the eye could see, but
Monique's paperwork had been processed on the flight, and transmitted in
advance to the proper authorities. So barely ten minutes after landing, she
was inside the Changi Airport terminal, and on her way toward the exit.

Changi brought back fond memories; she loved the glass-and-pillar
architectural design, which managed to still look modern despite its age.
Walking through Terminal 3 reminded her of a human chess game she
had played with her mother when she was young, jumping from square to
square across the irregular black-and-white floor patterns while shouting
Checkmate! at the top of her lungs. She must have been seven or eight

years old at the time. Her mother had just taught her to play chess, and had laughed along with her as they pranced through the concourse. They had traveled to Singapore a few times since then, and each of the trips had been a memorable one. Of course, all of her trips with her mother had been memorable.

Monique shook off the thought as she walked out the door into the humid, overcast skies of the early afternoon. It was warm, even for Singapore, but it wasn't raining and Monique didn't mind the heat. There was no line to speak of for the waiting taxis, and Monique jumped into the first one available.

"Destination, Marina Bay Grand Hotel, Bayfront Avenue," she said as she slid into the seat.

"Confirm destination, please." The autocab responded in English without missing a beat.

The display on the screen in front of her showed a map and location for the hotel, as well as an aerial view of the hotel itself. It was hard to miss.

"Confirmed," she said. The car eased away from the curb and deftly maneuvered its way through the congestion; Monique kept a tight hold on the inside door handle until they were through the worst of it. Soon enough, they were running at speed, past the neighboring golf courses, and along the East Coast Parkway. Her home in the DC suburbs was far from any coastline, so she only got to see open water when she travelled. And even now, her view was mostly obscured by trees, buildings, and the occasional glimpse of a flood wall running parallel to the road. But even the infrequent, partial view across the Singapore Strait was a welcome sight.

Monique relaxed her grip on the door handle, and looked down at her purse in the seat next to her. On an impulse, she reached into the front pocket and withdrew the drawings she had made the day before.

Months ago, she had started drawing pictures of her visions. At first, the visions were hazy. The early drawings were an attempt to decipher what she had seen; making use of her art training was an unexpected side benefit. Over the months, the visions had crystallized–to the point that the drawings were no longer necessary. But she had drawn this last set all the same, as much from habit as need.

They were pencil on paper, though her talent gave even these simple drawings a substantial degree of nuance. The first was her drawing of the Marina Bay Grand Hotel, stark in its contrast against the sky, and drawn alone, without background or other adornments. The second was the street marketplace she didn't recognize; in her vision, the sounds and smells had been as much of the sensations as was the visual setting. She had visited a few marketplaces on her previous trips to Singapore—her mother had loved to cook—but this one wasn't familiar.

And finally, there was the man. Asian descent, dark hair, thin nose, and the scar along his chin. Monique would have said he was in his early twenties, but she had never been good at guessing ages. She had no idea who he was or how she would find him, but here in the car, she felt a sense of *rightness* to her search. She was no longer afraid of where her path might lead.

She looked up as they crossed a bridge, and the road slowly curved to the left, exposing the triple-towers of the hotel in front of her. In a few more minutes, the autocar had expertly navigated its way to the entrance, again avoiding the swarm of pedestrians, bicyclists, and motorized vehicles that crowded around them. She placed the drawings back into her purse just as a bellman arrived to open her door.

"Welcome to the Marina Bay Grand Hotel." A hand extended to help her from the vehicle.

"Thank you," she said.

"May I help you with your luggage?"

"No luggage. I'm fine, thank you."

"Registration is just through the door and past the waterfall. Enjoy your stay."

Monique nodded and made her way through the sliding doors. The hotel had been sold and renovated since her last visit; it took her a moment to get her bearings. What had once been a large, circular seating area inside the lobby was now an architectural marvel—an enormous waterfall, cascading down from unseen heights and ending in a large oval basin on the floor. But the genius was not in the waterfall itself. Rather, it was in the utter lack of noise from where she stood, just twenty feet away. A waterfall of that size should have made conversation all but impossible; instead, she could hear an older couple having a conversation, barely ten feet away. The technology was unfamiliar to her, but the effect was impressive. It said to her, *"We have spared no expense to make this your quiet retreat."* She liked the new design immediately; it engaged nearly all her senses, and connected with her in a way that couldn't simply be filed away by her mind.

Monique skirted the waterfall and made her way to the reception desk. A short young woman with her hair in a bun was waiting for her. Without being asked, Monique removed her ID card from her wallet and pressed her thumb to the scanner.

"Thank you," the clerk paused to look at her screen. "Miss Durand. And welcome back. I see you are staying in one of our suites. Unfortunately your room won't be ready for another few hours. Would you like to take advantage of the pool, or perhaps the spa?"

Monique shook her head. "No thanks, I'll just take a walk. You'll let me know?"

"Of course. We have your number on file."

As Monique turned to walk away, an idea struck her. She looked back at the clerk.

"Has the concierge desk moved?" she asked.

"It's right over there, across the hall." The clerk pointed to a bank of desks.

Monique made her way across the lobby to the concierge desk. There were eight desks, each of them attended by a holographic concierge. Four men and four women, identically dressed, actively responded to guest requests. A lone human concierge–a woman–sat at a desk behind them. Monique was impressed; a more typical ratio was three or four to one.

Monique sat down at the only open desk, across from one of the holographic women.

"My name is Julia," the woman said. "How may I help you?"

"I was hoping you might recognize a local marketplace from a drawing I have?" Monique unfolded the drawing from her purse, and held it up in front of her.

"If you would hold it still, I will try to find the location," Julia said. She studied the picture, though in reality a small camera and processor were the ones doing the studying. Monique looked around briefly and saw no sign of the electronics; even the source of the hologram itself was a mystery.

"This is a wonderful drawing, did someone give it to you?"

Stalling for time. Monique smiled.

"Yes, a friend. She said I should visit this market but couldn't remember the name." She wasn't about to share the details of her visions with a hologram.

"I may have found something for you. In fact, if this is a match, the market isn't far from here. Are you familiar with the area?"

"A little," Monique said.

"Good." She pointed to a map that was under the glass on her desk. "It's here, not far from the hotel. I can upload the address and a map to your account if you'd like."

"That would be great, let me give you the number."

"We have your number, Miss Durand. I'll send it now." Monique's net lenses activated, displaying a confirmation in her peripheral vision.

"Thank you," Monique replied as she stood. She gave a brief wave to the human concierge, who hadn't moved since Monique's arrival. The woman didn't seem to notice.

● ● ● ● ●

Just as the concierge had told her, the market wasn't far. The driver pulled to the curb, and she paid the fare before stepping out into the early afternoon crowd. Her initial reaction was mixed–the view from where she stood was nothing like her drawing, but the smell of coriander, the sounds, and the *feel* seemed right. This was the place, she was almost sure. Her arrival at the hotel hadn't given her the same sensation. But now, a visceral sense of *knowing* swept through her. She soaked it in, hardly noticing as other shoppers were forced to step around her.

Reluctantly, she let the moment slip away. She hadn't expected the feeling of confirmation, and she debated her next steps. With her hand still on the taxi door, she considered returning to the hotel, where she could rest and get a fresh start in the morning.

No. She was here. She would at least spend a few minutes to get her bearings and look around.

She shut the taxi door, and began a slow, deliberate walk through the marketplace. Sights, sounds, and smells continued to float past her. There weren't nearly as many home-bots and other robotic shoppers as she was used to seeing–but there were a few. The diversity of artificial, lab-grown meats, however, far surpassed the typical Washington DC grocery store. Monique doubted it would ever gain this level of popularity at home–the meat industry had labeled it *fake-steak*, and spent a fortune ensuring that no self-respecting American would buy it. To date, the campaign had been surprisingly effective.

As she perused the stalls, she briefly weighed the idea of showing her drawing to one of the vendors. But she dismissed the idea just as quickly; too awkward. She had plenty of time for that tomorrow. Or the day after. She was in no rush. Instead, she followed her sense of smell and feel, letting the aromas and a growing sense of *rightness* guide her direction.

Eventually, her wandering brought her to a dead-end at the back of the marketplace, so she turned to retrace her steps. As she glanced about to re-orient herself, another feeling of déjà-vu flowed through her. Suddenly, the marketplace took on the scene from her vision—in sight, as well as sound and smell. In fact, the smell of coriander was even stronger from this end of the market. It seemed to be coming from somewhere to her left.

And in that instant, she saw him.

Wearing a white smock over a black T-shirt, he was busy serving customers at a small but tidy spice stand. He didn't look in her direction; in fact, she lost sight of him more than once as he worked his way up and down the counter. Her drawing could have been a photo—right down to the nose, jaw line, and short, ruffled hair. She couldn't see the scar from this distance, but she was sure it was there. She stood rooted in place as months of procrastination and doubt were washed away. He was here, and he was real. She squeezed her eyes shut for a moment, holding on to the rush of adrenaline that surged through her body. The boulder she had imagined on the cliff's edge had begun to teeter—and she was ready to give it another nudge.

She approached quietly, stopping behind a small group that was shopping at the stand. They were a mix of what appeared to be locals and tourists; he was helping an older woman with her order. They spoke rapidly, in a crisp, staccato-style Chinese dialect. This small corner of the market appeared to serve primarily Asian customers, along with an occasional tourist. In contrast to the hotel—and most of Singapore—she heard Mandarin Chinese spoken almost exclusively by those around her.

Monique reached into her purse, retrieving the translation devices she had brought along with her. They were a bit antiquated—only capable of providing real-time translation in English, Spanish, and Mandarin. But since more than half the world's population now spoke those three languages, she had hoped they would suit her needs. It was a safe bet, here in Singapore. The device looked similar to her net-phone earpiece. Current earpieces, and most implants, now included universal translation functions. But Monique rarely used the feature, and preferred a more simplistic earpiece for day-to-day-use. She removed her regular earpiece, and placed one of the translation devices over and behind her ear.

When she looked up, he was staring at her. Their eyes locked for the briefest of instants before he looked away. She took a half-step forward and to the right, wanting to make sure that the translator locked into his voice.

"How can I help you?" he said. In perfect English.

Monique smiled. He was helping a young couple standing next to her. From their dress and mannerisms, Monique guessed that they were British; apparently he had come to a similar conclusion.

"We're just looking, thanks. The smells are absolutely brilliant!" The couple slid to their left, and Monique moved into their vacated space. She took the translator off her ear, and put it back into her purse.

"Surprised you?" he said.

"Sorry, I shouldn't have presumed," Monique said. "I bet you speak more languages than I do."

"No, just English and Mandarin. Around here, that's ninety percent of what I need." He paused for a moment before continuing.

"How can I help you?"

"Well, actually, I have a bit of a strange request. I was hoping for a few minutes of your time.

"Privately," she added.

He didn't answer immediately, giving her a quizzical look.

"Can I ask what it's about?"

"It's a little hard to explain. I have some pictures I'd like to show you, and a story that goes with them. Just a few minutes of your time, unless you decide to stay longer. We can grab a table right over there." She pointed to the café next door, where a few tables were empty.

"I'll buy the tea," she smiled as she finished.

He glanced briefly at an old-fashioned wrist-watch, as her request played out at the corners of his eyes.

"Let me ask to take a short break. Would you mind waiting? I'll join you over there in a bit."

"Great. My name is Monique. I'll see you in a few minutes?"

"I'm Bhima," he said. He turned to help an older man standing next to her.

Monique walked over to the café, selecting a table away from the crowds, but still visible from the spice stand. As she watched Bhima work, she saw him occasionally glance in her direction. *The curiosity must be killing him.*

The waitress came by and Monique ordered a green tea for herself. She also pulled the three drawings from her purse, and left them folded on the table. She made sure the drawing of Bhima was at the bottom of the pile.

Last chance to run, she thought. She had come to the market on a whim, only because her hotel room hadn't been ready. The theory of finding this man had collided head-on with the reality–just a few hours after landing in Singapore. And yet, her breathing was slow. Her mind was clear. She was at ease, and she was ready.

Monique was less than halfway through her tea when Bhima arrived at the table. He had removed the smock, and was now dressed in just the black T-shirt and a pair of black slacks. Monique also noticed his black shoes, which were polished and well cared for, though well worn.

Bhima pulled out the chair across from her, and sat down.

"Thanks for joining me," Monique said. "Can I get you some tea?"

"No thanks, I'm fine."

They shared a moment of oddly comfortable silence. Monique took a sip of tea and collected her thoughts. *Here we go.*

"Just so you know, I don't usually ask strangers to join me for tea."

"Sure," he replied. "You normally offer coffee."

Monique laughed; Bhima seemed to be at ease as well.

"No coffee for me. Not my cup of tea."

"Me either," Bhima responded, leaning forward in his chair. "So you said you had some pictures?"

"I did. Along with a story. I don't want to bore you with my life history, so I'll start from a few years ago, not long after my mother passed away. For that and some other reasons, I began to practice meditation."

Monique paused for a moment, looking down at her tea. She had rehearsed this speech many times, but here in person, it was much more difficult than she had imagined; a warm flush had risen to her cheeks. She took another sip of tea before continuing.

"Sorry, this is harder than I thought it would be."

"I'm still listening."

"Thanks. But bear with me; it's going to sound a bit strange.

"Not long after I started meditating, I began having visions–things I saw and felt while I was alone and in a kind of *inner place* I had found. At first they were hazy and difficult to interpret, but over time they became clearer, to the point where I thought I understood what they meant, and what they were trying to tell me."

"So I drew them out on paper."

As she spoke, she unfolded her drawings on the table.

"That's the Grand," Bhima said as he looked at the top drawing. "You're quite an artist."

"Thanks. I know the hotel; in fact, I'm staying there now. As the images became clearer, I knew it was Singapore. So I flew over here. Just today."

She slid the hotel drawing to the bottom of the pile.

"That's the market here," he said. "Impressive. I can even see the outline of our spice stand."

Monique nodded. "This I didn't recognize, but the concierge at the hotel did. She sent me over here. I didn't see it when I first arrived, but when I got to this end, I turned around to walk back out–and there it was. Just like I had seen it."

Bhima was nodding, and studying the drawing of the market. *Now or never.* Monique pulled it away, exposing the drawing of the young man.

Bhima leaned forward, looking up at her. And back down at the drawing. And up again. The market had fallen away; now, it was just the two of them, and implications yet unspoken.

Bhima finally broke the silence. "You drew this? And not just now?"

"I drew it in Washington DC. Yesterday. But I've been seeing this vision for months."

"Are you sure it's me?"

"Yes." She paused, choosing her words carefully. "Yes. If you want, we could sit here the rest of the day and see if anyone walks by that even remotely matches this drawing. But they won't. I can feel it. It's you." She let the last words linger in the air between them.

Monique couldn't tell what Bhima was thinking. He hadn't run off, which had been her biggest fear. But now what? She pressed ahead.

"Bhima, I don't have all the answers. All I know is that these visions compelled me to find you. I resisted for months, but here I am. Here we are. What do you think it means?"

Another long silence hung in the air between them.

Bhima leaned back in his chair. "Sorry, it's a bit much for me to process. Honestly, I have no idea what to think, or whether that really is me in the drawing. Though I have to admit, the resemblance is hard to ignore.

You said you're staying at the Grand Hotel, right? Maybe we could get together and talk some more. I could try to find some time."

"I suppose," Monique replied, trying her best not to sound disappointed. "I know this sounds a bit crazy."

"You'd be surprised," Bhima said. "But I believe what you're saying. I just don't know what it means."

Monique could feel the moment slipping away–from the thrill of finding the man in her visions, to the cold reality that neither of them knew what to do next.

But Monique wasn't entirely unprepared. Since her decision to find Bhima, she had imagined this meeting, and the many possible ways that it might unfold. If their roles had been reversed, she would have reacted in much the same way–it was a lot to take in. But no one–not even Gloria–knew the full extent of her visions. And if she was truly taking a leap of faith, it was time to reveal the rest of her secret.

She leaned forward in her chair, taking a long, slow breath–in and out. She could already feel the intensity building inside of her.

"Bhima, I understand how you feel. I don't blame you. But before you go, let me show you one other thing."

She stared into his eyes, while reaching inside and accessing the place–her place. She could feel the pure, quiet heat growing from within. Then she focused on the cup of tea. And with the slightest of efforts, she used her power to slide the cup of tea across the table, from in front of her to in front of him. It was the smallest of demonstrations, but she might as well have pushed the moon out of orbit. She never moved, and her gaze never left his eyes.

Bhima looked down, eyes wide. She struggled to read his reaction. Shock? Confusion? She couldn't be sure. But it wasn't what she expected.

His eyes returned to hers. A scraping sound reached her ears, and she broke her gaze to look down. She saw the tea cup slide back across the table, coming to a stop precisely where it had started. The look of relief on Bhima's face was palpable; they shared a knowing smile.

Monique felt the beginnings of a new sensation–a mix of power and purpose, coursing through her veins, like liquid fire. She wanted to shout–

to scream at the top of her lungs. But she resisted the urge. Instead, she uttered two simple words.

"Join me."

●●●●●

They returned together to the hotel, finding a pair of relatively secluded seats, behind the waterfall, where they could continue their conversation. Of the million scenarios Monique had envisioned, discovering that Bhima shared her strange power had never been one of them. She was still processing the data–still trying to understand the full implications. And although Bhima had been happy to come back with her to the hotel, the thought of leaving Singapore, and returning with her to Washington DC, remained a different matter.

She listened as Bhima described his upbringing. Like Monique, he was an only child, and adrift from what little family remained. He had never known his father, and his mother had recently succumbed to one of the many drug-resistant viruses that plagued Southeast Asia. In fact, his mother's family had abandoned him to care for her during the final weeks of her suffering. Since her death, he had been living with the couple that owned the spice market.

"What about your family?" Bhima asked her.

"My mother passed away about five years ago. It was a skiing accident. She was with a friend; they said she hit her head in a bad fall. They were in the back country, so it took hours for someone to reach them."

"I'm sorry to hear that. Sounds like the two of you were close. Like I was with my mother."

"We were."

"And your father?"

Monique sorted through her stack of pre-processed answers. But almost as quickly, she cast them aside. *He deserves better than that.*

"You and I seem to have that in common as well," she said. "I'm not in touch with my father, either. My parents were divorced when I was young. It was messy. I lived with my mother after that."

Why was that simple truth so hard?

"So what do you do for a living?" Bhima asked. "Besides hunting down professional tea cup pushers, I mean."

"I manage an art gallery in Virginia, outside of Washington DC. But I'll be honest with you. My father was wealthy, and when my mother passed away, I inherited her entire estate. So I'm fortunate, in that sense."

Bhima gazed across the broad expanse of the hotel lobby. When he did finally respond, it was without the usual jealousy or barely-concealed hatred she had come to expect in these situations.

"Must be nice," was all he said.

"I wish it were that simple," she replied. "And believe me, I paid a heavy price. Plus, I never felt like I was putting the money to good use. Until now. This trip has felt more *right* to me than all of my last five years of charity work. And I want it to continue. For both of us."

"I know," Bhima said. "You've said that. But it's no small thing for me. Everything I know is here. I've never even been outside of Singapore."

"I get that," Monique said. "Really, I do. It took me months to get up the courage to come here. So I can wait. Even if it takes you two or three more hours."

He laughed; she returned his smile.

"But seriously," she continued. "I didn't just come here to talk. I want to do more. I'm *supposed* to do more. My visions, the power—there's a purpose behind them. Something much bigger than the two of us."

Monique weighed her next words—and just how much she should open up to him. *Tell him,* she thought. *He's just like you.*

She took a deep breath.

"Bhima, I know this might sound crazy. But you and I are going to change the world. Don't ask me how yet, but I can *feel* it. And I want you to be a part of it."

Bhima remained quiet; several seconds passed before he spoke.

"Give me some time," he said.

They continued their conversation, through dinner at the rooftop restaurant, through the orange glow of the evening's sunset, and over a few drinks back in the hotel lobby. By the night's end, they had come back to the subject of their peculiar power. The discussion ended in a series of pranks— wall paintings askew, doors curiously shut, and drinks suddenly just out of reach. But when Monique went a bit too far, pushing a stranger's drink off the edge of a table so that it shattered on the floor, Bhima was abruptly quiet.

"Sorry," she said. "That was my fault."

"It's okay," he said. "But we should probably stop. Besides, it's getting late. I should get home."

Monique lowered her head, before gathering herself and standing up. Bhima did the same.

"Bhima, I've had an amazing day. I really enjoyed meeting you. I hope I get to see you again–as soon as you're ready." She held out her hand.

Bhima smiled, and reached out to give her a hug. She returned his embrace.

"Don't worry," Bhima said, stepping back. "I'll see you tomorrow. And probably every day after that.

"I'm in," he added.

ELEVEN

There is nothing nobler or more admirable than when two people who see eye to eye keep house as man and wife, confounding their enemies and delighting their friends.

– Homer

It was a fine way to live, Victoria had to admit–blue skies, a warm breeze, and sand between her toes. Further down the beach, the girls were preoccupied with a small Caribbean reef octopus they had discovered lurking under a large, rusted anchor. From the sounds that drifted back to her, Victoria wasn't sure which of the three was most petrified.

The private island was apparently a perk of Rudy's new position, and a welcome getaway for the family after his first full week as CEO. It wasn't far from the city, just a short flight. And the private jet was still there, waiting on the tarmac whenever they were ready to leave. Not that Victoria was quite ready to go, of course.

They were alone on the island–save for the staff, whose service rivaled that of any five-star resort. And not just the human staff; even now, a beach-bot passed nearby, systematically cleaning and grooming the already pristine beach around them. They had also availed themselves of the island's various high-tech toys; at one point, she and Rudy had staged an aerial dogfight in hover-bubbles, while Sonja and Shae launched foam-tipped anti-aircraft missiles at them from the beach. Victoria had nearly crashed from laughter when she heard Shae yell, "Die, you dogs!" through her earpiece. They hadn't had that much fun in ages.

Now she was lounged in a beach chair, soaking up the mid-day sun. Rudy was inside, organizing dinner plans–or more likely, sneaking in a few minutes of work. She had tried her best to give him a long leash over the past week; he had a lot to digest, and his work ethic was a big part of his success. At the same time, though, Victoria knew where that led, and she was determined that their children would be raised by *two* parents, and not just one. They needed a dad, not an absentee business executive, as her own father had been. As much as she still loved her father, they could never get those years back. So instead, she made sure that her girls had the full benefit of Rudy's influence. Especially during their teenage years. Rudy had asked to marry her for life–an unusual gesture in a world of limited-term marriage contracts. She had been swayed by the romantic gesture–and his unwavering commitment. She fully intended to honor her side of the bargain.

She heard a noise from behind her, and turned to see Rudy, walking across the sand to join her. He was idly flipping his net-phone into the air with one hand, and catching it with the other. She watched him do it a few more times before he reached the edge of her beach blanket.

"You know you're going to drop that thing," she said.

"Not a chance," he replied. As if to prove his point, Rudy tossed it up once more with his right hand, this time catching it behind his back with his left.

Victoria smiled. *Always the showboat.*

"Come join me?" She rolled out of her chair and stretched onto the blanket, claiming a patch of shade under the white beach umbrella that stood guard next to her. Rudy dropped down to join her.

"So what's for dinner?" she said.

"Lobsters again; it's what the kids wanted."

Victoria rolled her eyes; she should have guessed. She didn't mind Caribbean lobster, per se, but they were now on the endangered species list. Only a loophole in local regulations allowed the residents to spear fish for them. The kids loved them, and Rudy didn't particularly mind, either. *These days, what isn't on the endangered species list?* Rudy had said it with a wink, and his Cheshire-cat smile. But Victoria knew she would still harbor a twinge of guilt. So she changed the subject.

"Then we have a few hours until dinner," she said. "So tell me more about the new job."

"Like I told you, it's the same job, just more of it. What else do you want me to tell you? Right now, I'd rather enjoy the kids, and the beach. And you.

"But ask me a question and I'll do my best to answer it."

She knew he was avoiding the topic—even more so than usual. But she knew that game. She rose up on one elbow, enticing him with a closer view of her bikini-clad body.

"Tell me more about the island, then. Do we get to use it every weekend?" She gave him her best smile, while poking him in the ribs with a finger.

"No, we don't get it every weekend," Rudy said. "Nice try. It's shared by several companies, for use by the CEOs."

"Funny that Carl never mentioned it," she said.

"It is a bit strange. Maybe he felt guilty about it. Or he didn't use it much."

"Any other perks you haven't told me about?"

"I don't think so."

"What about the bonus?"

"What about it? I told you, on the flight down here."

"You told me *what*; you didn't tell me *why*. You just took the job. It seems a bit unusual." *There. Now it was on the table.*

"Sorry, I thought I explained it. But really, at this point, the money's not for us, right?" He pointed toward the girls. "It might not even be for them."

"That's exactly what I mean," Victoria said. "I'm starting to wonder what you did to deserve it. After all, I've seen you in action." She gave him another poke, and a smirk.

Now Rudy rolled his eyes. But he was still smiling, which was a good sign.

"Vic, you're the only woman in history to complain about a hundred million dollars. The company earns almost a billion a day in profits. It's not unreasonable."

"Don't be naïve, Rudy. I didn't say it was unreasonable. But that money comes at a price. Believe me, I know."

"I know that. But so has all the money before this. And we're doing fine." Rudy squeezed her knee, seemingly for emphasis.

"Sure," she said. "But this isn't about the private islands and Manhattan penthouses. This is about family, and especially the kids. You know how I feel about it. We might have as much money as my parents at this point."

They both looked out to the water, as Sonja and Shae tried to coax the octopus into a yellow bucket. Victoria could see they were giving it a valiant effort, but only so much progress could be made when neither one of them was willing to get within three feet of the slippery beast. It was mostly an exercise in frantic screaming and laughter. She turned back to Rudy; he was still watching the girls.

"I hear you," he said at last. "Let's just agree to keep the dialogue going. I know you'll tell me if things start to get out of whack."

"Don't worry, I trust you," she said. "But you didn't grow up like this—like I did. Just promise you'll trust me and my judgment about the impact on the kids."

"I promise," he said. But his gaze was still elsewhere; even his voice sounded distant.

"I'm not kidding, Rudy." Her voice was a bit louder than she had intended—but now she had his full attention. "Money without discipline is a bad combination. Believe me, I know."

"Hey, if you had been the proper daughter, I never would have had a chance." Now it was his turn to poke her in the side; she deftly deflected his hand.

"We got lucky," she replied. "I got lucky. My penchant for troublemakers like you could have ended somewhere very different. We're not taking that chance with our girls."

"I get it, Vic. You're beating the drum again."

He was right; it wasn't the first time she had made this speech. But men were men—and repetition never hurt. She stood up, brushing some sand from her arm.

"Okay. So let's go see them," she said. "They're having way too much fun. We can talk more after dinner."

"You bet," Rudy said. He stood up, brushing sand from his own hands. But before they could take a step, she heard the all-too-familiar chirp. It was a bit different than the usual tone, but the meaning was undoubtedly the same.

"You're kidding me." She shifted her weight to one foot, arms crossed. She tilted her head for added effect.

"I'm sorry, Vic. But I've been good all weekend, right? I just need to deal with this one call. Ten minutes, I swear. I'll be right back."

She shook her head, but kept her smile. She knew when to push, and this wasn't the time.

"You've been great. Take whatever time you need. We'll be out here when you're done–unless the octopus gets us first." She gave him a quick kiss, and headed for the water.

●●●●●

Rudy watched her walk away, admiring the elegant stride and easy confidence that came from her privileged upbringing. He knew the risk he was taking by keeping Victoria in the dark–and getting on the wrong side of her family wasn't a place he wanted to be, either. Rudy hated lying to her–and he could only imagine the explosion if she–or worse yet, her father–found out his bonus was being held at the Global Bank of Middle Africa. GBMA had been a thorn in her family's side since its inception, having put a serious dent in her father's own banking empire. But Arthur had insisted, and Rudy had eventually agreed. The payment, he realized, was a simple and effective reminder of their arrangement. *Immeasurable wealth. Unquestioned loyalty. And silence.*

All things considered, though, his first week with the Consortium had been a good one. Arthur had been right–so far, the job had been one hundred percent aligned with his role as CEO. On his first day, a message had come to divert additional resources to a research effort in the Power Division–an as-yet unsuccessful study related to anti-matter propulsion. Rudy made a few phone calls, and truth be told, it was a good decision. The research showed promise, and probably should have been plussed-up even sooner. That evening, Arthur sent him an invitation to a local charity event. He added it to his calendar; Victoria would enjoy it.

Throughout the rest of the week, he received a handful of other missives. None were difficult; a few he even considered amusing. One asked him to fast-track a reality show that was going to follow a crazy trillionaire– the one building his own, floating nation-state in the middle of the Pacific. They were calling the show *Atlantis Rising.* Rudy couldn't imagine that the world needed another reality show, but apparently it was a common tool, used by the Consortium to distract the masses. The call took less than a minute. In fact, the executive at the other end sounded incredulous that Rudy was engaged at such a low level of detail. But word soon spread, and Rudy knew it would help keep people on their toes.

All of the messages came anonymously through his new net-phone. The Consortium had done their homework–it looked identical to his old model, and worked with his existing net lenses. But when he pressed and held his index finger to a precise, invisible spot on the back shell, it accessed a completely separate operating mode; it was all he could do to resist taking it apart. Arthur had given him the net-phone as they left GRI headquarters last week.

His second gift from the Consortium had been a bit more problematic–a tiny microchip, injected under the skin in his right hand, between his second and third knuckle. It was non-negotiable, Arthur had said, and barely the size of a snowflake. It was integrated with his new net-phone, and gave him access to Consortium facilities, among other things. It was the *other things* that gave Rudy pause. Logically, he knew that implanted technology was all but standard practice–from communication and tracking devices to replacement body parts and monitoring tools, like *myHealthScan*. But up until now, he had resisted–perhaps because he knew too much about the potential for abuse. But Arthur had insisted–it was for his safety, he said. Rudy had finally acquiesced.

Today's message was like the others–a brief burst of text that disappeared almost as soon as he read it:

Wine cellar. 10 minutes.

He had yet to try sending a response–all of the messages had been clear and precise. They arrived, he read them, and they disappeared. The larger question, of course, was who was sending them? Arthur? The Chairman? Or someone else? He had no way to know. Rudy had spent more time over the past week pondering these questions than he had in acting on the various requests. And he was no closer to an answer.

He left the beach, passing through a veranda and into the dining room, before descending the stairs that led to the wine cellar. He was confident he knew what he'd find there; in fact, he was mildly surprised that the message hadn't come until today. The only question was whether anyone would be there to greet him.

Not surprisingly, it was Ajay, the House Manager. He was waiting patiently at the bottom of the stairs. Rudy and Victoria had toured the cellar when they first arrived; they were both fond of good red wine. And the cellar didn't disappoint–though not exceptionally large, it made up in quality for what it lacked in quantity. Ajay had told them it held more than ten thousand bottles, with an average value of about two thousand dollars per bottle. He and Vic had tried their best to put a dent in the collection.

"Welcome, sir." Ajay's white teeth and broad smile were in stark contrast to the subdued lighting of the room, and his own dark complexion.

"Thanks, Ajay. I was wondering when I'd be back down here."

"It's been a pleasure to serve your family, Mister Dersch. And to have you join *our* family."

Ajay turned and walked to the west wall, reaching between two dusty bottles. An instant later, Rudy heard a faint whirring. The rack of wine directly in front of him gradually descended through the floor, disappearing below them. The wall behind the wine had also disappeared, revealing a ten-foot hallway that culminated in a door at the far end.

"I hope all that motion doesn't spoil the wine," Rudy said.

"No chance, sir. I do store some of the lesser wines in that particular rack. But it was designed to drop rather than slide in order to minimize the disturbance."

"Shall we?" Ajay gestured to the hallway.

Rudy followed behind as they walked down the hall, stopping at the far door. It bore a striking resemblance to the entrance under GRI headquarters–right down to the keypad, the cameras, and the multitude of small openings around the door.

In a moment, the green light appeared, and Ajay punched a code into the keypad. Again, Rudy heard a metallic click, and Ajay pulled the door open. Both of them stepped through.

Deja-vu. The room was similar to the one underneath GRI headquarters–perhaps a bit smaller. But the separate processing room was identical–stacks upon stacks of pure processing power. *How many of these rooms do we have?* One of them was enough to stagger the imagination; now he knew the Consortium had at least two. And probably many more.

"Arthur is waiting, sir." Ajay gestured to a seat at the conference table.

Rudy crossed the room and sat in the nearest chair. As he did, a holographic image of Arthur joined him in a seat across the table. At

Arthur's arrival, Ajay excused himself and went back through the door. Rudy heard the familiar click as the door closed behind him.

"Greetings, Rudy. I hope I'm not disturbing the family weekend. Are you enjoying the island?"

"It's been fantastic. The location, the food, the service–everything has been perfect. Victoria and I are grateful."

"Wonderful," Arthur said. "Then let's get through this call so you can get back to them. Any problems after your first week?"

"Not really," Rudy replied. "Pretty straightforward stuff. I might even call it a bit mundane."

"True enough," Arthur said. "What you'll discover is that our business is all about a thousand little things. We've learned over time that lots of little changes are easier, and far less likely to raise eyebrows. Any one of them, when viewed on its own, is barely worth paying attention to. But put them together, and they can move mountains.

"The challenge," Arthur continued, "is catching things in time so that little adjustments are sufficient. Which brings me to the reason for the call."

"Which is?"

"Do you by chance know a GRI scientist by the name of Martin Fletcher? He's in your robotics division."

Mention of the robotics business sparked his interest. The name, however, didn't ring a bell.

"I don't think so," Rudy said.

"He's on the software side, mostly working with the law enforcement product line. He's been a big contributor to some of the algorithms behind our tactical support droids. He even testified in front of Congress at one point. He's become well known in the advanced AI community."

"Sounds like a great asset."

"Yes. Or at least, he was. Unfortunately, we've run into a bit of a problem."

"How so?"

"In simplest terms, we have some Consortium assets in the robotics industry–though not at GRI. These assets monitor, and in some cases tweak, the AI controls in certain classes of robotic intelligence. It's one of those thousand little things I told you about."

The revelation was a bit unsettling; Rudy could imagine several ominous ways that robotic controls could be *tweaked*.

"So what's the problem?" Rudy said.

"Here's the thing. Our people are good–the changes we make are subtle, and spread across multiple modules. But this guy–he's smart, and he understands enough of the big picture to ask questions. The wrong kind of questions." Arthur let the last statement linger in the air between them.

"I see." Rudy paused to consider the implications. "So what exactly are you recommending that I do?"

"Well, Arthur said, "this isn't the first time we've had to deal with a curious scientist. Frankly, it's not the hundredth. I've come to you because Carl preferred to handle these things personally, when it involved someone at GRI. The fewer involved the better, he would always say. So I thought I'd bring it to you before we did anything else. Especially since it involves the robotics division."

Rudy considered his words. Arthur was right; Carl was a *do it yourself* kind of guy. And this sounded a lot more interesting than fast-tracking a meaningless reality show.

But he wanted some more information first.

"Can you tell me a bit more about these *tweaks*?" Rudy asked. "I'll tell you, it sounds a bit ominous, particularly where law enforcement droids are concerned."

"Of course," Arthur replied. "It's mostly a reporting mechanism. Years ago, we realized that droids could be the eyes and ears of the Consortium–and not just law enforcement. It's an incredibly cost-effective way for us to keep an eye on things."

"And less risk than recruiting humans," Rudy added.

"Precisely."

Rudy could see the logic. Not only law enforcement robots, but drones, traffic cameras, security cameras–they were everywhere, and already tied into the Net. He could easily imagine embedding code in existing communication protocols to divert data to other sources. As long as no one looked too closely–and as long as you could control the overall programming and integration effort. Which of course, GRI already did.

"Okay," Rudy said. "I can take care of it. But just to be clear, I think persuasion and the proper leverage will be more than adequate. He just needs some help seeing the big picture. I'll make sure he gets back into his own swim lane. And stays there."

"Excellent," Arthur said. "We'll look forward to hearing how it goes."

"And I'll look forward to learning more about this *we* you keep mentioning."

Arthur smiled. "Touché. Next time we talk, when you're back in New York, we'll find some time to do that."

"Fair enough," Rudy said. As he pushed back from the table and stood, Arthur's hologram winked out, leaving Rudy alone in the room. He made his way back through the door, returning to the wine cellar. Ajay was there, waiting patiently.

"How are things, sir?"

"Great," Rudy replied. He glanced around the room. "How about we grab a couple bottles for dinner?"

"Anything in particular?"

"Something expensive. Red. But lighter, to go with the lobster. Pick one you like. Or better yet, pick two."

"Very well sir," Ajay said. "And your family is still on the beach, if you'd like to re-join them."

"Fantastic. Then there's still time to rescue the kids from that monstrous sea beast."

Rudy bounded up the stairs, leaving Ajay behind.

TWELVE

A true friend is one soul in two bodies.

– Aristotle

Monique and Bhima spent several more days in Singapore, while Bhima wrapped up his affairs and obtained the necessary travel papers. Each evening, they would meet at the café, or in the hotel lobby. Often, they would sit in silence, mulling the implications of the growing connection between the two of them. But they also shared stories; Monique even found herself talking about her childhood, when she and her parents had seemed happy. Bhima added some of his own stories, and recollections from his younger days. There was a casual ease to their conversations–like childhood friends, eager to catch up. But when Monique tried to probe about their moment in the cafe–their shared power, the visions, and their potential meaning–she sensed a continued reluctance. So she dropped the subject.

On their final morning in Singapore, Bhima met her at the hotel, and they traveled together to the airport. She had booked an early flight, scheduled to arrive in Washington DC the evening prior to their departure– the unnatural result of supersonic flight combined with a crossing of the International Date Line. So it was almost midnight by the time they arrived at her home, and both of them were exhausted. After a quick tour of the

house, she set Bhima up in one of her guest rooms, and they both drifted
to sleep.

● ● ● ● ●

Monique awoke early the next day, despite her kitchen-bot's best efforts
to put away the morning food delivery as quietly as possible. Bhima must
have heard the noise as well; he joined her in the kitchen, wearing loose
cotton pants and a dark t-shirt, and looking rested and relaxed despite
their trip halfway around the globe. Monique had thrown on a tank top
and a pair of her favorite yoga pants; it was a casual look that matched her
morning mood.

"Tea?" Monique asked. Bhima had never been outside Singapore, so
she was doing her best to help him with the transition. Gloria would have
laughed at the sudden spike in her maternal instincts.

"Thanks. That would be great." Bhima sat down at the table, directly
across from her.

Monique made the tea herself. As she did, they both absent-mindedly
watched her personal video feed. In the brief time it took her to brew the
tea, she was offered a reduced-rate return trip to Singapore, as well as some
other exotic travel destinations. There was even an introductory offer to
visit one of the new space hotels. The travel offers were interspersed with
a few news stories from the art world, and one about a visiting yogi from
Thailand.

She set two cups of tea on the table. "Don't go sliding these around,
they're full."

Bhima smiled. "Thanks."

"Any plans for the day?" Monique didn't want to push him, but she
was ready for the next step.

"Not sure. Still waking up, I guess."

Monique was quiet for a moment, as they each drank their tea.

"I told you a little about my visions when we were in Singapore," she
said. "But the power we have–I didn't discover it until much later."

The moment was chiseled in her memory, as real as the cup of tea
in her hand. Her visions that day had overwhelmed her. Disoriented,

frightened, and lost, she had reached for a glass of water that was at the far side of the room. And then it was in her grasp—and all over her shirt, as she recalled.

Monique continued. "You've had this ability for years?"

"Just a few years. Right after my mother died."

Monique nodded. "What happened?"

Bhima paused. She could see the internal debate playing out in his features. But before she could offer additional encouragement, the words were tumbling out.

"I was at the crematorium," Bhima began. "Picking up my mother's ashes. There was a line, and the person in front was arguing with one of the workers. It was hot, I was angry, and I was feeling lost. I wanted her with me. I'm not even sure I formed a complete thought, but the urn came to me. I don't even remember seeing it move. There was so much pandemonium around me, no one even noticed."

Monique nodded again; now she understood the small vase that Bhima had retrieved from his luggage last night. He had placed it carefully on the window sill in his room.

"And after that?" she asked.

"Little things. Mostly parlor tricks. Once I pulled a chair out in front of a man that had stolen something from our shop. Broke his arm. That's why I'm a little paranoid about it; I toned it down after that. I never told anyone else."

Monique nodded; now Bhima's reaction to the broken glass in Singapore made more sense.

"And you've never had visions of any kind, like the ones I've described to you?"

"No," Bhima said.

Monique paused for a moment, considering her next words. For her, the point of no return had come and gone when she boarded the plane to Singapore. But she could tell that Bhima was still struggling to understand it all. His mind was at odds with his inner self—it was holding him back. She knew how that felt.

"Bhima," she said. "I know it's a lot to take in. The whole thing is crazy, if you step back and think about it. But that's the mistake—we have to stop thinking, and start to follow our gut. The inner voice that I know you have—just like I do."

Bhima looked directly into her eyes. "I wouldn't be here if I didn't get that. But it's easier said than done."

"I know," she said. "So what if I showed you something that might help? My private studio is downstairs; it's where I practice my meditation–releasing myself from the limitations of the mind. It's where I found you. There is no obligation, and it may lead us nowhere. But I promise it can help you become more relaxed and comfortable about being here."

She watched as Bhima weighed her words. She had pushed the teetering boulder as much as she dared; now it was up to him.

"Why not," Bhima said at last. "Let's try it."

● ● ● ● ●

Bhima followed her through the gym and into her small meditation studio. No one else had ever been inside; a tingle ran up Monique's spine as they passed through the door. What had always seemed empty to her was, in reality, overflowing with drawings, tapestries, and other art that all but covered the walls. It was like a window to her soul, and not one she had necessarily intended to open.

Bhima gazed around the room, lips parted and eyes wide.

"Wow," he said at last.

She closed the door. His simple word and casual smile helped put her at ease.

"I guess you could call this my sanctuary," she said. "First, you should make yourself comfortable. I stand up when I meditate, but that's a little unusual. You may want to sit, or even lie down. It's up to you."

"I'll try standing," he said. "Seems like I should follow your lead."

"Sure. But if it's not working, try something different. Your posture should complement your practice, not be a distraction.

"What works for me," she continued, "is to close my eyes, and focus first on breathing; it helps me relax and to be open. Breathe in through the nose, loosen your muscles–begin at the scalp and work your way down. Then, once you feel completely relaxed, start to shift your focus to your inner self–a place where you can get in touch with your true Being, separate from your mind. Almost to the point of turning off the mind, in fact."

"I'm not sure I follow that last part," Bhima said.

"I know. It's hard to explain. Think about being fully conscious and in the *Now*–letting go of the past and the future. The present moment is all that matters. Concentrate on that place. Hopefully, a door will open–like it did for me. It's the only way I know to get where we want to go."

Bhima was quiet, caught in his own thoughts.

"I'll give it a try," he said at last. "But most of the time I spend on my own is spent thinking about stuff. My future. My problems. Things like that."

"I understand. It may take some time. But I'll be right here. We'll see where it goes."

Bhima remained standing, leaning against the far wall for support. He closed his eyes, and began a pattern of slow, even breathing. At first, he lasted less than a minute before his eyes would open–shaking his head, a flustered look on his face. After more encouragement, he was able to hold his focus longer, but never beyond a minute or so.

"Time out," Bhima said as he opened his eyes again and frowned. "This is harder than it sounds. I think I'm starting to understand what *not* to do–I can tell when my mind wanders or starts to take over. But turning it off is really hard."

Monique nodded. "Absolutely. A lot of people never truly master it. Don't be frustrated. Some say it helps to embrace the distraction–to put all your attention to it. When you do that, it will dissipate, and you can return to your primary focus."

"Maybe it would help if you weren't standing there staring at me," he said. "It's a bit distracting."

Monique laughed. "Good point," she said.

Monique crossed the room and began to stretch. She normally liked to exercise before meditating, but today she'd stick to stretching. She worked her way through an abbreviated routine.

"That's not helping, by the way." Bhima had stopped to watch her, a sheepish smile on his face.

Monique put her hands to her hips and gave him a look, while also trying to fend off the blood rushing to her cheeks.

"Very funny," she said. "But if you had your eyes closed like I told you, this wouldn't be an issue."

Bhima laughed. "Sorry, I'll try. Actually, I'm having fun. And I appreciate your help. Like you said in Singapore, it does feel right."

"Good," she said. "And you're welcome. Just don't make me have to come back over there."

"I get the feeling that would end badly for me."

Monique waved him away. "All right, back to work."

She finished her stretching. Out of the corner of her eye, she could see that Bhima had his eyes closed, and was breathing deeply and slowly in a relaxed, easy posture. She closed her eyes, and began to do the same.

She had practiced her meditation a few times in Singapore, but distractions and her own thoughts had gotten in the way. Now, she was quickly sinking into her place of peace; all her thoughts fell away. She could feel the transformation, and her return to an enlightened state of consciousness. There had been too much thinking–too many *what if's*– over the past several days. Now, they were swept away as the energy and connectedness of just Being flowed through her. She was alone, and back in her familiar place; Bhima's presence no longer registered in her awareness.

Or did it? At the edge of her consciousness, there was something different–an *essence* that extended just beyond her own. At first, she ignored it, assuming it was a subtle intrusion of her own thoughts. But the feeling persisted and, if anything, grew stronger as she settled into the comfort of her inner place. As of yet, the dancing light that would carry her through The Leap was nowhere to be seen.

Monique soaked in the energy; as she did, the ephemeral shape at the fringe of her awareness seemed to pulse; or at least, it connected with her for the briefest of instants. After a moment's hesitation, she reached out, extending her own Being and sense of self toward the source of this new sensation.

She couldn't be sure, but the hazy essence seemed to drift in her direction; it was the kind of dim light that Monique might see if she squeezed her eyes shut too tightly. It floated closer, like a kite on a winding spool, dancing in a soft breeze.

Bhima. The feeling came to her unheeded, though she immediately grasped its fundamental truth. She was still in her place, still felt the calm, the joy, the enlightenment of Being. But now there was also a connection, a link to something that was both part of her and separate. She didn't want to lose the moment by trying to understand it–so she simply embraced it.

And then, the dancing light was there, urging her to follow and make The Leap. She felt a surge of energy as she let go and accepted the transition, opening herself to the visions that she knew would come.

She was not disappointed. But the sights and sounds of Singapore had been replaced. Now she saw an eerie twilight, enveloping a wide and busy thoroughfare. A famous but long-gone iron edifice towered in the background, as a poignant feeling of loss washed over her. The view zoomed to a neighborhood, and then a mixed-color brick building, iron bars on the windows, crowded in amidst a busy city street. The accompanying sounds and smells struck a familiar chord in Monique's senses. Then, two faces—a boy and a girl. Teenagers, a bit gaunt but resilient, staring back as if they were daring her to find them. Their features looked similar enough to be brother and sister.

All at once, she was back in her studio. She took a moment to collect her thoughts—to transfer the feelings and intensity of the vision to her active mind. It was then that she noticed Bhima, sitting against the wall, eyes wide.

"I guess we're going to Paris," he said.

THIRTEEN

Love your enemies, for they tell you your faults.

– Ben Franklin

Jonas's apartment was small–and without the functionality-per-square-foot ratio that transformed small into trendy. It was the most basic of bachelor pads, with a bedroom, bath, galley kitchen, and a modest, adjacent living room. There were no shifting walls, self-adjusting windows, multi-function appliances, or morphing, claytronic furniture elements to maximize the use of space. Instead, the highlight was a view of his neighbor's balcony, a few feet away. But Jonas didn't mind; it was less to clean.

He was slouched in one of his two kitchen chairs, staring at the holophone on the far shelf. It was the most expensive item in the room–and he swore it was mocking him as it sat atop its lofty perch. Even with his doctoral degree and successful small business, Jonas knew where he stood in the world. The company behind his research grant had begrudgingly loaned him the holophone–but only after he promised not to miss any more of their monthly status calls. It was an uneasy truce, to say the least.

Jonas waited for the call, dreading the necessary evil of their regular jousting sessions. It wasn't ideal to take the call at home, but it would be far worse to take the call from Hanssen Scientific, where his staff had to suffer through it as well. Plus, he never knew what Brent might say.

It was a few minutes before nine, still early for him but mid afternoon on the east coast. Jonas glanced through his notes one last time, making sure he had sufficient scientific data and other hocus-pocus to distract them from the larger issues. At the back of the stack was one additional page of notes–the one he had spent the majority of his time preparing. He wished he had the additional data back from Planck III, but it had barely been a week and he was still waiting for the second set of results. He'd have to make do with what he had.

Right on time, the holophone chirped. Jonas reached up and tapped his earpiece; a figure flickered into existence in front of him. Lester White was the executive in charge of Jonas's research grant, a fact that he rarely let Jonas forget. Lester knew just enough science to be dangerous, but not nearly enough to be of any real use. And worse, Lester was not the decision maker. Or at least, as far as Jonas could tell, he was authorized to say *no* but not to say *yes*.

"Good morning, Lester," Jonas said.

"Good afternoon, Professor Hanssen."

"Will Rolland be joining us today?" Jonas despised these calls regardless, but they were worse when Lester's boss, Rolland Hughes, didn't attend. At least he could reason with Rolland.

"No," Lester said. "He's tied up in some more pressing matters."

Jonas didn't bother to hide his disappointment. They had discussed this topic several times before; Lester knew where he stood.

"Sorry to hear that," Jonas said. "But thanks again for letting me do this from the house. It's much easier for me, away from the distractions and commotion of the office. I do appreciate it."

"No problem. Please go ahead with your update."

Jonas glanced down at his notes one last time, and then back to Lester. True to form, Lester was still standing–the king lording over his subject. Fortunately, the holophone only projected participants, and not their surroundings–so Lester couldn't see the apartment. Jonas leaned forward, launching into his speech.

"I'm sure you've seen the most recent data we sent, but let me run through the highlights–"

"I'm not sure I'd use the word *highlights*," Lester interrupted.

"I understand how you might reach that conclusion, but allow me to explain." *Not a good start.*

Jonas continued. "You're right, we still haven't found a suitable asteroid for large-scale mining. But let me tell you what we have found. Obviously, we've eliminated thousands of potential targets–some of which your competitors will likely pursue. To their regret.

"And, we have all of those asteroids mapped and logged, just in case mineral prices or other economic factors suddenly make one or more of them feasible. As you know, a few of the asteroids are within five percent of our minimum parameters."

"And as you know," Lester said, "We have no interest in spending billions on an asteroid that's within five percent of break-even. Or worse." Lester's expression mimicked his impatient tone.

"Understood. Which is why we're also monitoring the latest in mining technology. And in propulsion. And other technologies where cost reductions could alter the fundamental formulas for return-on-investment."

"Professor Hanssen. I get all that. Same as I told you the last time we spoke. So please understand me. My business is supposed to be a profit center–not a cost center. I'm not in the business of funding R&D efforts; I'm in the business of delivering profits. We need a target asteroid. The mining equipment is already in near-Earth orbit, ready to launch. New mining technology is irrelevant to equipment already in space. The only thing that's relevant to me, right now, is that I have underutilized assets sitting out in space. And on my balance sheet."

Lester leaned in toward Jonas, lowering the volume of his voice just a fraction of a notch.

"Look, Jonas. This is the part where I'm supposed to tell you that time is running out. I can't continue to hold your hand every month–I've got orbiting hotels to finish, and a new space elevator getting started in the Galapagos Islands. You should try dealing with the carbon nanotube issues we have down there. Not to mention the damn environmentalists.

"The bottom line is this," Lester continued. "We've given you three months. You have one more. If you can't find a suitable asteroid in the next thirty days, we'll be forced to find someone else who can."

Jonas felt the muscles in his arms tighten; he was gripping his notes like a gale force wind might tear them away. It was all he could do to control his growing frustration.

I'll tell you what you can do with your carbon nanotubes.

But Jonas fought back those thoughts, trying his best to salvage the conversation.

"Is this coming from Rolland?" Jonas asked.

"It's coming from me. Which is all that matters."

"Lester, don't be hasty. Our track record to date speaks for itself. We nailed the numbers on the test asteroid. And you hired us to avoid an expensive mistake—to make sure you don't spend billions on a wild goose chase to a worthless iron-filled rock. Give us the time, and we'll deliver."

"Four months may be hasty in your world, Professor Hanssen. But I can assure you, it's not at all hasty in mine."

Lester put up his hand. "That's all the time I have, Professor. I have another call. I'll talk to you again in a month." The holophone winked off, leaving Jonas to stare at the empty space that had previously been Lester White.

Shit.

Jonas's frustration boiled over; he grabbed his empty coffee mug and flung it toward the wall. But the handle got caught in his fingers, and it sailed well left of his intended target. With a thud, it scored a direct hit to the holophone. He watched helplessly as the holophone teetered, then slid off the shelf and fell, seemingly in slow motion, before shattering into several pieces on the floor.

Jonas leaned back in the chair, his eyes rolling to the ceiling as he expelled a long breath of air. His gaze returned to the table, where he saw his last page of notes protruding from the pile.

So much for dark matter funding.

He yanked the page from the pile, crumpling the helpless sheet into a tiny ball. With an effort, he whipped the crumpled ball at the trashcan across the room.

It bounced on the floor, three feet short.

FOURTEEN

A man always has two reasons for doing anything:
a good reason and the real reason.

– J.P. Morgan

It was Rudy's second week as CEO, and already it seemed the honeymoon was over. He was through the first round of reviews with key staff; a good showing for a company that generated nearly six trillion dollars in annual revenue. A few loose ends still remained, including a few executives who would need to be let go. But those plans were already well under way.

The family had returned from the island late Sunday night, after the lobster dinner. Ajay had even given the girls two extra lobsters to smuggle home with them. Victoria wasn't thrilled, but the damage was already done and she eventually conceded. She refused to concede, however, on their departure time, and they left shortly after dinner–or more precisely, after the kids had finished off the key lime pie. The final slice vanished on the flight back to Teterboro airport. From there, Bond had whisked them straight through the Giuliani Tunnel and home to their penthouse on Central Park West. All in all, it had been one of the best family weekends in ages.

And then came Monday. Rudy had arrived to work early–but not early enough. The backlog was immense; he had asked not to be disturbed over the weekend except in an emergency, and now he was paying the price. There were business partners to mollify, investment decisions to review, acquisition targets to vet, and key positions to fill. And the media, of course—today they wanted his thoughts on the latest death in space—another construction worker at one of the new space hotels. But not one of his hotels, thankfully.

And these were just the items that filtered through to him. Rudy's staff tackled the majority of requests, led by his state-of-the-art Virtual Chief of Staff, Grace. Nearly ninety percent of the messages he received were handled by her deft touch, a percentage that had increased steadily since she had been deployed. He knew this because her AI algorithms had been developed at GRI, and under Rudy's direct supervision. Even when he had finally approved her design for mass production, Rudy had withheld a few of the more complex algorithms for his own use, along with the prototype's unique voiceprint. Grace was truly one of a kind, and he'd be lying if he didn't give her some of the credit for his eventual rise to the top.

So it was mildly amusing when Grace announced an ad hoc meeting with Sandy Kent, one of the senior executives in the advanced robotics software division. She was a long-time colleague, and one of Victoria's favorites. In fact, her son and Shae were the culprits behind the infamous *birding* incident—having attempted to launch a 3D-printed bird from the penthouse roof. It dive-bombed an unsuspecting tourist, costing the man a day at the local health center. It had cost Rudy quite a bit more than that.

"Hello Sandy," he said as she arrived. "I hope you didn't back-door poor Grace just to get in here."

"Rudy, please," Sandy said. "You know I don't need the back door. I'm perfectly capable of talking my way through the front."

"True," Rudy replied, waving her over to the smaller of his conference tables. They both sat down.

"Forgive me," Rudy said. "But I'm swamped. What can I do for you?"

"No problem," Sandy said. "We miss you downstairs, and you know I wouldn't come up here if it wasn't important. I just need you to green-light our offer for that company in Detroit."

Rudy ran her words through his mental rolodex, but he drew a blank.

"Sorry. Way too much on my desk. Refresh my memory."

"It's the *DreaMaker* company. You know, the product they claim allows you to choose your dreams."

"I thought we decided it didn't work," Rudy said.

Sandy smiled, and shook her head. "You didn't read the report I sent over the weekend, did you?"

"Give me a break, Sandy. I'm still catching up. Just fill me in."

"I know, that's why I'm here. Personally, I think the jury's still out on the product itself. It works on some people, but not on others. And they still aren't sure why. It might even be genetic."

"So why do we want it?"

"For the software," she said. "Turns out they are doing some pretty interesting stuff with direct human-to-computer interfaces. We think it may have direct applicability in our current AI work. Like I said, Grace has the details."

Rudy smiled. "Okay, I got it. I'll get back to you before the end of the day."

"Great. Have Grace let me know."

"Will do," Rudy said. But her mention of the AI group had struck a chord; he held up a hand as she started to rise from her chair.

"Hold on, Sandy. A quick question?"

"Shoot," she said.

"Do you by chance know a Martin Fletcher? Works in the AI group?" Rudy had yet to deal with Arthur's request; Sandy's call might turn out to be a fortuitous turn of events. She was on a short list of GRI executives that he trusted implicitly.

"Sure, he's an up-and-comer in the AI integration group. Sharp, a bit of a loudmouth, but usually backs it up. Why?"

Rudy paused. He hadn't really thought this through yet, and he needed to approach it delicately.

"I've heard the same thing," he said. "In fact, the description reminds me a bit of someone else we know."

Sandy laughed. "Funny. It hadn't occurred to me, but you're right. Except that Martin might be a bit smarter than you. And not as loud."

It was Rudy's turn to laugh. "Nice. As usual, a lack of flattery will get you nowhere."

Now for the hook.

"Do me a favor?" Rudy continued. "I've heard a few comments to that effect, and I'd hate to see his career derailed by some youthful over-exuberance. Tell him he's getting noticed, but he needs to keep his head down and deliver. Play by the rules and everybody wins. You know the drill."

Carl had done the same for Rudy, many years ago. It was good advice; he hoped Sandy would take the bait.

"You bet," Sandy said. "He'll be grateful for the message. And the opportunity."

"Thanks. Let me know." Another message from Grace had popped up on his net lens display; he made a face toward Sandy, pointing at his eye. Sandy nodded and waved before opening the door, and letting herself out.

One more off the list. He was sure Sandy could take care of Martin.

Rudy returned to his desk, using his net lens to scroll through his latest messages as he crossed the room. Nothing seemed immediately urgent; instead, he took a moment to find Sandy's notes on the *DreaMaker* acquisition. He transferred the files to his desk monitor with a quick stare, drag, and double-blink. He still had a lot of Monday left on his plate; it was time to get to it.

F I F T E E N

Never doubt that a small group of thoughtful, concerned citizens can change the world. Indeed, it is the only thing that ever has.

– Margaret Mead

They had been back from Singapore for less than a day, but Monique saw no reason to delay the trip to Paris any longer than necessary. Bhima had agreed. As it turned out, an Elite Airlines flight was available late that evening, arriving in Paris early the next morning.

That afternoon, Monique pulled out her drawing supplies, again putting her visions to paper. Bhima joined her, adding his own recollections. Without question, they had both experienced the same vision. Monique was at a loss to explain it, but Bhima described with absolute clarity the moment when he felt her presence, and the sensation of her reaching out to draw him in. He hadn't seen the dancing light, but he clearly made The Leap, nonetheless.

The first vision had been the Eiffel Tower–or more accurately, the Eiffel Tower as it looked before its destruction almost twenty years ago. Monique remembered the details as if it was yesterday; the explosions, followed by the slow, agonizing collapse of the tower as it toppled into the Seine. The story had dominated the news feeds for months, but no perpetrators–or even a motive–had ever been identified. Monique had been there several times as a child–mostly with her mother. So it had saddened her all the more when the French government made the decision not to rebuild it. They had given several reasons; too costly, too much concern it would happen again–and most surprising of all, too much apathy from the French people. The rich didn't need it, and the rest didn't want to pay for it.

Another example of our slow decline.

She and Bhima briefly discussed the potential meaning. Bhima had no personal connection to the events–he was only a few years old at the time. And Monique was equally unsure. Was it just a way to identify the location–like the hotel in Singapore? Or was it a deliberate attempt to trigger her emotions? If so, it implied she was being more than just led. Was she also being manipulated? The visions felt *pure* to her, as much as they felt *real;* she refused to believe that they were anything but benevolent. And she was sure–deep in her gut–that she would discover their purpose, if she just continued down the path.

The second scene centered on a single, mixed-color brick building, crowded amongst several others on a busy city street. It felt like Paris to her; Monique guessed it might be the 12th or 13th arrondissement. She could imagine passing through the area on her way to Vincennes Park. Even more interesting was the small, white sign on the wall of the building: *Orphelinat du Cœur.* An orphanage. She and Bhima searched the Net for the name; much to her surprise, no such name existed. But she was sure she could find it once they arrived in the city.

The final part was easier to draw, especially given Monique's talent for portraits. They gazed together at the finished drawing–the teenage boy and girl staring back at them with a determination that she found a bit unsettling, and yet strangely compelling. She and Bhima had discussed the children at length–the obvious conclusion being that they were wards of the orphanage. They both agreed that they looked like brother and sister–the commonality of features was hard to ignore, particularly in the eyes.

With the drawings complete, they departed for Dulles Airport. Given the lateness of the hour, the metro train was less than full, though the airport terminal was once again overcrowded. Monique purchased tickets while Bhima stood behind her, watching the scene at the south end, where a mass of travelers were being herded through various checkpoints. Monique saw the conflicted look on his face.

"Everything okay?" she asked.

"I guess. It's a bit strange to be over here. I feel out of place. And those tickets are a lot of money."

"Bhima, like I said in Singapore, I don't want you to worry about the money. I've always enjoyed spending money on a good cause. And I'll let you in on a little secret—as far as I'm concerned, it's not really my money."

"Really?" Bhima said. "Then whose is it? I thought you said it came from your mother?"

Monique took a deep breath. "It did, but it's not quite that simple. It's a long story. At the right time, I promise I'll tell you about it."

"Is it stolen?"

Monique laughed. "No, but thanks for the show of faith. It's not stolen, I promise."

Bhima was silent, and Monique left him alone with his thoughts. The silence continued through security, and on the tram to the gate. Once again, the flight was boarding as Monique arrived. Bhima finally spoke as they joined the small line that had formed.

"So you think this is a cause?" Bhima asked. "That we're on some kind of quest?"

"I do. It feels like more than just some wild goose chase. But what do you think?"

"Well, the visions didn't seem random to me. It feels like they have a purpose. But I'm just a beginner. So I'm still not quite sure what I think."

"I get it. We'll take it day to day. And you're always free to go back to Singapore. Remember that."

They passed through the gate area checkpoint, down the jetway, and onto the plane. Bhima gawked at the jet interior, eyes wide. It was his second time on an Elite Airlines flight, but the novelty had yet to wear off.

"Actually, I think I'm good," he said. "I don't need to go home just yet." He gave Monique an exaggerated grin.

She shook her head.

They stowed their bags and settled into their seats. Less than thirty minutes later, they were on their way.

● ● ● ● ●

During the flight, they used the in-seat Net devices to continue searching for the orphanage. There was still no luck finding the name, but Bhima was convinced he found the building on a satellite image, in the heart of the 12th arrondissement, just north of Boulevard Diderot. It was impossible to tell for sure, thanks to the reduced granularity of satellite images on the public internet. The irony didn't escape Monique; it wasn't so long ago that she had spent her own time and money to help gain passage of the Digital Privacy Act. She certainly didn't miss the private drones and voyeur-cams that were so prevalent before the law had passed, but that level of detail certainly would have been helpful to them now.

Regardless, they studied the satellite images and compared them to the drawing. The mix of red and tan exterior brick work, the ornate entrance, and the green doors—all of it matched. According to the Net data, the building in question was a small school. Monique wrote down the address; it was as good a place to start as any.

They landed just before dawn. Given the early hour, they remained on the plane and lingered over breakfast. By the time they had finished, Elite staff had processed their paperwork, and they breezed through immigration and customs, eventually exiting the airport into a cold, rainy morning in Paris.

Outside, Monique searched the taxi queue to find a human driver; there was little chance the driver would recognize the orphanage, but little was better than none. And she had the address as a start.

"Going to the city?" A vehicle had pulled up in front of them. An older man leaned out the window, his arm casually draped over the door.

Monique frowned. Even in Paris, strangers addressed her in English. *Face it—you're just another American now.*

"Yes, the 12th arrondissement. Are you familiar with this address?" She handed him a slip of paper.

"I know where it is," he said.

It was the answer she expected—though not the one she had hoped to hear. She motioned to Bhima, and they both climbed into the back seat. The driver loaded their bags, and they were on their way.

It was morning rush hour; the traffic increased as they approached the city. Monique stared at the passing scenery, awash in childhood memories. She even wondered, just for an instant, where her father might be at this very moment.

"You okay? You seem distracted." Bhima's question brought her back to the present.

"Sure, I'm fine," she said. "Did I tell you that I was born in Paris?"

"No, I would have remembered that. How long did you live here?"

"Not long. We moved away when I was young. My father's company was acquired by an American firm. But we visited occasionally, after that."

"Do you think this is a coincidence? Coming to Paris?"

"I'm not sure. I had also been to Singapore before–though I never lived there. But I think it's more about the people than the place."

"What are we going to do if this isn't the place?"

Monique pondered the question. They had a lot of options.

"Well, we can ask around," she said. "Show people the picture. Or we can go to the hotel. Maybe we go there, check in, and start with the hotel staff."

"We could be here a while," Bhima said.

"We could. Or this could be the place. We'll know soon."

Monique looked back out the window; they had finally exited the Boulevard Périphérique that encircled Paris, and had entered the city proper. She glanced around to get her bearings. With a start, she realized that they were already past Rue de Reuilly, and were continuing down Boulevard Diderot, deeper into the city.

Now I'm a tourist? Monique leaned forward in her seat.

"I think we've done enough sightseeing. Turn at the next intersection and take us directly to the address I gave you. *Merci boucoup.*"

Her reward was an icy stare from the driver, who glanced back for just an instant. But he knew better than to argue, just as she knew better than to expect an apology. This was still Paris, after all.

The driver turned right at the next intersection, and soon the vehicle traffic all but disappeared. On the side roads, cars were replaced by all manner of individual transportation, from bicycles and scooters to lightweight motorboards. Monique was caught off guard by the rapid transition; even the character of the neighborhood had changed. During her early childhood, Paris was increasingly the domain of the wealthy–or at least, what was left of the upper middle class. But things had changed, and a general malaise had clearly begun to invade the outskirts of the city proper. She was sure it wasn't unique to Paris–just the inevitable march of too few with means, and too many with needs. Even now, she could see the decay in the buildings, and in the disrepair of the streets. But especially, she saw it in the eyes of the residents themselves.

She knew the look; she had seen it in Singapore, and even back home in Washington DC. It was a blank stare—people going about their routine, oblivious to the world and people around them. Disconnected. And she could feel it—like an absence of hope.

The driver turned again, and again, now weaving through back alleys in a not-so-subtle attempt to find a more direct route and curry favor from his passengers. They were passing an old hospital, and fast approaching Rue de Reuilly, albeit from the opposite end of the block.

"Stop the car," Monique said. Bhima gave her a curious look. The driver glanced back and slowed down, but didn't stop.

"*Arrêtez, s'il vous plaît.*" That got his attention, and the car slowed to a stop. The driver turned to face her.

"Madame, we're almost there. This is not the place to get out."

"We'll be fine," she said. "You can take the luggage to our hotel. It's not far from here." She gave him the name, along with an additional tip. She also made a show of recording the taxi number, as well as the driver's name. He watched her as she did, an impatient frown affixed to his face.

"When you arrive at the hotel," Monique said, "Tell them to hold the bags for Monique Durand. I have two rooms reserved. Can you remember that?"

The driver nodded, mumbling something in response. He gestured down the block, pointing them toward their destination, before climbing back into his car and driving away.

"What was that all about?" Bhima asked. It had stopped raining, though the air was still cold. Bhima stuffed his hands into his jacket pockets; he was clearly unaccustomed to the colder weather. They began to walk in the direction that the driver had indicated.

"Do you feel it?" Monique stopped and took a few deep breaths, closing her eyes and trying to slow the acceleration of her heart.

"I don't think so. What do you feel?"

"This is the place. I can feel it. You don't feel anything?"

"Maybe, I don't know. I'm not sure what to look for."

"Don't look," Monique said. "Don't think. Feel. When I came to the market in Singapore, I wasn't sure I was in the right place until I saw you. But now, I can feel it. And it's the same feeling I had when I first saw you. Some kind of connection, maybe. I'm still not sure what to call it. But someone else like us is definitely nearby."

"Or maybe two someone else's," Bhima said.

"Good point. Maybe that's why I can feel it already."

They walked down the block, approaching the next intersection. As they reached the corner, Bhima pointed ahead and to his left.

"There," he said.

It was the building. The mixed brick work, the green doors, iron grills over the windows, and a white sign on the front wall. Monique couldn't read the sign from where they stood, but she didn't need to. She knew what it said.

She jogged the short distance to the door; the feeling was strong enough now that it seemed to pull her down the street. She had already rung the doorbell by the time Bhima joined her on the doorstep.

At first, no one answered. Monique began to worry about the time; it was not yet nine o'clock. Still, she rang the doorbell again.

Finally, one of the large green doors swung open. An elderly woman stood in the doorway, her hair pulled back in a tight bun. The door cast a shadow across her face, making it difficult to distinguish her features. But even so, Monique could see her expression–mouth open, eyes wide. Seconds passed before the woman spoke.

"It *is* you. You're here. *Mon dieu.*"

Monique looked at Bhima; he shrugged his shoulders. The implications swirled in her head.

"*Bonjour, madame.* My name is Monique Durand. This is my friend, Bhima. We were hoping we might come in and have a word with you?"

The woman barely hesitated, opening both doors and stepping back to allow them in. Monique followed her inside, with Bhima right behind her. It was clearly no longer a school, though Monique could see that it once had been. The architecture was mid-twentieth century, perhaps a bit older. There was a large room to her right; in front of her, a hallway was marked by several doors on each side. At the end of the hall, a staircase led to the second floor. Paint was peeling from the ceiling, and a few of the chandelier bulbs were out. But the place was clean; Monique could smell the disinfectant as if some had been spilled in the entryway.

"Please, follow me. I'll take you right to them." The woman waived for them to follow. At the end of the hall, she climbed the stairs. Monique and Bhima were close behind.

At the top of the stairs, the hallway turned back to the front of the building. In front of them were three doors; the woman chose the one on the right. She knocked three times on the door before opening it. The lights were already on, so she pushed the door open and gestured for Monique to step inside.

It was a bedroom. There were two single beds, with a dresser between them. But Monique barely noticed; it was the walls that grabbed her attention. They were covered with drawings–at least a hundred of them. And every single one of them–from the smallest of sketches to the largest of portraits–was a drawing of her. Monique. It was overwhelming; she had to remind herself to breathe.

The woman extended her hand. "It's a pleasure to finally meet you. My name is Adele." They shook hands.

"I'll go fetch Ana and Pierre," Adele continued. "They're downstairs at breakfast. As you can see, they've been expecting your arrival."

Adele was still shaking her head as she left the room.

Monique walked to the near wall, studying the closest of the drawings. There was talent in the hand that drew them–and not just technical skill. The nuance of textures and facial expressions was on par with Monique's own expertise. How long had it taken to draw them all? Months? Years?

She heard the pounding footsteps long before she saw them. All at once, they burst into the room–a boy and a girl, teenagers. Monique guessed they were in their early teens. They were the same height, with the same narrow features, thin, dark hair, and the same wiry build. In fact, she now realized, they were twins.

They launched themselves at Monique, enveloping her in a fierce hug. She returned the embrace. Strangely, the feeling she experienced out on the street had diminished; in its place was simpler, more comfortable feeling of familiarity.

"We knew you'd come!" The boy, Pierre, looked into her eyes, a broad smile stretching across his face.

"No one else believed us," Ana said. "Well, except maybe for Miss Adele." Her smile might have been even wider than Pierre's.

"How did you find us?" Pierre asked.

Monique stepped back, and reached into her purse for the drawings. She laid all three on the bed next to them. Ana and Pierre nodded vigorously, studying each of the drawings with intense interest.

"It's so wonderful to meet both of you," Monique began. "My name is Monique Durand. I was born here in Paris, but I've been living in America for most of my life. And this," she pointed to Bhima, "is my good friend, Bhima. I found him the same way I found you."

"Through a vision?" Ana asked.

Now it was Monique's turn to nod in agreement. "Do both of you have these visions?"

"Yes," they answered in unison.

"But Ana did most of the drawings. She's the artist," Pierre added.

Monique took another look around the room. Clearly, the two of them had been having visions for much longer than she had.

"The drawings are amazing, Ana. You're very talented. How long have the two of you been having these visions? There must be a hundred drawings on the walls."

Ana and Pierre exchanged a look; after a moment's hesitation, Pierre reached under one of the beds, and pulled out a low, clear container. It was large—nearly the same size as the single bed. Pierre lifted the lid.

More drawings. Hundreds more. All neatly stacked and organized inside the container.

"Are we leaving with you?" It was Ana's voice. Monique saw the look of anticipation on her face, but her eyes also betrayed a hint of trepidation.

Adele had returned to the room; she cleared her throat to get the group's attention.

"Miss Durand and I will need to discuss that," Adele said. "Why don't the two of you go finish breakfast?" She gave them both a warm smile.

There were a few protests, but eventually Ana and Pierre went back downstairs. Monique didn't expect they'd be gone long.

Adele turned back to Monique and Bhima.

"Well," she began, "I can't say that I understand any of this. Did you really see them in your own vision?"

"We both did," Monique said, glancing at Bhima. "Along with the orphanage. That's how we found you."

"If I hadn't seen it myself, over these past few weeks," Adele said, "I'd never have believed it. In fact, I'm still not sure I do."

"Weeks?" Monique asked. There was no way these drawings had been done in a few weeks.

"Yes," Adele replied. "The twins have only been here a few weeks. And to call this an *orphanage*, I'm afraid, is a bit of a stretch. Even with the fancy sign outside the door."

Monique could see that Adele was building to a longer story; she waited patiently for her to continue.

"Ana and Pierre's parents were killed in a car accident, about two years ago. They were scientists at a small research facility here in Paris. Unfortunately, they had no other family, and it was difficult to place the kids into the foster care system."

No family. The string of coincidences was starting to feel like much more than that.

"Why couldn't they be placed?" Monique asked.

"A number of reasons," Adele replied. "They're old, and they refused to be separated. But most of all, because of this."

Adele waved her hand across the room.

"They started having these visions, not long after the death of their parents. So they didn't stay long at the first facility. And on top of that," she continued, "The system here in France is overloaded–not that we're any different than most. There just isn't anywhere for them to go. So for now, they're here with me."

"So what is *here,* exactly?" Monique asked. "The sign does say *orphanage* out front."

"It does," Adele said. "And this used to be an orphanage. But it was shut down, about a year ago. Budget cuts. So now it's just me, the caretaker. Until they decide what to do with the building."

"And what about the kids?"

"Their parents and I had a mutual friend. It's a long story, but the short version is that they're here with me–unofficially–until I find them something more permanent. I have plenty of room, and I don't expect anyone from the government will be checking on us here, at least not anytime soon. So I took them in. About a month ago."

There was pause in the conversation; Adele seemed to be collecting her thoughts.

"So now what?" Monique finally asked.

Adele appeared lost in thought; Monique waited for her to respond.

"So now," Adele said at last, "You try to convince me to let you take them with you. *N'est-ce pas?*"

Monique smiled; she appreciated Adele's directness. She saw Bhima grinning as well. *Déjà vu.* Even the kids had known why she was here.

Teenage twins. I've officially lost my mind.

The boulder at the edge of the cliff wasn't just teetering; it had started to careen down the hill.

"Adele, thank you," Monique said. "And you're right; I am here to convince you. I'd be honored to give it a try."

S I X T E E N

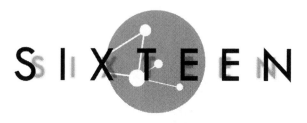

*The oppressed are allowed once every few years
to decide which particular representatives of the
oppressing class are to represent and repress them.*

– Karl Marx

Jonas arrived at Kat's apartment just as the morning sun had crested Wa'ahila Ridge, spilling its first rays into the Manoa valley. He had called her as early as he dared–and after a fitful night of sleep. He took one of the bike shares from his neighbor's building–they had been nice enough to give him access, and he wouldn't be putting his life on the line at this early hour. Kat had offered to make coffee; he could use the friendly ear.

The two of them had been near-constant companions over the past several days. The first evening at the coffee shop had turned into a second, followed by a third. She was easy to talk to–charming, unassuming, and full of youthful exuberance. They had a lot in common–after a difficult childhood, she had put herself through college, arriving in Honolulu with a master's degree and barely enough money for bus fare. She had lucked into the small apartment near campus–it belonged to the family of a close college friend. She only paid the utilities, and she had the place to herself. This was his first time in her apartment; he took a quick look around as she let him through the door. It was small, but neat and well appointed. It was a notch or two above his place—smaller, *and* more functional. Plus, it came with a rudimentary, early-model maid-bot. Jonas was already jealous.

Over coffee, he filled her in on the call with Lester. He had let go of his initial anger; truth be told, he just didn't care that much about finding asteroids for the rich. But the work paid the bills and, more importantly, allowed him the time to pursue his dark matter research. Plus, there was his team to consider. They counted on him to keep the grant money flowing.

Coffee soon turned into breakfast. She had made haupia, one of his favorite local dishes. She ate hers straight from a cup, but Jonas poured the pudding onto a leftover brownie he found in the fridge, and drizzled some chocolate on top. Kat just stared at him, shaking her head. After breakfast, Jonas made a show of trying to help with the dishes, but the maid-bot would have none of it.

Kat went back to her room to finish getting ready for class. He glanced at his watch; he needed to head to the office soon. The team needed to know about their looming deadline, and the implications. They were already burning the candle at both ends—he wasn't sure how much more pushing he could do over the next thirty days. Plus, the Planck III data was due back any day. *Timing is everything.*

"Are you leaving soon?" Kat was standing in the kitchen doorway, looking even better than she had when he arrived.

"I need to get to the office," he said. "Sorry I came over and dumped on you; all this shop talk must be getting old."

"Not at all," she said. "But maybe next time we could try something other than the spectroscopic properties of precious minerals."

"I see," he said. "So for the record, you're not a fan of precious stones? That's good to know."

"Funny. We'll see how you like it tonight, when you get to help me study for my quantum mechanics exam."

"You think so?" Jonas replied. "Is that your best attempt to ask me on a date?"

"Oh, I'm not asking," Kat said. She was giving him that look again; he doubted anyone had ever said no to that look. He certainly wasn't going to try.

"Of course I'll help. Not that you need it."

She smiled and joined him in the kitchen.

"Thanks," she said. "But believe me, I could use the help. So go if you need to."

"I have a few minutes," he said. "Besides, I'm really not looking forward to telling the team."

Kat pointed to a chair at the kitchen table; he sat down while she finished in the kitchen. Already, her close proximity was improving his mood.

"Everything will be fine," she said. "I'm sure you'll find a big, fat, juicy asteroid soon."

"I hope so. The alternatives aren't so great."

"What's the worst that can happen? I bet another mining company would hire Hanssen Scientific in a heartbeat."

"Maybe. But I worry about Brent and Kahli. I know they live paycheck to paycheck."

"Don't we all," Kat said. She was quiet for a moment, as she helped put some dishes back in the cabinet above her head, where the old-fashioned maid-bot couldn't reach. Jonas watched as she stood on her tiptoes, stretching to slide plates onto the top shelf. He probably shouldn't have been staring, but he couldn't help himself.

"Doesn't it bother you?" Kat continued. "Working with this huge company, and all the money you've made for them? How can they pay you so little? You should be making a fortune."

Oh, it bothers me. It was a decision that ate at his gut nearly every day. But that was behind him; he was resigned to the realities. For now, though, he wasn't ready to burst Kat's bubble.

"Sure, it bothers me a little," he said. "But it's a choice I made. A tradeoff. For them, it's simple supply and demand. They have a global marketplace for the kind of expertise I offer; technology allows them to buy it from anywhere in the world. So I don't have much leverage."

"But you have your algorithms," she said. "And a great team. No one else has that."

"It's not that simple. Unfortunately, they own the rights to the algorithms. And the data. It was part of the deal we agreed to up front. We could have tried to keep the rights, and get paid for results. A cut of the profits from asteroids we found. At the time, we weren't in a position to take that risk. So we sold the rights in exchange for some security."

"But you keep improving the algorithm. Without you, the data isn't worth nearly as much."

"I appreciate that you think I'm so special," Jonas said. He gave her a wink. "But the reality is that there are thousands of hungry physicists out there, just like me. Or close enough for their purposes. With what they already have, I doubt they would miss a beat."

"Thousands?" Kat looked incredulous. "So are you saying I made a mistake by coming here to get a Ph.D.?"

So much for Kat's bubble. He should have known; she was too smart to miss the implications.

"Look, you know I'm thrilled that you're here. You don't have to listen to me; I'm a skeptic. But it's simple math. Robotics and other technologies mean fewer jobs. And a single computer chip now has more processing power than the human brain. So governments react with enormous education subsidies, especially low-cost classes over the Net. So college became the new high school. Or maybe grad school is the new high school."

Might as well give her both barrels. Jonas plowed ahead.

"Here's the best part. People like me generally have enough money to get by. We're far better off, and better educated, than any previous generation. And we're taught to be self-sufficient; what college graduate wants to admit he can't make a decent living? So we get along, barely, in a world expertly balanced to provide just enough to keep us from causing trouble. And wait, it gets better. People over sixty-five are now more than a quarter of the population. But they are over *fifty* percent of the voting population. So every extra dollar goes to helping them live past a hundred–and not to us twenty and thirty-somethings. We have no voice."

Kat had stepped away from the dishes, watching him intently as he spoke.

"Well, that was quite a speech," she said. "So the American dream is dead, is that what you're saying?"

"Sorry," Jonas said. "I'll get off my soapbox. I don't usually pull it out until I've been dating someone for at least a month."

"Don't worry. My dreams aren't so easily squashed."

"That's good. Because statistically speaking, getting rich is more than one hundred times less likely than it was just a generation ago. And over a thousand times less likely than it was fifty years ago."

"Then I guess we'd better double down on that dark matter research, huh?"

"You know," Jonas said, standing up and crossing the kitchen to wrap his arms around her waist, "You might be worth keeping after all."

"Thanks," she said. "Though the jury's still out on you. Now get moving, or you'll be late again."

She was right; Kahli and Brent would be waiting for him.

"Do you still want me to call you if the Planck III results come in?"

"What do you think? Absolutely."

"It's got to be in the next day or two. I tightened the parameters to make sure we could confirm a match, but I'm surprised we still haven't received a return signal."

"Jonas," she said.

"What?"

"Go. You can't keep being late for everything."

"Funny. Because I'm pretty sure I can."

"That was then. This is now. I was sent here to whip you into shape. Get a move on."

Jonas leaned in for a kiss.

"How can I resist a woman who threatens to whip me?" he said as he walked out the door.

Maybe we can beat the odds.

She was certainly making the case to try.

SEVENTEEN

We do not have a money problem.
We have a values and priorities problem.

– Marian Wright Edelman

Tuesday started on a better note, as Rudy awoke to enjoy an early breakfast with the kids. Rosie had each of their favorites ready–a fresh fruit smoothie for Sonja, chocolate chip waffles for Shae, and sugary-sweet Texas red grapefruits for Rudy. His favorite producer had a waiting list now–and the outrageous prices to go with it–but they were worth every penny. Rudy always ate two on Tuesdays, the morning after his weekly shipment arrived.

The three of them ate in near-silence. He relished their quiet mornings–and spending time with his girls as they prepared for another whirlwind day. They left for school at seven; he would follow them down to the lobby, and Bond would whisk them off to school. They were in the three percent of New York children enrolled in a traditional school setting–he and Victoria were strong believers in a full-fledged classroom environment. Of course, it helped that they could afford the six-figure tuition.

The thought of school led Rudy's mind back to Carl. They had first gotten to know each other during the campaign for education reform, and the Digital Education Act. Rudy had still been young; it was an eye-opening immersion into bare-knuckle politics. Ultimately, they had overcome the National Education Association's last-gasp effort to protect an outdated educational model. And even more important, they had scored an enormous contract for GRI's digital education platform, which was now the educational solution of choice for the vast majority of U.S. public schools. And the resultant uptick in U.S. standardized test scores had been clear vindication. It was Rudy's first big-time contract, and it had kick-started his career. As well as his relationship with Carl.

His thoughts were interrupted by Victoria, who had arrived to join them at the kitchen table.

"Paid the price last night for our little getaway, did you?" She may have been late to breakfast, but she was never late with the morning jab. She gave him a quick kiss as she sat down to eat.

"I suppose," Rudy replied. "But I was here to make breakfast for the kids. Not a bad tradeoff."

"Dad, Rosie made breakfast," Sonja corrected.

"Well, I programmed her. Doesn't that count?"

"A dog with some notes could program her," Victoria said. "Which you know, since you designed her."

"So I'm a victim of my own success." Rudy winked at the girls; they both rolled their eyes. Even at a young age, they were grizzled veterans of the regular sparring sessions between mom and dad.

Victoria shook her head–though the smallest hint of a smile gave him the all-clear sign.

"I shouldn't be too late tonight," he said. "That was the other reason I wanted to stay last night."

"Dad, can we make something on the new printer tonight? I have some awesome ideas." Shae gave him an expectant look; he could only imagine what nefarious schemes they had concocted for the poor, innocent nano-fabricator.

"Maybe. Ask me again tonight after your homework is done."

"Yes!" Shae exclaimed. She and Sonja exchanged a look; they knew from experience what *maybe* meant.

Rudy and the girls grabbed their things, and took the elevator to the ground floor, where Bond was waiting. Rudy gave them a hug before they sped off to school. Then, he climbed into his own waiting sedan for the short trip to GRI.

• • • • •

At the office, his morning was relatively uneventful; Grace had worked through the night, optimizing his schedule and delegating lesser items wherever possible. The day started with a holophone conference between the heads of their European businesses, led by their Istanbul-based President of European Operations. The group lobbied him to let them take over GRI operations in Antarctica. Rudy understood their desire–it was one of GRI's fastest-growing units, and the current leadership wasn't meeting its growth goals. But Rudy worried that the stodgy, old-world mentality of the Europeans wasn't a good fit for Antarctica–since the expiration of the last environmental treaty, it had become the new Wild West, with a business culture that rewarded an act-first-beg-forgiveness-later mentality. GRI had taken advantage, of course, with several mineral and water projects well underway. Rudy told the group he would give them an answer in a few days.

Afterwards, he sat for an interview with a worldwide business news feed–one of the few in which GRI had no ownership interest. Those were always tricky, so Rudy had done his homework. The topic was GRI's desalinization business, and whether raiding the oceans to quench the world's growing thirst was preferable to strategies that reduced consumption. But Rudy had tackled this topic before; GRI had an entire public relations army to provide him with relevant facts, figures, and amusing anecdotes. It had been an easy affair. So it was past eleven when Sandy stopped by, poking her head in the doorway.

"Grace said I could have a few minutes." She came in and shut the door before he could answer.

"Sure. You got my approval of the acquisition terms, right? Is there a new wrinkle?"

"No," she said. "That's proceeding as planned. The owner is going to accept the offer; you could see it in his eyes."

"Great. So what's up?"

"It's that other thing," she said. "Martin Fletcher. I spoke with him last night, and I'm sorry to say it didn't go as I expected. So I thought I should come up here and fill you in personally."

"Sure. Go ahead." Rudy turned back to his desk, trying to hide his disappointment.

"Well, I tracked him down in the AI lab last night; he was working on some revisions to the latest law enforcement protocols. He's been making some amazing progress, you know."

"Like I said, I had heard. But go on."

"I started casually, checking in and asking about his work. He gave me an opening to mention you, and I used it to give him the pep talk we discussed. His reaction surprised me."

"How so?"

"He got angry. Started ranting about his latest updates, and how they were being undermined by one of our business partners. He thinks they are trying to circumvent some of his algorithms through a sophisticated web of counter-commands."

"Do you believe him?"

"No idea. I'd have to spend a week sorting through all the code. And I'm sure I'd need help. But he's certainly convinced."

"I assume the partner is Alpha Robotics? Any idea why he'd think they would do this?" Rudy was taking a risk now, but he had to ask the question. It would look more suspicious if he didn't.

"Marty thinks they want to take credit for his work; he's petrified their name will go on these latest updates. He also thinks the changes pose some kind of danger. But without further investigation, I can't say whether that's the case, or it's just his ego talking."

Good. No full-fledged conspiracy theory. Or at least, not yet.

"Thanks, Sandy. I appreciate the update. You can't really blame him for wanting to protect his work." Rudy paused a moment to consider his next steps. He needed to tread carefully.

"The last thing I want to do is put you in the middle of a mess with Alpha Robotics. I know how important they are to the business. So let me handle it from here. I can do some poking around without getting either of our hands dirty; I'll deal with Alpha Robotics myself if and when the time comes."

"Are you sure? What about Marty?"

"Yes, I'm sure," Rudy said. "Marty will be fine. He'll get over this ego thing, and eventually he'll see the intent of your message. And if any of his claims prove to be true–which I doubt will be the case–we can deal with them then."

"Got it," Sandy said. "Sorry this became a bit of a mess." She turned and walked to the door.

"Not your fault. Like I said, I'll take care of it. And one more thing."

"Yes?" she said.

"Are you ready to admit you were wrong now?"

"About what?"

"It looks like Marty is a bit louder than me, after all."

"It's a horse race, I'll give you that." Sandy shook her head as she walked out the door.

He could only hope the humor would put her back at ease.

● ● ● ● ●

Rudy leaned back in his chair, trying to collect his thoughts. Their talk wasn't a complete disaster, though he knew it was far from the result Arthur was expecting. His net-phone sat on the desk, and Rudy stared at it, contemplating his next course of action.

A direct confrontation with Martin was out of the question—even more so now than it had been at the outset. Martin's internal radar was no doubt on high alert now, and a visit from the CEO would only set off more alarm bells. Sandy was one of his most trusted associates; if she couldn't manage to get him back in line, then he doubted anyone else would be able to, either. And he couldn't give anyone else the added context that would help get the job done. So from his desk as CEO, he was stuck.

And there was no need to call Alpha Robotics. Their engineers were changing the algorithms, exactly as Martin had implied—though perhaps not as skillfully as Arthur might like to believe. It wasn't yet a crisis, but it had advanced beyond the mildly troublesome stage that Arthur had described on Sunday.

Rudy despised having to ask for help. He was only a few weeks into the new role; these most recent events weren't going to impress Arthur, let alone the Chairman. But he was also a realist. The problem was still relatively trivial, and likely containable with the added resources of the Consortium. They could back off the algorithm changes for now— or perhaps find an alternative way to achieve the same outcome. Rudy could see no other path that didn't lead to additional risks, or additional questions. Or worse.

Rudy considered, for a minute, what the Consortium's end game might be. Arthur had called the changes *tweaks to the reporting mechanisms*. If that was the case, why were they in the integration layer? Unless, of course, it was for that very reason–because no one would think to look there. And how important were these changes? How far would they go to ensure they were in place? He was about to find out.

He picked up his net-phone, and held it with his index finger pressed firmly to the hidden spot on the back shell. After a few seconds, the net-phone silently switched modes, self-authorizing through the chip in his hand. A menu appeared; he pressed the option to dial Arthur, and waited for the connection to complete.

Arthur's voice came on the line. "Good morning, Rudy."

"Good morning." A small green LED was lit, activated by a combination of voice recognition software, and the chip implanted in each of their hands. As long as the light remained green, the line was secure, and both parties were positively identified. They could speak freely.

Rudy got right to the point. "I have an update for you regarding Martin Fletcher. Unfortunately, not a good one."

"I see. Let's hear it."

"I had a trusted colleague from the AI division approach him, rather than doing it myself. That would have been too out of place. We agreed on the message she would deliver; it was couched as a pat on the back, combined with a reminder to stay focused on his work and the big picture. A few minutes ago, she stopped by to tell me that he didn't take it well. He's convinced that something fishy is going on with the AI algorithms."

"What did he say, exactly?"

"The good news is that he thinks the whole thing is an attempt by Alpha Robotics to take credit for his ideas. The bad news is that he's adamant about it. Either your guys at Alpha are sloppy, or he's just a lot smarter than they are. He also said that the changes were somehow dangerous."

There was silence on the line as Arthur digested the news. Rudy waited patiently.

"The people at Alpha are not sloppy," Arthur said. "I can promise you that. Martin is a talented scientist. You were right to call me–offhand I don't see any way for you to take this further without an undue level of risk."

Rudy nodded; they were in agreement on that.

"Fortunately, this is a scenario we contemplated, and we have a contingency plan in place. It will take a few days to execute, but we should have this resolved before the end of the week."

"Hold on, Arthur. What do you mean by *resolved*?"

"I mean as in fixed. We'll take care of it."

"How? Given the situation, I think I should know a bit more than that." Rudy wasn't sure he wanted the answer, but he had to ask.

"I'll do you one better, Rudy," Arthur said. "We're going to show you."

Rudy was taken aback. "Show me what?"

"Relax, Rudy. You're off to a great start, and we don't want this small setback to put you off in any way. These things happen all the time; it's human nature. As I've said, we're all about a thousand little changes, not major events. You'll see. Plus, this will help provide you with some additional context as to how we do things. Don't worry, it's nothing to lose sleep over.

"Give us a few days," Arthur continued. "We'll send you a message. And thanks again for the call. It was the right decision." Rudy heard a click on the line as the call ended.

Rudy leaned back in his chair. He had no idea what had just been set in motion, but he could feel the hairs on his neck rise as he thought about the fate of Martin Fletcher. Somehow, he doubted that the Consortium's definition of *little changes* was going to seem so little to Marty.

E I G H T E E N

A solitary fantasy can totally transform one million realities.

– Maya Angelou

 Monique was glad to be home; she was even happier to be stealing a few minutes of quiet time, no matter how early the hour. A fresh cup of tea helped to clear her mind.

The last few days had been a whirlwind. Not just in the logistics of returning to the U.S., but also in her transition to some bizarre form of pseudo-motherhood. She imagined that the twins would be a handful for even the most seasoned of parents—and she was anything but. Fortunately, they were good kids at heart; she had already become quite fond of them.

Relaxing over her cup of tea, she reflected on the events of the past few days. She had spoken at length with Adele, explaining what she knew, and providing some of her own background. Adele had asked some tough questions, but was ultimately swayed by her story—and by the twins, who were busy packing. The constant reminder of the drawings, piled on each of their beds, most likely also contributed to Adele's decision. In the end, Adele had admitted that the twins would soon be taken from her care—one way or the other. And Monique seemed a far superior option to the current realities of the French foster care system.

All that had remained was the mountain of paperwork–though at Adele's suggestion, Monique also made a sizeable donation to the foster care program itself. Adele was well-versed in the intricacies of the French bureaucracy, and assured her that the money would all but guarantee a smooth return home. It had been surprisingly easy for Monique to transfer the funds–any guilt she might have felt was more than offset by her growing sense of *rightness;* it was simply another step in the journey, and another way to put her wealth to good use. And sure enough, they flew home without incident, just a few days later.

Monique sipped her tea, letting her thoughts continue to wander. Since finding Ana and Pierre, there had been scant opportunity to ponder her next steps. But now, fresh from a full night's sleep and alone in the kitchen, her mind began to race. She had always been quick to embrace a good cause, and this certainly felt like one–though to what end, she was still unsure. What was the underlying purpose? The *real* purpose–not just the wanderings of what felt like a modern-day Noah. Besides, her ark was now out of spare bedrooms.

She heard noises from down the hall; probably Bhima, though perhaps the twins were also early risers. She wondered whether the group would be ready to take the next step with her.

There was one way to find out.

On cue, Bhima strode into the kitchen, followed by Ana and Pierre.

"So when are we going to see the next vision?" Ana asked, before she had even reached the table.

Over the past few days, they had discussed their visions, and in particular how Monique's had changed immediately after finding Bhima. Ana and Pierre were both eager to see if it might happen again, but Monique wanted to wait. It was enough just getting the twins back home; she didn't want to inject any additional complications. But now, she was ready. "We can go downstairs as soon as everyone is ready."

Pierre looked around the room. "Why downstairs? Why not right here?"

Monique considered his words. She had meditated all over the world, but she had never had the visions anywhere but in her studio. Early on, she preferred it that way–it was a controlled and safe environment. But things had changed.

"We could try that, sure," Monique said. She looked at Pierre. "Have you ever done this with more than just the two of you?"

"No," he said. "We've tried to include others–like Adele. But they were closed to us. There was no connection."

"What do you think makes us different?" Ana asked.

"I'll tell you what I think," Bhima said. He looked around the table. "You've been at this for a while. But the other day was my first time. I think it has to do with being able to turn off your mind. That's probably automatic for all of you, but it's hard. We're wired to be tightly bound to our minds; it's who we are. I doubt many people can let that go. *You are what you think,* right?"

Monique nodded; it did make some sense.

"Without your help the other day," Bhima continued, "I don't think I would have gotten there. Not until you reached out for me. Or whatever you want to call it."

"Tell us more," Monique said.

"It was like being adrift–alone–and you threw me a life line. But it was more than that. Because at the same time, there was a pulling sensation–like you were helping me to separate from my thinking self. Leaving my mind behind. Without the help, I don't think I would have been able to do it. Or at least, it would have taken me a long time to figure it out for myself."

"Pierre and I started having our visions at the same time," Ana said. "So we never tried to connect like that. Or maybe, we already were connected."

"Interesting," Monique said. "After my visions started, I spoke with a few of my former instructors. Not about the visions, but about the place I had found, and the intensity of the experience. The sense of joy, but also the strong feeling of *purpose*. A few of them claimed a similar experience. Yet somehow it didn't sound the same to me. They would use words like serenity, or tranquility, or peace. For me, it's more than that–like a feeling of urgency, or maybe, unmet intentions. Does that make any sense?"

The other three nodded their heads. It was time to press forward.

"Is everyone ready?" Monique said.

There was a tangible excitement in the room. Monique took a last look at Bhima, who sat next to her. He had already closed his eyes. She briefly considered standing up, but didn't want to disrupt the momentum of the moment. So she remained in her seat, and closed her eyes as well.

She slowed her breathing, and turned her focus inward. Much more quickly than she expected, the journey began. The separation from her thinking self was almost immediate; the abruptness of the transition startled her. She was in her private place—though it was no longer private. She could sense the others, and could even discern their identities as they approached. First was Pierre, by far the strongest aura. Ana was beside him, fainter and yet in some ways just as closely connected. And then Bhima, less defined but there, nonetheless. Without knowing how, she sensed a type of communication between them. Not thoughts—more like feelings, intertwined with instinct. They built on the sense of purpose that continued to grow inside her—a common thread that urged her on.

A familiar light approached. Monique steadied herself for The Leap, and the surge of energy that came with it. All at once, they were across.

The visions came in a rush. She saw a sprawling city astride a wide river, awash in a haze of sun and sand. The ancient and instantly recognizable pyramids were barely visible in the distance, juxtaposed against the glare of the rising sun. The vision shifted, and a building appeared. It was a T-shaped, neo-classical building in faded red stone, abutting an open space that combined green gardens, statues, and paved walkways.

And then, there was a face. It was a lone woman, with an olive complexion and long, black hair. Her dark, midnight-sky eyes peered back at Monique, unblinking. She wore a red scarf, wrapped around her head and neck.

The image faded, and with a rush, Monique was back at the kitchen table. She looked around at her companions; Bhima's eyes were still closed, but Ana and Pierre were already staring back at her. Pierre could barely contain the grin on his face.

"What's so funny?" Monique asked.

"Don't be mad," Pierre said, stealing a quick look at his sister. "But it was so awesome not to see your face again."

● ● ● ● ●

They remained at the kitchen table, discussing the vision and comparing notes. The location was obviously Cairo, Egypt; a quick search on the net confirmed the building to be the Museum of Egyptian Antiquities—more commonly known as the Cairo Museum. None of them had been to Cairo before, including Monique; she was surprised at her own sense of relief, with the journey now set to diverge from her early childhood travels. She wasn't sure why, but the anonymity of a trip to Cairo somehow put her at ease. Not that a trip to Cairo should put anyone at ease.

"Can we leave today?" Pierre wasn't wasting any time.

"I'm not sure we all need to go," Bhima said.

"One step at a time," Monique said. "Ana, can you draw the woman we saw? Let's get that done before we forget any of the details. I don't think we need to draw anything else."

"Sure!" Ana said. "I'll go get my stuff." After a moment's hesitation, Pierre slid from his chair and followed after her.

"What are you thinking, Bhima?" Monique wanted to take advantage of the few minutes they would have alone.

"I'm not sure. Everything is moving so fast. I just don't think we want to be traveling the world like it's a family vacation."

"Do you want to stay behind with the twins? I could go to Cairo on my own."

"No." Monique detected a trace of defensiveness in his tone.

"Well, I don't want you to go alone either. And we're obviously not leaving the twins here, or with a stranger. So I think it's best if we stick together, at least for now. After we find this woman, we can reconsider. Does that make sense?"

"I suppose. Cairo just worries me."

"I know. Me, too." Monique couldn't blame him for the concern; it was one of the reasons she had never been there. Central Africa's quick and surprising rise as a world banking power had left Egypt and other countries of northern Africa far behind. The result was a country still struggling to find its place, and stuck in a decades-long cycle of revolution and regime change. Now that she thought more about it, and with the addition of two teenagers, she would have preferred a trip to almost anywhere else.

Bhima still wasn't finished. "And what about–"

Monique held up her hand. Ana and Pierre were returning to the kitchen; Ana carried a sketch pad and pencils in her hands.

"We can do the drawing together, while we plan the trip," Pierre said. "Lucky for us we haven't even unpacked yet!"

"I'll take a look at flight schedules while the two of you work on the drawing. Bhima, any chance you could make some breakfast?"

"Depends. If you want me to make breakfast, then yes. But if you're asking me to program that robot of yours, then probably no."

Monique laughed. "Fine, I'll look up the flights from here. You figure out what everyone wants to eat and then we'll decide how to make it. Careful, though. You might learn something along the way."

Bhima shot her a look, eyebrow raised. He turned to the fridge and began a search for breakfast options. Monique did her own search, scrolling through the Net for available flights to Cairo. She found a flight that evening, and added a suggested hotel in the heart of downtown; she updated the request to include three rooms, and tapped the Purchase button.

Number Four, here we come.

● ● ● ● ●

Bhima proved to be fairly adept in the kitchen; his blended breakfast drink was surprisingly good–although the twins had required some coaxing before they would try it. Bhima revealed that bok choy was the source of the pale green color, but he refused to divulge the spices or any other ingredients he had used. "Family secret," was all he would say.

During breakfast, the group worked on the drawing. They argued over the details–the thickness of the eyebrows, the contour of the nose, the fullness of the lips. At every phase, Ana was forced to draw and re-draw until all agreed it was right. In the end, the drawing was exactly as Monique remembered, right down to the mole below her left eye.

Ana pushed the drawing to the center of the table. They sat together in silence, staring at the completed work. Looking at each of the others, Monique could sense a shift–an almost perceptible readiness to move ahead.

"Can I ask a question?" Pierre said at last. He was looking at Monique, still holding his empty glass.

"Sure, go ahead," she said.

"I get that your job is to find people. Ana and I have the visions." Pierre looked at Bhima.

"So what does Bhima do?"

Monique suppressed a smile. Pierre certainly wasn't shy. But she had an idea where this was headed. Bhima jumped in before she could speak.

"Can I show him?"

Monique considered the question. *Why not?*

"Go ahead," she said. "But be nice."

Pierre had a confused look on his face. Bhima turned to face him.

"It's true, my room wasn't plastered with drawings of Monique when she came to get me. I didn't know about the visions. I was more surprised than she was when she found me. But we did have something else in common."

"What was that?" Pierre said.

Bhima looked over at Monique; she nodded her head. He turned back to Pierre and held out his clenched fist over the table.

"This," he said.

Pierre stood up from his chair to get a closer look; Bhima still hadn't opened his hand.

"What?" Pierre pleaded. "Show me!"

"You bet," Bhima said. He opened his hand, which was empty. At the same instant, Pierre was lifted off the floor, knocking over his chair as he sailed through the air. There was a dull *thump* as he hit the far wall; he was suspended three or four feet off the ground. Monique would have sworn an invisible hand had shoved him from the table, and they were watching the replay in slow motion.

Pierre's look was a mix of panic and confusion; Ana sat rigid in her chair, mouth agape in disbelief.

"What are you doing?" Pierre yelled. "Put me down!"

But apparently, Bhima wasn't done. Pierre began a clockwise spin, back against the wall, his arms and legs flailing freely. When his head reached the six o'clock position, Monique finally broke in.

"Bhima, enough."

To his credit, Bhima let him slide gently to the floor, where Pierre collapsed in a heap. Ana chose that instant to let out a short, high-pitched shriek. Monique nearly jumped out of her skin.

Bhima's been practicing. Good for him.

Pierre was already standing up, pulling his shirt back down over his exposed midriff. He looked to be fine, save for the slightly bruised ego.

"Are you okay, Pierre?" Monique asked.

"Sorry if I got a little carried away," Bhima added.

"I'm fine, I'm fine," he said, looking at Ana. She seemed to have relaxed; Monique could see the tension releasing from her neck and shoulders. Pierre turned to Bhima, eyes wide.

"Dude, you have *got* to teach me that!"

NINETEEN

No great discovery was ever made without a bold guess.

– Sir Isaac Newton

Tuesday raced past, still without word from the Planck III satellite. It was just as well–Jonas spent the day with his team, running full diagnostics on all of Hanssen Scientific hardware and software. They had decided to shift the search to another region of the asteroid belt, not far from the previous location, but closer to Earth. This required shifts in the telescope trajectories, as well as updates to various search parameters. The initial programming had taken most of the day.

It was late Tuesday night before they finished the initial recalibration work. He had called Kat and begged forgiveness. She told him to go home and get some rest, which he did. He was exhausted.

Wednesday was much the same–more calibrations, more testing, and more frayed nerves. Kahli in particular was on a short fuse, with funds running low and the team still calibrating, rather than searching. Finally, on Wednesday night, they re-initiated the search. Even Kahli had succumbed to the need for a bottle of champagne. They toasted to luck; they would need it.

It was now more than a week since he had sent the new instructions to Planck III. Jonas was officially concerned.

Thursday arrived as a different sort of beast; now they were in waiting mode, with less than four weeks until the deadline. Jonas wondered whether the others had quietly begun testing the job market; he couldn't really blame them. In their position, he probably would have done the same.

When his earpiece finally did make the long-awaited chirping sound, he nearly knocked his coffee off the table. He tapped the button, and the computer-generated voice at the other end provided confirmation–the Planck III data was coming in. Brent and Kahli knew the sound; they each nodded, and Jonas was out the door before a single word was uttered.

Jonas had borrowed his neighbor's bike share again, so he rode it to the lab, bobbing and weaving through the late morning traffic. It wasn't that far–just a few miles, and he stuck mostly to side streets. But the ride was more uphill than not, and combined with his level of urgency, he was fortunate to arrive in one piece, and only three-quarters exhausted. Nevertheless, he left the bike leaning against a wall, and headed for the lab at a sprint.

Inside, he skidded to a stop at his computer terminal. The computer recognized his presence, and the screen came to life. As he caught his breath, the data came in a rush–just as it had before. It would take time to do a full comparison, but he didn't need time to understand the immediate implications. It was the same data. The same readings.

Confirmation.

Stay calm. Don't jump around like an idiot. People are watching.

He glanced around; there were maybe six or eight others in the lab. A jumble of thoughts swirled through his head. Next steps. Calling Kat. The opening line of his Nobel Prize acceptance speech.

A high-pitched chirp interrupted his stream of thought. It was the team back at the office. He reached up and tapped his earpiece.

"Hello, this is the brilliant and soon-to-be-famous Professor Hanssen speaking."

It was Kahli on the other end of the line.

"Funny, Jonas. Sounds like you got some good news over there."

"You could say that," he said. "But still a lot of work to do."

"Well, speaking of work, you might want to sit down. Because there is more coming."

"What?"

"Brent told me to call you. We have something. I think the exact words he used were *mother lode.*"

Jonas wasn't sitting, but he did now.

"You're serious? Wow. Talk about timing." Jonas rubbed his eyes; his head was starting to hurt.

"I guess so," Kahli said. "He's running around here like a crazed lunatic. You need to come back. Soon."

There was a sudden cacophony at the other end of the line; Jonas could hear Brent arguing with Kahli in the background. Then Brent's voice was on the line.

"Jonas, you need to see this. It's the perfect asteroid–only better. You wouldn't believe the initial valuations even if I told you. And I'm not going to tell you until you get back here." Brent was talking so fast that Jonas could barely understand him.

"Brent, slow down. What's perfect? The mineral composition? The water? The location?"

"All of it. And more. I'm telling you, you're not going to believe it until you see it for yourself."

"Amuse me. What's the first iteration value?"

"Get back here and you'll see. But I'll tell you this–it doesn't end in trillion."

Jesus.

They hadn't even thrown around *quadrillion* as a joke. Granted, subsequent iterations would probably bring the value down, as they accounted for market price changes due to increased supply. But *quadrillion* was a hell of a place to start.

"Okay, I'm coming," he said. "Can you put Kahli back on the line?"

"I'm still on," Kahli said.

"Let me pull some things together over here. It may take a few minutes. But I'll be back in the next hour or so."

"Is that an actual hour, or a Jonas-hour?"

"Funny. If I swear to be back there in an hour and a half, can you live with that?"

"I suppose. But Brent really wants to call Lester and tell him the good news. It's already close to the end of the day on the east coast."

Jonas couldn't explain it, but Kahli's words sent alarm bells to his head. Possibilities were suddenly materializing; doors were opening. He wanted the time to look behind all of them.

"Jonas, are you there?" Kahli was waiting for a response.

Jonas leaned forward in his seat.

"Kahli, listen to me. Let's wait and be sure before we call Lester. I don't want to be hasty."

"Believe me, Jonas. We're not being hasty. The data came in just after you left. Brent is one hundred percent certain."

"I understand, but let's think this through. Until now, they've held all the cards. And when we give them this data, once again we'll have nothing. Maybe they ask us to look for more. Or maybe they won't. Especially if this is the mother lode, like Brent said."

"What are you saying?" she asked.

"I'm just asking you to please not call anyone, at least until I get there. Let me think this through while I'm on my way. Trust me on this. We don't want to just give it away."

"You mean the data?"

"No. I mean the leverage."

There was a long pause. Jonas held his breath. He knew it was a lot to ask, especially from a by-the-books accountant.

"I see your point, Jonas. We won't call until you get here, I promise. But please hurry. The inmate is going to be running the asylum pretty soon."

Jonas laughed. *She gets it.*

"Thanks, Kahli. We'll talk through all of it as soon as I get there. And congratulations to you as well, you're just as big a part of this as any of us."

"Now you're just kissing my butt. You should have quit while you were ahead."

"Don't be so cynical. I'm serious. We wouldn't be here without you. I would have spent all the money months ago, and Brent would have quit."

"Maybe. But you do always seem to find a way."

"I find good people. They find the way."

"Enough, enough. Compliment accepted. Now let me go round up the inmate, before he does something we regret."

"Deal. See you soon." He tapped on his earpiece and ended the call.

●●◌●●

Jonas was determined to get back to the office as soon as possible. Keeping his promise to Kahli was at the back of his mind, but making sure they didn't jump the gun and call Lester was his top priority. The beginning of a plan was forming in his mind, but it was still loose tendrils and frayed ends. He needed the time to think through the details–and he needed some help. These weren't amateurs they were dealing with; all the possible scenarios needed to be run.

He offloaded the Planck III data to his net-phone, where he could study it back at home. He glanced at the clock; *still plenty of time.*

Up to this point, he had only included Kat in his dark matter research–and his personal life, of course. Now he wanted to drag her into his work at Hanssen Scientific. Would the others go along? And even if they did, was it the right thing to do? His gut–and the plan that had begun to incubate in his head–said *yes.* But he'd known her for barely two weeks. The math didn't necessarily add up. Brent's accusation of an *obsession* flashed through his mind again; he was sure he'd get another earful when he arrived back at the office. And yet–

He tapped his earpiece.

"Call Kat," he said.

She answered almost immediately; the sound of her voice only strengthened his resolve.

"Hey, Jonas. Are you calling to hear about my incredible test scores?"

"Of course," he said. "Not that I need to ask. But it sounds like we both have reason to celebrate."

"Really? The satellite data?"

"Yup. Just as we hoped. Except it gets better. We also stumbled on an asteroid today. Brent already gave it a name. The mother lode."

"Whoa," she said.

"Listen, are you done for the day? I'm just leaving Watanabe Hall, headed back to the office. Could I swing by and pick you up?"

"Sure, I'd love that. What's up?"

"I have an idea, but I think I'm going to need your help. This is our one chance, our only leverage. Are you in?"

"You bet I'm in," she replied, without the slightest hesitation.

"I can't wait until you tell Lester," she added. "It'll be great to give GRI a taste of its own medicine."

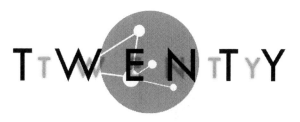

TWENTY

*Problem solving is hunting. It is savage
pleasure and we are born to it.*

– Thomas Harris

The message came early Thursday afternoon, instructing Rudy to be in the Consortium facility at four o'clock. The timing caught his eye–it was the only open window on his calendar. When he asked Grace whether anyone had asked for that time slot, she said no. The coincidence was a bit much to swallow.

Rudy wrapped up a few items, and let Grace know he'd be unavailable for an hour or so. He took the elevator to the ground floor, and crossed the lobby to the boardroom. With the microchip now embedded in his hand, access to the Consortium facility was a simple matter–until he reached the final doorway. There, he needed to enter his private access code on the keypad, while the green light was still flashing. *I should remember to ask Arthur what happens if I get the code wrong.*

He held his breath as he entered the code; to his relief, the familiar *click* told him the door was unlocked. He pulled the door open, and stepped inside.

No one else was there; even Liu seemed to be gone. Rudy shrugged, glancing at the time display on his net lens. It was just a few minutes before four o'clock. He walked to the fridge and helped himself to a protein drink before settling into one of the nearby chairs. Still, there was no sign of anyone.

Rudy shook his head. The cloak-and-dagger secrecy of the Consortium was beginning to wear thin—he had little patience for wasted time. Especially his own.

Without warning, the large central monitor came to life. Rudy caught his breath; it revealed a drab, barren room, with nothing on the walls but a single video screen, hanging from a small bracket in the far corner. The room itself was empty, save for a single chair at the center. Someone was tied to the chair, partially concealed by a cloth bag, placed over their head. It was only then that Rudy heard the audio feed; he detected the faintest sound of labored breathing. No other sounds escaped the room.

Martin. After the meeting with Sandy, he had looked up Martin Fletcher in the corporate directory, and on the Net. He was sure it was him, though he saw nothing in the video to confirm his belief. Rudy sat forward in his chair, mesmerized by the scene—for all he knew, the room could be in this very building. A chill ran down his spine at the thought.

There was a metallic *click*, followed by the sound of footsteps. He counted six steps before a man came into view, walking past the chair before turning to face it. Rudy would have sworn the man paused to look directly at him, as if to be sure Rudy got a good look. It was hard to tell how tall the man was in the otherwise empty room, but his bald head, narrow eyes, and cold look would be difficult to miss. The man's age was hard to place—he could have been thirty, or fifty, or anywhere in between. His mannerisms suggested someone accustomed to command; Rudy could see the calm, easy confidence in his motions. He wore a loose black shirt, and dark grey pants with an assortment of pockets.

With a flourish, the man swept the cloth bag away. It was Martin; his eyes darted back and forth as he took in his surroundings. How long had Martin been in the room? He seemed calmer than Rudy would have expected.

"Hello, Martin. My name is Pax."

"Pax?" Martin's eyes continued to survey the room.

"Yes, Pax. It's Latin for Peace." The seemingly well-practiced line was delivered with a straight face.

Martin's shoulders appeared to droop; his eyes fixing on the man now standing in front of him. Rudy heard him take a deep breath.

"Are you going to tell me why I'm here? Wherever here is." Rudy admired Martin's resolve.

"I am," Pax said. He crouched down on the balls of his feet, resting his elbows on his knees, fingers interlaced, eyes even with Martin's. Pax spoke in a soft voice; Rudy turned his head slightly to hear him more clearly.

"We have a problem, Marty. Can I call you Marty? And I'm the guy they call to fix problems."

Martin stared ahead, silent.

"Here's the thing. You're a smart guy, Marty. Maybe even too smart. So I'm guessing you know why you're here."

"Because you don't like what I'm doing with the AI protocols."

"In part. But what you fail to understand, what you don't see, is the bigger picture."

"I see the changes," Martin said. "Each one is innocuous enough, but as a whole, it creates a dangerous back door at the cross-droid integration level."

"We see how you might reach that conclusion. And we've tried to explain how we address it at the system level. It's a more elegant approach. More flexible. But you've stubbornly refused to listen."

"I've listened," Martin said. "I just don't believe you."

Pax smiled, glancing up at the camera again.

"Precisely," Pax said. "So here we are. And I'm sorry to say, you've left Alpha Robotics with no other choice."

Pax stood. At the same time, Rudy saw Martin stiffen. Now there was an unmistakable look of fear. Even Rudy froze in his chair, hands tightly wrapped around the armrests.

"Wait!" Martin pleaded. "I'm sure we can find some other way to deal with this."

"We've offered other options. You refused."

"I've changed my mind!" Martin eyes darted about the room, looking for a miracle that didn't seem likely to come.

"I don't think so," Pax said. "This is the only workable solution now." Pax straddled the chair, putting his left hand on Martin's shoulder. Rudy could see Martin trying to move, but Pax held him still; now Martin was whimpering. With his right hand, Pax reached into his back pocket. Martin's eyes were squeezed tightly shut. He shook his head back and forth, like a toddler refusing his spinach.

Pax's hand emerged from his pocket, withdrawing a small slip of paper. He held it directly in front of Martin's face.

Martin's eyes were still glued shut; he was oblivious to what was unfolding before him.

"Martin. Open your eyes." Pax didn't yell, but the force in his command caused Martin to comply.

"Look at the paper I'm holding."

Martin made a face; he seemed to be trying to focus on the paper, just a few inches from his nose.

Rudy was transfixed. He couldn't see what was on the paper—so it was impossible to tell what was running through Martin's mind. But now Martin's mouth hung open, as if he was struggling for words.

"It's—it's a lottery ticket."

Pax released his hand from Marty's shoulder. He stepped back, dropping the ticket into Marty's lap. Marty looked lost. His head lolled back and forth, as if drunk. Rudy himself was struggling to keep up.

Pax returned to his crouching position, leaning forward, elbows on his knees, staring directly at Martin.

"Here's the deal, Marty. This is a ticket for tomorrow's lottery. It's a winning ticket—all seven of the numbers will match. Trust me on this. And don't ask me how I know. As of right now, it's the only winning ticket. There's a small chance some lucky son-of-a-bitch will buy another winning ticket between now and tomorrow night, but I wouldn't bet on it. By tomorrow night, the owner of this ticket should be worth a hundred million or so. More than enough to set them up for a comfortable life.

"Congratulations," Pax added.

Martin stared blankly at Pax. He looked down at the ticket. Rudy could almost hear the gears turning in Martin's head as he tried to sort out his sudden change in fortune.

"Here's how it works," Pax continued. "We're going to take you home. And you're in no condition to work, so you'll stay home tomorrow. Tomorrow night, they'll announce the winning numbers. Those numbers. They'll also say that the ticket was purchased at a small store on 40th and 8th—video will show you entering and leaving that store last night. You stopped there around seven o'clock. Not coincidentally, you did walk right past that store right at seven. I'm sure you know the place.

"Are you with me so far?" Pax put a hand on Martin's knee. Martin was nodding, though Rudy wasn't sure the words were fully registering. But Pax pressed on.

"Good," he said. "On Saturday morning, you'll call a lawyer to help you manage all this newfound money. Here is his card." Pax dropped the card on top of the lottery ticket.

"He'll be with you through the rest of the process. As you can probably guess, he's one of us. He was referred to you by a colleague at GRI. He's superb at what he does—he'll handle the media, set up a trust for your family, and help you with your relocation. And of course, he'll be reporting back to us."

"Relocation?" Martin's tone was tentative, but Rudy sensed that he was beginning to gather himself.

"Yes, relocation," Pax said. "You can't stay in New York. You'll have some options to choose from, and you can take the extended family if you want. Your choice."

"And then what?" Martin asked.

"And then you live your life. Hard as that is to believe."

"But what if these numbers don't win?" Martin asked.

"They'll win," Pax said. "You'll have to trust me on that. We have a one hundred percent success rate."

Rudy could see Martin processing the implications. He was doing the same.

"There must be some kind of catch," Martin said.

"No catch. But there are a few rules. First, you'll talk to no one but your wife and kids from the moment we drop you at home until the moment the winning numbers are drawn. No one. Understood?"

Martin nodded.

"Second, you'll contact our lawyer first thing Saturday morning. And third—" Pax stood up now, taking a stance that somehow appeared both casual and yet deadly serious.

"You will never, ever discuss this with anyone. Including your family. You'll retire and become part of the conspiracy. And let's face it—who would believe that you were handed a winning lottery ticket? Alpha Robotics has nothing to do with the lottery, right?"

Martin sat still. It was a lot to process; Rudy was amazed at how well he seemed to be handling the ordeal. An eternity seemed to pass before Martin finally spoke.

"I understand," he said. "I can follow those rules. No problem."

Pax stepped back, and again glanced up in the direction of Rudy's video feed. Rudy would have sworn Pax was giving him some kind of signal.

"I know you can," Pax said. "But just to make sure we're on the same page, I have one more thing for you."

Pax looked to his right, where the lone video screen was mounted to the wall. Martin followed his gaze. There was a flicker, and an image appeared. It was a woman and two small children, sitting at a round table. They appeared to be having dinner, oblivious to the surveillance equipment that was expertly concealed in the room. Rudy didn't need to ask who they were; the color had all but drained from Martin's face.

"Understand this, Marty. Alpha Robotics can be quite generous. But this is no game. And like that lottery ticket, they don't like to take chances. So consider what you see on the screen, and how easy it was for us to snatch you off the street, rig the lottery, and monitor your family. They aren't a group to mess with. And not just for your own sake; I hope this video image is something you never forget."

Martin was still watching the video as Pax reached down to retrieve the hood, placing it back over his head. Rudy's video feed ended, and the screen went blank.

Rudy took a deep breath, the flood of implications still swimming through his head. He had to admire the inventiveness of the plan. No missing person, no risk of investigation or discovery; Martin was now just as complicit. And even better, he had Martin convinced that Alpha Robotics was behind the entire scheme. Rudy could only wonder how many other times the Consortium had resorted to this particular ploy.

Kidnapping. Assault. Embezzlement. He had entered a new phase with the Consortium; he was sure this was just a first, small peek down the rabbit hole. Now, larger questions began to form in his mind. How far would he be willing to go? How much did *he* believe that the ends could justify the means?

And how long until Victoria figured it out?

TWENTY ONE

*Three things cannot be long hidden:
the sun, the moon, and the truth.*

– Buddha

Team Hanssen was already huddled at the conference table when Jonas arrived. He had kept his promise; it was barely an hour since he had spoken with Kahli. And he had even managed to pick up Kat along the way–dumping the bike and splurging on a taxi. The two of them burst into the room together, amid a mix of surprise and confusion.

"I'm impressed," Kahli said as she glanced at the clock. "Kat, you're a miracle worker."

Jonas couldn't explain it, but Kahli had taken an immediate liking to Kat. He wished he could say the same for Brent, though he wasn't surprised; Brent had made his feelings known from the outset. And bringing her to this meeting probably wasn't going to help.

"I thought we were discussing next steps?" Brent asked.

"We are," Jonas said. "Kat's here because she and I have some other work to do when we're done. But I think she could help us–she understands our work, and she brings an independent perspective. One we can trust."

Brent didn't appear to be convinced. There was an awkward silence, as Jonas and Kat continued to stand just inside the doorway.

"I think it's a great idea," Kahli said as she stood up. "Kat, come sit over here. There's an extra chair."

Jonas exhaled. Brent, however, remained standing.

Kat still stood in the doorway; her gaze shifted between Brent and Kahli as she spoke.

"Thanks, Kahli. But you two barely know me. Maybe it's best I wait outside. That way you can talk freely. Besides, whatever hare-brained scheme Jonas has cooked up this time, I'm sure the two of you can straighten him out."

It was all Jonas could do to keep a straight face. He watched as Brent did the math, weighing Kat's words against his own track record in arguing with the boss. It wasn't calculus; this was simple arithmetic.

"No, no, no," Brent said at last. "Kat, please stay. Kahli is right; we could use your perspective."

Jonas jumped at the opening. "Great. Let's get started."

Kat circled the table to sit next to Kahli; Jonas strode to his usual seat at the end of the table, but didn't sit down. Instead, he pressed both hands to the hard metal surface, and leaned in toward the others.

"All right, here's my take. To put it simply, we're finally in the driver's seat. If the initial numbers are right—and I know they are—this is by far the most valuable asteroid ever discovered." Jonas looked around the room; all three heads were nodding.

"So now what?" he continued. "Well, we can call GRI, and let them know. That's the easy answer. My guess, they'll thank us. Maybe even pay us a small bonus. And we'll be out of a job in a month."

"What?" Brent looked incredulous. "You can't be serious. We find a rock worth hundreds of trillions, if not more, and they fire us for it? That makes no sense."

"Think about it, Brent," Jonas said. "This thing is going to consume all of their resources. So why keep us around? They won't be able to handle anything else—for a few years, at least."

"But they could queue them up, right?" Brent asked. "They can lay claim to everything we find."

"Not really," Jonas said. "You know the rules. They have to begin mining operations within six months of discovery, or they lose the rights and it goes to auction. They can't hoard asteroids. I don't think they can handle everything we're going to find. They're better off shutting us down. Buying some time."

Kahli jumped in. "I think you may be underestimating GRI's resources. And their appetite." Brent and Kat both nodded in agreement.

"Maybe," Jonas said. "Maybe not. But what if we had some other options?"

"Like what?" Brent asked.

"Like taking advantage of the leverage we finally have."

"How?"

"By making them pay," Jonas said.

The room fell silent. Brent glanced over to Kahli, and then back to Jonas. His mouth hung open, though no sound escaped. It was Kahli who finally spoke.

"You do understand, Jonas," she said, "that we've already been paid. Like it or not, we made a deal. And believe me, our contract is ironclad. No pun intended," she added.

Oh, I'm aware, he thought. Jonas tried his best to hide his frustration. It was the only time he had let the team overrule his better judgment–his gut. Jonas had wanted to roll the dice, to get paid when they found an asteroid. But the rest of the team wanted the safe bet, the guaranteed paycheck.

"I know that," Jonas said. "We made that decision together. What I'm saying is that there's no harm in asking. Given the size of this thing, why not? It's going to make everyone rich but us."

"They'll see it as blackmail," Brent responded. "It's a lot of downside for minimal upside. One way or the other, they get the asteroid. All we'd get is unemployment. Or worse."

"What do you think, Kat?" Brent looked expectantly across the table.

Here we go. Jonas held his breath.

"Well, keep in mind this isn't my money, or my risk," she said. "But I think Kahli is right. It's just too much risk, for minimal reward. And even if they do fire you, after a find like this, someone else will pick you up. I'm sure of it.

"Sorry, Jonas," Kat added. "You told me to be honest."

Jonas looked to Kahli and Brent; they were nodding in agreement.

"Sure," Jonas replied. "I hear they're looking for some good scientists down in Antarctica." He tried to infuse just the right level of sarcasm into his voice.

"It won't come to that," Brent said.

"It's okay," Jonas said. "Actually, I agree with you. Which is why I don't recommend that option, either."

Jonas could see their confusion; Brent threw his hands into the air.

"Then why are we having this discussion?"

Jonas collected his thoughts. *Option two, here we go.*

"I have another option. One that has enormous potential upside."

"This should be good," Brent said.

Jonas ignored his comment, leaning forward again, palms now pressed to the edge of the table.

"What I propose we do," he said, "is to shop this asteroid with a few close friends–outside GRI. Not the asteroid itself–just the location. We sell the location for a big finder's fee. We delay telling GRI for a week or so, until after we close a deal. No one will be the wiser."

There was a brief instant before anarchy erupted in the room. All three voices exploded at once, though Brent was the loudest and most insistent.

"Are you crazy?" he howled. "No way can we do that!" He folded his arms and leaned back in his chair, planting his feet firmly on either side, like giant redwoods.

"That's a bit crazy, even for you, Jonas." Kahli looked more disappointed than angry.

All eyes turned to Kat. She seemed lost in thought, and took a few moments before breaking her silence.

"Sorry," she said. "I agree with both of you, but something else Jonas said caught my attention. He said *delay telling GRI*. And it got me thinking."

"What if you delay telling them," she continued, "just for a few days? And instead of asking for extra money for something you've already found, what if you ask them to let you intensify the search?"

The group digested her idea; Kahli was the first to respond.

"So tell them we are working around the clock for the next three weeks, which isn't part of our agreement."

"Right. I think they're more likely to agree when it's all hypothetical, as opposed to a negotiation that has the solar system's most valuable asteroid as the centerpiece. And then maybe ask for a bonus if you do find something."

"We'd still be misleading them." Brent continued to lean back in his chair, shaking his head.

Jonas jumped back into the debate.

"Right. We would," he said. "It's a nice idea Kat, but it still has a lot of risk. And not as much upside. I still say we take a few days to shop this thing and see what we can get."

There was another prolonged silence.

"If those are the choices, then I vote for Kat's idea," Kahli said.

"I'm still voting we tell them now," Brent said. "It's the most valuable asteroid ever found. GRI will take care of us."

"And I still vote we go shopping," Jonas countered.

"How about this," Kahli offered. "Brent–if Jonas is willing to come off the cliff and agree to Kat's suggestion, would you be willing to do the same? I think it's a good compromise; we ask for more pay, and a future bonus. That's it. Minimal risk."

"I think we're walking away from a huge opportunity," Jonas said.

"I think we're crazy to do anything but what we've already been paid to do," Brent responded.

"So, are we agreed then?" Kahli looked at them both, pushing the issue.

Jonas looked at Brent, who still hadn't moved. Jonas was going to have to extend the olive branch.

"I can live with it, I suppose," Jonas said.

Brent finally set his chair back down.

"Promise you won't cost me my job," he said.

"Trust me, Brent. I got you this job. I promise you'll still have it next week. And next month. And next year."

Brent frowned, but nodded his head. Jonas jumped at the opening.

"How about if everyone heads home and gets some rest," he said. "It's been a big day, and I need to put some notes together. Kahli, set up a call with GRI. Just tell them I want to provide a quick update and get a few questions answered."

"No problem," she said. "I'll let you know when I get a time."

The meeting broke up, but not before Jonas shared a handshake with Brent. They were often at odds, but in the end, they would make it work. They had complementary skills; Jonas knew he needed Brent as much as Brent needed him. Each of them had an important role to play.

Kahli approached him as they left the room.

"Nice job," she said. "Sorry you didn't get exactly what you wanted. But Kat sure helped, didn't she? Good thing she stayed. Who knows what would have happened if she hadn't been in the room, right?"

Kahli held his gaze for an extra few seconds, giving him an exaggerated wink before she left the room.

● ● ● ● ●

Jonas remained behind, taking notes and gathering his thoughts. Kahli returned a few minutes later; the call with Lester was set for Monday morning.

More time to prepare, he thought. *Even better.*

Before long, Brent and Kahli departed, leaving Jonas and Kat alone. Nevertheless, he closed the door to the conference room, just to be safe.

Jonas felt the adrenaline rush as he approached her, reaching around her waist and lifting her off the ground in a fierce embrace. It was followed by a kiss.

"Kat, you were amazing! Amazing. Academy-award worthy. You were right—Brent was never going to agree without the threat of an even crazier option. Jesus, he nearly had a coronary when I said we should shop the asteroid."

"Thanks," she said. "I just hope you know what you're doing. They're counting on you." She stepped back, a look of apprehension on her face.

"I know. Believe me, I know. But there is no way I'm letting GRI just walk away with this. It's too big. We deserve our share."

"I hope you're right." She looked around the room. "Now, how about we move on to more important stuff?"

"Oh," he said, returning her gaze. "I thought you wanted to talk about dark matter." He reached back out to her; she pushed him away with a gentle shove.

"Funny. You know that's what I meant."

"How about this—let's wrap up here; there's one more thing we need to do. Then we'll go back to my place, make dinner, and I'll show you the dark matter data."

Kat grinned. "So I finally get to see your apartment?"

"Yup. It's all downhill from here. Now follow me, I'm going to need your help."

He grabbed her hand as they left the conference room, returning to his work station. The screen lit up as he approached.

He punched up the day's data, his eyes lingering over the immeasurable beauty of the mother lode.

You are going to change the world, he thought. *Or at least, my world.*

He motioned for Kat to sit.

"The others don't know this, but GRI uploads all of our data every night. So we need to erase all signs of the mother lode. Now."

Kat gave him a long, deliberate stare. The implications were now laid bare–in his words, and on the screen in front of her.

"I guess I'm all in now, aren't I?" she said.

"And then some." He gave her a wink.

TWENTY
TWO

Power attracts the worst, and corrupts the best.

– Edward Abbey

Rudy lingered inside the Consortium facility, lost in his own thoughts. Though it seemed like an eternity, he had been there barely an hour; his dinner event with Victoria was still a few hours away. So he sat alone, struggling to reconcile what he had seen with his own sense of morality.

Was it really any worse than what he had done to get approval for the *myHealthScan* device? He wasn't sure. The confrontation between Pax and Martin was real, and personal. His device had impacted many, but they were faceless, and nameless. And what about Martin? A year from now, would Martin call this the worst day of his life? Or the best? In both cases, it could easily be argued that the end did justify the means. Martin would eventually see that, Rudy had to believe.

It's not what happened in that room–it's the larger implications. And the questions it raises. It was time for some answers.

Rudy pulled the net-phone from his pocket, activated the secure channel, and dialed Arthur. The answer came almost immediately.

"Hello, Rudy," Arthur sounded almost jovial.

The green light was on. "I was hoping we could talk. I've got some questions."

"Of course," Arthur said. "I see you're still in the facility."

Rudy ignored his comment; he knew the Consortium tracked his location. It wasn't hard.

"I assume you were watching the video?" Rudy asked.

"Yes. I think our problem is solved, don't you?"

"Ignoring the fact that GRI is about to be short one very talented AI expert," Rudy said. "But tell me, who is Pax?"

"He's what we call a *Fixer*. We have several in our employ. They come from different backgrounds, with different, unique skill sets. Each has a particular history that binds them to us. We take care of them, give them interesting work, and they reciprocate with discretion and their unconditional loyalty. In Pax's case, as you can probably imagine, he's ex-military. With a few interesting twists."

"Twists?" Rudy asked.

"He was special forces, but injured on a covert mission in Asia. We used some experimental new technology to help fix him up, so to speak. Pardon the pun."

"But he is still human, right? He's not a robot."

"Of course not," Arthur said. "You know as well as anyone that robots built to resemble humans are illegal. We'd never take that risk. Plus, robots can't carry weapons."

Rudy considered Arthur's words. The story behind Pax was of less immediate concern; he needed answers to some larger issues.

"So help me understand what I just saw. Does the Consortium do that every day? Or was it unusual? Was it what you'd call one of your small changes, or was that a big deal? It's time I understood better what I've gotten myself into."

"Fair enough. It wasn't the first time we've used that particular ploy. But we don't do it often. Off hand, I'd call it maybe a four on a one-to-ten scale of the things we do, in terms of magnitude and risk. Does that help?"

Rudy tried to imagine what Arthur might constitute a ten–but just as quickly, pushed the thought aside. *Later.*

"So Martin really is going to win the lottery?"

"He is," Arthur said. "Honestly, rigging the lottery is simple; you'd laugh if I told you how. We never thought it would go on this long. Frankly, it should have been discovered a long time ago. Typical government incompetence. But rest assured, we've anticipated that eventuality, and the trail will lead far, far away from the Consortium. And any of us."

Rudy shook his head. He was beginning to wonder what wasn't easy for the Consortium.

"Okay, enough about Martin. And Pax. Let's talk about the big picture. The real purpose of the Consortium."

"Like I told you that first night," Arthur said, "Our goal is to preserve the *status quo*. To protect humanity from itself, in a sense."

"Define status quo."

"It's a phrase we use. It means a world of civility. Of ever-increasing quality of life. And minimized chaos."

"Quality of life for whom?" Rudy asked. "For the elite?"

"For everyone. Sure, some of us are always going to have more than others. That's human nature. And only fair. But you can't argue the results of the past forty years—quantum leaps in education, higher average income, new first-world economies all over the globe, and amazing new technologies. Humanity's average life span has never been higher. If anything, you might argue that humans now live *too* long."

"Maybe. But some would argue that the vast majority of people have just enough to get by. And that it won't last much longer."

"They might say that. Just as I'd argue that the masses can't be trusted to run things. Look at the first half of the 21st century. Around the world, the masses consistently elected leaders that were patently incompetent. Or corrupt. Or both. Why? For one, because the skills needed to get elected no longer had anything to do with the skills required to be an effective leader. A *real* leader could never get elected. So we had a world full of empty, talking heads. And worse, these leaders were wasting enormous amounts of capital—squandering huge amounts of money and other assets on election campaigns, or on failed projects—all with little if any return on investment. It was a death spiral."

"So in steps the Consortium. A few benevolent dictators who know what's best for humanity."

"I prefer to call us an invisible hand," Arthur responded. "The world has enough quasi-elected dictators. We don't *rule;* we *adjust.*"

"Give me some more examples. You gave me a few that first night. Tell me some of the bigger ones. The tens, on your scale."

There was a moment of silence. They weren't using a holophone, or the room's holographic projector, so Rudy had a limited ability to judge Arthur's reactions. But he was going to press the issue, one way or the other.

"I don't think we've ever gone to ten. But one example might be the Global Bank of Middle Africa. From day one, GBMA was critical to our plans. Truth be told, it still is. We need instant, worldwide, and untraceable access to our financial resources."

Arthur paused for a moment before continuing.

"Establishing GBMA required an enormous amount of our financial reserves," he said. "And our political capital. But we transformed a third-world economy into one of economic prosperity. We created a bank that was sophisticated and global, but also independent–impervious to political pressure or threat of sanctions. It's called the black hole of banking for good reason."

"But there were a lot of people involved in that effort," Rudy said. "Their names were all over the news. They can't all be part of the Consortium."

"Of course not," Arthur said. "With just a few exceptions, they were all oblivious to our role behind the scenes."

Rudy considered the implications. Most of his friends had accounts with GBMA; he had only resisted because of Victoria, and her family.

"You understand my problem with GBMA. Victoria. Or more precisely, her father."

"We do," Arthur said. "At our level, it's a small world. You know that. It's nothing we can't handle."

Easy for you to say. But again, Rudy put those thoughts aside; he still had more immediate issues to address.

"I'll grant you, GBMA was well thought out," Rudy said. "A poor nation gets handed near-instant prosperity, and is all but immune to outside economic threats. They're a self-sufficient island. And the media was entirely focused on the *what*. They largely ignored the *why*."

"That was no coincidence, as you already know. But what you saw in the news was maybe five percent of the story. The battle to establish GBMA played out almost entirely behind the scenes, and between wealthy nations, and in some cases even wealthier individuals. Many, many accommodations were reached. But again, we were the grease. Not the gavel."

"Interesting," Rudy said. "So that's one example. How about some others?"

Now Rudy could hear the first hints of frustration in Arthur's voice.

"Rudy, we could do this all evening. And I'm certainly not authorized to give you the entire forty-year history of the Consortium. If I asked you to name the ten biggest political, economic, or environmental events of the past few decades, you can assume we had a hand in eight or nine of them. And just as important are the things that we prevented. Regional conflicts, in some cases. Or small uprisings that could have become much worse. We once recovered a nuclear device from a Russian terrorist cell–an honest-to-god nuclear bomb. In fact, you can thank Pax for that, if you ever meet him."

Rudy wasn't going to let the topic go so easily; he had his own set of frustrations. But there was no sense in pushing too hard in one direction; he could switch tacks.

"Don't get me wrong, Arthur. I appreciate what you've already told me. It helps. But maybe one more thing? You said at the outset that I'd be working directly for the Chairman. When is that going to happen?"

"Soon, Rudy. Maybe sooner than you think. Let me talk to him and we'll see where he is on that. I think he wanted you to get your feet wet first."

"I think the water's up to my waist at this point."

"I'll talk to him," Arthur said. "But that does remind me, I've got a couple other items for you. Do you have a few more minutes?"

"Sure. Go ahead."

"First, I believe you received an invitation to a charity event on Saturday, correct?"

"I did. Victoria and I are going."

"Excellent. One of the other attendees is going to be a man by the name of Joseph Gratz. He's the Chief of Staff for Senator Anthony Pavesi."

"I know Tony," Rudy said.

"Then you know that he chairs the Senate Appropriations Committee. Joe is one of our key conduits to the Senate. Over the years, we've found senior staffers to be potent allies."

"I think Tony is also someone we could trust," Rudy said.

"Believe me, Rudy. Elected officials are a bad idea. Like I said, the vast majority are either incompetent or corrupt. Early on, we went that route. But they just can't be trusted–other than to serve their own self-interest. Which changes daily. So we turned to the staff. They're far more reliable."

"So what's your point?" Rudy asked.

"We need you to deliver a message to Joe. Even in this day and age, we prefer face-to-face meetings with the more senior politicians. And it will be much more effective coming from you. I'll send the details to your net-phone."

"Anything else?"

"One more thing," Arthur said. "And this is a bigger deal. Maybe a six on your scale. Remember when we first spoke at the funeral? I mentioned that Carl was in the midst of some critical work? I was talking about Consortium work. We think you're ready to pick one of those up."

"What is it?" Arthur had piqued Rudy's interest.

"You remember Gunnar, right? Our economist. One of the key components of his research has been the development of what he calls Target Wealth Bands. It turns out, there is a direct relationship between free cash flow in an economy, and that society's relative stability. He calls it the *Wealth Ratio*.

"Sure. More money in the system makes everyone happy."

"Actually, it's not that simple. What he's found is that there can be *too much* money. Or at least, there are alternating bands of stability and instability, as you climb up the wealth ladder. When an economy spends too much time in an unstable band, bad things happen. Protests. Or even outright revolution. My point is, he's proven that economies with more wealth can actually be less stable than those with less."

"That makes no sense," Rudy said.

"We didn't understand it either. He thinks that the unstable bands are maybe where the added wealth creates an unmet need for more–rather than simply satisfying needs. But the data speaks for itself, especially over the past fifty years. Just look at Russia, or Venezuela. It's incontrovertible.

"If it's so incontrovertible, then why isn't it public knowledge? Other economists should have stumbled on it by now."

"Are you sure?" Arthur responded. "Think about it. First, the data isn't as clear more than fifty years back. And beyond one hundred, it doesn't hold. But that shouldn't be surprising. Twentieth century data collection was rudimentary, at best. A lot of self-reporting. Worthless, in my opinion. The correlation gets better as the data gets better. And now we have access to truly accurate data–data collected without human intervention. Without our ability to skew the facts.

"But there's another reason," Arthur continued. "What if we announced that more money could be bad for an economy? How do you think that would go over?"

"But if the data clearly supported it," Rudy began.

"Please," Arthur interrupted. "Do you know how many good ideas, supported by reams of data, have been shot down by public opinion? Or public ignorance, I should say? Remember the childhood immunization crisis in Southern California?"

Arthur had a point. Rudy had lost track of the number of new technologies they had been unable to commercialize, for all sorts of perverse or otherwise ridiculous turns in public opinion. And fueled by the media.

"Okay, so let's assume that it's true. What does it have to do with me?"

"Here's the thing," Arthur said. "Iran has been stuck in an unstable band for over a year now. Usually, economies seem to either run through these bands to the next stable level, or they naturally drop back. But not this time. And I'm sure you've seen the consequences."

Rudy wasn't surprised by Arthur's comment; there had been an unusual level of unrest in the region for the past several months. But GRI had relatively few high-value assets in that area, so he had largely ignored it.

"So Iran is unstable," Rudy said. "That's not exactly news. But you're claiming something bad may happen?"

"Not *may,* but *will.* I can guarantee it. It's just a matter of time. Carl was working with us on this very issue, when the accident occurred. We need you to step in and complete his work."

"And what work is that?" Rudy asked.

"To be blunt, we need to step in and reduce the Wealth Ratio. Get it back to a stable band."

A moment of silence passed between them, as Rudy digested Arthur's words. Implications swirled through his mind, like an icy wind through the trees. He could feel a shift—the sudden, increased gravity of their discussion. He drew a deep breath, choosing his next words carefully.

"Why not increase the Wealth Ratio?" Rudy asked. "Help push them up, not down. Seems like that would lead to better long-term stability."

"Believe me, if we could, we would. Ten years ago, when the Maldives had all but sunk beneath the sea, we helped facilitate the relocation of their population. It cost us a fortune, but it stabilized their economy. And better yet, it showed the world that humanity could overcome some of the biggest problems we've created on our own planet. It helped preserve the status quo. If there was a similar solution for Iran, we'd use it. But we've run the models. Absent a crisis like the Maldives, injecting capital into an economy isn't easy. And we just don't have the time. A reduction can be done in weeks. If not days."

"How?" Rudy regretted the question almost before he had finished asking.

"A small, controlled, natural disaster."

Rudy put his head in his hands, leaning his elbows against the table. *This can't be happening.* He took another deep breath, opening his eyes to what was suddenly a much smaller room.

"You're joking, right? Is this some sort of test? Before I can meet the Chairman? You can't be serious."

"It's not a test, Rudy. And I promise you, it's as serious as you can possibly imagine. Like I said, Carl was personally leading this same initiative. We were days away from launch. Obviously, we couldn't dump this on you on day one. But, we brought it to you as soon as we thought you were ready."

"Brought what, exactly?"

"We're planning an earthquake in Northwest Iran, along the Caspian coastline. The recent tremors in that area have given us the data we need– not to mention the cover story. And GRI has the equipment we need to make it happen. This has been months in planning, Rudy. The event has been precisely designed to minimize loss of life, but to cause enough damage that cleanup and rebuilding will reset the economy's wealth ratio to a safe range. We're very confident in the numbers. We just need you to help with some GRI resources. We can't do that without you."

"People will die, Arthur."

"It's likely, yes. We've discussed this. A few people–not thousands. Or worse. Don't focus on the few who might die. Think about the thousands you'll save. This is about saving lives, Rudy. Not ending them. And not just by stabilizing the economy. Our controlled event may also help to avoid a more massive earthquake in the future."

Rudy's head was pounding; he wasn't sure he had room for many more of Arthur's rationalizations. But there was one question he had to ask. No matter what the cost.

"Arthur, I have to ask you. Did Carl really support this idea? I've known Carl for years; I'm having trouble believing he'd do this. And then he's killed in a car accident. It's hard not to connect the dots."

An even longer period of silence passed between the two men; when Arthur responded, it was in a slow, steady tone.

"I understand the implication, Rudy, though I won't say I like it. Two things. First, Barbara and Lilly were in that car. I hope that's all I have to say on that topic. It crushes my heart just thinking about it. But second–this isn't the first natural disaster we've orchestrated. Recall Nicaragua a few years ago–the volcano. Carl led that effort."

Rudy considered his words. Not even the Consortium would go after a member's wife and child, would they? It would have been easy to target Carl alone, if that had been the intent. Still, he wasn't entirely convinced. But he did recall the events in Nicaragua–the earthquake and subsequent eruption had killed surprisingly few people. With existing technology, it was plausible. Though it was also unnerving, to say the least.

Rudy took a deep breath, and shifted tacks.

"Are you really asking me? Or are you telling me?"

"We're asking," Arthur replied. "We need you with us, Rudy. We can't coerce you, it wouldn't work over the long term. You need to be committed. Like I am. I'm here to help you get there."

"So I don't need to decide right now?"

"No, of course not. But every day increases the risk. We really do believe that."

"How about this, then," Rudy said. "Can I get a copy of Gunnar's data? So I can evaluate the strength of the case on my own?"

"Absolutely. And I'll provide you with an outline of the plan, and the GRI resources we need. But let me ask you this. If we provide you with the data, and you agree that the facts are incontrovertible–that it really is a matter of sacrificing a few for the sake of many–are you prepared to do it?"

That's the heart of the matter, isn't it? Arthur was good; it was a fair question if he wanted to see the data. Rudy took a moment to weigh his options. For now, he saw but one path forward.

"Yes. I am."

TWENTY
THREE

I am now convinced that theoretical physics is actually philosophy.

– Max Born

It took them more than an hour to expunge all evidence of the asteroid. Then, Kat watched as Jonas reconstructed a plausible data set as a substitute. It wasn't hard to build a set of data that showed nothing; he'd been looking at those kinds of results for months. After he was finished, they took the bus back to his apartment–another taxi might have broken the bank. It was late when they arrived, though as he opened the door, the fading twilight was still more than enough to illuminate the reality of his bachelor lifestyle.

Jonas stood in the doorway, chagrinned. He had hoped to better orchestrate this moment; Kat's eyes grew wide for the briefest of instants before she collected herself and smiled.

"Sorry, the maid was supposed to come today." Jonas did his best to keep a straight face.

"I've seen your office, Jonas. This is your office with a kitchen. I've seen worse. Well, except maybe for that."

She pointed to a spot next to the sink, where Jonas had re-created the Leaning Tower of Pisa in a canted, gravity-defying stack of dishes, rising almost a third of the way from the counter to the ceiling.

"Would you believe me if I told you it was a physics experiment?"

"Not likely. Biology experiment, maybe. But how about I go freshen up, and when I come back I'll give you a hand with it."

Jonas directed her to the bathroom. Fortunately, he was much more fastidious in that small space–even he had a simple bath-bot. Kat gave him an approving smile as she closed the door and disappeared.

He immediately launched himself at the pile on the counter; the last thing he wanted to do was spend the evening washing dishes. He had no illusions that he could wash them in the time she was gone–but with a modicum of creativity and the inventive use of some empty cabinet space, in short order the tower had all but vanished.

Jonas canvassed the rest of the apartment, his radar attuned to other potential distractions. As he collected the odd stray sock, empty food wrapper, and assorted other detritus, his thoughts returned to the woman tucked away in his bathroom. A month ago, she hadn't even existed. Now, his idle thoughts consisted of little else. There had been an air of anticipation since her performance in the meeting–further heightened by their close proximity on the bus. They had barely spoken a word during the ride; the body language had been more than enough.

She emerged from the bathroom, nodding her approval as she walked through the kitchen to join him. They sat down together on his only couch.

"Wow, you may have a second career as a maid," she said.

"Don't count on it. And I wouldn't open any of the kitchen cabinets. They've officially been declared a health hazard."

Kat gave him a look, head tilted. Jonas found it endearing.

"Seriously, how do you manage to be both cute and disgusting at the same time?"

"It's a rare talent," he said.

"Well, at least half of it is."

"Ah hah. And which half is that?"

"That's what we'll have to figure out, I guess."

"And how should we do that?"

The words floated between them; it was all Jonas could do to wait for her response. Finally, Kat broke the silence.

"We should at least talk about the dark matter data, you know."

"Should we?" he said, leaning in closer. He vaguely recalled an important discovery from a far-away satellite, sometime earlier in the day.

She shoved him playfully. "Come on, you've waited twenty years for this! I've waited almost twenty days." She gave him a devilish smirk. "I'm dying to know what you think it all means."

Before he could react, she grabbed him by the shirt and gave him a rough kiss, lingering on his lips just a bit longer than necessary.

"Don't worry," she said, locking her eyes on his. "I'm not going anywhere."

Jonas leaned back on the couch, giving his brain a moment to descramble.

"You're a piece of work, you know that? Most girls want dinner and virtual reality. But you demand particle astrophysics. Go figure."

"There's nothing wrong with dinner," she replied. "It's just farther down my list of priorities. Much farther," she added with a smile.

Jonas laughed. "Okay, you win. Let's talk particle astrophysics. It wouldn't hurt to share some ideas with you, before my brain gets any more muddled."

Kat turned sideways on the couch, laying her legs across Jonas's lap and putting her head on the armrest. She used her arms to wiggle her way up the couch until she found a comfortable position.

"Great," she said. "Lay it on me."

Jonas looked at her, smiling and shaking his head. *A piece of work—and then some.*

"Okay, so we have confirmation of the initial readings; this second set of data is similar. The problem, though, is that it's also different. I haven't really studied it in detail yet, but it's clearly not an identical set of readings. Something is there—some kind of pattern, but the individual readings vary. Does that make sense?"

Kat seemed to be lost in thought; again, Jonas was amazed at how quickly she could switch gears.

"I suppose. Maybe like a snowstorm? At a distance it's just snow, but up close the individual flakes and patterns are different?"

"I'm not sure that's the right analogy, but I don't have a better one. At least, not yet."

"So does this change your thinking?"

"Not really. We still have something unexpected out there—something that's interacting with the laser. Back when we were trying to find dark matter on Earth, we used a super-dense element like germanium, hoping that a dark matter particle would smash into its relatively huge nucleus. But that was like an archer trying to hit a bull's-eye from a mile away. In some ways, the laser on Planck III should be even less likely to find something—but obviously, it did. So clearly we're looking in the right place, and in the right way."

"And between our solar system and the Oort cloud is the right place? The middle of nowhere?"

"Exactly. Think of dark matter as the scaffolding of the universe; it holds things together. Where are we most likely to find dark matter, working to prevent galaxies from flying apart? Wouldn't that be in the space between the stars?"

"Plus, that's where there are plenty of cosmic rays. High-energy radiation. Right?"

"Very good," Jonas said. "Another reason it was a promising place to look."

"Okay, so assume we've found dark matter," Kat said. "The question still remains—what is it?"

"Yup. That's the trillion-dollar question. Our discovery may be the answer to *where* dark matter is. But I'm still not sure it gets us any closer to *what* it is."

"Doesn't the *where* help us figure out the *what*?"

"Of course. You have to find it before you can study it. Plus, we have an enormous amount of data to analyze—who knows what we may find? But it could take us months."

He ran his hand along her leg, admiring the curves he found along the way.

"Or years, if I somehow lose my focus," he added.

"You could lose more than your focus," she said, grabbing his hand. But the look in her eyes belied her words.

"Well, first things first," he said, trying not to skip a beat. "We need to prepare for the call on Monday. We may have convinced the team of our plans for the mother lode, but now we have to sell it to GRI."

"I'm not worried about that. You sold me on it."

"True. But my goal with them is a little different than it is with you."

"Really?" she replied. "Because I would have sworn your goal was to screw us both."

Jonas laughed as their eyes met. Neither of them spoke as he leaned closer; she wrapped an arm softly around his neck. The friendly banter was swept away.

Now we're both all in.

TWENTY FOUR

*We only become what we are by the radical and deep-seated refusal
of that which others have made of us.*

– Jean-Paul Sartre

The Cairo heat was oppressive–even hotter than Singapore, though not nearly as humid. On top of that, Monique wasn't thrilled to have all of them together in such a dangerous city–but Bhima had been adamant. "No way you're going alone," were his final words on the subject.

At the airport, she hired a private limo service, with an armed driver, to escort them to their destination. The service had been recommended by someone she knew from the gallery; he did occasional business in Egypt. She paid the driver in full, in advance, to stay at the museum until they were ready to leave. She hoped it wouldn't be too long.

The Museum of Cairo was downtown, tucked against the east bank of the Nile, about thirty minutes from the airport. Their driver had snaked his way through morning traffic, finally pulling to a stop at the edge of an open plaza. The museum's red, hulking stone façade dominated their view.

Gazing out the car window, Monique understood Bhima's concern. There was another demonstration scheduled for today in Tahrir Square, just a stone's throw from the museum. Scanning the plaza, Monique could already see several groups milling about. They seemed largely disorganized at this early hour, but exuded an ominous presence, nonetheless.

They piled out of the car and into the plaza. Several sets of eyes followed as the group made its way across the open expanse; Monique did her best to ignore them. With any luck, the crowd would have left the museum plaza for Tahrir Square by the time they were ready to leave. *Or so we can hope.*

They weaved their way through the uneasy crowd, arriving without incident at the museum entrance. Monique glanced briefly at the twins, who were wide-eyed but seemingly eager to continue. Bhima gave her a nod when she looked in his direction. She gestured for the group to follow, and they passed through the massive, arching entrance and into the museum proper.

Monique scanned the entranceway, noting that the layout was exactly as described on the Net. There were two floors, with the central hall open from floor to ceiling. The top floor could be seen directly above them, with a railing of miniature gothic columns running like a racetrack around the central hall. Museum employees were easily identified by their bright uniforms, to include a red beret for the men and a scarf for the women—exactly as they had seen in the vision. An even larger number of security staff, guns at the ready, was dressed in far less festive attire.

Monique turned to the group. "How about we split up? Ana can come with me; Pierre can go with Bhima. We'll cover twice the ground that way; I don't want to be here any longer than necessary."

Bhima appeared torn. "I'm not sure. Maybe we should stick together."

"Bhima, I know you can take care of yourself. Pierre knows that as well." She smiled at Pierre. "It's a limited, controlled space, with lots of security. Let's take advantage of that."

The twins were nodding; even Ana seemed to agree with the idea. Bhima was silent for a moment before finally relenting.

"Fine. Pierre and I will go upstairs; you two search the ground floor. But tell us the instant you see her."

"We will. I know she's here. I can feel it again, just like I could in Paris."

Monique watched as Bhima and Pierre crossed the hall and began climbing the nearest set of stairs; once they disappeared, she turned to lead Ana into the ground floor displays. Ana had stopped to stare at the colossal statues of Amenhotep III and his wife, Tiyi, staring back at them from the far end of the hall.

"Pretty impressive, aren't they?" Monique asked her.

"They look like they're smiling," Ana said.

"You would, too, if you ruled all of Egypt."

Monique wandered toward the statues, trying to stay focused on people and faces. Ana didn't have to be told to stay close–though she was clearly fascinated by the countless ancient artifacts. The two of them worked their way to the far end of the hall, finally reaching the stairs below the enormous pair of statues. She and Ana climbed the few stairs and circled the statues, emerging into a section of newer relics and sarcophagi in the room immediately behind them.

Monique spotted the woman almost immediately. Even without the red scarf, she was hard to miss. She was stationed at the door to the northernmost room, still as a statue and with hands clasped behind her back. As Monique walked toward her, their eyes met. It was the eyes that Monique recognized; a deep brown, the color of dark chocolate, yet warm and playful. And the mole below the left eye. The woman smiled as Monique approached, exuding an air of both surprise and recognition.

"It's you, yes?" the woman said in a soft, delicate voice. Monique was surprised by her tone–it was in sharp contrast to the intensity of her eyes.

The woman was glancing around the hall. "Where are the others?"

Monique was caught off guard; of the many questions she was prepared for, this wasn't one of them. But she quickly collected her thoughts.

"We're thrilled to meet you," she said. "My name is Monique; this is Ana. And if you don't mind, I'll take a minute to call the others. But how did you know there were more of us?" As she spoke, Monique activated her net lens and sent a short message to Bhima.

"My name is Tabia." She was silent for a moment, shifting her gaze around the room.

"Forgive me. As much as I've waited for this moment, it's a bit overwhelming–seeing you here in front of me, for real. As opposed to just visions. Is that how you found me?"

"It is," Monique responded. "But our visions are of one person. Never a group. What have you seen?"

"Well, first you," she said to Monique. "And two children, Ana and I'm guessing her brother?"

"My *twin* brother," Ana corrected.

"Of course," Tabia said with a smile. "And then the two men, a younger one with a darker complexion and a scar. And the other one, a bit older. With blonde hair and blue eyes."

Bhima and Pierre arrived as she spoke–their dash across the hall had garnered the attention of more than a few of the security guards. Monique gave Bhima a disapproving look; he gave her a defiant stare in return.

"Tabia, meet Bhima and Pierre," she said. "She's been expecting us. All of us," Monique added.

Bhima's eyes widened. "All of us?"

"And one more. Apparently, we're still one short."

Tabia nodded. "A man. Thin, short blonde hair, blue eyes. Probably in his thirties."

"That is so awesome!" Pierre said.

"Do you know where he is?" Monique asked.

"No," Tabia replied. "I just see faces. Believe me, if I knew how to find you, I would have tried." Her eyes continued to dart around the room as she spoke.

"Don't ask me to explain, but we only see one person at a time," Monique said. "Though we also see locations. With you, we saw this museum."

"I see." Tabia paused, looking at the others in the group. "So now what?"

"Well, we didn't see a vision of you until after we found Ana and Pierre," Monique said. "So I'm guessing we'll see this blonde-haired man next."

"Are you coming with us?" Ana looked up at Tabia with an expectant smile.

"I might, if I knew what that meant," Tabia said. "But my shift just started; it's safer for me to stay until the end of the day, when I can leave with a security escort."

Monique considered her statement. The scene outside was worrisome, though she guessed Tabia had seen worse. At the same time, she didn't relish an entire day at the museum–even if their driver was willing to wait that long. One last glance at the group, and the plethora of soldiers surrounding them, convinced her of their proper course. She turned back to Tabia.

"Tabia, I know this is sudden. It was the same way for Bhima, and for Ana and Pierre. But we'd love for you to join us. I'll be honest–we still don't know exactly what that means, or where this is headed–only that it *feels* right. There's a purpose to all of it, I'm positive. And I'm guessing you feel it as well. But right now, I want to get to our hotel. We have a car waiting. You could join us now, or you could meet us this evening. Or not. It's up to you."

Tabia looked at each of them. The hum of conversation and echoes within the large hall were the only sounds as she weighed her options.

"You're right," she said. "I do feel it. But I also have my job here. I'd like to join you tonight, if you don't mind. We can talk about it some more."

"I understand," Monique said. "It's a big decision. Meet us tonight, as soon as you're ready. We aren't going anywhere until tomorrow, at least." She gave Tabia their hotel information.

"Thank you," Tabia said. "I'll be there, I promise. I have more to tell you, as well."

"I'm sure you do." Her comment spurred Monique to another thought. "Speaking of more, have you ever shared your visions with anyone else?"

"No, just me," she said. "Have you?"

"We have, though it's new to us as well. But we'll wait for you at the hotel before we try again. Who knows—you may help us discover what this is all about."

"That would be wonderful. I'll see you soon."

Monique motioned for the rest of the group to follow. She could see the disappointment in Bhima's eyes; Ana was clearly upset. They were halfway across the main hall before anyone spoke.

"We shouldn't leave her," Ana said.

"Definitely not," Pierre added.

"We can't force her to come with us," Monique said. "And you heard her; she's going to join us tonight. So we aren't really leaving her. She has a job, and things to take care of. It's a big decision to walk away from life as you know it. Even a life here in Egypt."

Neither Ana nor Pierre looked convinced, though they didn't object. Bhima was quiet as well. Their silent march ended at the south exit, where a few other tourists stood watching the activity in the plaza. Monique sent a signal to their driver; he was still waiting where they had left him.

She gazed out into the plaza; the situation had clearly deteriorated. The crowd had swelled, to the point that she could no longer see their car. A slow stream of tourists filed past them; an exodus from the museum was well underway. She watched as a family attempted to cross the plaza, weaving their way through the expanding throng. They were soon lost from view, swallowed by a sea of growing animus. She caught a glimpse of a scuffle at the northwest corner of the plaza; whether it was between protesters or an attack on tourists, she had no way to tell.

Monique weighed their options. The size of the plaza crowd continued to rise; the situation was degrading with each passing moment. She turned to look at Bhima.

"It's not that far," he said. "We'll be fine." But his eyes didn't convey the same message.

Monique watched another group pass by them and enter the plaza; now she and the rest of her group were the only foreigners in the entryway. It was time for them to move. But as she made her decision, there was the light touch of a hand on her arm.

"Monique, look!" Ana was pointing behind her.

It was Tabia, though no longer dressed in her museum attire. Now she wore more traditional Egyptian garb–including a muted blue hijab that expertly covered her head and hair. The muscles in Monique's neck and shoulders relaxed as she smiled at their new companion.

"Change your mind?" Monique asked.

Tabia took a brief look outside, studying the situation in the plaza, before turning to face the group.

"Two years, I've been having these visions. Two years! Not every day, mind you, but often enough. To see all of you walk away–it was too much. I could *feel* something tearing inside of me. So here I am. Sorry to say, you're stuck with me."

Monique smiled. Ana gave Tabia a voracious hug.

"Welcome to the team," Bhima said. "Now maybe you can help us get out of here."

Monique looked at Tabia. "Could museum security escort us out?" she asked.

"No," Tabia said. "They won't leave the museum. Some so-called protesters used to stage fake confrontations, and when security came out to help, others would rush in to loot the place. So now the artifacts are the priority. Sorry."

"Which side would the guards help?" Monique asked. She was genuinely curious.

"Depends on the guard," Tabia replied.

"Great," Bhima said. "What about the military?"

"They're focused on Tahrir Square. They could help, once they arrive here. But it's no guarantee. Some of them are worse than the demonstrators."

Monique considered their options. It wasn't that far to the car–the plaza was much wider than it was deep, and the car was on the far side, maybe two hundred feet away. She considered a more circuitous route, hugging the south wall, around the protest, and then along the road back to the car. The distance was longer, though, and would lead them toward the skirmish she had seen earlier. In fact, she could now see the confrontation had spread, and was gaining the attention of others. She made her decision.

"Okay, we're headed for the car," she said. "Bhima, you lead the way. Ana and Pierre will stay right behind you, and Tabia and I will follow. Let's take as straight a route as we can, skirting that center island. After we get to the street, we can turn left to reach the car. Is everyone ready?"

The group nodded.

"Don't run," Tabia said. "It draws attention. Better to walk. But keep up the pace."

Bhima led the group down the entryway stairs and into the plaza. Monique's adrenaline surged as they plunged into the crowd. At first, the demonstrators parted in front of them, and Bhima made a beeline for the rectangular pool at the center of the plaza. Monique hoped that the pool would provide relief on their right; only a few demonstrators stood among the tall ferns at its center, and no one was standing in the shallow water. But the crowd pressed closer as they walked, and the noise continued to grow. Their pace had slowed to barely a walk.

It was when they arrived at the northeast edge of the pool that Monique realized her mistake. A tight line of demonstrators stood along the low cement wall of the pool, commanding a view over the plaza. They had probably arrived early to secure their spots, and were in no mood to move for a group of tourists. Amidst angry looks and shouts, Bhima was forced to his left, so that the mob grew on all sides. The men on the wall loomed over them, shouting in unison. She could no longer see a path in front of them, though Bhima still pushed ahead. The twins were glued to his sides, with Monique and Tabia close behind. As a group, they took up less space than a table for four. And yet, the crowd pressed closer still.

They neared the south end of the pool, and were passing between the pool's edge on their right and a small stone replica of the sphinx on their left. Now the demonstrators rose over them on both sides; they were forced to walk single file. Bhima's pace had slowed to a crawl. Monique kept her eyes locked on her friends in front of her; she could still sense Tabia at her back. The noise was reaching a crescendo, with a rhythmic chanting that was a heavy weight on her shoulders. The car was perhaps twenty paces away–assuming it was still there–but to Monique, it seemed beyond all possible reach.

Monique felt a rough tug as a hand grabbed her forearm, twisting her to the left. Her years of jiu-jitsu took over. Faster than her mind could form the thought, she lashed out–fingers together, her hand forming an open *shuto* as it whipped across her body, striking the Adam's apple of the man holding her arm, scant inches away. His eyes grew wide at the swiftness of her attack; he released her arm, grabbing his throat and falling back into the crowd. A split-second of stillness followed, as those nearby paused to process her reaction. But it was the briefest of instants–soon replaced by a surge of several more protestors, the closest a short, stocky man brandishing a heavy stick.

Monique focused on him first, transforming her hand to the *ippon-ken*, and driving her extended middle knuckle into the man's eye. Her speed also caught him off-guard, and he collapsed to the ground as a loud, long wail escaped his lips. Almost simultaneously, she spun, and her elbow connected with the ribs of a man now behind her. But there were too many, she knew. Even as she spun back toward the group, she could see that the cause was lost. A dozen men heaved toward her, a savage look in their eyes.

"Bhima!" she screamed, knowing all the while it was wasted breath.

What came next was a blur. Like a parting of the Red Sea, the crowd around her was flung aside, arms and legs askew, as they were launched over and into the demonstrators behind them. Suddenly, Monique could see Bhima, directly ahead of her–and holding tightly to Ana and Pierre, a wild look in his eyes. Just beyond them was the car, barely thirty feet away. An open path lay before them, as an eerie silence engulfed their end of the plaza. It only took Monique a moment to recover.

"Run!" she yelled, grabbing Bhima by the arm. Tabia passed by her, putting a hand on both Ana and Pierre, pressing them forward.

In a handful of heartbeats, they reached the car, and piled into the back seats. They sped from the scene as Monique peered out the rear window, watching the confusion in the plaza quickly disappear from view.

A shocked silence engulfed them as they each caught their breath. Monique was the first to speak.

"Bhima, that was incredible. You saved us–and no thanks to me. How did you do that?"

Bhima shook his head.

"That wasn't me. I thought you did it."

They stared at each other for an instant more, before turning their gaze to Tabia. She sat between the twins in the seat behind them, a sheepish look on her face.

"I told you there was more to tell," she said.

●●●●●

The driver looped around the museum and sped north, along the Nile Corniche. They arrived at the hotel just a few minutes later. As an extra precaution, Monique approached the hotel desk alone, while the others wandered through the lobby shops. There were no problems with check-in, however, and they were all soon re-united in their adjoining hotel rooms.

Monique took a moment to relax on the bed, replaying the museum events in her mind. How many had seen what Tabia did? Monique doubted that their driver had seen anything; he was sitting in the car, fiddling on the Net, when they had all piled in. But had anyone in the plaza captured the events on video? She was sure that the museum area was awash with cameras; at least a few had to be pointed in their direction. Let alone the likelihood of drones, covering the protest.

We'll find out soon enough.

Monique turned on the hotel video, accessing the various news feeds. It wasn't long before she found one covering the situation at Tahrir Square.

"What are they saying?" Bhima asked.

"So far, not much," Tabia replied. "They're calling it typical for Tahrir Square, maybe a bit larger than usual. And nothing about the museum."

"But it just happened," Tabia added. "If they get anything, this feed will carry it. They always do."

As if on cue, the picture cut away to a view of the Cairo Museum–and the plaza. The room was suddenly quiet, save for the announcer's voice.

"They're talking about a brief confrontation at the Cairo Museum," Tabia said.

"The crowd is a lot smaller now," Bhima said.

He was right. Most of the demonstrators had dispersed; it would have been much easier to cross the plaza now.

"They're saying that the plaza cleared out just after the clash occurred," Tabia said. "And that most of them went back to Tahrir Square for the main event."

"Maybe that other fight acted as a diversion," Bhima said. "Everyone was focused on that as we made our way to the car."

Could we be that lucky? At least a dozen demonstrators saw–or in some cases, experienced–what Tabia had done. But it was possible, Monique supposed, that none of it was caught on camera. The event had lasted just a few seconds; after that, it would have looked like any other crowd scene. Maybe they had gotten lucky, after all.

The video feed went back to Tahrir Square. They left it on, in case it returned to the plaza. Monique asked Pierre to keep an eye on it.

"Thank you, Tabia," she said. "It's a good thing you decided to join us. That was quite a demonstration."

"I told you, I couldn't imagine being left behind. But that moment back there, in the plaza–it surprised me, too. I've never done anything like that."

Tabia paused; she seemed to be mulling over her next words.

"I overheard you and Bhima in the car. What I did wasn't a surprise to you. Do you have the same power?"

"Not all of us. At least, not yet. But Bhima and I do."

Tabia smiled; her posture even seemed to relax a bit.

"I'm so happy to hear that."

"I think it's time we explore these powers," Monique said. "We were lucky this morning–and I don't like to rely on luck. We need to know what we're dealing with–what we can do. And what we can't."

"I agree," Bhima said.

"Fly me around the room!" Pierre had shifted his gaze from the video feed, and was looking eagerly at Bhima.

"Slow down, kiddo," Monique replied. "Let's take it one step at a time. How about if we experiment with the furniture before we start throwing kids around?"

"Sure, *now* we have to be careful," Pierre sulked back to his chair, though he continued to keep an ear to the discussion.

"First, let me ask a question," Monique said, looking at Bhima and Tabia. "Can either of you describe how you do it? For me, it's almost an extension of my arm. Like pushing, or pulling. But it doesn't come from a thought—like *push that desk across the room*. It's more of a feeling that you need something to happen. Does that make sense?"

"I've never tried to describe it to anyone," Tabia said. "But that sounds right. And I think maybe the intensity of my feelings impacts the power behind it. That might help explain what happened back there, at the museum."

"Maybe," Bhima said. "Or maybe our power increases as we have more of us together. Like the way you say the visions seem stronger and clearer when we do them together."

"Good point," Monique said. "And I think we can test all of that." Monique glanced around the room; the only freestanding piece of furniture of any size was the bed.

"But maybe not this second," she added. "It's a small space. We need more room to test our limits."

"Then let's see where we're going next," Pierre said. He was still following the discussion, a look of impatience now etched on his face.

"I agree," Monique said. "The sooner we know, the better. Plus, we could be on the news feed any minute, which would seriously complicate our ability to leave the country." She looked at the feed, which was still focused on Tahrir Square. For now.

"I'm ready," Ana said.

Monique turned to Tabia. "Would you join us? We've only done this together a few times, but it's not too different. You'll feel us pulling each other together. And I'd love to know whether we see anything you've already seen."

Tabia nodded. "I'd like to help. And to better understand what this is all about."

Everyone found a comfortable place in the room; Monique noted that Tabia also stood, while Bhima sat in a chair. Pierre and Ana leaned against the near wall, next to each other. After a last look at each of her newfound companions, Monique closed her eyes.

As before, the suddenness of the shift surprised her. In just a handful of breaths, she had shut down her mind, and separated from her thinking self. She could feel her body relax–the slowing of her heartbeat, the release of her anxiety, the connection to her inner place–things that used to take minutes, she could now accomplish in seconds. She registered all of this in a corner of her consciousness; more as *truth* than *thought*.

The others were arriving–as if drawn by her presence. They came together as the dancing light approached, hovering in front of them. For a moment, Monique sensed more–as if invisible tendrils of *purpose* spanned the distance between her and the light, tugging at the edge of her consciousness. She grasped at the strands, hoping to gain a purchase. But the light moved on, and in another moment, she was making The Leap.

The transition was abrupt. A tropical scene filled her vision–a gleaming cement-and-glass city astride the ocean, surrounded by a lush green canopy. A single, brown, monolithic peak rose majestically in the distance. The fractured scars down the sides of the mountain betrayed its volcanic legacy. Monique absorbed the sound and feel of the cool ocean breeze as she immersed herself in the vision.

The first image faded–replaced by that of a man. Blonde hair, pale blue eyes, mid to late thirties. He was a few days from his last shave, though the look was more carefree than unkempt. As usual, Monique didn't recognize him, though she was sure she would when they met.

Surprisingly, the vision didn't end with the man. It shifted again, now revealing what looked like an office, possibly for a technology firm. Banks of monitors filled the room. It was a small space–enough for a handful of employees, though no one was there now. The vision panned across the room, and Monique saw other items pass by–most notably a large telescope in the back corner. And behind the telescope, a placard that read *Hanssen Scientific.*

The vision shifted again. Darkness was followed by a blur of light. She could feel movement, as she did when making The Leap. But this was more, and different; the pinpricks of light were beyond count, though each one seemed to be both individual and part of the whole, traveling in unison as they raced past her position. They were traveling with her, it seemed–coming from behind and streaking ahead, into the distance–at a speed far exceeding her own. She had no absolute reference to judge their speed–or the passing of time, for that matter. It could have been seconds, or hours.

Once more, she had the feeling of oneness; the lights seemed to beckon–urging her to match their pace. She watched in wonder, letting the connectedness of the moment wash through her. For now, it was enough.

●●●●●

Monique opened her eyes; she was back in the hotel room. Pierre was the first to speak.

"Where was that place? We are so going to that beach!"

"Hawaii," Monique said. "Honolulu, to be exact. Diamond Head crater is hard to miss." She paused to see that everyone was listening. Bhima had already risen from his chair and crossed the room; the rest were watching her from where they stood.

"Did we all see the same thing?" she asked. "Tabia, was that the same man?"

"That was him. But I had never seen Honolulu before. Or the computer lab. Or what came after."

"That was the longest vision I've ever had," Monique said. "Usually they end once I see a face. I hope it means something."

"Jonas Hanssen," Bhima said. He was standing at the Net terminal in their hotel room, a grin on his face.

"Who?" Monique asked.

"Jonas Hanssen, of Hanssen Scientific," Bhima replied. "Did you see the sign? I just looked it up on the Net; it was him we saw. They have an office in downtown Honolulu. They do research on asteroid mining."

"We shouldn't have much trouble finding him, then," Monique said.

"I have the address," Bhima added.

TWENTY FIVE

Politics is the art of looking for trouble, finding it everywhere, diagnosing it incorrectly and applying the wrong remedies.

– Groucho Marx

"Feel free to join me if you ever emerge from your funk," Victoria said, rising from the table. She stood over him for a few more seconds, before gliding off to join a group of her friends, a few tables away.

She's right, Rudy knew. He was doing exactly what she had warned him about–letting his new job impact the family. And their relationship. Tonight's charity event wasn't the issue–normally, he'd put on his best smile and work the crowd, right along with her. But tonight, he resented that he was again on the clock–thanks to the Consortium. So instead of a relaxing Saturday night at the American Museum of Natural History, he was left to stew over his assignment–and how to deliver a message to a Senate staffer, with his wife none the wiser.

He continued to watch her, admiring how effortlessly she blended into the group discussion, radiating a casual ease and warmth. She looked spectacular–dressed in a floor-length, black sequined dress with a plunging neckline, and accentuated by a platinum and diamond necklace with matching stud earrings. He had wanted to wear his less formal tuxedo, but Victoria had arched an eyebrow at the idea—and he didn't have the energy to argue. So he had reluctantly donned his wool-and-mohair tux—along with his favorite, 007-logo vintage cufflinks. She hated those cufflinks.

It was hard to believe that barely a week ago, they had been enjoying the sand and sun of a private island retreat; that was now a distant memory. He had been behind the eight ball since their return, and Victoria wasn't thrilled with the hours he was keeping—he had barely said hello to the kids all week. It didn't help that he was hiding something from her. And it wasn't just a little something.

He looked up at the museum's immense blue whale replica, hanging above his head. It was an apt view; he could feel its weight pressing down on his shoulders. Arthur had sent over a pile of wealth band information, as promised, and Rudy had spent a good portion of the day reviewing the models. It was a fascinating study, but it didn't take him long to realize it was a pointless exercise. It would take him months to absorb the mountain of data—verifying sources, correlating timeframes, testing conclusions—and he didn't have that kind of time. *No wonder Arthur was happy to provide the data.* There wasn't any simple way for him to authenticate the findings. Frustrated, he had put the data aside.

A smattering of applause interrupted his thoughts, and he turned his attention back to the evening's assignment. Senator Anthony Pavesi and his Chief of Staff, Joe Gratz, were gathered with a small group, just beyond Victoria and her friends. Getting a private message to Joe wouldn't be easy, given Rudy's relationship with the Senator. Tony, like Rudy, was a long-time friend of Carl's. There was little chance he could pull the Chief of Staff aside, with Tony standing right there next to him. And with the event about to end, it was apparent that Joe wasn't going to leave Tony's side; Rudy was going to have to get creative. And that, unfortunately, meant that he needed Victoria.

He rose from the table, grabbing his drink as he left, and joined the group surrounding his wife. He painted a smile on his face; to her credit, Victoria gave him a warm smile in return.

"Hello, sweetheart," she said. "Your timing is perfect. I was just telling Sylvia the story of how we met."

Wonderful. She's going to make this difficult.

"I thought all of New York already knew that story."

"I've tried, but apparently I missed a few." She gave him a smile and a wink–to the rest of the group, he was sure it appeared endearing. But he knew better.

"Maybe Lois could finish the story," he replied. "I know she's got it memorized. I need to speak with Senator Pavesi before he leaves, and I'm sure he wants to say hello to you. He might not recognize me without you on my arm." Rudy could play the game, too.

"Really?" Victoria asked. She turned from Rudy to roll her eyes at the group. "These titans of industry. Sometimes I wonder how they manage to get themselves dressed in the morning." She gave Rudy another smile.

"Lois, you can finish the story," she continued. "But here's the punch line: the police only let him go after my parents told them he was with the evening's entertainment."

She got the usual laughs, though they were somewhat subdued with Rudy standing next to her. *Might as well go along,* Rudy decided. Maybe he could buy a little good will. He fed her a soft, underhand softball, right down the heart of the plate.

"You know, you never did pay me for that bet," he said.

"Sweetheart, I've paid," she replied. "Believe me, I've paid." She passed a knowing look to the rest of the ladies in the group, who laughed and nodded in agreement. He took his cue, rolling his own eyes and smiling, while taking her gently by the arm and leading her away.

"Will that story ever get old?" he asked as they walked toward the Senator.

"Only when you do."

Rudy stopped, pulling Victoria close.

"Listen, Vic, I know it's been a long week. And I'm sorry. Things will settle down, I promise. But right now, I need your help. I need you on my side."

Victoria returned his stare, but didn't immediately respond.

God, she's beautiful. It was all he could do to return her gaze.

"Victoria–"

"Of course I'm on your side," she said. "And yes, it's been a long week. We miss you. I'm just worried; you seem more pre-occupied than usual. More than I expected."

Rudy weighed his words carefully; he knew he was walking a very fine line.

"It's a big job, you know that. But we'll be fine. I need to speak with Tony's Chief of Staff. Then we can get out of here, and spend some quality time at home."

"I thought you wanted to talk to Tony?"

"I do. But I also need to speak privately with Joe, his Chief of Staff. Do me a favor and flirt with Tony for a minute, okay?"

"You're unbelievable. Have I ever told you that?"

"Every day." Rudy did his best to put on his humble-and-grateful face. Victoria leaned in, giving him a kiss on the cheek.

"Fine. Let's get it over with."

They approached the Senator's group, and Rudy extended his hand.

"Good to see you, Senator."

"How are you, Rudy?" Senator Anthony Pavesi was his own New York institution; five-term incumbent, part-time philanthropist, full-time bachelor, and a permanent fixture of the city's social scene.

"We're heartbroken over Carl and his family," the Senator said. "I know the two of you were close. Sorry I missed you at the funeral; busy day, I imagine."

"It was," Rudy said. "And thank you. I know you were close to Carl as well. I'm just hoping to continue his legacy."

The Senator smiled. "I'm sure you will, especially if you can manage to keep this lovely lady on your team. Hello, Victoria. You look absolutely stunning this evening. How many years are left on that marriage contract of yours? Rudy, you are one lucky man."

Rudy bit his tongue; it was par for the course with Senator Pavesi. But Victoria didn't skip a beat.

"Senator, you know that Rudy and I married for life. Call us old fashioned. But thank you so much for your support this evening; we do appreciate it."

"For you, my dear, anything. It's my pleasure."

Victoria took the smallest of steps to her right. Like a motion-sensing search beacon, the Senator spun to follow her; he probably wasn't even aware he had done it. Rudy admired Victoria's deft touch; she was a pro. Rudy turned to face Joe.

"Hi, I'm Rudy Dersch. With GRI." He extended his hand to the Senator's Chief of Staff.

"I know who you are. I'm Joe Gratz, the Senator's Chief of Staff. I was a friend of Carl's as well. We were heartbroken about the tragedy."

"Good to meet you," Rudy said. "It's been a difficult few weeks, but we're doing what we can."

Rudy glanced over at his wife; she and Tony were already engaged in an animated discussion. It would take a fire alarm, and perhaps even the accompanying fire, to distract the Senator's attention away from Victoria.

Delivery time.

"Like I told the Senator," Rudy continued, "I just want to continue Carl's legacy. My goal is to preserve the *status quo*."

Arthur's code phrase had the desired effect; Rudy saw the surprise in Joe's face.

"Interesting," Joe said. "I guess I should have expected as much. Why mess with success, right?"

"True. And we'd like to keep it that way. Which is why I'm here."

Joe raised an eyebrow. "You came to see me?"

"I did. Or I should say, we did."

Joe's eyes darted about the room. "We?"

"I'm delivering a message, from all of us. With Carl gone, I'll be your conduit. We have some important work to do, and we're expecting your full support."

"I've always done what I can," Joe said. "Your people know that. Like I've said all along, there are limits to what I can do from my position."

It was the response Rudy expected. Joe was a career Senate staffer—well versed in the art of saying both yes and no to the same question. But Rudy wasn't new to the game either.

"Joe, as much as I loved Carl, I think it's safe to say that he may have let his long-term relationship with your boss unduly influence his dealings with you. I'm not an unreasonable man, but I'm going to expect more. And don't worry—I'll never ask for anything that I don't know you can deliver."

Joe was silent for a moment, lips parted and eyes wide. Rudy guessed it had been quite a while since anyone had spoken to him that way. But he recovered quickly.

"I'm not sure where you've gotten your information, Mr. Dersch. But the Senator and I have delivered plenty for Carl, and for GRI. I think you may be misinformed."

"Call me Rudy," he said with a smile. "And spare me the party line. Just in the last year, you stood by while the Justice Department killed one of our acquisitions—and don't forget the failed appropriation for our new robotics plant. That was my project, you know."

Rudy could see the color rising in Joe's face. But his response was carefully measured and controlled; he was no amateur.

"That robotics plant wasn't in New York. You know that. Just like you know that the Senate is the legislative branch, not the Executive Branch. There's not much we can do about the Justice Department."

Now the hairs on the back of Rudy's neck were starting to rise. *I see why Arthur needed this done in person.*

"Carl may have bought that line, though I doubt it," Rudy said. "Sorry to say, I'm not that naïve. A five-term Senator and Chair of the Appropriations Committee damn well better be able to influence the Justice Department. And push through a simple funding bill—whether it's in New York or New Guinea. Sounds like you need to build some better relationships."

"We have plenty of good relationships, thank you. But they won't stay that way if we abuse them every time you say *jump*."

"No one said anything about abuse. This is about preserving the status quo. Which is a big part of what keeps you in office. You should remember that."

"I can promise you, the Senator and I aren't going anywhere. But I assume you already knew that."

"I'd be careful about making assumptions," Rudy said. "Especially ones that underestimate what I'm capable of."

"I'm not sure I like what you're implying."

"I'm not here for you to like me. Just to be sure that when I say *jump,* you jump."

"That's not going to happen." Joe's voice had begun to carry, as the intensity of their conversation rose. The other conversations around them suddenly came to a halt.

I think we just set off the fire alarm. Rudy turned to look at Victoria; she and the Senator were staring at him.

"What's not going to happen?" Victoria said.

Rudy hesitated, but only for an instant.

"Sorry, Joe here was rambling on about the Giants, and how this was finally their year to win the Super Bowl. I told him the Eagles would be providing all the fireworks this year."

Rudy flashed a big grin. To his credit, Joe did the same. There were a few laughs, though more nervous than genuine.

"I think Rudy has far too much faith in the guys from Philly," Joe said. "In case you've forgotten, they haven't won a Super Bowl since the advent of unlimited forward passing. Your team is a relic."

Now Rudy laughed, though even to him, it sounded a bit forced. He knew it wouldn't fool Victoria.

"True," Rudy said. "I'm a bit old fashioned. I prefer the days of a single quarterback–one guy in charge. Just don't underestimate the guys from Philly; I still think they're going to have those New Yorkers jumping."

Joe was still smiling, though he continued to shake his head.

"You should be more concerned about Philly's new medical team," Joe replied. "I'm hearing they made a mess of the team's pre-season drug regimen. Philly may have to learn the hard way–just because you *can* do something, doesn't mean you should."

Before Rudy could respond, Victoria put a hand on his arm. "Enough with the football," she said, glancing around at the rest of the group. "Leave it to the kids on the playground. And speaking of kids, we've got a couple of teenage girls at home. I think it's time we departed." Her casual tone and soft smile had expertly diffused the situation.

Rudy laughed, giving her arm a squeeze. She was right. And he had delivered his message.

"Joe, it was good to meet you," he said, holding out his hand. "I'm sure we'll talk again soon.

Joe extended his own. "Good night, Rudy. Good luck to you as well."

They said their farewells to the others, including Senator Pavesi. Rudy signaled for Bond, and they began to make their way to the museum entrance. They had gone less than twenty paces before Victoria spoke.

"What the hell was that all about?"

"Sorry, we got into some business. It was my fault. Remember the robotics plant in Michigan? The one that didn't get government funding? I told him he owed me one; I don't think he appreciated it."

"Well, that was slick. Lucky for you the Senator likes us. Or one of us, anyway."

"I noticed that. I was about to go get him a napkin. To stop the drooling."

"Stop it," Victoria replied. "You think this is a big joke? You know better than that. We don't need Tony's Chief of Staff to have a hard-on for you."

Her language surprised him—this wasn't about the conversation with Joe. She was venting again.

"Vic, relax. I know what I'm doing. Joe was pushing me, seeing how far he could get with the new guy. He and Tony knew Carl well; I think the relationship was more to their benefit than to ours. That's going to change, and Joe needed to know that."

"You could have been a bit more delicate," she replied.

"No, I couldn't. Not if I wanted to get my message across."

Neither of them spoke as they crossed the remainder of the hall.

"I guess we'll never know," she said at last.

Rudy collected their coats at the Rotunda entrance, and they passed through the doors and out into the cool night air. Bond was already waiting. Rudy followed Victoria into the car, confirmed the destination, and sat back in his seat. It was a quiet ride home; neither of them was in a talking mood.

Rudy replayed the conversation with Joe in his mind. *Arthur had better not have screwed me.* He had pushed it to the limit, just as Arthur had advised. Victoria had been right; he never would have gone that far on his own. But Arthur had convinced him it was necessary—Senator Pavesi was an important asset, and Carl had let their hold on him slip. Hopefully, tonight's effort would bear fruit—and get the relationship headed in the right direction.

Where he was headed with Victoria, however—that was another matter entirely.

TWENTY

SIX

*He who is not contented with what he has, would not be
contented with what he would like to have.*

– Socrates

Jonas was up early on Monday, surreptitiously cleaning the last
of the dishes he had stuffed into the kitchen cabinets. They
had spent most of the weekend sequestered in his apartment–
managing to devote a fraction of that time to the dark matter data, as well
as to preparations for the call he'd soon be taking.

Kat emerged from the bedroom, hair still wet and wearing one of his
button-down shirts and an old pair of running shorts. She had made a
quick trip home on Saturday to pick up some things, but seemed equally
happy to rummage through Jonas's closet. He didn't mind.

"I might keep this shirt," she said as she sat down to a quick breakfast.
"I love the texture."

"It's yours," he said. "Now eat. My call is in twenty minutes."

They finished breakfast, and Kat helped clean up. They cleared a place
on the table for Jonas to spread his notes; it was a few minutes before nine.
Kat sat at the table as well, directly across from him.

"Don't forget, you're not here," he said.

"Relax, I'm just moral support. Now focus. And remember not to push
too hard. Just set the stage for the next call. That's all."

"Yes ma'am. It's not my first rodeo, you know."

Kat glanced around the room. "Sure. I can see you're an expert at this. Go get 'em, cowboy."

Ouch. He gave her a glare out of one eye, but resisted a more pointed response. Instead, he took a final look through his notes.

It wasn't long before he heard the familiar chirp, and tapped on his earpiece to answer.

"Hello, Lester. Thanks for making yourself available on such short notice." Jonas was determined to be on his best behavior, no matter how hard it was.

"No problem at all, Professor Hanssen. I'm hoping you have news to report? Aside from the broken holophone, of course."

So much for a good start.

"My apologies, Lester. I spoke to someone earlier in the week and told them what happened. Totally my fault, I bumped into it and knocked it off the shelf. Apparently I'm a lot better at math than I am maneuvering in my own kitchen." He hoped to elicit a laugh, but there was no such luck.

"In any case," Jonas continued, "Like I told your assistant, I'll pay for the damage. Take it from our next payment."

"That won't be necessary," Lester said. "These things happen; we've already shipped another one. Call it a gesture of good will. I know I can be difficult, but Rolland and I want you to know that we believe in your team. We still consider you to be a good investment."

Jonas and Kat exchanged glances. Kat nodded, pointing to his notes.

"Thank you," Jonas said. "I feel the same way. Obviously we wouldn't be here without you and GRI. Which brings me to the reason for the call."

Jonas took a deep breath. *Here we go.*

"After the call last week, we decided to pull up stakes and move to a new set of coordinates. We ran a whole bunch of numbers, based on what we've learned over the past few months, and decided to target a different area. We've been sweeping that area since the end of last week, and continuously monitoring the data. Nothing jumped out immediately, but in general what we've found so far is significantly better than what we had been seeing at the previous coordinates. So we're cautiously optimistic."

Jonas paused to make sure Lester was keeping up. It was a bit strange without the holophone; normally, Lester was an easy read. But now there was only silence–a prolonged silence, in fact. At last, Lester spoke.

"Okay, I appreciate the update. But my assistant mentioned you had a few questions?"

"Yes, we do. As I said, we're now in the monitoring phase. And without the deadline, we would continue to monitor as we have been, watching and reviewing data during the day, making adjustments, and then leaving the equipment and computers to do their thing overnight.

"But now, with the deadline looming, the team feels we should be monitoring and adjusting around-the-clock. Our chances to find something in the next three weeks are hugely increased if we maximize every hour in that window. We can tweak at eleven at night, rather than the next day. Our odds of success will increase by about two hundred percent."

"So you're asking whether you can work overtime."

"I suppose you could say that. And as I'm sure you've already guessed, we'd like to get paid for that time as well."

Jonas paused for Lester to mull over his request. Kat might still have doubts about his negotiating abilities, but he was smart enough to know that filling the silence was the sure sign of an amateur.

Jonas looked to Kat, who held up two fingers. He nodded; he wasn't going to forget the second item. But he needed to get through this one first. He was surprised by the time it was taking for a response. Normally, Lester wasn't much for listening; he was just waiting to talk.

"Professor," Lester began. "I can see how our call from last week has created a sense of urgency. I'm appreciative of your dedication to the effort. But at the same time, I don't want your team to overwork themselves, or to make a mistake at three in the morning that could have catastrophic financial consequences. We need to have absolute, one hundred percent confidence in your data."

"I can promise you, Lester, there won't be any risk with the data. We can manage it."

"Maybe you can. And don't get me wrong, the money isn't the main issue here. There are a lot of other factors at stake." Lester paused for a moment; now Jonas really wished he hadn't broken the holophone.

"I'll tell you what," Lester said. "I want to give you every opportunity to succeed. So for now, go ahead and put in the extra time; we'll pay you for it. In the meantime, I'll go back to Rolland and see if we can't find some additional accommodations. Maybe even slip the deadline a bit. Like I said, we want you to succeed. I'll get back to you before the end of the week."

"That's great, Lester. And we'll manage the hours without any increase in risk. The team will be thrilled."

Score one for the good guys. Jonas was surprised by the response; normally, GRI bent over backwards to pinch every penny. Lester's answer was effectively a blank check–just a vague cap on the number of hours. *They must really need this asteroid–which means more leverage.*

"Is there anything else?" Lester said. He was clearly eager to end the call, and get back to more pressing matters.

"Just one more thing. I hesitate to even mention it, but I promised the team I would."

"Go on," Lester said, though his tone didn't match his words.

"We were hoping to revisit the topic of a bonus. Not for you to make a decision right now, but just for you to take away and consider."

Lester's frustration was unmistakable. Even without the holophone, Jonas could visualize the look on his face as he spoke.

"Jonas, we've been over this. We offered you that option, and your team chose to take the safe route. So we're paying you whether you find anything or not. You can't go back now and have it both ways."

Jonas anticipated the response, though it was less vitriolic than he'd expected. He took a quick look at Kat before pressing forward.

"I know that. But here's the thing. We're looking at the big picture, and the potential return on investment. All we ask is that you consider–when the time comes–the value we've delivered, versus the price that you've paid. Not what you're contractually obligated to do, but what we think is the right thing to do."

"The right thing to do is to find an asteroid. Otherwise this whole conversation is moot."

"True. I'm just planting the seed. So when we do find that asteroid, you'll remember my speech."

Lester laughed. "Sure, plant the seed. And I'll go back to GRI and see if I can find someone to water it. I'll pass on the message."

"Thanks, Lester. I really appreciate it. We all do. We won't let you down."

"Great. So is that it? Or do you also want a piece of the asteroid itself?"

"No, the asteroid is all yours. Maybe you can ship us a souvenir once you're done with it."

"I'll add that to the list. And now, I really do have to go. Thanks for the call, and good hunting. Like I said, I'll get back to you before the end of the week."

Lester disconnected; Jonas took a deep breath, leaning back in his chair as the tension released from his neck and shoulders.

"What do you think?" he asked Kat.

"Not bad. He committed to more pay, and promised to consider the bonus. Nice job."

"At least it didn't blow up in our face. But frankly, I expected a lot more pushback. I wonder if he's already written us off."

"Don't be so paranoid. They just shipped you a brand new holophone; those things cost a fortune. They wouldn't have sent one if they had already given up on you.

"And don't forget," she added, "He said they might extend the deadline. That was his idea."

"I suppose. So we'll call it a ground-rule double. Maybe I'm just disappointed because I was swinging for the fence."

Kat reached across the table and took his hand. "It was a good at bat. Now let's go tell the others. I'm sure they're waiting to hear from you."

Kat was right. Plus, they needed to work out a plan to *discover* the asteroid, so to speak. That was going to take some time.

Still, it was a good start. Things were beginning to fall into place.

TWENTY
SEVEN

To the mind that is still, the whole universe surrenders.

– Lao Tzu

Monique paced the hotel lobby, watching and waiting for the cars to arrive. She had positioned herself near the door, with Tabia and Ana by her side; Bhima and Pierre were stashed further down the long entranceway, partially obscured by a large planter.

It was time to leave Cairo–or at least, to make the attempt. The last forty-eight hours had tested her patience–along with her problem-solving skills. A video from the museum had finally appeared on the news feed; it was shot from a distance, but clearly showed the five of them, racing through the plaza. In retrospect, they were fortunate to have seen it–otherwise, the group of them traveling together would have been easy to spot.

Equally fortunate was the video itself, which turned out to be incomplete. It had been shot by someone filming the fracas along the museum's south wall. The sound of a scream could be heard, and the camera wielder spun to the south. But by then, Tabia had already acted, so the video showed only the aftermath–bodies strewn about, an empty section of plaza, and the group of them as they scurried into the waiting sedan. Their backs were to the camera throughout; even the car had been largely obscured by the crowd and the ongoing commotion.

Tabia had spent the next several hours watching the news feed, providing them with regular updates. Interviews with those at the scene added little; the few who had witnessed the event itself were largely dismissed by the commentators. At one point, it was announced that a search was under way for the five individuals seen leaving by car, but no one from the police or military was ever interviewed to confirm or deny the report. Tabia confirmed that the only description provided had been, *"...a man, two women, and two children."*

The group discussed their options. Tabia had already agreed to fly back with them; truth be told, Monique was fairly sure she made that decision at the museum. Tabia had no family in Cairo; she had been adopted by an elderly couple as a baby. They had provided her with a good education, but little else. Tabia left the hotel on Saturday morning to collect some things, and say goodbye to a few friends.

After Tabia left, Monique had turned her thoughts to the trip home. She didn't want to take any chances, so she found two separate flights back to the U.S.–one to Washington, one to New York–and just forty minutes apart. Unfortunately, the flights weren't until Monday evening. But it was their best option, so she booked two tickets to DC for Bhima and Pierre, and then three to New York for herself, Tabia, and Ana. The twins had to be separated; otherwise, they would draw too much attention. Bhima even decided to stop shaving; by Saturday, a hint of patchy stubble had begun to appear. Monique wasn't sure whether it was an effective disguise–or simply drew additional stares. But she wasn't going to tell that to Bhima.

She also decided that they should switch hotels; too many people had seen the five of them together. She selected a hotel at random; one on a small island, called Gezira, in the middle of the Nile. It somehow seemed removed–safe–from the rest of Cairo, as she stared at the city map. Before leaving, they each purchased a change of clothes–items more in line with local custom. They went to the new hotel in two separate taxis, and arrived without incident. Once there, she called a different car service, using the hotel concierge, to reserve two separate cars for the trip to the airport on Monday.

On Sunday, Tabia had returned. She told them the news feeds were still reporting that a search was underway. But as far as they could tell, it hadn't been picked up by any feeds outside of Egypt. So far, they had been lucky. But Monique still insisted on the separate flights. And to be safe, they spent the entire day sequestered in their hotel rooms.

By the time the cars arrived on Monday afternoon, they were more than ready to leave the hotel–and Cairo. As planned, Bhima and Pierre went out the door first, passing by her with a final wave before jumping into the first vehicle. The driver sped away as soon as the door was shut. Monique watched them go; with any luck, she'd see them both at her house, by this time tomorrow night. With a nod to the others, Monique led the way out the door, and climbed into the second car. Tabia and Ana followed.

They left the hotel, heading south and west, away from the airport. They had agreed to take a circuitous route–past the Egyptian Pyramids– adding about an hour to their drive. In addition to Monique's desire to see the famous site, it would also separate their arrival at the airport from that of Bhima's. They were three tourists, squeezing in one last trip before their flight home.

They crossed the bridge from Gezira, turning south along the Nile, toward Giza. The road soon wrapped around Cairo University, and the driver took them west, slicing through the dense cityscape and along King Faisal Street. As they approached the pyramid complex, the driver exited the main road, expertly guiding them down several side streets, until they emerged at the Sphinx, almost directly in front of them. Monique couldn't help but stare; even the desert haze couldn't diminish its majesty.

"How did they *do* that?" Ana asked.

"Wonderful, isn't it?" Tabia said. "I used to live here in Giza, when I was young. I saw them every day. This is where I first got interested in our history, and the Cairo Museum."

Tabia paused for a moment before continuing.

"These were built over four thousand years ago, in honor of the great Pharaoh Khafra. The pyramid directly behind the sphinx is his burial site; it took about 20 years to build. There are a lot of theories on how it was done–the most popular is that some kind of sled was used to pull the massive blocks of stone. And they used water to wet the sand in front of the sled. It made the blocks easier to pull."

They drove past the Sphinx at a slow clip, then past the Great Pyramid, before leaving the site and joining the traffic on Ring Road. But Monique's thoughts lingered at the pyramids, long after they faded into the distance behind them.

Four thousand years. The rise of western civilization, globalization, our ascent into space–none of it was on display here. It made her wonder–how much had humanity really changed in all that time? Sure, technology had changed, but *humanity* was still the same–ruled by our minds–or emotions, or often just instinct. Was that all we would ever be? She was sure her visions were telling her otherwise–that humanity was capable of so much more. More than just monuments to our intellectual and physical prowess. The alternative was too depressing.

Monique glanced at the time on her net lens display. It was getting late; Bhima and Pierre should be to the airport by now. But from thirty miles away, all she could do was wait. And hope.

Monique glanced to her companions. Ana was reading a book; Tabia stared out the window. But she must have sensed Monique's gaze; she turned to face her.

"Are you going to miss this place?" Monique asked her.

"Yes and no. I'll miss a few people. And Cairo will always be my home. But the visions have haunted me. I need to understand what they mean. I can feel some kind of *intent* behind them. I know you do, too."

"I do. The visions pointed me to you, but it's the feeling–the sense of purpose–that convinced me to come find you. Along with these strange powers."

Monique took a moment to frame her next question.

"Can you tell me how you discovered yours?"

But before Tabia could reply, there was a chirping sound. *Bhima.* Monique held up a finger, tapping her earpiece to answer.

"Bhima, is everything okay?"

"I'm not sure," he said. "We're here at the airport; the driver went inside to take a look around. He says they have extra military inside, comparing people in line to a photo they're holding."

Monique closed her eyes, taking a few deep breaths to control her pulse. From the outset, she had feared that the Egyptian authorities might bypass a search of the city, concentrating instead on the airport. The video may not have shown their faces, but it was clear they were foreigners; their escape would almost certainly pass through Cairo International. With the few extra days in Cairo, she had hoped the events in the plaza had been largely forgotten. Apparently, that wasn't going to be the case.

"Monique? Are you there?" Bhima was waiting for her to respond.

"Sorry, I'm here. Just thinking it through. We could go back to the hotel–or maybe a different one. Wait them out. They can't keep looking forever. Or we could go ahead with our plan."

There was silence on the line; Monique could imagine Bhima, carefully weighing the options. He was the one at the airport; she wasn't going to push him.

"I think we should go ahead," he said. "The two of us will be fine. I really don't want to spend any more time in Cairo."

Monique glanced to Tabia, who was following the conversation. She nodded her head.

"Be careful," Monique said. "Call us as soon as you're safely on the plane."

"We will," he said. "You be careful as well. See you soon." The line went dead.

Monique leaned back, taking a few slow breaths. Soon, the three of them were going to run the same gauntlet. She could already see the trepidation in Ana's face. She needed something to distract them; they were still a good distance from the airport, with no way to help or monitor Bhima's progress. She turned back to Tabia.

"Sounds like we're going to have some fun at the airport. But we'll be fine, I promise. We can certainly take care of ourselves, right ladies?" She smiled directly at Ana, who managed a weak smile in return.

"Tabia," she said. "Would you mind telling us about your powers? How you found them?"

"No, I don't mind," Tabia said. "But it's a little complicated. Given the audience." Tabia was still looking at Monique, but her eyes briefly darted to Ana.

Uh oh. Monique had an uneasy feeling that she knew where this was headed.

"Maybe you could just summarize?"

Tabia paused for a moment before responding.

"I was at the museum. It was at the end of a closing shift, so it was late and only a few of us were there. One of the security guards had been bothering me, and that night he went a little too far. So I pushed him away."

"Like you did to help us?" Ana asked.

Tabia grinned. "Yes, just like that."

Monique had little trouble imagining the scene, even from Tabia's brief description.

"Sounds like he wasn't your type," she said.

"Actually, none of them are."

Monique laughed; even Ana joined in.

"Boys are a lot of trouble," Ana said. "Sometimes I wonder why any of us like them."

Tabia reached out and ruffled Ana's hair. "Patience, Ana. Boys have their place. Either way, you'll figure it out, I'm sure."

"Did this happen recently?" Monique asked.

"No. Maybe a year ago."

"Have you used the power much since then?"

"I practiced. A lot. You could say I was highly motivated."

"Do you think you could teach others?"

"I know I could. Assuming they have the ability."

"Do you think you could teach me?" Ana asked.

"I could certainly try," Tabia said, giving her a warm smile.

"When I met Bhima," Monique said, "He had the same power, but not the visions. I taught him to find his inner place; it was easier than I expected. What I wonder is whether the two are related–a package, so to speak. I think they are."

"So do I," Tabia said.

"When we get to Virginia, I think it's time for some experimenting. And some training."

"Pierre is dying to learn," Ana said.

"I bet he is," Tabia replied.

They continued on in silence. As the minutes passed, her concern for Bhima and Pierre grew. She couldn't call him; that would raise a flag–especially if he was being questioned.

There was nothing to do but wait.

●●●●●

The sun had nearly set by the time they arrived at the departures terminal–a crescent-shaped, low-slung building that sat bluntly amongst the rock and sand just east of the city. Their driver ignored the drop-off area, pulling through to the far end of the terminal and parking in a spot clearly marked Official Use Only–in both English and Arabic. He gave Monique a smile.

"I'll escort you in," he said.

Monique wasn't going to complain; they'd be less conspicuous with the local driver as part of their group.

Inside the terminal, she saw no sign of Bhima or Pierre. She did see a few members of the Egyptian military–one with a large, hulking dog on a short leash. It could have been a k-bot, programmed to detect fugitives; she couldn't tell from such a distance. But there was no commotion; no obvious sign of anything wrong. Still, it concerned her that Bhima hadn't called again. His flight should be boarding.

"Follow me," her driver said. They set off across the short expanse of the stark-white terminal, weaving their way through the evening crowd. Unfortunately, Elite Airlines didn't fly to Cairo, so they were traveling on a traditional carrier–which meant the traditional immigration and security lines. Plus, they were flying in coach, which she hoped would help them blend in. It wasn't far to the passport control lines, which were less crowded than she expected.

"This is as far as I can go," the driver said.

Monique shook his hand to thank him, and they joined the passport control line. Just like the twins, Tabia had never been outside her home country–and yet she had her passport ready, somehow knowing this day would come. It was another testament to the power of their visions–how else to explain leaving all you know behind to join a stranger on some ill-defined crusade?

They inched their way through the line, trying to remain inconspicuous. *Be small*, she had advised them. Ana appeared to be taking the advice literally; she was slouched over with her sweatshirt hood partially obscuring her face. Monique and Tabia kept a wary eye on the guard standing at the immigration desk–the one with a photo in his hand. There was a fine line between actively avoiding his gaze and staring too intently. Monique tried to walk that line, but as they approached the desk, the line felt more like a tightrope–stretched over a dark abyss.

And then, they were past, and standing at the immigration desk.

"Passports?" a woman behind the desk asked them. Tabia produced all three passports; they had agreed that she should do the talking.

But there was no talking to be done. Three cursory looks through the passports, three stamps, and they were waved through. Monique took a deep breath–possibly her first since they had stepped up to the desk. They picked up the pace, walking forward to the security line.

"That wasn't so bad," Monique said to no one in particular.

"Easy!" Ana agreed. "Are we done?"

"Almost," Tabia responded. "Just a little further."

The security line was straight ahead, and relatively quiet. The equipment was decades old–a simple full-body scanner and an x-ray machine for the bags. And she saw no sign of extra staff, or the military. They placed their bags on the conveyor, and then stepped to the scanner. Ana went first, followed by Tabia, then Monique. All clear. Again, Monique caught herself breathing a sigh of relief.

Which made the hand on her arm all the more unexpected. She turned, her body making an involuntary jump.

"Is this your bag?" A tall, lanky man in an airport security uniform held Monique's purse in his hand. His breath enveloped her like a mushroom cloud; it was all she could do to return his gaze.

"Yes. Is there a problem?" She tried to remain calm; she could see Ana, frozen in fear, just behind him.

"Please follow me," he said. He walked to a door behind the security area, holding it open for her.

"All of you," he said.

Monique glanced at Tabia, who looked as confused as the rest of them. *Not good.* But what choice did they have? There was no getaway car here; no obvious path of escape. Monique put her arm around Ana, motioning Tabia to follow.

Inside the room, another security guard was there to greet them. He was bigger than the first, and made no pretense of a friendly greeting. But her gaze left him almost immediately–she was focused on the man in military uniform, leaning casually against the wall. A gun was slung over his shoulder, with a hand resting casually near the trigger.

There was a soft click as the door shut behind them. Monique pulled Ana close to her. Tabia remained still, a step or so to Monique's right. The room was small, barely enough for the six of them, let alone the table that sat in the middle of the room. Elbowing his way past Monique, the thin guard handed her purse to the larger man.

He grabbed at it, leaned forward, and dumped the contents onto the table. Monique watched as her things clattered and bounced on the metal surface; a few of them skittered off the table and onto the floor. He wasn't done—he began to fish through her things, as if looking for something in particular.

"Can I help you find something?" Monique tried to keep the ire from her tone, but there was only so much a woman was willing to tolerate when it came to her purse.

His hand clamped onto an item, and then another. He held them up so she and the others could see. It was her translation units.

"Do these belong to you?" He leaned even further forward, as if to challenge her response before it was made.

Monique hesitated; she had no idea why they would ask about her translators. She never took them out of her purse at the museum, she was sure of that. *Let's start with the truth.*

"Yes, they belong to me. Is there a problem?"

The man stood to his full height, giving Monique a long, deliberate stare. He didn't appear the type to carefully consider his words, but several seconds ticked by before he responded.

"Someone reported one of these stolen. All of you will have to stay here, until we can sort this out. You'll have to catch a different flight."

Monique did her best to ignore the shiver crawling up her spine.

"We can't do that," she said. "We have important business back in the United States." The words tumbled out in a rush.

"I'm sorry to hear that," he responded. "But we have our procedures. We have to wait for the police to arrive."

Monique and Tabia exchanged glances. She felt Ana's grip tighten on her arm.

"How long will that be?" Monique asked.

"We don't know. You'll have to wait."

Monique took a deep breath, glancing again at the security officer against the wall. He stood motionless, feet apart, staring back at her with an indifferent ease. His hand remained draped over the trigger mechanism.

Monique returned her gaze to the man in front of her, who was still holding both translator units in his meaty hand.

"I promise you, those are mine," she said. "I use them for my work. I'd be happy to show you; I know how to use them."

The guard shook his head, shooting a furtive glance to the clock on the wall. He turned to his colleague, and they conversed for a moment in low tones. He then tapped his own earpiece, holding another murmured conversation with someone on the other end. Time pressed on; Monique expected someone else to barge in at any moment. She could sense the tension in Ana's grip, and in Tabia's eyes.

Finally, the man turned back to face them.

"I've been authorized to allow you to leave, but only if you leave these items behind. You can provide us with your personal information, and we'll return them to you if they turn out to be yours."

Allow us to leave? All at once, the truth hit her. *It's a shakedown.* She did her best to hide her anger; she would happily join the façade.

"I would appreciate that," she replied. Let me give you my name and address and we'll be on our way; we really must make our flight."

She filled out the form; they made no effort to verify the information. She doubted the slip of paper would survive their next cigarette break. She scooped her things from the table, putting them back in her purse; none of them lifted a finger to help. The items on the floor, she left behind.

The thin man opened the door for her. Tabia and Ana squeezed out first, with Monique closely behind. The door shut the moment she crossed the threshold.

"That was insulting," Tabia said as they set off for the departure gate.

Monique nodded, though she was more relieved than insulted. They could have the translators. But before she could respond, her earpiece chirped. It was Bhima.

"Bhima?" She picked up her pace, motioning for the others to follow. "Where are you? Is everything okay?"

"We're fine," he said. "Sorry it took a few minutes to call. The gates are a madhouse. We barely got to the plane on time. I just thought it would be better to make sure we were on the flight before we called."

Monique saw Ana's expectant look. "They're fine," she said. A wide grin broke out on Ana's face.

"*Now* are we safe?" Ana said.

"Almost," Tabia told her.

"Monique? Are you there?" Bhima was still on the call.

"Yes, we're here. We just got through security."

"No problems?"

Monique looked at her two companions, who were directly in front of her, on a beeline to the gate.

"No problems. Or at least, nothing a little charity couldn't solve.

"We'll see you soon," she added.

TWENTY
EIGHT

Nothing is more difficult, and therefore more precious,
than to be able to decide.

– Napoleon Bonaparte

Rudy stood at his office window, staring at the New York City skyline. From his corner office, the top-floor view looked west and south–over the financial district, Battery Park, and eventually the Statue of Liberty. He could even see a few of GRI's robotic cranes, hard at work on the entrance to the transatlantic tunnel. It would be ten more years–at least–before the tunnel was complete, but he was looking forward to his VIP seat for the vacuum-train's maiden voyage. The trip to London would take barely an hour. Of course, he was also looking forward to the one hundred billion dollars to be earned by the various GRI divisions that were hard at work on the project.

An icon flashed in his net lens; Rudy scowled as another meeting appeared on his calendar. It was beginning to look like ancient hieroglyphics– so many entries that even Grace's best efforts couldn't squeeze meaningful content onto the display. Mondays were becoming all too predictable–no matter how much he got done, the pile of work remaining was larger than it had been when the day began. The dearth of empty space on his calendar only added to his mood, which had been sour since the previous weekend.

But he had a knack for compartmentalization–he would sit down with Victoria when he got home, and they would eventually work things out. Right now, he had a company to run. And a big decision to make.

As he glanced through the schedule, he was surprised to see a meeting with Rolland Hughes; he was sure it wasn't there the last time he looked. Rolland was a trusted associate–perhaps not part of his inner circle, but trusted enough to be running a key unit in the Space business. If Rolland needed a spur-of-the-moment meeting, it was undoubtedly important. He glanced at the always-present icon that connected him to Grace.

"Hi Grace. Tell me about the meeting with Rolland Hughes?"

"He said it's about an asteroid," she replied. "He's on his way. He also said a man named Lester White would be with him. I've attached his bio."

A picture and short bio appeared in Rudy's display; Lester was a Vice President in charge of several third-party R&D efforts, reporting directly to Rolland.

"Thanks, Grace." Rudy disconnected, wondering whether he'd ever break the habit of thanking a computer.

Not likely. It was the least of his bad habits.

Rudy left his desk and walked to the smaller of his conference tables, as Rolland pushed through the door. From the body language alone, it was clear they wouldn't be popping any champagne; Lester looked like he had just left a funeral.

"Thanks for seeing us on such short notice," Rolland began. "This is Lester White. He oversees the project we'll be discussing."

Rudy shook Lester's hand. Rolland continued.

"First, let me give you the good news. And it's *really* good news. One of our outside research firms has discovered an asteroid–and not just any asteroid. They've already christened it the *mother lode.* It's on the inner fringe of the asteroid belt. And to say it's loaded would be a serious understatement. It's far and away the most valuable asteroid ever discovered. By orders of magnitude."

"That is good news," Rudy said. "Great news, I'd say. But by the look on your face, I'm guessing there's some kind of catch."

"Unfortunately, yes," Rolland said. "Two of them, actually."

"One at a time," Rudy said.

"Here's the first problem. The group doing the research is a company called *Hanssen Scientific.* Professor Jonas Hanssen is the owner; he's been on our payroll for a few years. They discovered the asteroid last Thursday. He initiated a call with us for earlier today; we assumed he would be announcing the discovery."

"So what's the problem?" Rudy asked.

"We had the call a few hours ago. Hanssen never mentioned the asteroid. Instead, he asked for a raise, plus a bonus if they find anything. After the call, we went back to look at his data, and sure enough, he had erased all the evidence."

Rudy took a moment to digest the news. *These damn scientists are going to give me an aneurism.* He could feel the pressure building above his eyes.

"So we hired an idiot?" Rudy said, a bit louder than he had intended. "He must know we'd catch him."

"Not exactly," Lester said, jumping into the discussion. "Until recently, we uploaded the data from his systems on a nightly basis. And he knew that. But a few months ago, we upgraded to a real-time interface, which he doesn't know about. So we had the data as soon as he did. As far as he knows, we know nothing about his discovery."

"Hold on. You said he discovered the asteroid last Thursday. So how am I just finding out now? Four days later?"

Lester paused to look at Rolland, but Rolland knew better. Lester had jumped in and grabbed the bull by the horns, and now he was stuck in the saddle. Rudy waited patiently for Lester to continue.

"Well, the discovery was late Thursday," Lester said. "So we saw the data on Friday. And by then, Jonas had already scheduled a call for Monday. We assumed it was a call to deliver the good news. So we waited to get the full analysis and results from him."

"And despite this real-time interface, you never noticed he deleted the data?"

"No sir," Lester said. "The interface just sends us new data. It doesn't go back and look at old stuff. We didn't see any reason for it."

"I bet you see a reason now," Rudy said.

"Yes, sir," Lester replied. "But at least we know about the asteroid. Without the new interface, we wouldn't even know that."

"Well," Rudy answered. "Congratulations then." He glanced at Rolland, who gave him an almost-imperceptible shake of his head. Rudy decided to shift gears.

"Tell me exactly what Hanssen said on the call."

"He asked for overtime pay," Lester said. "We had put them under deadline and they were working extra hours. We have a fixed-price contract with him. He also asked for a bonus, if and when they found an asteroid."

"And you didn't confront him?" Rudy asked.

"No sir," Lester said. He looked over to Rolland, a plea for help etched on his features.

"This is where the second issue comes into play," Rolland said.

"Wonderful. Tell me."

"Six months ago," Rolland said, "Carl made the decision to shift most of our resources away from near-Earth orbit, and toward the asteroid belt. The consensus was that the best near-Earth asteroids had all been claimed, so we should move to get ahead of the competition in the belt."

"I know that," Rudy said.

"Hanssen Scientific is the research lead on this effort. They have some unique technologies to precisely value distant asteroids. But they've been searching the asteroid belt for months now, with nothing to show for it." Rolland paused.

"Go on." Rudy said.

"So a few weeks ago, we decided to take our fleet of probes off line, so that we could perform some hardware and software upgrades."

Christ. Rudy started doing the math in his head, and the numbers didn't look good.

"Off line for how long?" he asked, trying to stay calm. He knew the answer before it came.

"About two months," Rolland replied. "Two or three weeks from now, at our absolute best."

"Who the hell decided to take the entire fleet of probes off-line?" Rudy asked, semi-rhetorically. He stood up to pace the room.

"It was my decision to take the probes off-line," Rolland said. Rudy didn't need to look to know that Rolland was lying.

"So you're telling me we found the most valuable asteroid in history," Rudy continued. "And we can't get there to claim it until after the sixty-day legal deadline. So the damn thing will go to public auction."

"Maybe," Rolland said. "Or maybe not."

Rudy stood up, and started pacing the office.

"Explain," he said.

"Since Lester didn't confront Professor Hanssen, you could argue that we don't know about the asteroid yet." Rolland lowered his voice. "So the sixty-day clock to land a probe on the asteroid hasn't started."

Rudy considered Rolland's words. It was a good point—and potentially redeemed Lester's decision not to confront Professor Hanssen. Given all the facts, it was a good spur-of-the-moment call. Or maybe the guy just got lucky? At this point, it didn't matter.

"How many people know?" Rudy asked.

"At GRI, you're looking at them," Rolland said. "The engineer who normally reviews the Hanssen data was out last week, so Lester reviewed it himself. He was the one who discovered the asteroid data for us, before Hanssen erased it."

Either this guy is a lot smarter than I thought, or he's the luckiest bastard on the planet. Rudy sat back down at the table. Now he had something he could work with.

"Just for fun, give me a ballpark as to what this asteroid is worth," Rudy asked.

Lester must have been eagerly awaiting this question; he jumped in without hesitation.

"It's orders of magnitude beyond the value of any previous discovery. It's an M-type asteroid, loaded with rare elements, plus more than enough water to power mining operations. On top of that, it's on the inner fringe—closer to us than over ninety-nine percent of the belt asteroids."

"So what's the number?" Rudy asked again. He was still having trouble warming up to Lester.

"It's big enough to have a sizeable impact on the world market for several elements, so an exact number is difficult. But given the potential to accelerate construction of the new moon base, space stations, and our own orbital hotels, demand should be through the roof. The value could be more than a quadrillion."

Rudy took a deep breath. It was the mother lode. And a game changer. A rock that size would solidify GRI as the most powerful corporation on Earth. Not to mention his own legacy. But in the wrong hands, it would create a potent new competitor. Just a few weeks into his tenure, Rudy knew this was a defining moment. And the kind of moment that was right in his wheelhouse.

"Okay," Rudy said. "Here's what we're going to do. Lester, you are going to get two probes operational. Not one—two. And you're going to do it in a week. I don't care what it takes; all the resources of GRI are at your disposal. I'll pull engineers from NASA if we have to. Say the word, and you'll have what you need."

"Rolland," Rudy continued. "I want you to quietly check with the appropriate friends on Capitol Hill. See where we are with our efforts to extend the sixty-day claim window. It was fine for near-Earth asteroids, but sixty days to reach the asteroid belt is ridiculous. I know you're already on this, and it's probably too late in this case, but let's check anyway. Just be delicate. You know what I mean."

"And what about the Professor?" Lester asked. "And the others at Hanssen Scientific? There are two others in the company."

"Do they all know?" Rudy looked at Lester, who glanced over to Rolland.

"They do," Rolland responded.

Rudy took a moment to consider the implications. Hanssen and his team were certainly a risk—and one he couldn't fully control.

"How did the call end?" Rudy asked. "Did you give him the money he asked for?"

"I didn't roll over," Lester replied. "But yes, I told him that we'd treat him fairly. He was happy; he has no idea we know the truth."

Rudy nodded; he hoped that was the case. But he saw the look that passed between Rolland and Lester; there was more to the story.

"Thank you, Lester," Rudy said. "Would you mind giving me a few minutes with Rolland? You can wait for him outside."

Lester stood up, a look of disappointment on his face. Rudy rose and circled the table to shake his hand. *Time to throw him a bone.*

"Lester," Rudy said. "We don't really know each other, so I can't say whether you made some good decisions here, or just got lucky. But it doesn't matter now—you're here, and you're in the game. You've got a big opportunity in front of you. Run with it, and the sky's the limit. This could be a turning point for GRI. And you're in the middle of it. Don't let me down."

"Thank you, sir. I won't," Lester said. Rudy walked with him to the door, shutting it behind him as he left. He turned back to face Rolland.

"Can we trust that guy?" Rudy wasn't in a mood to mince words.

"Yes," Rolland said. "I'll admit, he's not a superstar–you saw that for yourself. But he's solid, and a hard worker. And more importantly, he's loyal. Extremely loyal. And in this situation, I think loyalty is the thing we care most about."

"You're right about that," Rudy said. "I just don't get a great vibe from him."

"I hear you," Rolland said. "But trust me, he'll get this done. Or better put, I'll personally ensure that he gets this done."

"That's what I want to hear." Rudy sat back down at the table. "So tell me about Hanssen Scientific, and this Jonas Hanssen. Are we one hundred percent sure they all know about the asteroid?"

"We are. When we upgraded the interface, we also installed one of our new, nano-surveillance systems. We've done it at a handful of outside firms that are critical to our long-term strategy, and where we own the facility. Carl approved it–*Trust but verify,* he said. Hanssen Scientific is one of those firms. Lester knows, but he doesn't have access to the feed. Only I do. So when he came to me, I checked the video before I came up here. It took some time, but I found it."

"Found what?"

"On Thursday, after they discovered the asteroid, Hanssen held a meeting to discuss what to do. All of his staff was there."

"So they all decided to blackmail us?"

"Sort of. But it's not quite that simple. In fact, Hanssen himself lobbied to sell the asteroid to the highest bidder."

Son of a bitch.

Rudy could feel the steam shooting from his ears.

"You've got to be kidding me. This guy is insane."

"I'm not so sure. If you watch the whole meeting, I think he used that option as a ploy to arrive at a middle ground. To ask us for more money. It was quite a show, actually. He's inventive."

"Inventive or not, it complicates things."

"I know. The good news is, Lester says this Hanssen is also a loyal guy. He'll keep his word to the team. He won't shop the asteroid, and he'll keep it quiet. Until he's ready to tell us."

"When will that be?" Rudy asked.

"Hard to say. But soon. He's got no real reason to wait–other than to cover the fact that he's already found the thing. Calling us tomorrow would look suspicious."

"True. But that's not good enough. We need to buy a week or so. At least. As soon as he notifies us, the clock starts ticking."

"We can put him off," Rolland said. "When he's ready to tell us, he'll call. He won't send a message; he'll want the satisfaction of announcing the find personally. So we can delay the call a bit."

"That will help. But it may not be enough. Let me think about it some more, and I'll get back to you. Tomorrow at the latest. In the mean time, let me know if anything changes. Monitor that video feed. And get those damn probes fixed."

"Will do." Rolland stood, and walked to the door.

"Just one more thing," he said.

Rudy rolled his eyes. "Now what?"

"Something else from the video. There's a fourth person at Hanssen that knows about the asteroid."

"Who?"

"Hanssen's girlfriend. A graduate physics student from the local University. She was in the meeting."

"A graduate physics student? Hanssen needs to get out more."

"You might change your mind if you saw *this* particular graduate physics student."

Rudy smiled, waving Rolland out the door.

"Go fix those probes," he said.

Maybe this Professor Hanssen isn't so crazy after all.

TWENTY
NINE

We are just an advanced breed of monkeys on a minor planet of a very average star. But we can understand the universe. That makes us something very special.

– Stephen Hawking

No amount of cajoling could convince Kat to skip her morning classes, so eventually, Jonas had given up. She had been impressed with the way he handled the call with GRI–but not *that* impressed. In fact, she all but demanded that he go immediately to the office, and inform the others. She did promise to return to his place at the end of the day, so they could dig further into the Planck III data. It would have to do, for now.

Jonas borrowed one of the bike shares again, arriving at the office to expectant looks from the rest of the team. Kahli joined them in the lab; she looked to be as anxious as Brent.

"Do I still have a job?" Brent asked.

"You have a job, and a raise," Jonas said. "The call went great. GRI agreed to the extra pay. And they'll consider the bonus. Lester said he would get back to us."

"That's it?" Brent said. "Did he seem suspicious at all? Ask why we were calling now?"

"I told him that the deadline was forcing our hand," Jonas said. "And that we wanted to put every spare minute to use. In fact, he also offered to re-think the deadline. He said maybe they would push it back. I forgot about that."

"Not sure that matters much now," Brent said.

"No, but it says they want us to succeed. That we're not one step from the streets. I'd even say we could have pushed harder. Lester was surprisingly amicable. I thought he'd put up more of a fight."

"Maybe you wore him down," Kahli offered. "He'd rather spend more money than more time on the phone with you."

"Funny," Jonas said. "So are we happy now? We've still got a few small details to iron out."

They spent the rest of the morning locked away in the conference room, discussing the timing and logistics behind a re-discovery of the asteroid. They eventually settled on a discovery date of Sunday–six days away. This had the added benefit of demonstrating that they were working on the weekends. Jonas had argued to wait longer, but the others wanted to end the ruse as soon as possible. Plus, they added, GRI wasn't likely to ask questions once the mother lode landed in their laps. They would send a message to GRI on Sunday night; the call would most likely be scheduled for Monday. One week from now.

Once the decision was made, they spent some time further analyzing the asteroid itself. If size was all that mattered, this asteroid would have a Napoleon complex, being small on the celestial scale at just under five hundred feet across. But that was the magic number–big enough to justify a mining mission, yet small enough to potentially bring back to Earth. By international treaty, no asteroid larger than five hundred feet was allowed into Earth orbit. A mistake with a five-hundred-foot asteroid would level a city. But much larger, and the entire planet could be at risk. Corporate and environmental factions had fought tooth-and-nail over the size limit; most agreed that it was yet another battle won by big business. A five-hundred foot-wide asteroid might still be small to some, but it was nearly double the volume of a four-hundred-foot-wide rival.

The asteroid's other characteristics were also ideal. It's location on the inner fringe of the belt put it at less than one hundred million miles from Earth, with a trajectory that was bringing it closer, rather than farther away. And its shape was a nearly perfect sphere, with minimal spin–which considerably simplified a host of issues associated with mining operations.

In the end though, size, shape, and trajectory paled in comparison to the ultimate measure–composition. And there wasn't much peeling of the onion needed–as Jonas liked to say–to see that this was no ordinary rock. First, the water composition would provide enough energy for mining operations, as well as other fusion-based energy needs. When added to the mineral-rich ores, the value quickly rose off the charts.

Kahli had spent the past few days trying to solidify the value of the asteroid. It was no small task, given the huge potential swings in key variables–things like the current market price for various minerals, anticipated arrival dates, and mining costs. By mid-afternoon, her exasperation was on full display.

"Honestly, I think monkeys with darts could do a better job than me," Kahli said.

"You're doing fine," Jonas said. "Besides, does it really matter? Hundreds of trillions, a quadrillion–in either case, GRI is launching a probe. It's a no-brainer."

"I'm not doing it for this asteroid, dummy." Kahli gave him a pointed look. "I'm doing it for the next one. Somewhere down the road, my estimate will be the difference between a go and a no-go. And I want them to have faith in my numbers. Starting with this one. That's how *I* become indispensible."

Jonas nodded. She had a good point. And she deserves just as much of the credit.

Not that she ever believes me when I tell her as much.

"Keep at it, then," he said. "But err on the side of big. Let's be the first quadrillion-dollar rock. That's all anyone will remember."

"We'll see. You'll be the first to know, I promise. But I plan to keep iterating until the last minute."

"You do that. I still need to get started on that data file, and the original asteroid data. That's going to take some work. Especially knowing how much GRI will be poking around on this one."

"You're going to start that now?"

Jonas looked at the clock, giving Kahli a wry smile.

"No. I'm meeting Kat at my place," he said. "But I'll get to it first thing tomorrow."

Kahli grinned. "I'm sure you will."

•••••

After a quick stop for takeout, Jonas was back at his apartment, enjoying an early dinner with Kat. He had splurged on a potpourri of Hawaiian food–lau lau pork, lomi salmon, poki, fried rice–and extra haupia. With all that was going on, both of them had skipped lunch, so the food disappeared in rapid fashion. And best of all, they ate the entire meal without a single plate or utensil from his kitchen.

No dishes–the perfect meal.

"You really know how to treat a girl," Kat said as they cleaned off the table.

"Are you complaining?" Jonas asked. "I told you it was the best takeout in all of Honolulu. They put the *wow* in lau lau."

Kat rolled her eyes. "Please tell me you didn't just make that up. And no, of course I'm not complaining. You were right, it was great."

"Of course I was right. Now get over here and let's get a look at more of my brilliant work."

Jonas grabbed the half-empty bottle of wine, along with both wine glasses, and sat down on the couch. The Planck III data was already spread across the table; it had been there all weekend. Truth be told, they hadn't spent much time looking at it. *Four days, it's all but languished here. Who would have thought I'd ever do that?*

Kat joined him on the couch, and they stared for a time at the reams of data in front of them.

"Where do we start?" she said. "It's a bit overwhelming."

"Well, let's pick up where we left off."

"You mean last weekend? Here on the couch?" Kat gave him a smoldering look; it was all but impossible to ignore.

"Funny," Jonas said. "You know what I mean. We were talking about the differences in the data between the first and second results, and what it might mean."

"We were talking about having information on the *where*, but not much on the *what*."

"True. And we need the *what*. But the more I think about it, I think the differences between the readings are important. This comes from deep space–outside our solar system. It's a void, for all practical purposes, in the places I took the measurements. And that's confirmed by the baryonic data. So what could be causing these non-baryonic particles to act differently in the two locations?"

"What does the data say is out there?"

"A lot, in a relative sense. Space abhors a vacuum–*horror vacui*, as Aristotle said. In this case, we've got hydrogen, helium, and other heavier atoms, for one. In fact, high-energy cosmic rays can interact with these atoms and create chemical reactions out there. And don't forget the space dust."

"Is it possible that different types and sizes of the large space dust molecules are causing the different readings?" Kat asked.

"It's possible, but I was careful to try to eliminate those. There are collectors on the Planck III satellite, so I can filter results based on what they find."

Jonas waited as Kat seemed to sift through her own thoughts. He hoped she would have a moment of inspiration. Because he certainly wasn't.

"Maybe we should think about this differently," she said at last. "Maybe the answer isn't staring us in the face. We have some facts–non-baryonic particles out there, behaving in strange ways. But maybe we still don't have enough data. If that's the case, what more information could help us crack the code? What else can we test for?"

It was a good question. Jonas pondered her line of reasoning for a minute before responding.

"Maybe you're right. I wonder if we could push the limits of Planck III even further?"

"In what way?" she said.

"What if we could somehow interact with these particles? Not just detect them? What if we tried to do what we were doing here on Earth, decades ago?"

"You mean collisions?"

"Exactly," he said. "Maybe there are enough of these particles to do what could never accomplish in the colliders here on Earth. A collision to measure mass, spin, and other quantum properties. Communicating with them–so to speak."

"Can we do that?" Kat asked.

"Good question. I'm not sure."

They sat in silence, as Jonas pondered his options. Until a few weeks ago, he had been alone in his dark matter quest. Kat had been a welcome addition—for a number of reasons. But in general, he had been loath to share the effort with others. Maybe it was time to do just that.

"I think it may be time to get some help," he said at last.

"Help? From whom?"

"Someone intimately familiar with the Planck III satellite, and all its capabilities. Someone who was part of the team that launched it."

"You know someone like that?"

"I do. And so do you."

"What? Who?" Kat sat up on the couch, her interest piqued.

"Professor Kaito Matsui."

"The head of my physics department? The guy that put us together?"

"The same. How do you think we're able to access the Planck III data feeds from a lab at the University of Hawaii? Not just because of my good looks, that's for sure."

Jonas watched as Kat processed the information.

"Professor Matsui doesn't seem old enough," she said.

"If I told you how old he was, you'd fall off the couch. But yes, he was a doctoral student at the time. A brilliant one, mind you. And he remained with the project, long after the launch."

"So he might have some ideas on our next steps? How to devise more tests?"

"I hope so. At a minimum, he'll enjoy learning about our discovery. I owe him that. In fact, it seems I owe him on more than one front."

Kat blushed ever so slightly, giving him a friendly push to try and cover the fact.

"Should we call him?"

"Later," he said, pushing her back down onto the couch.

"Much later."

THIRTY

In theory, there is no difference between theory and practice.
In practice there is.

– Yogi Berra

Monique arrived home just as the sun peeked over the tree line at the end of her street. The three of them stepped out of the autocab, retrieving their small bags. As Monique turned toward her home, the front door opened and Bhima emerged, followed closely by Pierre. An impromptu reunion ensued; she was relieved to see everyone in good spirits, and together again.

The remainder of their trip had been uneventful, other than the discomforts of traditional commercial travel. During the flight, she received a message from Bhima that he and Pierre were safely at her home. The three women cleared customs in New York, and then caught a high-speed train back to Washington DC. From the downtown station, it was a short cab ride home.

Despite the circumstances of the past few days, Monique felt refreshed; in fact, she and the others had managed to sleep through most of their eleven-plus-hour flight. Bhima and Pierre had done the same. The twins were clearly no worse for wear–Monique could barely keep up with their staccato-style conversation, as they traded stories about the trip, and who had the better virtual reality experience during the flight. With a bit of coaxing, she herded all of them back into the house.

Once again, her kitchen-bot had kept the refrigerator stocked, so breakfast was another Bhima concoction, just as good as the last. They sat around the kitchen table, trading more stories about the group's adventures in Cairo, and the trip home. Tabia continued to be apologetic about the hooligans assigned to Cairo security; Monique countered with stories of Ana's bravery during the ordeal. Throughout the discussion, Pierre fidgeted in his chair. Finally, he could control himself no longer.

"Ana said you would teach us your powers?" he blurted out, looking at Tabia.

Monique laughed. "I'd say it's as good a time as any. Would you agree, Tabia?"

Tabia nodded. "Like I said, I'm happy to give it a try."

Monique stood up from the table. "Okay. Let's do it right, then. The back yard is fenced, with plenty of space. We can treat it like a science experiment."

The group followed Monique into the back yard. On the way through the house, they collected a range of objects–mostly fruits and vegetables from the kitchen, but also a chair and a heavy bronze bust. Out in the yard, these items were piled next to a few lawn sculptures, including the yard's centerpiece–a large stone statue of a winged cherub, trumpet raised in salute. Monique nodded, satisfied.

Tabia picked a large grapefruit from the pile.

"You'll need to have some patience; I've never tried to explain this to someone before." She was still, staring at the grapefruit in her hand. Then, without warning, it rose from her hand, floating to eye level. There it froze, as if placed on an invisible table.

"I think Monique is right," Tabia said. "I don't do this with my mind; it's not a thought. It's hard to describe, but I can *feel* it rise from my hand. Maybe it's similar to the visions. That might be a place to start.

"But watch this."

The grapefruit rose further into the air–first quickly, and then slowing until it was half again as high as the house. There it stopped, though not quite perfectly still. Tabia spoke again.

"Right now, that's just about the limit. If I really concentrate, I might be able to push it a bit higher. But not much. The power is very localized–at least for me. I haven't been able to do anything outside of that radius. But I can do this."

The grapefruit floated back down, close to her eye level. Then, it rose as if shot from a cannon–a missile headed for the heavens. Tabia made no attempt to retrieve it; they watched as it disappeared out of sight. Monique waited for the sound of a crash, or a scream; thankfully, it never came.

"Close up, I can use a lot of force. That's how I can push things like that grapefruit with such velocity. But at that speed, once it was above the house, I had no way to control it. Like an arrow. One shot, and it's gone."

Monique and Bhima each grabbed a grapefruit. Both of them were able to push it into the air; Bhima was quickly able to reach the roof. Monique was close, but not quite as high. After a minute, Monique let hers drop to the ground. *No need to assault any more neighbors.* A moment later, Bhima did the same.

"Now let me show you something else," Tabia said.

This time, she grabbed several pieces of fruit. One of the grapefruits, as well as an apple, an orange, and a lemon. In one swift motion, she tossed them into the air–where all four remained, suspended together like a small fruit basket–without the basket.

"Like in Cairo," Tabia continued, "I can also affect multiple objects at the same time. But only as a group. I can't make the apple go up as the lemon goes down. I can't even drop just one of them; it's all or nothing. But like you saw, in close proximity you can have the same effect on a lot of objects."

All four of the fruits dropped to the ground.

"What about the head?" Pierre said. "Can you pick up that head? I could barely get it out here."

On cue, the bronze bust rose into the air, hovering in front of Pierre.

"That is so cool," he muttered.

"What about the statue?" Bhima asked. Monique thought she might have detected a hint of jealousy in his voice.

Tabia lowered the bronze bust carefully to the ground, and turned to the center of the yard. She stood silently, studying the statue as if she was trying to find the best handhold. After about thirty seconds, she looked away.

"No, it's too heavy. I haven't spent a lot of time experimenting with big objects. So I don't know why I can't move that statue, but I can move a dozen people who probably weigh as much."

"Interesting," Monique said.

"Is it our turn now?" Pierre and Ana had been watching the proceedings from the patio, near the back door. Pierre looked as though he might explode from the pressure of his pent-up expectations. Ana seemed excited as well, having risen from the chair she'd brought into the yard to stand alongside her brother.

Tabia retrieved two grapefruits, placing them side by side in front of the cherub statue, in the center of the yard. She stepped back, turning to face the twins.

"Take a breath and relax," she said. "Maybe start in the same way you have the visions. I think the power comes from the same place—or the same source. Whatever it is. But instead of focusing inside and the connection to your own Being, focus outward. Focus on the grapefruit. And keep your mind out of it, just like the visions. Don't think; feel."

The others watched as Pierre and Ana tried to move the grapefruits. At first, they stood casually, arms relaxed; both of them had their eyes closed. But despite their efforts, the grapefruits remained motionless. Before long, Pierre opened his eyes, a look of disappointment on his face as he saw the grapefruits, lifeless as the statue. Then he was scrunching his face, raising his arms, changing his stance. All without effect. Ana remained still, now with her eyes open, but with a similar lack of results. After a few more minutes, Pierre threw up his hands.

"I'm horrible," he said.

"I'm not sure what to do," Ana added. "Or what I'm doing wrong."

"It's alright," Tabia said. "We can keep practicing. I bet we'll figure it out, together."

"In the meantime, I have an idea," Monique said. "It might even be fun." She walked across the yard, picking up two tomatoes and a stalk of celery. She handed a tomato to Bhima, and gave the celery to Tabia.

"Let's play some keep away," she said. "Bhima and I will try to avoid Tabia's celery. Tabia, you try to hit us. We'll stay within the yard, to make it fair. And to stay out of trouble," she added.

In a moment, the two tomatoes and the celery were floating just above their heads; Monique and Bhima quickly sent their tomatoes to the far end of the yard.

"It's the battle of the vegetables!" Pierre yelled. He took a front row seat at the edge of the patio; Ana sat back down on her chair.

Like an arrow bolt, the celery surged toward Monique's tomato. The suddenness caught her off guard—and, she realized, her control at this distance

was reduced, just as Tabia had said. Still, she was able to move at the last instant, dodging to the left and narrowly missing Bhima's tomato in the process.

A bizarre sort of dance followed–full of feinting and dodging, diving and swerving, speeding and slowing. Ana and Pierre were active spectators, though clearly rooting for Tabia. *Smash the tomatoes!* was a common refrain.

As the minutes passed, Monique noticed an increased sense of control; the game was having its desired effect. Practice was going to help build their skills, just as Tabia had described. The thought, though, nearly cost her the game. Tabia feinted toward Bhima, then swerved at her from below. Once again, she barely dodged in time. She refocused her efforts–it may have been just a game, but she had no intention of losing.

Bhima also appeared to be improving his skill. At that moment, he changed tactics, launching his tomato far into the sky. It was technically still in the yard, and he recaptured control as it returned to the earth, before it could smash to the ground. He did this twice, smiling at the others while his tomato was far out of reach–and clearly impressed with his own ingenuity.

The third time, however, was his downfall. Tabia was ready this time, positioned above the house, as high as she could still control the celery. She waited there–like a baseball player, poised in the batter's box, sitting on a juicy fastball. And a fastball it was. She accelerated the celery, before Bhima could regain control, and the tomato exploded. In a fitting finale, the pieces rained down on Monique and Bhima, with the largest one splattering onto the side of Monique's neck.

Infectious laughter filled the yard; Pierre ran over to Tabia, grabbing her arm and raising it above his head.

"The winner of the first-ever vegetable war!" he said.

Monique and Bhima stood side by side, brushing bits of tomato from their clothing.

"Are you a little tired from all that?" she asked Bhima.

"I am," he said. "Not like I ran a marathon, but like I'm *drained*, somehow. I'm not sure exactly how to describe it."

"Me too," she said. But it was good practice, don't you think? We got better, no question."

"Absolutely. And you can tell how far Tabia is ahead of us. We need to catch up."

"Agreed. But first, I'd like to try one other thing."

Monique gathered all of them together on the patio.

"Tabia wasn't able to move that statue on her own. I'd like to try it together, as a team. We already know that the visions are better as a group; I'm hoping it's the same with this power. Agreed?"

Bhima and Tabia nodded.

"Can we try too?" Pierre asked.

"Of course," Monique replied. "Maybe, like the visions, it will help the two of you find your powers as well."

They stood next to each other, intent on the statue. As the moments passed, Monique felt the familiar sense of oneness—a growing connectedness—amongst the group. She could *feel* Bhima and Tabia beside her—like in the visions, but somehow also different. It was more *intense*, in the moment, than if they were simply standing outdoors, discussing the weather.

At any moment, Monique expected the statue to rise from the ground. But it didn't. The cherub was stone-still, mocking her with his tiny trumpet.

Monique shook her head, drawing a deep breath. The others did the same. *I was sure that was going to work.*

"My turn," Bhima said. "I have an idea."

"Spread out," he added.

Bhima crossed the yard. Monique moved to her right, so the three of them formed a wide triangle. Pierre and Ana filled in along the sides.

"Let's try it again," Bhima said.

The effect was immediate. Without a sound, the statue rose into the air, turning slowly until it settled in place, a few feet above the ground. Now Monique distinctly felt a *flow* between them—a means of communication that allowed them to share in the effort. It was like nothing she had felt before; she knew instinctively where to push, how to pull, where to help—so that the statue remained locked in place, floating above the yard.

With an unspoken signal, they began to lower the statue. On a sudden whim, Monique lifted her side instead, holding on while the others released. The statue somersaulted to the ground, landing top first. At impact, the cherub's neck snapped. They watched as the head bounced once and rolled across the yard, coming to rest a few inches from Monique's feet.

She placed one foot atop the cherub's nose, arms crossed, striking a triumphant pose.

No one mocks Monique Durand, she thought with a smirk.

She was ready for Hawaii.

THIRTY ONE

The question isn't who is going to let me;
it's who is going to stop me.

– Ayn Rand

By the next morning, Rudy was willing to find a silver lining just about anywhere he could manage. Today, it came in the form of a large stuffed rabbit, staring at him from his desk as he arrived at the office. The rabbit had a carrot in one paw, and a folded piece of paper in the other.

Rudy removed the piece of paper as he sat down, unfolding it to read the inscription.

How High? Regards, Joe.

Rudy leaned back in his chair, a broad grin on his face.

Looks like Joe got the message after all.

It was good news. Rudy had been having second thoughts since their confrontation on Saturday night–especially after the earful from Victoria. But this was his vindication; he stuffed the note in his pocket, making a mental note to show it to Victoria that evening.

Thoughts of Joe and Senator Pavesi brought him back to the Consortium, and to Arthur. But most of all, to the decision still heavy on his mind. He had spent more time last night reviewing the wealth ratio data. If you believed what was on the paper, the evidence was compelling. But there was just no way for him to independently validate the data itself. At least, not in his lifetime. Plus, Victoria had again complained about his bringing work home. She had scowled at the stacks of data staring back at him from the desk.

"That doesn't look like the kind of thing a CEO should be doing," she had said.

She was probably right. But that didn't help him solve the problem.

On top of that, he still hadn't found a solution to the Hanssen Scientific issue, and what to do with the others that knew about the asteroid. The longer the charade played out, the greater the risk became. Even after the find was announced, he realized, Hanssen and his team would continue to be a loose end.

Rudy thought through the timing. If GRI claimed the rock at close to the sixty-day window, as he expected they would, the whole world would be watching. And given the money at stake, someone was bound to do some poking around. And that would be a problem.

He had done his own poking around, studying Professor Jonas Hanssen on the Net. Born in the Midwest and an only child, he seemed to have spent his childhood in relative obscurity–no easy task in this day and age. A prank he pulled in grad school had made the news–along with his more recent scientific achievements. But none of it appeared to have translated to financial success; his home address–and the pictures Rudy found–was ample evidence of that. Rudy had also pulled GRI's contract with Hanssen. Lester had been right–it was fixed-price, with terms that were extremely favorable to GRI. Rudy could see how that might work against them–he doubted it would take much to get Hanssen to admit to the true discovery date.

A loose end. No question about it.

Rudy rubbed his eyes. There was a common theme running behind all of these thoughts–one that was increasingly at play in the recesses of his mind.

He pulled out his net-phone, and activated the Consortium channel. He tapped once more to dial.

"Hello Rudy," Arthur answered almost immediately. The green light on the net-phone was glowing.

"How do you manage to answer every time I call? You're beginning to make me paranoid. Like I'm being monitored, 24-7."

Arthur laughed. "If I only had the time. I bet it would be interesting."

"Not lately, I can assure you. But do you have some time now?"

"Of course. How can I help?"

"Funny you should ask. I've got three things, actually. First, I wanted to let you know that the message to Joe Gratz was a success. I got a note from him this morning. He heard us, loud and clear."

"Excellent. And good timing. We may need a follow-up with him in the next week or so."

Rudy pressed on. "The second item is a little more complicated. I was hoping I might ask for your thoughts on a GRI issue. And maybe even some help."

"Should I put my GRI Board hat on?"

"Maybe," Rudy replied. "Maybe not. Here's the thing. I just learned that one of our research teams has made a major discovery—an asteroid out in the asteroid belt that is orders of magnitude more valuable than anything ever found before. It's a game changer—hundreds of trillions, if not more."

"Fantastic. That would really solidify our space business."

"And then some. But we have a couple of problems. Potentially big problems."

"Go on," Arthur said.

Rudy filled Arthur in on the duplicitous plans of Hanssen Scientific, as well as GRI's own issues with its probes. Arthur was silent until Rudy had finished.

"What have you done so far?"

"I've got a full-court press on the probe efforts. The good news is that Rolland has already found some ways to improve the probe's speed, while we're at it. The cost is too much to retrofit the entire fleet, but for the two we're getting ready to launch, it will buy us a few days, maybe more."

"Good," Arthur said. "And what about Hanssen?"

"They met yesterday, and decided to send us a message on Sunday. It's not clear whether the message would constitute formal notification—Rolland thinks this guy wants to tell us real-time. But either way, that's going to be cutting it close. Too close. If the clock starts Sunday, it's fifty-fifty that we can get there in time."

"I see," Arthur said. "And you're one hundred percent sure that this knowledge is contained to Hanssen Scientific? Plus the girlfriend?"

"Ninety-nine percent. He'd be crazy to tell anyone else. But we don't have all of them under continuous surveillance, so we can't be one hundred percent certain. The girlfriend is a wildcard. And don't forget Lester and Rolland at GRI."

"Right," Arthur responded. "That's a lot of people." There was a period of silence on the line; Rudy waited patiently for Arthur to continue.

"Rudy, here's how I see it," Arthur said at last. "First, your judgment continues to impress; I appreciate that you called me. It's not a simple problem. And there are some nuances you aren't aware of. But I think we can rectify that."

"Please do," Rudy said. He was tiring of the cloak-and-dagger.

"How about this," Arthur continued. "Give me an hour or so; I'd like to run it up the chain, so to speak."

"To the Chairman?" Rudy asked. "How about we just call him together? I have the context."

Time to cut out the middleman.

"I understand your position," Arthur responded. "But calls only come *from* the Chairman; I can't call him. Not directly, in any case. What I will promise to do is make the case to him. I agree with you, it's time that you had direct access. Either way, I'll get back to you shortly."

Rudy wasn't thrilled with the result, but it was a start.

"I can live with that," he said. "And the sooner the better. The clock is ticking."

"You had mentioned a third item?" Arthur asked.

"I did," Rudy said. "Iran—the wealth ratio data. I've been thinking about it."

"And?"

"The data is compelling; I can't argue with the conclusions. Assuming the data is legitimate, of course."

"Rudy, I give you my word that it's legitimate. And so would the Chairman. Not to mention Gunnar; this is his life's work. There is nothing we take more seriously, believe me."

"So," Arthur continued, "Do you have a decision for us?"

Truth be told, Rudy still had more questions. But a door had suddenly opened, and he wasn't going to miss the opportunity to walk through it.

"I'll tell you what, Arthur," he said. "Get back to me soon on the asteroid; I can give my answer to both you and the Chairman when we speak."

Once again, there was a brief silence on the line.

"Well played, Rudy," Arthur said. "I'll pass your message along, and get back to you shortly."

"Thanks, Arthur. I do appreciate it."

The line went dead. Rudy leaned back in his chair, looking again at the oversized rabbit, still crouched on his desk.

Maybe, just maybe, he was beginning to get the hang of this.

THIRTY
TWO

The best argument against democracy is a five-minute conversation with the average voter.

– Winston Churchill

The house was impressive, but not overly so. Most of what made it so unique was well hidden, or buried deep below the surface. Visitors saw the gilded, ornamental gates, but not the army of robotic security, concealed in the shadows. They saw the occasional video camera, but not the fleet of private satellites orbiting overhead, collecting feeds from millions of other cameras around the world. Inside, they saw the tasteful décor of a modest, nine-thousand-square-foot private retreat–but not the fifty thousand square feet of pure processing power that lived and breathed below.

The Chairman sat peacefully in his study, enjoying a large snifter of cognac. He was still ruggedly handsome, particularly given the ninety-six years that he carried on his sturdy frame. Even those who knew better would swear he was no older than seventy; he attributed it to good genes, clean living, and the absolute best in medicine and biogenetics that money could buy.

To the casual observer, the Chairman's study was an elegant and well crafted mix of technology and comfort–but no more than that. The dozen or so large monitors were evident, but unobtrusive; most of the time, they simply carried news feeds from around the world. They gave no indication of any additional capabilities.

On an otherwise ordinary mirror, a red LED flashed. Someone in the Consortium was sending him a direct message. The signal had been sent a full five or six seconds earlier; before arriving at his retreat, it was anonymously routed across a massive private network, completely independent of the public Net and invisible to the world at large. Even the technology was unique, and not yet available to the general public. With luck, it never would be.

Fewer than ten people in the world could send that message, and none knew its final destination. Some of them knew *who* he was, of course—that was unavoidable—but not *where* he was. He had dozens of homes just like this one, and moved between them on a regular basis. It was partly precaution, but also due to his love of travel. He had arrived here, at his home outside Tuscany, just the night before.

The message was from Arthur Knowles. He had his hands full with their newest recruit—and during a critical phase in the Consortium's long-term plans. He placed a return call, over the same private, encrypted network. It was answered almost immediately.

"Good afternoon, Arthur," the Chairman said.

"Good morning, sir. Let me guess—Europe?"

"Or thereabouts. And how are things with Rudy? We have an answer, I hope?"

"We're close. He's a sharp chap, but you knew that. Eventually it will serve us well—you might even say it already has. But at the moment, I believe he's using the decision as leverage."

"Leverage for what?"

"To work with you directly. Like I said before, he's not big on layers. I don't think it's personal, but he'd love to cut me out. He didn't put it in so many words, but that's the gist."

"It's not personal. He knows Carl and I spoke directly—you told him that. So he's expected the same since day one."

There was a momentary pause in the conversation, as both men considered next steps.

"There is another factor," Arthur added. "I just finished a call with him. He's asking for help with the asteroid, just as you expected he might.

One small piece of new data–Hanssen plans to announce the asteroid on Sunday. So we have four or five days."

"Good. So we help Rudy with the asteroid, get his agreement on Iran, and then give him the access. If all of that goes as planned, he'll be fully committed to us, I'm sure."

"So we move on the asteroid situation, as we discussed?"

"Yes. Let Rudy know–give him some guidance on making the call to Hanssen. I'll take care of our end."

"Yes, sir. Anything else?"

"No. You know what's at stake; we're approaching the end game. And this asteroid is a critical piece of the puzzle."

THIRTY THREE

The devil can cite Scripture for his purpose.

– William Shakespeare

Jonas was slouched in a conference room chair, hoping his morning coffee would kick in before the call from Lester did. It was rare for him to be in the office at this early hour, but Lester's assistant had called at the crack of dawn, requesting a follow-up discussion. Less than twenty-four hours had passed since they had last spoken; Jonas was surprised by the quick turnaround.

They want to move forward–just like we do.

He was cautiously optimistic that there would be some good news to share with the team.

So he was at the office, alone in the conference room, and staring at a brand new holophone. It had been delivered the previous evening, along with a second, identical unit–and a roll of duct tape. In the box had been a note:

For future calls, without the falls. – Lester.

Jonas rolled his eyes, setting aside the second unit, and the duct tape, for his return home. He already had plenty of the latter, of course. But there was no such thing as too much duct tape.

The chirp of the holophone interrupted his thoughts, and he pressed the button to answer the call. To his surprise, both Lester and Rolland materialized before him. They were in dress shirts, but without a jacket or tie. It was a casual look, particularly for a couple of GRI executives. Of course, casual was relative term–he doubted either of them was wearing a pair of flip-flops.

"Good morning, Professor Hanssen," Lester said.

"Hello Lester," Jonas said. "And Rolland. I didn't know you'd be joining us."

"Lester thought it would be helpful," Rolland said. "Since I've missed the last few calls. I hope you don't mind?"

"Not at all," Jonas replied.

Assuming you're here to deliver good news.

"I see you received the new holophones," Lester said. "Did you take the other one home yet?"

Jonas twisted his face in a look of confusion. "Sorry, but I couldn't find the instruction manual for that round, gray roll of sticky stuff. You may have to come out and give me a hand to install it."

Lester laughed. "I'm betting you'll figure it out."

"I'll do my best. And I appreciate the replacements."

There was a moment of silence; Jonas sensed a shifting of gears.

"Thanks for getting back to me so quickly," Jonas said. "Does it mean you have some good news?"

"I think so. But we have a couple of follow-up questions."

"Fire away."

"First, we wanted to be sure that the whole team is on board. We don't want any of you to burn out–especially you, Professor."

"I can assure you, we're all fully committed."

"Great," Lester said. "What will your schedule look like? We want to be able to support you from here, in case you need anything."

"We were thinking twelve-hour days, six days a week, for at least the next two weeks."

"Sounds good. We'll pay you for the extra hours. But we need everyone to be committed–and to be there. Especially you, Professor. We know you have some outside interests, including other research projects; you've discussed one of them with us before. We just want to confirm that this work is going to be your top priority. And that you'll be doing the work at Hanssen Scientific."

Now they pay attention to the dark matter research. Perfect.

But he'd let that go, for now.

"You have my word." He tried his best to keep any frustration from his voice.

"Don't get us wrong, Jonas." Now Rolland joined the conversation. "We have complete faith in you. We just want to be sure this is done right, and with the long term in mind."

"In fact," Rolland continued, "We were wondering if there was any way to further accelerate your progress. Are there any additional resources that might help?"

The question was unexpected; Jonas chewed on it for a moment before an idea struck him.

"Actually, there is one other person. A woman in the graduate physics program here at the University."

"How can she help?" Lester asked.

"She's already been helping–in some cases just a fresh set of eyes, but also to offload some of the more routine tasks. She's been a quick learner."

"Sounds like a good opportunity to me," Rolland said.

Jonas watched as Rolland and Lester exchanged a quick glance. *Good thing Rolland is on the call.*

"Consider her the newest addition to your team," Rolland said. "We'll send you the revised paperwork. Anything else we can do?"

"I don't think so," Jonas said. "I just want to say again, how much I appreciate the support. We won't let you down."

"You haven't yet, that's for sure," Rolland said.

"And one more thing," he added. "Lester told me you asked about a bonus. Like we had originally offered."

Jonas winced, though not in a way that Lester or Rolland would have noticed. He understood the inference–truth be told, he knew full well he was asking to have it both ways.

"Don't get me wrong," Jonas said. "It's just something for you to consider. We'd have to earn it first."

"Fair enough," Rolland said. "We'll commit to another discussion, if and when you do."

"That's all we can ask."

"So are we all set then?" Lester leaned in from his seat, glancing back and forth between Jonas and Rolland.

"I think so," Jonas said.

"Agreed," Rolland replied. "Jonas, we'll look forward to your next call. Make it a good one!"

The holographic image of Rolland and Lester winked out. Jonas leaned back in his chair, breathing a sigh of relief. Their agreement was going to cost him some time with the dark matter research, but otherwise the call went as well as he could have hoped.

He left the conference room and gathered the rest of the team in the lab. They listened intently as he shared the details of the call.

Brent was the first to speak. "All this subterfuge for a few extra bucks," he said. "I know you mean well, Jonas, but I'll be happy when Sunday has come and gone."

"It'll be more than a few bucks by the time we're done, I promise you," Jonas responded.

Brent shook his head, but walked back to his station and continued with his work.

"He'll be fine," Kahli said. "But he's right, we'll all be happier once this is behind us."

"Me too," Jonas said. "Me too."

Jonas walked back to his own workstation, looking at the clock as he crossed the lab. Kat should have just finished her Theoretical Physics lecture, with a few free minutes before her next class. He tried giving her a quick call; she answered almost immediately.

"Well?"

"Well, it looks like you are officially the newest employee of Hanssen Scientific. Congratulations."

"What?"

"Not only did we get the extra hours, but they asked if we could use any additional expertise. So I told them about this smart, sexy grad student that brings a whole new meaning to the word *expertise*."

There was a moment of silence.

"I hope you didn't say that. For your sake."

"I'm kidding. But I did get you on the payroll. I assume that's okay?"

There was another pause on the line.

"I guess so. But maybe next time you could check with me before accepting a job on my behalf?"

"Ouch. Are you getting tired of me already?"

"Of course not. I just want to manage my time. And keep *you* from getting sick of *me*."

"Not going to happen. I'm having way too much fun."

"So no problems on the call?"

"The only issue was that they want me to make this my top priority–they specifically mentioned the dark matter research. We'll have to get creative to find time for it."

"But otherwise, they're still in the dark?"

"We're all set. They have no idea."

● ● ● ● ●

Half a world away, Rudy answered a similar call. It was Rolland on the other end of the line.

"We're all set. They have no idea," Rolland said.

T H I R T Y

FOUR

An onion shared with a friend tastes like roast lamb.

– Egyptian Proverb

The three of them lounged on the back patio, drinks in hand. A full day of practice had left them exhausted, though also much more attuned to their newfound powers. Bhima, in particular, was nearly a match for Tabia–as proven by the tug-of-war exercise they had devised in the afternoon. Monique did what she could to encourage them, while also trying to help Ana and Pierre. Unfortunately, the twins had no such luck.

At the peak of Pierre's frustration, they had taken a break to meditate, and to revisit their current vision. It remained the same; all of them watched again as the scenes swept past. Afterward, they drew a single picture of Jonas, while debating the meaning of the final moments–the blurred lights, racing past and into the distance. They didn't reach much of a consensus– except to agree that it would most likely change again, after they found Jonas Hanssen. He was a physicist–perhaps he would have some answers. In the meantime, Ana and Pierre went back inside. Ana wanted to read; Pierre was most likely still trying to lift a grapefruit, if Monique had to guess.

She stretched out her legs under the table, enjoying the camaraderie of the moment. She wasn't much of a drinker, though she did keep a few bottles of wine at the house. They had just opened their second bottle of Icelandic Riesling–crisp and dry, with hints of apple combined with floral undertones. Despite the onset of fall, there was still a warmth in the air, even at this hour. And the wine contributed to the effect. Monique felt as relaxed as she had in weeks; certainly since her fateful encounter with Charles Jones at the art gallery. It was hard to believe that had been just a few weeks ago. It seemed like months.

"Beautiful evening," Monique said, to no one in particular.

"We don't get much weather like this in Singapore," Bhima said. "This is nice. Maybe a little cold, though."

"Cold?" Monique said, eyes wide. "It's sixty degrees! What you miss is the Singapore humidity; that's what gets to me."

"Did you live your whole life in Singapore?" Tabia asked him.

"I did. Never left the island until Monique brought me here."

"Did you leave any family behind?" Tabia said.

Bhima glanced briefly at Monique before answering. "Not really. My mother passed away a few years ago, and I was never close to the rest of my family."

"Sounds familiar," Tabia said. "I never knew my parents."

"Brothers and sisters?" Bhima asked.

"Not that I know of."

"Quite a coincidence," Bhima said. "We're all only children, with no real family to speak of. Pierre and Ana fit the same profile."

"They have each other," Monique said.

"True, but no one else." Bhima said. He leaned forward in his chair.

"What about you, Monique?" he said. "You haven't told us much about your family."

True. Bhima was right; she avoided the topic as best she could. But it was time; they deserved to know at least some of it.

"I think you know I was born in Paris. It was a pretty good childhood, at least early on. But then my father sold his company, we moved to the United States, and the relationship between my parents was never the same. They were divorced soon after that."

"Did they both pass away recently?" Tabia asked.

"No. My mother passed away about five years ago. It was a skiing accident." Bhima was nodding his head.

"I'm sorry to hear that," Tabia said. "Were you with her?"

"No," Monique admitted. The call from her mother's boyfriend still echoed in her mind.

Monique, I have some terrible news. You should sit down. It's your mother. I'm so sorry.

"And what about your father?" Bhima asked.

"He's still alive. Though calling my father alive might be an oxymoron." The others gave her a quizzical look.

"You know, an oxymoron," Monique said. "Like Glacier National Park."

"So you don't talk to him?" Tabia asked.

"The divorce was bitter." Monique was doing her best to temper the acidic tone in her voice, but it was proving difficult. "During the divorce proceedings, my father told me he didn't want to be stuck with me. I was ten years old at the time." His words still rung in her ears—*You make a better negotiating chip than you do a daughter.*

"My mom got full custody, along with a sizable financial settlement. Though less than she deserved," Monique added.

"So your father is wealthy?" Tabia asked.

"He has money, but he's nothing special," Monique said. "When my mother died, I inherited her estate. That was her money, as far as I'm concerned. She earned it. And it's more than enough for me. So I have no need for my father, or his money."

"Is he still here in the States?" Bhima asked. "As far as you know?"

"I have no idea," she replied. "He retired a long time ago. And I haven't seen or spoken to him in years. He didn't even come to the funeral."

Monique reached across the table and grabbed the bottle of Riesling, pouring herself a healthy glass. A bit of it spilled onto the table as she poured. She took a small sip, then another. The cool, refreshing tang helped to calm her nerves.

"After my mother's death," Monique continued, "I tried to bury myself in worthy causes. Fighting climate change. Hunger. The Digital Privacy Act. I thought it would help me to forget—to feel good about myself. But it wasn't that simple. I was drifting, in a sense."

"You don't seem like the *lost soul* type," Bhima said. "What changed things?"

"The visions. My mother introduced me to meditation when I was younger. But I didn't take it seriously. I moved here not long after she died, and built the studio downstairs. That's when I really committed to finding a place where I could reconnect with myself; a place to be at peace. And that eventually led to the visions."

"Interesting," Tabia said. "My visions started not long after my parents both passed away."

"And I found my powers right after I lost my mom," Bhima said. "But not the visions. I didn't discover those until a week ago—when I met Monique."

Monique considered the similarities—and the potential implications. She had no idea what it meant, but it was worth filing away.

Bhima grabbed the bottle of Riesling, pouring what little was left into his glass.

"So we're ready for Hawaii? And Jonas Hanssen? After Hawaii, I get a feeling we're moving to a new phase."

"Maybe," Monique said. "We'll know soon enough.

"But as far as Hawaii goes," she continued, "I don't think Ana and Pierre should go, given the events in Cairo. And given the fact they still don't have our powers."

It didn't take long for Tabia and Bhima to grasp the implications. They stared at each other, as if sizing up the competition. It was Tabia who spoke first.

"I think you're right," she said. "And I guess it should be me that stays here with them. I can continue the lessons. With any luck, they'll be a match for the two of you by the time you get back."

"I appreciate that," Bhima said. "And the sooner the better, as far as I'm concerned."

During lunch, Monique had done a quick search on the Net. "Elite Airlines has a direct flight tomorrow afternoon. We can be there this time tomorrow."

"Let's do it," Bhima said.

Monique stood up; Bhima and Tabia followed her lead. Tabia gathered the empty bottles and took them inside; Bhima was right behind her. Monique stopped for a moment, taking one last look at the yard. The statue was upright again; they had picked it up and put it back in place earlier in the evening. The cherub's head, however, still lay on the ground, not far from where she stood. Almost as an afterthought, she used her power to gently lift the head, floating it back across the yard. When it reached the fountain, she rotated the piece until the head aligned with the neck. She put it down slowly, meticulously aligning the cracked pieces. When she released her hold, the head stayed in place. She stopped for a moment to admire her handiwork.

Brute force isn't always the answer.

If only her father had understood that.

THIRTY
FIVE

What can you do to promote world peace?
Go home and love your family.

– Mother Teresa

They were back on the private island, and as far as Rudy was
concerned, it wasn't a moment too soon. The mid-week trip
was exactly what the Dersch family needed–work and school
be damned. Sonja and Shae ran up and down the hallway, screaming with
delight, when Rudy made the announcement. Even Victoria's cold shoulder
showed signs of an early thaw.

Arthur's return call had come earlier in the day; Rudy had made the
necessary arrangements, and then cleared his schedule. Arthur seemed
almost eager to okay their use of the island retreat.

He probably thinks it will help sway my decision.

Rosie helped them to throw together a few bags, and Bond whisked
them to Teterboro, where the jet was waiting. They enjoyed a late dinner
on the flight–lobster, of course. This time, Victoria didn't say a word. Ajay
was there when they landed. He loaded the car, and escorted them back to
the compound. By the time they arrived, it was almost midnight, and the
kids went straight to sleep. The adults, however, did not.

Damn fine way to live, Rudy thought as he drifted off, sated and spent.

Wednesday began with a veritable breakfast feast–fresh fruit, juices, omelets made to order, and crepes drenched in lemon and sugar. It was followed by a family swim, though Rudy was careful not to stray too far from his net-phone. The island getaway, of course, had come at a price–he needed to be available when Arthur called.

Sure enough, the call came just before lunch. They were finishing an enormous sandcastle–although Shae had tired of the project an hour ago, and was inspecting the powered toys further down the beach. Rudy stood up, brushing the sand from his hands and shorts.

"Sorry girls, I did my best to wipe the whole day clean, but I have to take this call."

Victoria gave him the eye–but there was a warm smile behind the look.

"We'll give you a pass. But just this once," she said.

"Don't take forever, dad," Sonja added. "The tide's coming in!"

Rudy jogged across the sand, stopping for a moment on the veranda to throw on shoes and a shirt. He made his way down to the wine cellar, where Ajay was already waiting.

Ajay reached between the bottles, and once again the wine racks fell through the floor. Rudy followed Ajay down the narrow hallway, where they stood silently before the scanners. Ajay keyed in his code, and the green light illuminated. Then he opened the door, and stepped aside for Rudy to pass.

"You're not coming in?"

"No, sir. I'll be waiting for you back in the cellar."

"I won't be long," Rudy replied.

Rudy shut the door, closing himself into the facility. Nothing had changed since his last visit, barely a week ago. *Seems more like a year.*

He walked to the far side of the room, assuming Arthur would join him again at the conference table. Sure enough, the holographic projector soon came to life, and Arthur materialized in the seat next to him.

"Good morning, Rudy," Arthur said. "It's still morning there, yes?"

"Close to noon, I think. Tough to keep track on this island. Especially down in this room."

"I won't keep you long. But first, we have someone joining us."

There was the faintest buzz, and another figure appeared, seated comfortably in a chair across the table. He had the look of a non-descript, middle-aged man–thin, graying hair, perhaps a bit younger than Rudy.

His steel-gray eyes were offset by a warm, pink glow to his skin. He was wearing an off-white linen jacket and tan shirt; his hands were together, fingers intertwined, elbows resting on the table.

"Rudy, I'd like to introduce you to the Chairman." Arthur didn't attempt to conceal the grin on his face.

"Or should I say," Arthur continued, "His randomly-generated, holographic representation."

"It's a pleasure to finally meet you, Rudy." The Chairman spoke in a metallic timbre; there was no attempt to soften its obviously computer-generated tone.

"Thanks for joining us," Rudy responded. "Or sort of joining us, I suppose."

"Don't be fooled, Rudy. I'm here next to you, the same as Arthur. The only difference is my image–a randomly generated replacement. I don't even know what it looks like. We've found it's safer that way; no chance of subconsciously exposing something."

"That's good to know," Rudy said. "For a minute, I thought you were younger than me."

The Chairman laughed. "Trust me, Rudy," he said. "Not even close." He cleared his throat before continuing. "But don't get any ideas. I plan on occupying this seat for a few more years. You can't have it quite yet."

"Don't worry. I don't want it. Yet." Rudy gave him a friendly grin.

"Fair enough," the Chairman replied.

"But enough small talk," he continued. "We've got some business to discuss. Arthur filled me in on the matter of Hanssen Scientific. It may be bigger than you realize–we've asked Gunnar to run some models, and the economic impact of this asteroid is enormous. We cannot let this rock fall into a competitor's hands. Period. So we've developed a plan. First, we have two of our own probes that can be launched today. We'll swap them with two of yours–they'll be fully documented as GRI resources. They'll reach the asteroid safely inside the sixty day window."

"You have your own probes?" Rudy asked. "How is that possible?"

"Are you asking how we made them, or where we hide them?"

"Both, I guess."

"Well, we built them from GRI plans, which Carl gave us. And we hide them amidst all the space junk up in Earth's orbit. They blend right in–as long as the Space Junk Treaty never gets approved and implemented. And

I can promise you–it won't. You'd be amazed how much stuff we're able to hide up there, amongst all the debris."

"Well, it's fantastic news. Thank you." *Interesting that Arthur never offered, though.*

"The second item is the matter of Hanssen Scientific," the Chairman continued. "Frankly, I think this is a situation that calls for the unique skills of a Fixer."

"Like Pax," Rudy said. He had hoped this wouldn't be the answer, but it would be a lie to say it wasn't at the back of his mind.

"Exactly like Pax," the Chairman said. "And just as it was with Martin, it's best you don't know the precise details. This is too big–and too important–to leave any loose ends. Pax understands what that means, and will develop his plans accordingly."

Rudy did some quick calculations.

"Okay, but assuming your probes can get there in time, is all this even necessary? If we can get to the asteroid before the true sixty-day window expires, then we're in the clear. We could even expose Hanssen, fire all of them–take the high road. And our hands would be completely clean."

The Chairman shook his head. "The stakes are too high–it's too much risk. I can think of a dozen ways Hanssen could throw a wrench into our claim on that asteroid. Plus, it's not guaranteed our probe reaches the asteroid by the true deadline. We need the extra days this buys us. We need a guarantee."

"In that case," Rudy responded, "What about the two executives at GRI? They're in the middle of this as well. One of them is a friend–Rolland Hughes. What do we do with them?"

"They're a different matter. One, they're already complicit. Plus, they have a lot to gain, without the baggage that Hanssen brings. So I think you can handle the GRI staff. Agreed?"

Rudy considered the Chairman's logic. Rolland wasn't a problem; he could be trusted. But Lester? Rudy wasn't so sure. Rolland claimed he was loyal–but loyalty without talent was an empty promise. At least in Rudy's book. But he could handle that, as well.

"Agreed," Rudy replied. "I can deal with the GRI folks."

"Good," the Chairman said. "We'll move fast on this; we need to act before Hanssen announces the asteroid. At that point, the cat's out of the bag."

"Once Pax has solved our problem, so to speak–" Rudy paused to look at both men, "–how do we officially announce the asteroid discovery? That could be tricky."

Arthur leaned in to join the conversation. "Your team has all the original data, correct?"

"We do," Rudy said.

"Then we can re-insert that data at the appropriate time. With or without the Professor. And by then, we should have a precise arrival date for the probe. We can plan out the discovery with that data in hand."

"I'd suggest another call, when we reach that point," Arthur added.

The Chairman nodded, looking to Rudy for concurrence.

"And who's on that call?" Rudy asked.

Might as well get it all on the table.

"Good question, Rudy," the Chairman said. "Arthur has relayed your impatience to communicate directly with me. I can appreciate how you feel. I should tell you, though, that Arthur has been a trusted associate for many years. He does speak for me, and will continue to do so."

"I understand that. I'm just not big on layers," Rudy responded.

"Carl said the same thing. So that brings us to our last topic. Iran. And the wealth ratio. Have you made a decision?"

So there it is. A quid pro quo.

"I'm close," Rudy said. "I wish there was more time. I'll be honest with you–the whole thing feels a bit like a test–can the new guy be trusted? I don't like making decisions of this magnitude without a full grasp of all the facts."

"Rudy, you've seen the numbers," the Chairman said. "It's not some two-bit sales pitch when I say we are trading no more than a handful of lives to save thousands. Gunnar's data is irrefutable. And we proved it in Nicaragua. I realize you're late to the table, and you don't have the history. Or the years of effort that got us to where we are now. This was supposed to be Carl's decision. But here we are, and we need you."

"It just seems a bit strange," Rudy said. "You have your own asteroid probes. You created a global banking enterprise from whole cloth. But you need GRI to deal with Iran?"

"The plan has been a year in the making, Rudy. It's an incredibly complex problem, even with today's technology. We need specific resources from GRI, across multiple divisions. To include some satellites. The Consortium could build all of it, of course, but that takes time. Time we don't have."

There was logic to the answers, Rudy knew–but that didn't stop it from feeling like body blows to his conscience. And the more he wavered, the more persistent the tiny voice at the back of his mind became. *What would Victoria say?* He knew the answer to that question.

"You're right," Rudy said at last. "I am late to the table. And no one's ever called me indecisive. But this is no run-of-the-mill decision. It's something I have to live with for the rest of my life."

Rudy paused, looking to Arthur, and then back again to the Chairman. Their images were stone still, awaiting his answer.

"How about we deal with the asteroid, and resolve the Hanssen Scientific issue," Rudy said. "I'll give you my answer on our next call. In the next day or two, I expect."

The Chairman leaned back in his chair, shooting a quick glance to Arthur. Even with the holographic overlay, Rudy could see that the Chairman wasn't accustomed to hearing much other than *Yes, sir.*

"Rudy," the Chairman said, "I understand your reluctance. And I'll agree to wait. But know that every day is a risk. Gunnar can't predict when a region might pass the *tipping point*. It could be tomorrow, or a month from now. But it's coming. I can assure you of that. To not act would be a serious risk to the *status quo*."

"I get it," Rudy said. "You'll have my answer soon enough. Just keep me in the loop on Hanssen Scientific; the resolution is going to impact how I handle the GRI folks."

"Of course," Arthur said.

"Enjoy the beach," the Chairman added. He leaned toward the holophone, and his image winked away. Arthur's image disappeared a moment later.

Rudy sat alone, gathering his thoughts.

The noose is tightening. And he was running out of gimmicks to slip the knot.

●●◦●●

Back outside, Rudy reinserted himself into the sandcastle project. Shae had returned, having been unable to convince Victoria to let her take out a mini-jet boat on her own. The three of them were adding parapets to the outer walls, aided by four small buckets that served as the foundation. But Sonja was right—the tide was fast approaching. Buckets or no buckets, their effort would soon be for naught.

Rudy watched Sonja and Shae working together on one of the towers, while simultaneously trying to maintain the moat that kept the tide at bay. Victoria had stopped to watch them as well; she smiled as her own parapet began to collapse.

Here, watching his family, Rudy realized the truth. He had already made his decision about Iran. He knew what he had to do—no matter the cost. The security of his family would always come first.

He returned Victoria's smile, and squeezed her hand.

THIRTY
SIX

Celebrate your successes. Find some humor in your failures.

– Sam Walton

"Quiet, you drunken fools!" Jonas bellowed as he rose from the table. "I'd like to make a toast." Kat raised an eyebrow and stared at him in mock disdain. He was fortunate not to spill any of the wine from his nearly overflowing glass.

The four of them had just finished a dinner at *Kuloko Hou*–or *Loko,* as it was known to the locals. It was the loud, trendy new restaurant and place-to-be-seen in downtown Honolulu; they had scored a table through a friend of Jonas's, who happened to be the on-duty manager that evening. The restaurant served a variety of food-as-art regional dishes–with prices to match.

They deserved a celebration, Jonas had decided, and so the wine had flowed as fast as the conversation. Even Brent was enjoying himself, Jonas noted with satisfaction. And no one had complained or even commented on Kat's inclusion; she was part of the family now.

"A toast!" Jonas said again. "To the best damn science team–" he paused for effect, "–in this entire restaurant!"

A chorus of jeers followed; Brent threw a napkin in his direction. Jonas saw Kahli whispering something into Kat's ear. He brushed them aside with a sweep of his left hand, holding his glass high in his right.

"Seriously," he said. "Thank you for being here; we needed this. I know we're not quite to the finish line yet, but things are going to get busy soon. This may be the last chance we have to relax. For a few months, at least."

Now Kat was whispering something back to Kahli; they again exchanged knowing looks, a wide grin on both of their faces.

"What's so funny?" Jonas finally asked.

"Nothing," Kahli replied. "It's nothing. Sorry, please continue."

Jonas narrowed his eyes, shifting his gaze back and forth between the two of them.

"We're all friends here," he said, a bit too loudly. "You can share, I don't mind."

"It's nothing, Jonas," Kat said. "Go ahead with your speech."

Jonas spread both hands wide; now he did spill some of his wine, narrowly missing Kat, who was sitting just to his right.

"Please, I'm begging you. Tell us!" he asked again.

Kat gave him an apologetic look.

"You pants are unzipped," she mumbled.

Jonas couldn't control his involuntary reaction; he looked down, confirming the accusation. The table erupted in laughter. He sat down as a flush of red broke across his cheeks.

"Hey, soon I can hire someone to keep an eye on that for me," he said with a laugh.

"I wouldn't bet on it," Kat countered, waving a finger in his direction. Her response set off another roar; even in the loud restaurant, nearby tables were taking notice.

"Okay, okay," Jonas said. "You two are killing me. Here I am trying to open up, and you run me clean through with a saber."

"Poor baby," Kahli said. "I promise we'll behave if you want to embarrass yourself some more."

"Tell Kat about your last year at school," Brent offered. "You know, the football stadium."

"What is this, a mutiny?" Jonas asked. He was beginning to wonder if they were conspiring against him—as punishment of sorts for his scheming, perhaps.

They all stared at him, a look of expectation on their faces.

"Come on," Jonas said. "I haven't told that story in years."

"All the more reason," Brent added.

The entire group now stared at him, expectantly. Jonas leaned back in his chair, defeated.

Might as well finish in style.

"Fine. Here's the short version. It was my last year of graduate school, and I was buried in debt–as in forget-the-shovel-bring-in-the-excavator buried. I was maxed out on loans, which in those days was quite an accomplishment. Though I'll admit, not all of that money went strictly toward tuition." He winked at Kahli before continuing.

"Anyway, a friend got me a job at the University computer center. The money stunk, but I would take the late shifts, and sleep there overnight; otherwise I was basically bouncing between friends at the time. Needless to say I was there a lot.

"It was one of those late nights, alone and bored, that I found it."

"Found what?" Kat asked.

"A back door to the football stadium computers. They were all interconnected, and I found a security hole to the stadium scoreboard. So I took advantage of it."

"How?" Kat looked genuinely intrigued.

"Well, during the first game, we ran a few funny messages, with accompanying graphics. CHEER IF YOU LOVE A GOOD TIGHT END. But then a business school friend got the idea that we could sell advertising space. Anonymously, of course."

"And you didn't get caught?" Kat seemed incredulous.

"Not for a long time. It was a good set-up; double-blind, cash-only, through a small network of close friends. We made good money. Legitimate local businesses even started advertising with us. It became *cool,* so to speak. Advertisers got a huge return on their investment."

"So what happened?"

"The school was embarrassed because they couldn't close the security breach. Before each game, a professor would come in and declare they had fixed it. And then during the game–we ran more ads. Each week I left a breech for them to find and fix, but kept a new one hidden. I don't think they ever would have figured it out."

"Someone turned you in?"

"No," Jonas responded, a little too sharply. "No one ever said a word. In fact, they never knew anyone else was involved."

"They hired the big guns," Brent said.

"The best that money could buy," Jonas said. "They spent a small fortune on a firm from San Francisco, found the real back door, and tracked it to me."

"Did they arrest you?" Kat asked.

"Yes and no. Eventually we worked out a deal, but not until after the last football game."

"Tell her what they did," Brent said, a broad grin on his face.

"You're enjoying this, aren't you?" Jonas retorted, staring down the barrel of his index finger as he pointed toward Brent. But in all honesty, he was enjoying it as well; Kat was hanging on every word.

"So for the last game," he continued, "they let me believe I was still in command of the scoreboard. I sat at my station as usual, but when it was time for the first ad, what ran instead was a video feed they had set up from my location. So the whole stadium watched as they came in and arrested me. I tried to escape; apparently, it was pretty funny."

"What was the deal you made?" Kat asked.

"Oh, that was the best part," Jonas said, with more than a touch of sarcasm in his voice. "I was a local hero, so they didn't want the bad publicity of prosecution. The businesses agreed to pay the school for the advertising, so the school made money and looked like the good guys. They even let me graduate."

"So they just let you go?"

"Not quite. Remember my student loan? The one that was maxed out? Well apparently it was only maxed out for me. They took the cost of the consultants, and added it to my student debt."

"What about your business school friend?" Kat asked. "He never got caught?"

"You can ask him that question yourself. He's sitting right next to you. Except that *he* is a *she*."

Kat turned, eyes wide. Kahli was sporting her own sheepish grin.

"They offered to forgive the money if he turned in his accomplices," Kahli said. "For months, all the way until graduation, he swore he acted alone. Now you know why I put up with him."

"Why the rest of us still do is an open question," Brent said. He grinned as he spoke; Jonas used two fingers to pull ice from his water glass, hurling it across the table. This time, he was on the mark–catching Brent square in the chest.

"So now you know," Brent said, raising his glass to Kat. "You're dating a delinquent."

"He's not so bad," Kat replied. "I kind of like that he stands for something."

"I'm not sure he can stand for much of anything at this point," Kahli said. She shook the empty wine bottle in front of Jonas, as if daring him to prove otherwise.

Jonas didn't bite. "Hey, I resemble that remark," he retorted, leaning back in his chair. "But I promise you, this time the little guys are going to come out on top."

There was a momentary lull, as each of them was lost in their own thoughts. Kahli finally broke the silence.

"Speaking of," she said. "It's getting late, and we've got a lot to do tomorrow. I need to get home and get some sleep."

"Are you coming in tomorrow to help?" Brent asked, looking to Kat. Jonas nodded, leaning back even farther in his chair.

"I think so," Kat said. "I have a few early classes, but I should be there by late morning."

"Great," Brent said. "I'm going to save some data entry stuff for you; it would be a big help."

Jonas paid the bill, and they left the restaurant, emerging onto King Street. It was late, and the traffic on the one-way street was relatively light. It took several minutes to flag down a taxi. They put Kahli in the first one. Brent decided to walk, as he lived less than a mile from the restaurant. Jonas and Kat were left alone on the curb.

"Great people," Kat commented.

"I know," he replied. "You fit right in."

"I hope so. I was worried they might resent working with me, but even Brent seems to have warmed up. It's nice."

"We need your help. We have a lot to do in the next few days, and we need to triple-check everything we do. We can't afford to make any mistakes."

A second taxi arrived, and they piled into the back seat. Jonas gave the driver his address.

Home stretch, he thought, looking at Kat as she gazed out the taxi window. Next week, after the announcement, they would spend more time on the dark matter results. Jonas was already formulating a plan in his head–one that would require her help. And Kaito's.

Things were moving fast—and not just for the business. He stole another glance at Kat; she was absorbed in the night sky, her features a shadowy elegance in the pale moonlight. For just an instant, a dangerous four-letter word flickered across his conscious.

Slow down, he had to remind himself. The time for those words would come. But for now, they had a big week ahead.

THIRTY
SEVEN

If the people knew how hard I had to work to gain my mastery,
it wouldn't seem wonderful at all.

– Michelangelo

The first message had come several days ago. It was an early notice, nothing definitive, but Pax had begun the planning process, nonetheless. There were three of them—two scientists and an accountant. He did his homework, using both public and private sources to build a dossier on each. When he had finished, he evaluated a dozen or more possible solutions, weighing the various pros and cons. He formulated notional plans around the top three alternatives—all with a projected success rate of over ninety-eight percent.

In his line of work, however, ninety-eight percent was far too much risk. So he revised his plans to include a trusted associate. And when a subsequent message revealed he would be dealing with four individuals, rather than three, his penchant for over-preparation was once again rewarded. He built a dossier for the female grad student, and awaited further instructions.

Two days ago, those instructions had come; the mission was a *go*. He reviewed his plans, and based on current parameters, he devised an optimal solution. Along with contingency plans, of course. He spent the rest of the day running scenarios, fine tuning the plan, and gathering the necessary equipment. He sent a final plan up the chain; it was quickly approved.

He also contacted his associate, who would meet him at a private airstrip the next day. Her name was Deuce–and like Pax, it was an apt label. She was short and stocky, but surprisingly quick–in more ways than one. She kept her thick, dark hair as short as she could without drawing undue attention; her mixed heritage and otherwise unremarkable features also served her well.

They had last worked together in Nicaragua, a job that Pax counted among his finest. It had required all of their diverse skills–from the precise placement of the devices, to handling the local resources they had employed for the job. Two years had passed, and it was still thought to be a natural eruption–albeit a very singular and unexpected one. Exactly as they had planned.

Yesterday, they had boarded a private jet for the long haul to Honolulu. Pax didn't mind the flight; in fact, it gave him an opportunity to do a bit more research, and to rest. He and Deuce hardly spoke; theirs was not a business of small talk. He did give her the device containing the dossiers, as well as the outline of his plans. She studied them, even offering a few suggestions. But for the most part, they slept. And waited.

The jet landed at Honolulu International Airport in the pre-dawn hours of Thursday morning. They exited the plane at precisely 4am, bags and equipment in hand. An autocab was waiting–no driver meant one less set of eyes. The roads were nearly empty at that hour, and they made good time into downtown Honolulu, arriving at their destination precisely ninety seconds ahead of schedule. They unloaded, and crossed the sidewalk to a small apartment building.

The main door was unlocked, as expected. An immediate left took them to the stairwell entrance. Deuce jimmied the door, and they began their ascent. At the top floor, Pax stopped to listen. A full ten seconds passed. Hearing nothing, he pushed open the door, and peered down the hallway. It was empty. He glanced at his watch; it was 4:47am, precisely as planned. Statistically, this was the time of day they were least likely to encounter someone in the hallway. The odds were remote, but it was high on his list of measurable risks. And without cameras in the building, they weren't able to track the daily patterns of the other residents, inside the hallways. Of course, the lack of surveillance also worked in their favor. Fortunately, no one was about, and they hustled down the hallway to the last door on the right. He entered the key code to gain access to the apartment. They were in.

They stood still for a moment, letting their eyes adjust to the near-darkness. The street lamps provided just enough light to discern the apartment's meager furnishings. Pax glanced at Deuce, pointing down the lone hallway to their left. But it was unnecessary; she was already moving to search the few remaining rooms. She was back in less than thirty seconds.

"Clear," she said, joining him in the small living room. They walked to the set of windows overlooking the street below.

"There it is," he said. It was still dark, with nary a hint of the sunrise soon to come. But the occasional car and street lights were enough to distinguish the sign on the building just across the street: *Hanssen Scientific*.

Their observation post wasn't ideal; he'd prefer to be closer. But this was the best they had found—an unrented apartment, in a building without surveillance cameras, and a clear view from less than one hundred and fifty feet away. It would have to do.

Pax opened his bags to unload the equipment. First, he set up the video cameras and tripods—three small but high-powered video feeds that would catch all activity in both directions on the street below, as well as the Hanssen entrance. He then unpacked his computer system, setting it on the table next to him. In less than five minutes, he had all of the equipment interconnected and operational, with the video feeds recording, and displayed on the monitor. In addition, he tapped into the private Consortium network, gaining access to the GRI feeds from inside Hanssen Scientific. A set of headphones would give him access to the audio. He flipped through each of the videos feeds, and was pleased to see the office was empty, as expected.

Deuce was going through a similar exercise with her equipment, which she had laid out on the table. Each of her items, however, was for the next phase.

Pax pulled a chair to the window. It was barely 5am. They had several hours until everyone arrived. And based on the surveillance footage he had received while on the plane, it wasn't likely any of them would arrive much before nine. In fact, his biggest fear was that one of them might not come to work at all today. But he had contingencies for that, as well.

"We're still on plan," he said. "We'll monitor the entrance in shifts: twenty minutes on, twenty minutes off. Study the dossiers and the building plans when you're off watch." He left the handheld device with the dossiers on the table, within easy reach.

Deuce nodded; she had already settled into the chair to take the first shift.

Pax took a seat at the dining room table and pulled his net-phone from its designated pocket. He pressed his finger to the hidden location on the back, and sent a brief message.

In position.

The response, and any last-minute instructions, would come soon enough. In the meantime, he picked up the top folder, labeled *Katherine Steele*, and began flipping through the pages.

THIRTY
EIGHT

Technological progress has merely provided us with
more efficient means for going backwards.

– Aldous Huxley

Jonas was sure it was a subtle form of mockery; there was no other conceivable explanation for the way Kat bounded out of bed before six o'clock each morning. Worse yet, she was up, showered, and off to her first class before Jonas had more than stirred. Her final affront was to brew coffee, but leave it in a large mug on the kitchen table, where it would soon be cold. Some days, the smell was enough to get Jonas moving–but not today. He lay sprawled across the bed for almost an hour after she left, enjoying the warmth of the sunrise through the bedroom window. It was a good feeling.

Eventually, he crawled out of bed, feeling better than he probably had a right to. The coffee was even tolerable, once it had been reheated. After his own shower and breakfast, he caught a bus to Hanssen Scientific, arriving just before nine. Not surprisingly, the others were already there. He poked his head into Kahli's office.

"Morning, boss," she said. "You just won me lunch–Brent was convinced you'd never make it by nine." She looked at the clock. "Cutting it pretty close, though."

"Nice. In that case, you can split the lunch with me."

"Deal. The usual?"

"Of course. And don't forget the haupia. In fact, make it a double. We're not paying, right?"

Kahli grinned. "He's waiting for you in the lab. Chomping at the bit, so to speak. Better get to it."

"Yes, ma'am," he responded.

Kahli was right. Jonas pushed through the door to the lab, where Brent was sitting impatiently at his station, like a grade school student anxiously awaiting the teacher's arrival.

"Great, three minutes before nine," Brent said. "That figures. Did she call you?"

Jonas ignored his comment. "Morning, Brent. Ready to bag us an asteroid? I have a good feeling about today." He winked, just for effect.

"Funny. Can we get started now? The sooner we put this together, the better."

"Yup. Let's do it."

Jonas retrieved his net-phone, where he had entered the details of his plan. He transferred the data to his computer screen.

"First, let's run through the big picture," he said. "GRI pulls our data every night. So we can't go back and change anything that's already been uploaded. But what we can do is change what they see between now and Sunday." He pointed to the numbers on the screen.

"I've looked at the last week of data, and even without the mother lode, what we've been finding has been slowly decreasing in value since we did the recalibration. I think we can argue that it would be reasonable to shift the telescopes again, back toward the original coordinates. Or more precisely, back to where the mother lode will be located on Sunday morning."

"Why would we retrace our steps? That makes no sense."

"True," Jonas said. "But we can pick a new starting point, and plot a course to where the mother lode will be on Sunday, that doesn't retrace our previous search."

"That may be difficult."

"I know. But keep in mind, they don't have today's data yet. Or tomorrow. Or Saturday. If we need to, we can drop some breadcrumbs along the path. Give ourselves a better story for the path we follow."

"You do realize," Brent countered, "that this whole thing crumbles if they ever go back and retrace our steps. Or even just try to correlate past data to current observations. Anything we change won't match. We'll be screwed."

"I know that," Jonas said. "But for better or worse, we've already changed one day–last Thursday, when I wiped the original record of the mother lode. Hopefully, that's all we'll have to do. Or maybe, after Sunday, we could go back and restore the original data. And if they ask, we can just say we missed the damn thing. Either way, I'm thinking they'll be too busy–and too happy–to raise any red flags.

"Besides," Jonas added, "we'll be heroes!"

"I hope you're right."

"I'm right. Trust me."

Jonas dragged over a chair, planting himself at his work station, next to Brent.

"Look, I know we have a lot to do. I'm here to help. And Kat will be here later this morning. She can do a lot of the verification work. Maybe she could also monitor the current readings, and help us decide whether we need to tweak them. Add some breadcrumbs."

"I think you should monitor the readings," Brent said.

"Well, I was going to help you recalibrate the telescope course," Jonas responded.

"No offense, Jonas," Brent said, "But I can handle the telescopes. You told me to recalibrate, and I'm doing the recalibration. Like I always do. And if anyone ever asks, that's what I'll say.

"*Why* you asked me to recalibrate," Brent added, "That's for you to explain."

"I see," Jonas replied. "You were following orders."

"Exactly."

Jonas considered Brent's words. He couldn't really blame him–Brent was a reluctant participant, at best. In fact, in a worst-case scenario, they might all be better off if everyone else claimed to be out of the loop. It reduced the chance of contradictory stories.

What Brent didn't know, of course, was that Jonas had every intention of taking the fall on his own, if it came to that.

I know how that story goes.

"I get it," Jonas said. "It's a good plan. Get moving on the calibrations, and I'll monitor the new data. Just let me know if there is anything else I can do to help. Like you always do," he added.

"Thanks," Brent said. He paused what he was doing, looking up from his work with a bemused smile on his face.

"You know what the best part is?"

"What?"

"They're paying us extra to do this."

Jonas laughed. Even Brent had a smile on his face.

"You could say that," Jonas said. "But I'm not calling it extra pay. I'm calling it back pay."

Before anyone could respond, they heard the chime for the front door. Jonas glanced at the clock; it was still before ten. Kat must have skipped her second class. Either she wasn't feeling as well as she claimed this morning, or she was eager to get started at the lab. Either way, Jonas was glad to have her.

But a minute later, when the door to the lab opened, it wasn't Kat that pushed her way through. It was Kahli.

"Jonas, there are a couple of people here who'd like to speak with you. A Monique Durand, and her associate, Bhima. She says it's important."

THIRTY
NINE

Be like water making its way through cracks...
adjust... and you shall find a way around it.

– Bruce Lee

Pax was still at the window, eyes fixed on the street below. The morning had progressed exactly as anticipated, with the accountant arriving first, at seven-thirty. The scientists had followed, the first at eight, and the last, Professor Hanssen, just before nine. He confirmed the identities of each as they arrived, both visually and electronically. There had been nothing unusual to report, on the street or in the office. It was the start of another, mundane work day.

And then–in an instant–it wasn't. When the taxi pulled to the curb, Pax stood from his chair, anticipating that Katherine Steele had arrived. Instead, a jolt ran up his spine. A completely unexpected woman emerged from the car, along with a younger man. The woman paused on the sidewalk, appearing to take her bearings. Pax zoomed in for a closer look.

He blinked, and looked again. It had been years, but there was no doubt. Monique Durand. She was hard to miss, and he didn't forget a face. Especially that one. His thoughts raced as he processed the information–the Hanssen plan had suddenly become very fluid.

She passed through the door and disappeared into Hanssen Scientific, her companion in tow.

"Problem?" Deuce asked. She must have seen the look on his face. "That's not the Steele woman," she added.

"No, it's not."

He rose from the chair, grabbing his handheld research device and moving to a seat at the other end of the table.

"Take over surveillance," he said. "Keep watching the street. And tell me what's going on in there. We need to know why that woman is here. And who the man is."

Deuce grabbed the headphones, turning the monitor so her peripheral vision could watch it and the street simultaneously. She spun the chair to maximize her viewing angle.

Pax powered on his device and retrieved the dossiers, beginning with Jonas Hanssen. Page by page, deliberately, he flipped through all of them. Nothing. He dug into his database, retrieving the records for Monique Durand. They were out of date, and no more helpful than the others. He did a quick search on the Net, and found nothing of note. As far as he could tell, there was absolutely no connection between Jonas Hanssen, Hanssen Scientific, and Monique Durand.

Which of course, was obviously wrong.

"What's going on in the office?" he asked. He got up and walked to the window, watching the street so she could focus on the scene inside.

"Not much," she said. "Introductions. I don't think they know each other. There seems to be some confusion."

"What are they talking about? The woman's name is Monique," he added. "I know her."

"Is she a problem?" Deuce looked at Pax, a hint of curiosity on her face.

"No, nothing like that," he said. "She's not one of us. I know her through an assignment, years ago."

"So when we go in there, will she recognize you?"

"No, I don't think so."

Pax glanced down at the monitor. All of them were still standing in the center of the lab.

"What are they saying?" he asked.

Deuce was quiet for a moment, listening to the ongoing discussion inside Hanssen Scientific.

"Strange," she said. "Something about visions. The Monique woman is claiming she saw Hanssen in a vision."

Pax stared at the screen. Of all the possible answers he imagined, that wasn't one of them.

"Who is the other guy?" he asked.

"Someone named Bhima Yu," Deuce said.

The name didn't register; Pax did a quick search, finding nothing of obvious relevance.

Pax sifted through his options. There was a chance that Monique and her colleague would leave before Katherine Steele arrived–which would help to accomplish the mission, but wouldn't help him understand why she was here. Once he went inside, of course, he could question the members of Hanssen's team.

And what if she didn't leave?

"What's the plan, boss?" Deuce still had one eye on the monitor as she cast a questioning look at Pax.

Pax stared at the door to Hanssen Scientific. In more than a decade of work for this employer, he had never placed a call during an operation–and he wasn't about to start now. Besides, he doubted his contact could provide any more information than Pax already had. She hadn't been the target of that operation, years ago; she had been ancillary to his assignment. Stay in the business long enough, he knew, and it was bound to happen–the past overlapping with the present. Even in a profession where the past was often scrubbed clean, like sandpaper on soft wood.

But the questions still lingered. Why her? And why here? It made no sense.

Maybe it's a sign, he thought to himself. It wasn't the first time he'd considered it–whether it was time to move on. But he pushed those ideas aside, for now; he could deal with them later. At the moment, he had a job to do.

Another minute had passed. Deuce continued to watch the monitor, listening to the conversation inside Hanssen Scientific. She was a professional–she would wait for his instructions, rather than ask again. He could tell from her body language, however, that she was getting impatient.

He made his decision.

"Keep watching the feed," Pax said. "I've got some adjustments to make. And so do you.

"We're going in," he added.

F O R T Y

Experience is one thing you can't get for nothing.

– Oscar Wilde

Monique shifted again in her seat, unable to keep still on the ride through Honolulu. She saw the sign as they approached– *Hanssen Scientific.* This was the place. The taxi had barely come to a stop before she was out on the sidewalk, waiting for Bhima to circle and join her.

"Ready?"

"Let's do it," Bhima responded. They pulled open the door and entered the building. A chime sounded as they walked through the door.

Inside, a modest reception room held a tall, upholstered armchair, a glass side table, and a pale green lamp. A hallway led away from them, with three doors along the left wall. Monique was debating her next step when the nearest door opened, and a woman with long, dark hair, freckles, and a warm smile emerged to greet them.

"Hello! Welcome to Hanssen Scientific. How can I help you?"

"Hi. My name is Monique Durand." She held out a hand.

"I'm Kahli," the woman said. "Nice to meet you."

"This is my friend, Bhima Yu," Monique said. "We were hoping to speak with Professor Jonas Hanssen. Is he here?"

"He is," Kahli said. "I can see if he has a few minutes. Is he expecting you?"

"I don't think so," Monique said.

"In that case, can I ask what this is about?" Kahli's warm smile persisted, but Monique could see that she took her gatekeeper duties seriously.

"It's a little complicated," Monique responded. "I don't mean to sound cryptic, but it would probably be best if we explain it to him directly. It's important," she added.

Kahli stood her ground for a moment. Finally, she shrugged her shoulders.

"Okay," she said. "Let me see if he's available."

Kahli turned and walked back down the hallway, disappearing through the last door on the left. Monique and Bhima waited patiently; she was back in less than a minute, though her smile was somewhat tempered.

"Sorry for the wait," Kahli said. "Jonas wanted me to ask if you're here about the grant. Usually we get a call in advance, so we can prepare."

Monique exchanged a brief look with Bhima, who seemed equally confused. They both shook their heads.

"No, it's a personal matter; I doubt it has anything to do with his work."

Kahli seemed visibly relieved; a warm smile had returned to her face.

"Oh, that's great," she said. "Come on in. We are a bit busy today, but he said he could spare a few minutes."

They followed Kahli down the hallway, passing through the last door and into what appeared to be the research center. There were a bank of terminals in the center of the room; a large telescope was propped against the far wall.

Two men were in the room. The older of the two, though probably no older than Monique, stepped away and crossed the room. His short blonde hair, blue eyes, and engaging smile were hard to miss. Not to mention the flip-flops. Without question, he was Jonas Hanssen.

"Good morning," Jonas said, reaching out a hand. "Welcome to Hanssen Scientific. I'm Professor Jonas Hanssen."

So he doesn't recognize me. Monique thought back to her first meeting with Bhima. *Looks like I'll need to start from the beginning.*

"Monique Durand," she said, shaking his hand. "And this is my friend, Bhima Yu. Thank you for seeing us."

"My pleasure," Jonas responded. "You've already met Kahli, I see. Over there is Brent. We've got a lot going on today, and Kahli had said you wanted to discuss something personal. So Brent is going to keep at it, if you don't mind."

"No, not at all," Monique said. "That might be best."

"I'm going back to work as well," Kahli said from behind Monique. Jonas nodded, and she disappeared through the door.

"So how can I help you?" Jonas asked.

Monique gathered her thoughts, now wishing she had the others by her side. They had become a team, and her anchor. But it was just her and Bhima. She took a deep breath; she would make it work.

"This may sound a little strange," she began. "So thank you in advance for hearing me out."

She paused for a moment, but Jonas remained silent. She pressed ahead.

"A few years ago, I started meditating. Not long after, I started having intense visions. Not random, but pictures of specific people, and specific places. The first was Bhima. I found him in Singapore, a few weeks ago. There have been three others since then. We just returned from Cairo, where we met a woman named Tabia. After we found her, the visions shifted to Honolulu– your office, and an image of you. So we tracked you down, and here we are."

Monique could see the skepticism on his face, much like she had first seen with Bhima. She continued, before he could interrupt.

"I know it sounds crazy," she said. "But believe it or not, some of the others had seen me in their own visions, so they were waiting for me to arrive. Those were the easy ones. But with Bhima, I was a total stranger. I'm sure he felt a lot like you do now."

Bhima nodded vigorously. He opened his mouth to speak, but Jonas spoke first, glancing back and forth between the two of them.

"So you convinced Bhima to join you. That's not so hard to believe. Visions or no visions."

Monique felt a flush on her cheeks. Now it was Bhima who jumped in to speak.

"It wasn't what she said that convinced me," he said. "It was what she showed me. For one, she had drawn pictures of me from her visions. And of the place I worked."

Monique reached into her purse, withdrawing the sketch of Jonas and handing it to him. Jonas studied it for a brief moment before responding.

"It's a nice drawing. Looks just like the photo of me we have on the Net," he said.

"It's from our vision," Monique said, trying to keep any hint of annoyance from her voice. "I know it's hard to believe, but there's a purpose to us being here. I can feel it."

"And what is that purpose?" Jonas asked.

"I won't lie to you," Monique said. "We're not sure. But in this last vision—the one that included you—we saw something new. Something different. Small lights, lots of them, streaking past us from behind. Like traveling through the stars, but backwards, as if you are somehow in reverse."

Jonas's eyes grew a bit wider; for the first time, he seemed to show the slightest modicum of interest.

"Stars?" he said. "Interesting."

"Does that relate to what you do here?" Monique asked.

"No, not exactly," he said. "Not here, anyway."

Monique wasn't sure she understood his last comment, but there was clearly some kind of connection. Something she could use.

"So it might mean something to you?"

But just as quickly, the glimmer in his eyes was gone. He folded his arms and leaned back against a desk.

"I'm sorry, Miss Durand. I appreciate your cause; I really do. I'm sure you're doing something very important. And under different circumstances, I'm sure you could have convinced me to join you—for coffee, at least. But like I said, it's a bit of a busy time for us. Maybe we could pick this up again after we finish the current phase of our work. Sometime next week?"

Monique looked at Bhima. He gave her the smallest of nods.

What the hell.

"Professor Hanssen, I do understand your skepticism. But could I ask you to indulge me for just one more minute? There's one more thing I'd like to show you."

Before Jonas could respond, the chime at the front door rang again. All of them turned, waiting for the laboratory door to open. A few moments later, it did just that.

It was Kat.

●●●●●

Saved by the bell, Jonas thought. He smiled as Kat came through the door; his mood was already improving. She hesitated for the smallest of instants when she saw his two guests, but hardly missed a beat, crossing the room and giving Jonas a quick kiss. She waved to Brent as well.

"Good morning," he said, looking at the clock. "You made great time."

"I heard there was a party," she said. "I didn't want to miss it."

She turned to face the two newcomers, stepping forward and extending a hand to Monique.

"I'm Katherine Steele. I don't think we've met."

"Monique Durand. Nice to meet you."

Jonas watched as the two of them shook hands. It was like a chance encounter between snow leopards–two rare, intelligent creatures, confident and composed. Jonas wondered what thoughts might be crossing their minds; neither of them gave him the slightest indication. He'd have to remember to ask Kat.

The moment was interrupted by Monique's companion, who stepped forward to offer his hand.

"Hi, I'm Bhima Yu. A friend of Monique. It's nice to meet you as well."

Kat turned back to Jonas. "I didn't realize you were expecting visitors. Are they–"

"No," Jonas said, interrupting. "Monique is here on a personal matter. Unrelated to Hanssen Scientific."

"Personal?" Kat said. "That sounds interesting."

"I suppose it is," Jonas replied. "I should probably let her explain, but the short version is that she's been having visions. And apparently, I'm in them." Jonas handed Kat the drawing, which he still had in his hand.

Kat studied the drawing for a moment.

"She's been dreaming about you? Can't say I blame her." Kat smiled, handing the picture back to Monique.

"It's not dreaming," Monique said. "That would be a subconscious thing. This is a conscious act, during my meditation. Do either of you meditate?"

"No," Kat said. "At least, I never have." She looked at Jonas. "You?"

"Nope."

"Like I told Professor Hanssen, I know it's a little hard to believe," Monique said. "I tried to ignore it for months. I even stopped meditating for a while, which was a big deal for me. But the visions persisted. Eventually I saw specific faces. First Bhima, then teenage twins, then a woman in Cairo. And now, Professor Hanssen."

"What does it mean?" Kat asked.

"We're not sure. Maybe that's why we're here. We thought you might be able to help us."

"I'm not sure how," Jonas said. "We're scientists. We deal in facts. You know—math, physics, that sort of thing. Visions are way out of our league."

"What about the other part of the vision?" Monique asked. "The stars flying through space. That seemed to pique your interest. Or at least, you called it interesting."

Kat flashed him a look; Jonas put his hands out, palms upward, and shrugged.

"Maybe. I really don't know. I suppose there could be a connection—obviously we're out searching through space. But most of our research is paid for through corporate funding, and it's a highly competitive market. So it's confidential. If I told you, I'd have to kill you."

He smiled as he delivered the punch line; it wasn't clear that either of the visitors appreciated the joke.

"We're not here to steal any state secrets," Monique said. "And I doubt this has anything to do with the details of your work. It hasn't with any of the others. Like I said, we're just looking for answers. Or even for ideas. So far, there has been a compelling connection with each of the others. Starting with Bhima."

"What was your connection with Bhima?" Kat asked.

"I was just about to show that to Professor Hanssen, when you arrived," Monique replied. "If you don't mind, it will just take a second."

Kat looked to Jonas; he shrugged in resignation. But before either of them could respond, the conversation was again interrupted by the sound of the front door chime.

"You have a lot of visitors for such a top-secret operation," Monique said, a wry smile on her face.

"Kat works here," Jonas replied, a bit defensively. "And no, we really don't. Today is some kind of record."

Jonas glanced at the time. It was too early for the lunch delivery, so he had no idea who else might be coming to visit. But Kahli would deal with it, he was sure. *At this rate, we're going to be here all night.*

From beyond the door, Jonas heard an odd sound–a muffled thump, followed by silence. Before he could react, the door swung open. Through it strode a bald, muscular man, dressed in an odd sort of form-fitting shirt and pants that Jonas had never seen before. His narrow eyes seemed to absorb the entire room as he entered. A shorter, stocky woman, similarly dressed, followed behind him. The man moved to his left, so the two were a few paces apart. The woman remained still, blocking the door.

Jonas stared at the new arrivals.

They're not here to discuss a personal matter.

In fact, they looked to be all business.

FORTY
ONE

*The tree of liberty must be refreshed from time to time
with the blood of patriots and tyrants.*

– Thomas Jefferson

The Chairman sat forward in his chair, his usual glass of cognac in hand. The hour was late, but he was far from tired. More importantly, the events on the monitor were about to get interesting. He smiled as he took a small sip; decades of work were about to move into a final phase, and he wasn't about to miss it. The feed wasn't perfect; in fact, it was average quality, at best. But on the plus side, Pax had been able to cut the feed that ran to GRI. So this would be a private showing.

The Fixers were finally inside Hanssen Scientific. The two unexpected arrivals were a complication–to say the least–but nothing Pax couldn't handle. Pax and his partner now stood astride the only exit; Pax was the first to speak.

"Good morning, Professor Hanssen," he said. "My name is Pax. I was sent to discuss some important matters with you. Would you mind asking Brent to join us?"

Pax gestured across the room, where Brent was already standing. Jonas waived him over, and he crossed the room to join the others. It was Jonas who spoke next.

"Pax, did you say? I don't think we've met. Are you with Rolland's organization?"

"No," Pax replied. "You might say I'm the hired help. They call me a *Fixer*. I solve problems."

Jonas was quick to respond, lifting his hand to point towards the door behind Pax.

"In that case, maybe you and I could discuss this in the conference room. Whatever the problem is, I'm probably the cause. I'm sure we can work something out."

"I'm afraid we're past that point," Pax said.

Monique stepped forward to speak.

"Excuse me, but my friend and I are here on a personal matter. I assume this doesn't involve us?"

"It does now. You'll have to stay."

"Hold on," Jonas said. "The only person that needs to be involved is me. These were my decisions. No one else was involved."

"Involved in what?" Monique asked.

"It's just business," Jonas said.

Pax shook his head.

"A week ago," Pax said, "Professor Hanssen discovered a very valuable asteroid. Unfortunately, the Professor chose to hide this fact from the company funding his research–so he could extort some extra money from them."

Monique turned to face Jonas.

"Is that true?"

"Extort is a strong word," Jonas said. "It's a lot more complicated than that. But yes, we've found a new asteroid. One that will benefit all of humanity."

Pax shook his head again. "After it benefits you, of course."

Jonas pointed his finger at Pax.

"Look, we've worked our asses off. Our pay is a miniscule fraction of the profits. This is about fairness."

"Fair or not," Monique said, "It sounds like you have some issues. Maybe Bhima and I can come back later, after you've sorted this out."

"Sorry," Pax said. "You and your friend are involved now. You'll have to stay."

There was a moment of uncomfortable silence. Monique and Pax stared at each other, as if sizing each other up. Finally, Monique spoke.

"I don't think so. We're leaving. Let's go, Bhima."

Pax put his hand up. "It seems I'm not being clear enough. Perhaps this will help." His gaze shifted to his companion.

Words were replaced by chaos. First, the sound of a *thwack*. A low grunt escaped Brent's lips, and his left hand jerked to his side. He took a small step forward, his gaze locked on Jonas, before collapsing to the floor. At the same instant, a sharp cry arose from Monique.

"Bhima, the woman!"

As Pax and his companion turned toward Monique, they were torn from the ground and hurled backward, as if on the wrong end of a puppeteer's strings. They each slammed into the wall behind them, though Pax managed to absorb most of the blow along the length of his muscular frame. His colleague was not so fortunate–her head was first to hit the wall, with a sickening crack. She slumped to one side, seemingly unconscious. Or worse.

Another cry escaped Monique's lips.

"Bhima, help!"

Pax was still moving–using one arm to force his way down the wall–and he was making progress. There was a dull thud as his companion fell to the floor, motionless. An instant later, Pax's arms and legs were splayed flat, pinned motionless to the wall, like a spider on the windshield of a locomotive. He was no longer moving, though his bulging neck muscles betrayed his intent to do so.

The Chairman blinked, staring at the screen. The tumult had lasted just a few seconds. One of his people was down, and his best Fixer appeared neutralized. He watched as Jonas rushed to Brent, rolling him face up and putting a hand on his neck. Kat was close behind him. Brent didn't stir; Jonas turned back to look at Monique.

"What the hell?" he choked out, eyes wide. He turned to Pax, his voice reaching a crescendo. "What the hell!"

Pax returned his glare. "It appears you should be asking her that question."

Jonas turned to Monique, a volatile mix of anger, bewilderment, and fear on his face.

"This is what I wanted to show you," Monique said. "Though obviously, not *how* I wanted to show you. This power is my connection with Bhima– we both have it. I'm sorry we were late." She looked at Brent, still motionless on the floor, before turning back to Pax.

"Tell us what you've done," she said. Her voice had a calm tone of command, at odds with the chaos of just moments before.

The two of them glared at each other, unmoving, across the wordless gulf between them. Pax shifted his eyes to glance at his colleague before breaking the silence.

"He's been poisoned," he said, in a matter-of-fact tone.

"How?" Monique asked. "I don't see any weapons."

Pax glanced again at his colleague.

"Her name is Deuce," he said. "She's somewhat unique—even for my line of work. She's had some amputations done. In this case, both of her arms below the elbow."

"She has guns for arms?" Jonas sounded incredulous.

"Among other things," Pax responded. "But in this case, poison darts. Plus a powerful tranquilizer."

"Is he dead?" Jonas had found the dart, sunk deep into Brent's side, just below his right arm.

"Not yet," Pax said. "But they will be soon, if I don't give them the antidote."

Jonas stood, a stunned look on his face. Without a word, he sprinted to the laboratory door, disappearing from sight.

There was a camera in the hallway, but the Chairman didn't make the effort to switch the feed. He knew what was coming. A low, guttural scream pierced the air. It had barely finished before Jonas burst back through the door, Kahli in his arms. He put her down gently before launching himself at Pax; the look on his face left little doubt as to his intent.

"Stop!" Monique stepped in front of him, holding up her hand. The sharp crack of her voice, combined with the unspoken implication, brought Jonas to an abrupt halt. He managed only the smallest of sounds.

"Kahli," he said, barely above a whisper.

"We need answers," Monique said. "Killing him won't help us."

Jonas stared at Monique. It was a very different look than one he had given her just a few minutes before.

"You're as cold as he is," was all he finally said.

"Not true," Bhima replied. He spoke to Jonas, but his gaze was still fixed on Pax.

"Let's get some answers first," Monique said again. "Then we'll see how cold I am."

Monique turned back to Pax. He was still pinned to the wall, an impassive look on his face. But it was far from a look of defeat.

"Explain yourself," Monique said, in her own matter-of-fact tone. Her words and tone seemed to resonate; Pax answered almost immediately.

"I was sent here to deliver a message. This was part of the message."

"I offered to resolve this between the two of us!" Jonas again pointed at Pax, eyes ablaze.

"It wasn't up for discussion," Pax said.

"How long do they have?" Monique asked.

"Ten minutes. Twelve at most."

"What's the antidote?"

"It's not that simple. They've been poisoned, but it's a sophisticated concoction. Without the antidote I have, they'll die. And the autopsy will show it was a drug overdose."

Monique was quick to make the connection. "To shift suspicion from your employer."

Pax's eyes shifted briefly to Jonas.

"All three of them have a history of drug use," he said. "Combined with what will be found at their homes, it's an open and shut case. A major scientific discovery, followed by an excessive celebration. An unfortunate tragedy."

"Give us the antidote," Jonas growled. The look on his face hadn't changed since he had barged through the door.

"I don't think so," Pax said. "The antidote needs to be precisely administered. You'd kill them. Not to mention, we need to discuss a deal."

"You're in no position to bargain," Jonas said.

"I disagree. I'm still holding most of the chips. It's ninety-nine percent certain you won't harm me—not with your friend's lives at stake. Both of you have already made that clear. And, I have information you need. Other than this impressive parlor trick, you've got next to nothing."

"This is no parlor trick," Bhima said.

"What information?" Monique asked.

"Why I'm here," Pax said. "And what I can offer you. All of you."

"What do you mean, all of us?" Monique asked. "We weren't even supposed to be here. I have nothing to do with this asteroid. Or Hanssen Scientific. Why did you even demand that we stay?"

"I needed to understand why you were here," Pax said.

"Well, I guess you have your answer to that question," Monique said, the slightest of smirks on her face.

"Perhaps," Pax said. "Clearly, things have changed."

"So now what?" Monique asked.

"Now, given the circumstances," Pax said, "I have an offer for you as well."

"Given the circumstances, I doubt it will be persuasive."

"You might be surprised."

"Try me," Monique said.

"It concerns your mother."

Pax's ploy nearly worked—Monique took a step back, clearly shaken. For an instant, Pax was free. His arms swung forward, a savage intent written on his face.

"Monique!"

It was Bhima, and it was just enough. Pax was flung back against the wall. As before, he somehow managed to twist his body, avoiding a direct blow to the head. But a heavy thud attested to the severity of the impact. Still, he was fully alert, though his limbs were again locked in place, unmoving.

Monique approached Pax, stopping directly in front of him, with her own look of savage intent.

"Explain. Now."

"As I said," he replied, "We need to discuss a deal. My freedom for your freedom. And for information."

"You're in no position to broker for our freedom," Monique said. "We already have it."

"Don't be so sure," Pax said. "My employer would beg to differ. You won't ever be safe, once you leave this room."

"Your employer is screwed, once we leave this room." It was Katherine Steele who spoke now, and she looked every bit as serious as Monique.

"Maybe," Pax said. "So let's talk about a solution that could benefit all of us."

"Administer the antidote. Then we can talk."

Pax seemed to consider her words; the room was silent.

"I propose a temporary truce," he said. "I'm confident I can still accomplish my mission without harming anyone in the room. Give me the same assurance, and I'll save your friends."

"And then what?" Jonas asked. "We all walk out the door like nothing's happened? I doubt it."

"You can all walk out the door, yes," Pax said. "Though you may have to carry those two." He looked in the direction of Brent and Kahli. "Even after I revive them, they won't be in any condition to walk."

"Tell me what *accomplish your mission* means," Monique asked.

"Hanssen Scientific gets rewarded for discovering the asteroid. Handsomely rewarded. We'll announce the news together, tomorrow. You'll confirm the discovery as having been made today. We'll make sure the data supports this assertion. Then, after the commotion subsides, the group of you retires, away from the spotlight. We'll help with that as well."

"Wait a second," Jonas said. "Something doesn't add up. How do you even know about the asteroid? We didn't tell anyone. Something else is going on here. Something we don't know about."

The group was looking at Pax; a dispassionate stare was all they received in return.

"We need more," Monique added. "You just put poison darts into his friends. How can you possibly expect him to trust you?"

"Don't be so naïve. There are trillions of dollars at stake; of course there is more to it. More than any of us will ever know.

"Take the deal. Your options are limited. And we need you to legitimize the discovery. It makes sense."

"Why the hell didn't you just offer that deal when you walked in here?" Jonas asked.

"We calculated a less than twenty percent probability that you'd accept," he said. "You're a stubborn man, Professor Hanssen. Some might say, a bit obsessive. You like to make the decisions, and you don't like being told what to do. More incentive was required."

Katherine grabbed Jonas by the arm.

"Jonas, we need to make a decision. If he's telling the truth, we have about five minutes to revive Kahli and Brent. Less than five minutes for Kahli. We need to do that *now*."

"What about the two of us?" Monique asked, glancing for a brief moment to Bhima, a few feet away.

"Your situation, Miss Durand, is a bit more delicate," he said. "What I can offer is this. You and your associate can go. Assuming you stay out of this matter, I will give you my word not to harm you. Unfortunately, I can't make that same promise for my employer. But, you seem more than capable to deal with that yourself."

"That's not much of a deal. I can walk out of here now, with or without your help. We need more."

"That's why I'm offering you the information about your mother."

"How the hell could he know anything about your mother?" Jonas said, throwing his hands in the air. "He's bluffing. It's a lucky guess."

There was another drawn out silence; Monique and Pax stared at one another, as if searching for truth behind the other's façade.

"First things first," Monique said. "Save these two, and then we'll work out the details. I'm going to let you down. You are going to do what's necessary to revive them. Keep your back to us at all times. If you so much as make the slightest of turning motions, we'll tear you apart at the seams."

"The rest of you," she added, "should get behind those computer consoles. Just in case."

"I'm not going anywhere," Jonas said, though he did take a step forward and to the left, effectively placing himself between Pax and Katherine.

"Me neither," Bhima said.

"Allow me to check on Deuce?" Pax asked.

"Those two first," Monique replied. "But yes, of course. Same rules apply."

Pax slid down the wall, until he was standing on the floor. With an effort, he turned his back on the group; it was clear he was not entirely free of Monique's unseen power. Arms spread wide, he walked slowly backward, toward Kahli and Brent. He arrived at Kahli's side first, kneeling beside her and removing the dart. Deliberately, he held out his right arm. There was the slightest of whirring sounds, and small door opened at the top of his forearm. He removed what looked like a small syringe with his left hand, and began to work on Kahli as he spoke.

"For the record, Miss Durand, it's no small feat to pin down this arm. If you ever need a job, you should call me."

Monique didn't respond. She seemed entirely focused on the effort to revive both Hanssen employees.

Pax finished with Kahli, and slid a few steps over to Brent. When finished, he replaced the syringe and stood, crossing to Deuce—arms still wide, and always with his back directly to Monique.

He kneeled over Deuce, checking for a pulse.

"Are they okay?" Katherine asked as Pax stood, arms wide, still facing away from the group.

"Those two will be fine," Pax said. "Give them a minute to recover. But as for Deuce—no."

"I'm sorry," Monique said. "That wasn't our intent."

"Perils of the business," Pax said. "She knew the risks."

"So now what?" Monique said. "We just walk out?"

"Not until we know my friends are okay," Jonas growled. His anger remained fresh; every word from Pax seemed to reopen the wound.

At that moment, Kahli stirred, a soft moan escaping her lips. She rolled onto her side. A few seconds later, Brent did the same.

"They'll be fine," Pax said. "Gather them up and head to the door. As I said, don't underestimate my employer. Reinforcements could be here any minute."

Without warning, Jonas surged forward. In a few steps he was directly behind Pax, who remained with his back to the group. Before anyone could react, Jonas twisted his torso and launched a right hook, his fist on a collision course for Pax's head.

It never came close. In a single motion, Pax ducked, spun, and landed a vicious blow to Jonas's side with his left fist, shoving him aside in the process. He continued the motion until he was again standing at attention, arms wide, back to Monique. The blow knocked the wind from Jonas, who crumpled to the floor; it may have broken a few ribs.

"Jonas!" Katherine leaped to his side, holding his head. Jonas winced, struggling to breathe.

"That was my left," Pax said. "A blow with my right might have killed him."

"There was no need to hurt him!" Katherine yelled, a mix of fear and fury on her face.

"Self defense," Pax said. "I honored our agreement."

"As did I," Monique said. "But you can hardly blame him."

"He's right, Monique," Bhima said. "We need to get out of here. Who knows what's coming next."

"Then we have an agreement," Pax said. "The Professor will be contacted. Until then, you'll be monitored. Lay low. That shouldn't be a problem for him."

"Screw you," Jonas said through clenched teeth. As if to prove the point, he climbed back to his feet. He walked the few steps to Kahli, who was now sitting. He tried to help her to her feet, but it was too much; he clutched his side in pain, slumping down onto the floor next to her.

"Bhima, help Brent," Monique said. "Katherine, can you help Kahli?" She turned to Jonas. "I assume you can make it out on your own."

"I'll be fine," Jonas said. He stood up again, though just barely. His breathing was labored, and shallow.

They moved toward the door, except for Monique, whose gaze remained fixed on Pax.

"Tell me about my mother," she said.

"Not quite," Pax said. "As soon as I do, I'm of no use to you. And I've seen what you do with those you can't use."

Another brief silence.

"We'll have to trust each other," Pax said. "Join your group. I'll go across the room. Then I'll tell you."

"No," Monique said. "Stay where you are, back turned. You'll tell me when I say so. That's the deal."

Pax took a moment to respond. "Fine," he said.

She moved to the door with the rest of the group—Pax remained still, keeping his back to Monique.

"We're ready to go," Monique said. "Tell me what you know about my mother."

Pax paused, as if recalling the words.

"The skiing accident," he said. "It was no accident."

As he finished, Pax launched himself across the room—impossibly fast, and low to the ground, almost parallel to the floor. He seemed to vanish, like a ghost in fog, with only the smallest of scraping sounds betraying his very existence.

"Monique! Move, now!" It was Bhima again, grabbing her by the shoulder as he continued to support Brent. Monique pushed through the door, followed by the others. There was no sign of Pax. The door swung shut behind them.

●●●●●

The Chairman stood, switching the video feed to the hallway. He watched as the group made their way toward the exit. Monique was in the lead. Jonas was beside her, hunched over, arm to his side and in obvious pain. Katherine followed just behind, Kahli's arm draped over her shoulders, all but carrying the smaller woman as they shuffled down the hall. Bhima was at the rear, helping Brent, who was no more coherent than Kahli.

It was decision time. In rapid fashion, the Chairman weighed his options—the pros, the cons, the risks, and the potential rewards. Decision making was his forte, but there was usually more time. Especially in a situation as critical as this. But Monique had already reached the door.

His time was up. The scale tilted—ever so slightly—and he knew what he needed to do.

He pushed a button.

At first, nothing happened. Given the distance, the electronic signal should have arrived almost instantaneously. Instead, it took almost a full second. To the Chairman, it felt like an hour. In that time, Monique and Jonas passed through the door; Kahli and Katherine were close behind.

The explosion shattered the glass door and adjacent windows. Glass shards and debris flew inward, toward the Chairman's video feed. The scene shook; a cloud of angry red flame and smoke filled his entire view. Then, the signal was lost. A black, empty screen was all that remained.

The Chairman returned to his seat, retrieving his glass of cognac. The wheels were again in motion. He sifted through his decision, and the most immediate of implications. It wasn't the first time he had pushed a button— literally or metaphorically. And he knew it wouldn't be the last. He did what had to be done; the end game was in sight.

He picked up his net-phone. It was time to make some calls.

F O R T Y
T W O

The meek shall inherit the earth. But the poor are screwed.

– Anonymous

Professor Kaito Matsui put his fork down; it was the moment of the big reveal. As much as he enjoyed his daily lunch routine of homemade ramen noodles, the real reason he came home was to catch the latest episode of his favorite reality show–*Marriage Impossible*. It was a harmless addiction–one he shared with millions of others.

The number flashed on the screen: eleven percent. *Eleven percent!* It was the lowest score Kaito had seen in weeks. The two contestants–a young couple from Texas–wore looks of shock, disappointment, and frustration. The large red *11* flashed on the monitor above the couple's head, as if in silent rebuke. The video feed switched back to the show's host–her effervescent smile fixed, as always, across her ageless face.

"It's no match made in heaven," she told her audience. "In fact–I'm not sure this one's even made on Earth!"

Kaito smiled and shook his head; the signature tag line never seemed to get old. For better or worse, the love-struck couple's relationship was doomed; no marriage with a score that low had ever survived, as far as he could recall. Perfect unions, it seemed, were becoming as rare as marriage itself.

Kaito returned to his lunch. He was a simple man, leading a simple life—a fact belied by his half-century of work in leading-edge quantum physics. Though nearly eighty, he was still in his intellectual prime; or at least, no one had yet challenged him for his University of Hawaii Physics Department chair. And the dichotomy of his love for both physics and reality shows barely tugged at his conscience; if anything, they flowed together, like yin and yang, into a coherent and meaningful whole.

The daily lunch routine also allowed him to shut down, and relax in the uncomplicated familiarity of his small home. There were no Fourier transforms here, no PhD candidates vying for his attention. It was just him and his bowl of noodles, as warm and comforting as the Honolulu sun. He liked it that way.

So Kaito was caught off-guard when his video feed abruptly shifted to a local news feed; his gaze jerked up at the sound of the announcer. Like everyone else, he had configured his feed to automatically switch when it found higher-priority, live content. But he had pre-programmed only a handful of those rules—and there was almost nothing he had prioritized over *Marriage Impossible*.

A raging inferno filled the screen; the entire video feed was an angry crimson hue. It took a few seconds to process what he saw; it was a fire in downtown Honolulu. But not at the University—he could see that immediately. *So why am I getting the feed?*

And then he saw it—the familiar sign on the exterior of the building, now blackened and nearly illegible. Kaito knew what it said: *Hanssen Scientific*. A cold sweat formed on his skin as he increased the volume of the feed. A deep, colorless male voice was narrating the events as they unfolded.

"...officials on the scene are trying to contain the blaze to the original site of the explosion. Only fire-bots are inside the building; we're told it's still far too dangerous for humans. And no word yet on a cause."

There was a pause in the narration; Kaito's gaze remained locked on the screen. Even if he wanted to move, he wasn't sure he'd be able. His legs suddenly felt as limp as the noodles in his lunch bowl. A moment later, the announcer continued.

"Again, less than an hour ago, a powerful explosion in a downtown office building, followed by a fire that still rages as we speak. We're told the building contains the offices of Hanssen Scientific, a small research firm in the Manoa district. Hanssen does research related to asteroid search-and-discovery. Employment records indicate that there are three individuals employed by the firm, including its owner and founder, Doctor Jonas Hanssen. Hanssen is well-known in the field of asteroid research, with several significant discoveries to his credit."

Kaito took a deep breath, glancing down at his net-phone. He and Jonas had just spoken the other day–less than two days ago, in fact. Jonas had called to share his dark matter discovery; it was the most exhilarating news he had heard in years. Kaito could hardly believe it, and had said as much on the call.

"Jonas, slow down," he had said. "Tell me again precisely what you've found."

"Something is there," Jonas had replied. "We've reconfirmed with multiple readings. But only if you look inside very short time horizons. Less than an attosecond. Maybe that's why we've never seen anything before. My hypothesis is that the particles are intertwined with radiation, and travel through other dimensions, so they are only in our physical universe for the briefest of instants."

"Interesting," Kaito had said. "Though not an entirely new line of thinking. It's the relationship to radiation that intrigues me the most."

"Agreed," Jonas said. "And that's why I called you. We're wondering how we might be able to replicate these results here on Earth. Can we validate my hypothesis locally–in a way that would give us incontrovertible proof?"

Alarm bells had gone off in Kaito's mind–the kind he often heard when speaking to Jonas.

"Hold on," Kaito had said. "Who is this *we* you keep referring to? Have you brought the rest of Hanssen Scientific into this? I'm not sure that's a good idea, Jonas. You have a grant to pursue. Bills to pay, remember? I told you the lab was *yours*, in *your* spare time. Not as a second home for the entire Hanssen Scientific team."

"No, no, no. It's not them. But speaking of grants, the team may soon have some good news on that front as well. No, I'm talking about my new research assistant–Katherine Steele. You sent her over a few weeks ago, remember? To be honest with you, we kind of hit it off. She's amazing."

Kaito suppressed a small grin as he recalled the words. They had come in a jumbled rush, like a child with an overload of good news to share. Jonas had insisted that they get together next week–after the weekend, he recalled Jonas saying. It seemed a bit strange for someone as impatient as Jonas to want to wait that long, but Kaito had acquiesced. And now, as he watched Hanssen Scientific burn, he wondered if that had been a fateful decision.

He was pulled from his reverie as the announcer continued.

"We are now being told that the fire-bots have recovered at least three and possibly four bodies from the building. None have been positively identified, but we can only assume they are those of Professor Jonas Hanssen and his staff at Hanssen Scientific. Officials at the scene tell us that identification of the bodies will be difficult, at best."

Kaito leaned forward in his chair, head in his hands. *How could there have been an explosion at the lab?* There was nothing there but computer equipment. And some office furniture. It made no sense. Kaito's mind swirled around the possibilities. Had he inadvertently sent the young grad student–Katherine Steele–to her death? He could barely stomach the thought.

Kaito began to sort through his decade-long history with his friend. Jonas was a bit eccentric; Kaito knew that. Weren't most brilliant scientists? But he was also a good friend. Jonas was extremely dedicated, and loyal– almost to a fault. Kaito couldn't imagine that Jonas would keep anything combustible in the lab; there wasn't any reason for it.

Kaito raised his head; an idea suddenly struck him. He tapped his earpiece.

"Call Jonas," he said.

The phone rang. He held his breath, waiting for his friend to pick up and put an end to the cruel nightmare.

There was no answer. He tried a second, then a third time. Still no answer. He couldn't bring himself to leave a message.

Kaito leaned back in his chair, tilting his head back to stare at the ceiling. He closed his eyes and took a slow, deep breath.

Damnit, Jonas. What the hell am I supposed to do?

Jonas had no family–just a small circle of friends. And most of them were likely in that building. Kaito briefly considered going to Hanssen Scientific, but quickly put those thoughts aside. There was nothing he could do there, he was sure. Besides, investigators would soon be digging into Jonas's background, and the ownership of Hanssen Scientific.

Kaito knew they'd be calling him, soon enough.

FORTY
THREE

Who controls the past controls the future.
Who controls the present controls the past.

– George Orwell

Rudy knew the time before he even glanced at his net lens display–it was ten minutes past the last time he had looked. Most days at the office rushed by in a blur–but not today. All day long, he had deftly handled–or handed off–dozens of meetings and messages from GRI executives, while waiting for word from Honolulu. The morning was drawing to a close out in Hawaii; they should have received word from Hanssen Scientific by now. He was beginning to worry, despite himself.

In the big picture, though, things were actually looking up. Two days at the Consortium's island retreat had done wonders for his mental health–and for the health of his marriage. He and Victoria were back on speaking terms–and some non-speaking terms, he recalled with a grin. There was still some tension lurking below the surface, though. She knew he was hiding something–he could see it in her eyes. And although he could evade with the best of them, he was walking a fine line when he played that game with Victoria. She was no fool; her own father had given her a decades-long education in spotting half-truths and hidden meanings. She was the daughter of a global banking executive, who spoke the truth just a touch more often than the local weatherman. Hiding the Consortium from Victoria would be an on-going struggle.

As if on cue, the long-awaited tone chimed in his earpiece. Rudy retrieved his net-phone from the desk, and accessed its hidden mode. There was a message waiting; he read the text as he stood up from his desk.

Boardroom. Ten minutes.

Rudy wasn't surprised; they had several topics to discuss, and it was probably best to do it from the facility tucked away under GRI headquarters. He sent a quick note to Grace, letting her know that he'd be out for about an hour. She was more than capable to hold down the fort; in fact, Rudy secretly enjoyed the idea that his multi-trillion dollar enterprise was in the hands of a computer.

●●●●●

Rudy made the now-familiar trip to the underground facility. As he stepped through the door, he was surprised to see that no one was there–not even Liu Xhang, the Consortium's Technology Director. The endless rows of processing power stood sentinel, alone, in the room to Rudy's left.

A flicker of light caught his attention, and he turned his gaze back to the main room. Now there was someone with him–a thin, older man in a pair of loose trousers and a multi-colored, striped shirt. He had a sweater draped over his back like a cape, its arms hanging loosely down his chest. A small pair of old-fashion spectacles completed the look. Despite the short distance, Rudy couldn't identify the man–it wasn't someone he had met before.

As Rudy crossed the room, the man rose from his chair to greet him.

"Good evening, Rudy," the man said. Now Rudy recognized his colleague–the metallic tone of his voice was a dead giveaway.

"How are you, Mister Chairman," he said. "Sorry I didn't recognize you. You've aged a bit since we last met."

"How do I look?" the Chairman asked.

"Great for your age, I'd say," Rudy replied. "But you could use some fashion advice."

The Chairman's avatar managed a thin smile. "I'll have the developers get right on that."

Rudy took a seat across the table from the Chairman, who had returned to his own seat.

"Will Arthur be joining us?" Rudy asked.

"No, it's just you and me," the Chairman replied. "I said we'd be working together directly, and I'm a man of my word."

Rudy nodded; that was good news.

"How did we do at Hanssen Scientific?" he asked. "Are we all set?"

"It's probably best to show you," the Chairman said, pointing to the monitor on Rudy's right. "I'll play the video for you. But just to set your expectations, I'll tell you now that things didn't go precisely as planned. I think the end result is acceptable, though we still have some work to do. There are a few loose ends."

Rudy digested the Chairman's words, trying to imagine what *acceptable* and *loose ends* might mean to a man like him.

I'm about to find out.

The screen came to life; Rudy assumed the feed was coming from Hanssen Scientific. He recognized Professor Hanssen in the center of a small group. There were five people in the room; at the moment, a tall, thin woman with shoulder-length, dark hair was talking.

"Monique Durand," the woman was saying. "And this is my friend, Bhima Yu. Thank you for seeing us."

Rudy watched, mesmerized, as the scene played out–his confusion mounting with each passing moment. Meditation? Visions? Rudy glanced at the Chairman, who seemed unfazed by the discussion. *What is this? And who is this Monique woman?* A small knot was beginning to form in Rudy's stomach.

More people arrived–Hanssen's girlfriend, followed by Pax and his colleague. But this time, the *Fixers* did anything but. As the events unfolded, Rudy glanced to the Chairman–more than once. But his avatar remained seated, motionless. Even the massive explosion, which brought Rudy out of his chair, seemed to have no impact on the Chairman.

The explosion cut the video feed; only a dark screen remained.

Rudy was standing, his nerves like electrical lines dipped in water. The weight of the GRI empire–the entire building above him–seemed to press down on him. Yet the Chairman remained motionless, as composed and silent as a sniper.

"What was that?" Rudy choked out, pointing to the screen. "What the hell happened?"

"As I said, Rudy, things didn't go precisely as planned."

"No shit," was all Rudy could manage.

"I know it's difficult to watch with a dispassionate eye. So I'll give you a moment to collect your thoughts." The Chairman paused; it was several seconds before he continued.

"I take full responsibility for what you just saw. I made that decision. Professor Hanssen was a loose end. As were the others. Unfortunately, the woman was a complication we couldn't have predicted."

"What the hell did she do?" Rudy asked. "I've never seen anything like it. Doesn't look like Pax had, either."

"I don't know," the Chairman said. "But I'm looking into it. Impressive, to say the least. But it's probably moot at this point."

"They're all dead?" Rudy asked.

"At the moment, we're not entirely sure. I've spoken to Pax; he's fine. He cleaned up at Hanssen Scientific, so there is no sign of our involvement. And we have a contingency plan that's already getting underway. Pax said there were at least four dead, including his partner. But he hasn't been able to account for everyone. He's trying to do that now."

"Professor Hanssen?" Rudy asked.

"We're not sure."

"So killing them was our best option? I don't see how we keep our fingerprints off of this. The media is going to eat us alive. The trail leads right back to GRI."

"Not likely. Like I said, we have a contingency plan. And you're a critical piece of that plan."

The Chairman's eyes never wavered; he stared at Rudy as if his gaze alone could impose his will.

"In a few hours," the Chairman continued, "You'll hold a press conference, expressing your shock and offering your prayers for the victims and their families. Then, you'll announce Professor Hanssen's discovery of the asteroid. You'll provide the data as proof. And finally, you'll express your outrage at this apparent botched attempt—most likely by one of GRI's competitors—to steal his incredible find. And you'll pledge GRI's unconditional support in the investigation to expose those behind the murder of our beloved colleague, Doctor Hanssen, and his staff."

Rudy processed the words; he could almost hear the wheels turning–
the gears in motion–as the Chairman spoke.

"Where did we get the data? Technically, we don't even have it yet."

"Yes we do," the Chairman said. "Hanssen gave it to us yesterday. Why
else would we have launched the probes? There certainly isn't any data left at
Hanssen Scientific to dispute that fact. And the files at GRI will confirm it."

Of course. Rudy searched for holes in the story, but found none–
assuming Hanssen and the others were indeed dead. And that Pax had
taken care of the evidence in Honolulu. It was a clean solution–and in his
gut, Rudy knew he could pull it off. In fact, the media frenzy was going to
be a thorn in the side of his competitors for months. But the images from
the video still battered at Rudy's conscience.

"That might work," Rudy said. "But some good people–some innocent
people–are dead. How does the end justify the means? This is no rigged
lottery ticket."

"You're right, Rudy. I won't lie to you–our hands are dirty on this one.
It's not the first time for me, and it won't be the last time for you. Welcome
to the big boy's table. It's no small thing to preserve the status quo–and
those that do learn to live with some collateral damage."

"How does this preserve the status quo?" Rudy asked. "Seems like we're
just preserving GRI profits. Not that I'm necessarily complaining, mind
you." A small frown had appeared on the Chairman's face.

"Ask the ten billion people on this planet. We've nearly exhausted
the Earth's natural resources. You know that. Not to mention making a
mess of the planet in so many other ways. The asteroid buys us time; in
this case, a lot of time. This asteroid is central to our long-term plans. To
our survival, in fact."

"The asteroid would have been mined, regardless. Even if we didn't
get a probe there in time."

"Are you sure about that?" The Chairman's avatar stood up, and began
to pace the room.

"It would have gone to auction," he said. "At best, that costs us a year.
For this one, probably longer. And then, maybe it's traveled beyond our
grasp. Or maybe it's too late. You've seen some of Gunnar's work, Rudy.
And I can tell you, we don't have years. I can promise you that. So yes,
I'll sleep tonight–with some blood on my hands–knowing what we've
accomplished for humanity as a whole."

"You act like the world is on the brink of anarchy," Rudy said.

"I've seen Gunnar's full model. You haven't."

The Chairman stopped pacing, and turned to face Rudy. He leaned over, hands on the table between them.

"And speaking of Gunnar. That brings us to our other topic. Iran. And the wealth ratio. You still have a press conference to deal with, but the worst of this asteroid business is behind us. It wasn't ideal, I'll grant you, but it's done. So now we need to move to the next order of business. I'm here, dealing with you directly. And I'm asking that we move forward on the Iran situation. Immediately."

Even as a holographic avatar, the Chairman was a force–a rigid, physical presence. He could feel the weight of the words, the urgency of the Chairman's request. *The Hanssen thing is a debacle, and now I'm supposed to green-light an earthquake? Jesus.* Again, the moment pressed in on him, like rush hour on a crowded subway platform. He couldn't delay it any longer.

Rudy took a deep breath. He knew he had made his decision two days ago, as he sat on the beach with the three people he loved most in the world. If anything, he realized, the mess in Honolulu had only served to strengthen his resolve. The Chairman had handled the crisis with a deft touch–a calm efficiency that Rudy had to respect–and perhaps even admire.

The bottom line, he knew, was that he had his own status quo to maintain.

"I'm in," Rudy said. "In fact, the GRI resources are already in position. I gave the orders yesterday."

"Excellent," the Chairman replied. The look on his face said it was the answer he expected.

"I'll send you some notes for the press conference," the Chairman added. "After that's finished, we can focus our full attention on the asteroid. And any loose ends at Hanssen Scientific."

"Sounds good," Rudy said.

The call ended; Rudy was alone. Strangely, though, the weight of his decision had suddenly lifted. He felt good–like he did when he made big decisions from his office upstairs. This one really wasn't much different.

He glanced again at the time as he headed for the door. With any luck, he might even squeeze in a trip home before the press conference. Grace could work on the details as Bond drove.

There was one thing about Honolulu that still nagged at him, though–the moment when Pax and his colleague had been launched through the air, and rendered helpless. *How had she done that? And who was she?* The woman had taken control of a dangerous situation–and a very dangerous man. If she had managed to survive, she could be a serious problem. At a minimum, he should do a bit of digging. She was the kind of loose end, he knew, that they could ill afford.

FORTY
FOUR

*Anger is an acid that can do more harm to the vessel in which
it is stored than to anything on which it is poured.*

– Mark Twain

"Stop," Jonas said. "I need to stop, damnit."

Monique glanced in both directions; as far as she could tell, no one seemed to be watching them. She took a few more steps, and pulled Jonas into the shade of a narrow alley, where they were at least partially hidden from view. Jonas leaned back against the wall, arms wrapped around his chest, his breathing shallow and ragged.

"I know you're hurt," Monique said. "But look at it this way–the pain means you're still alive."

Jonas shot her a dark look–not the first since their miraculous escape from Hanssen Scientific.

"That's more than the others can say," he growled. His bitter tone cut deep into Monique's conscience. But Monique stood her ground, and returned his hard stare.

"I know. We're both hurt, as far as that goes. It wasn't easy to leave Bhima behind, either."

"Please," Jonas spat. "You've known him for a few weeks. That was my entire life we left back there!"

Monique could see the pain etched on his face, though she had no way to distinguish between his physical pain, and the emotional torment that was likely an even greater burden. Her mind went back to the explosion–an instant of malevolence that had flung them both away from the building, and into a parked car–ending together in a heap at the curb. Incredibly, she was largely unhurt, beyond a few bruises and scrapes. It was harder to tell with Jonas, who had remained on the ground next to her, curled in a ball and moaning softly. Glass was strewn across the sidewalk; Monique had been careful to avoid it as she struggled to her feet.

She had glanced about, frantically, for any sign of Bhima–or of Katherine, Brent, or Kahli. She saw none of them. She replayed the events again in her mind–the others hadn't come through the door, and must have been thrown back into the building. She looked to the entrance; the now-raging inferno made it impossible to get back in–or even to see past the door. A chill gripped her spine, working its way up her neck and to a growing lump in her throat. But even worse–she felt an acute sense of loss– of a broken connection. Despite the shock, the pain, the disorientation–she felt it, deep inside, strong despite her otherwise still-jumbled thoughts.

Bhima was gone.

She squeezed her eyes shut, and took several slow, deep breaths. The heat from the fire wrapped its tendrils around her, as if to draw her toward the flame. A thin film of sweat had broken out on her skin–though whether from the heat, or her growing sense of guilt, she couldn't be sure.

At that moment, a low, guttural wail had come from Jonas. Monique turned; he was up on one knee, fists clenched, eyes searching. He had also suffered some cuts and scrapes, including a cut along his scalp. Blood ran down his forehead in a few small rivulets; one had reached the bridge of his nose.

"Katherine!" Jonas shouted. Monique winced; she could see the devastation in his eyes. Even worse, she could *feel* the pain emanating from his body–like an apparition, trying to wrap its cold, dead fingers around its next victim.

She shook her head, trying to clear her own senses.

"Doctor Hanssen, we need to get away from here."

Jonas turned to her, eyes wide.

"What? They're still in there!" Jonas rose to his feet, grimacing as he stood; it was clearly an effort for him to stand up straight.

"I know," Monique said. "Believe me, I know. But there's nothing we can do. No way back in. And Pax could come out, or others could arrive. Any minute."

"Screw them. We need to find Kat. And Kahli. And Brent." Jonas spoke through clenched teeth.

"Jonas," Monique said. "Listen to me. There's no way we can get in there."

"Then use your power, like you did with Pax! Pull them out. Do something!" Jonas had grabbed her by the arm, and spun her to face the building. Monique turned her head to look at him, returning his hard stare.

"It doesn't work like that. I'm sorry. I can't affect things that far away—especially things I can't even see."

Plus—I know Bhima's gone. They're all gone.

She watched as Jonas processed her words—eyes still wide, jaw set. Finally, he shook his head.

"I can't just walk away." His voice had taken a softer tone—almost apologetic, Monique thought.

She took another look around. There was a small but growing crowd across the street. Traffic had stopped—empty cars were now blocking the road on either side. But she heard no sirens; as of yet, there was no emergency response in sight. She knew it was just a matter of time, though. As much as she hated the thought, they needed to leave. Soon.

She decided to change tacks.

"No one is asking you to walk away from all of this," she said. "I know it's your life's work. But there isn't anything else we can do here, or for the others. We have to go on. They would want that. I know Bhima would. None of them would blame you for that."

Jonas jerked his head around; a fire had re-kindled in his eyes.

"Blame me?" He jabbed a finger at her, stopping just a fraction of an inch from her nose.

"Blame me? This is your doing! Pax was here to make a deal with me, and you screwed it all up! You demanded to leave—you killed that other woman—you forced him into a corner! I've got nothing to hide. *You* leave if you want—I'm staying here and waiting for the police!"

The sudden force of his reaction took her by surprise—but only for a moment. Time was running out, for both of them. And now she had his attention.

"I suppose you could wait for the police–assuming they get here before Pax or his friends do," she said. "And assuming the police ignore the extortion claims against you."

"You have no idea what you're talking about. It was a business deal. We were just negotiating our fair share."

"And your business partners negotiate with guns, and poison darts? You need some new business partners."

This time, Jonas took a few seconds to respond.

"It's a big asteroid." He spoke in a low voice, almost mumbling the words. Monique wasn't entirely sure she heard him correctly.

"I may have underestimated its value to GRI," he added.

Monique caught her breath; there was a sudden tightening in her stomach.

"GRI?" Monique asked. "Pax works for GRI?"

"I assume so. They fund our research. We found the asteroid for them."

Monique's head began to spin; her urgency meter had just ratcheted up another notch. Or two.

"The same GRI that all but owns the media?" she said. "The one that manufactures all the police- and fire-bots that are on their way? The largest corporate conglomerate in the world? *That* GRI? We really do need to get out of here."

Now Jonas was silent, though his stare still spoke volumes.

One last shot, Monique thought.

"Jonas, we barely know each other," she said. "And I know we're both still in shock. But if we want any chance of ever getting to know each other–of understanding why I'm here, and how I might be able to help you and your research–then we need to go. Now. You can scream at me all you want after we're a couple of miles away."

The look in Jonas's eyes had softened–ever so slightly. He winced again as he relaxed his stance.

"Why do you even care?" he said. "Why don't you just go? You don't need me. I'll just slow you down."

"I told you, I saw you in my vision. Crazy or not, we're somehow connected. And I'll be damned if I'm not going to see this through. Especially now. My visions are connected to you–and to your research. I can feel it. There is a purpose behind them, and we're going to figure it out. To make sure our friends didn't die for nothing. And to hold GRI accountable."

Her words had finally broken through. Jonas nodded in response, though perhaps as much in resignation as agreement.

"Let's go then," he said. "Before I change my mind."

She did one last thing before they left–she tossed both of their net-phones into the burning building. It was going to be hard enough to hide from a company like GRI; she had no intention of making it any easier for them.

They left the scene as quickly as they dared–and as quickly as Jonas's injuries would allow him to travel. Few words were spoken as they walked; they had traveled several blocks before they heard the sirens. But no one had followed them, as far as she could tell. So when Jonas finally asked to stop, Monique had felt safe enough to step into the alley for a brief rest.

Jonas pressed his back against the building, eyes closed. She wondered if Pax had broken any ribs with the punch he had landed–but decided now wasn't the time to ask.

"Can you tell me about your research?" she asked. "How long have you been looking for asteroids?"

"I don't give a shit about asteroids," Jonas replied. "That was GRI's research. Mine is completely different."

Jonas went silent again, seemingly lost in thought. Monique couldn't tell if he was weighing his options, or just unwilling to share any more.

"What do–" Monique began.

"Dark matter," Jonas broke in. "I've spent my entire adult life hunting for dark matter. Katherine was helping me. She was my good luck charm. We had an incredible breakthrough, just a few weeks ago. We were out celebrating, just last night.

"Hard to believe," he added, almost to himself.

Dark matter, Monique thought. She was familiar with the concept. Could dark matter be the link between them?

She put her hand on his shoulder; Jonas looked up at her, his face still a grim mask.

In that moment, a new thought struck her.

"Jonas, can I ask a favor?" He was still looking at her; she didn't wait for an answer.

"Every time I've found someone from my visions, the vision has shifted. The woman I found in Cairo told me that you would be the last one. So I'm wondering what the visions will show me now. It may help us understand why we're together, and what we need to do."

She pulled her hand away from him and stepped to the side, turning to lean her back against the wall next to him. A month ago, there was no way she could have reached her inner place while outside–in broad daylight, in a strange city, and even stranger circumstances. But she was a different person now–stronger, and more connected. To her place, and to her power. She liked her chances.

"Would you keep an eye out for us while I try this?" she asked. "Shake me if someone sees us?"

Jonas continued to stare at her–she could only imagine what must be going through his mind.

"What the hell," he said. "Go ahead. I need a few more minutes anyway. Just don't take too long."

Monique leaned her head back against the wall, closing her eyes and beginning her slow, rhythmic breathing. Nothing happened at first–the surroundings continued to intrude on her conscience. The biggest distraction turned out to be Jonas–she could hear his labored breathing as he leaned against the wall next to her. And beyond that, there wasn't the same feeling of *connectedness* that she had with Bhima. Or the others. Jonas was a stranger–and not one she could necessarily trust. In fact, she realized, there was a chance he'd be gone when she opened her eyes again. But she pressed ahead, nonetheless. She may not trust him, but she did trust her instincts–and her visions. And he had been in them.

Her mind began to settle, and she let go of thought and time, focusing on the Now. The alley, the sounds, the city–even Jonas–began to wash away as she sank toward her inner place. The quiet peace was a welcome relief; she absorbed the energy it gave her, like a soft, cleansing rain.

The events of barely an hour ago, however, still lingered at the edge of her conscience. But instead of grief, she felt only a hardened sense of purpose. At her core, she strummed with potential–for things yet to be achieved.

She saw a faint light, and prepared for The Leap. But instead of approaching, the light remained still, just within her range of perception. Then it pulsed, ever so slightly. The realization struck her like an unwelcome truth, laid bare to all her senses.

Jonas.

After a moment's hesitation, she reached out, like she had with Bhima. He was separate–alone–yet somehow, connected. She felt his essence drift to her, become part of her. Then the dancing light appeared, and they made The Leap.

The power of the vision startled her–not in the content so much as the intensity–the sights, sounds, and smells. She saw a small town by the sea, plain yet strikingly beautiful, its landscape a slow transition from snow-capped mountains to forests, fields, and sandy beach. A multitude of low-slung buildings were capped by colorful roofs, sprinkled across the countryside like confetti. A few taller buildings sprouted near the shoreline. She heard traffic, birds, and the wind through the trees. As she took a breath, there was the slightest taste of salt in the air.

Her vision this time was in the third-person–Monique saw herself, standing at the edge of a small stream; Jonas stood on the other side. A swirling funnel of light danced between them. It stretched upward, as far as the eye could see. It was solid, then opaque–shifting and changing states as it danced, moving in a way that was unpredictable and yet perfectly choreographed. It spoke of power and elegance, of infinite specks of light, acting as one. A strange cacophony of sounds filled her head–it reminded her of the noise in a large concert hall, just before the show was to begin.

Monique marveled at the visual spectacle–but it was just a fraction of what she perceived. Deep inside, the vision tugged at her–far beyond what she had felt before. Her sense of purpose had redoubled–and doubled again. She was the boulder, now barreling down the hill at near-breakneck speed. She was the *answer*. She could feel it. All that remained was to understand the question.

"Monique!" She heard her name; it seemed to come from both inside and outside her vision.

"Monique! Wake up!" She opened her eyes; Jonas had grasped her by the shoulder and was shaking her, gently.

Monique took a moment to regain her bearings. They were still in the alley, still mostly hidden from view. No one seemed to have spotted them, and she heard no sirens or other obvious signs of pursuit. She turned to Jonas.

"Sorry," she said. "Give me a second. That was more intense than usual."

"No kidding. I was there, in case you didn't notice."

"What? Do you mean in the vision with me? You followed me?"

"I wouldn't say followed. *Dragged* might be a better word. I closed my eyes for a second, and suddenly I'm swept through the darkness into some small town. We were standing at a stream. And a funnel of light."

The two of them stared at each other; Monique wasn't quite sure what to say next. Jonas also seemed at a loss for words. Finally, Jonas leaned back against the wall again, head in his hands.

"What the hell am I *doing* here?"

Monique could only watch as Jonas continued to struggle, caught in the maelstrom of recent events. She felt her own emptiness where Bhima should have been–though clearly not on the order of Jonas's feelings for Katherine, or his team. She wondered how long Jonas and Katherine had been together.

Still, she had a purpose to fulfill–now more than ever–and lingering in this alley wasn't going to get her there.

"We shouldn't stay here too much longer," she said. "Any ideas where we might go? Somewhere safe?"

"If you're asking about the place in your vision, then no. I've never seen it."

"Me neither," she said.

"But I recognized that funnel."

"Really?" Now he had her full attention.

Jonas dropped his hands back down to his sides, taking a few more shallow breaths.

"I think it's dark matter. Crazy as it sounds, I used to have dreams like that as a kid–small particles dancing in a tornado like that. It's been years since I've had that dream, but I remember it like it was yesterday."

"Was anyone else in your dreams, back then?"

"No. Not that I recall."

Monique contemplated his words, and the implications. What if this was her purpose? To help him find dark matter?

No. It didn't feel right. There was more to it, she was sure. This was more than just a science junket.

"And I felt something, too," Jonas added. Now he looked right at her, his face a mix of loss and confusion.

"It's hard to describe," he said. "Like an *intention.* But that's not the right word. It was compelling me, somehow. Telling me to find it."

"I feel the same thing," she said. "A purpose. You and I are meant to do this. Not just to find dark matter. But to find the *purpose* of dark matter. A purpose, I think, that's going to change the world."

Jonas looked at her for several seconds. She had no way to know what he was thinking, but the truth in her words seemed to strike a chord; he pushed himself away from the wall.

"We need to go see Kaito Matsui. He's a friend–a friend we can trust. He can help us with the dark matter questions, and the vision. He may even know where this town is."

"Is he far from here?" Monique asked. "If he's a good friend of yours, they may already be there, waiting."

"It's not too far. And I doubt they've connected the two of us yet. Though I'm sure they're already searching my place, and maybe yours as well. But they won't be at Kaito's. Not yet."

The words were like a punch to the gut; Monique froze as the realization struck her full force.

Tabia. And the kids. Oh god, no.

And she had thrown their net-phones into the fire.

"Jonas, we need to go. *Now.* I have friends at my house. Children. I need to find a phone. *Please.*" She heard the suddenly frantic tone in her voice; she could only hope it didn't push Jonas even farther away.

Jonas only hesitated for an instant.

"It's less than a mile to Kaito's. Let's go."

FORTY FIVE

*An imbalance between rich and poor is the oldest
and most fatal ailment of all republics.*

– Plutarch

The press conference was entirely scripted–from the location, to the attendees, to the professionally-crafted remarks. They had chosen the GRI boardroom to make the announcement; it was convenient, it was well-equipped, and it was home turf. Rudy had called the head of GRI's media division, and she had agreed to send an appropriate cadre of reporters. The GRI staff moved with its usual speed and precision– led by his one-machine whirlwind, Grace. Less than two hours after his call with the Chairman, they were ready to begin.

Speed was important to their plan. The fire in Honolulu had yet to be picked up by any national feeds; Rudy wanted to be out in front of it, to control the story arc. Especially once the global significance became clear. So the sooner they made the announcement, the better.

The two hour window had also been just enough time to go home and see his family. He had explained the situation to Victoria–or at least, the Consortium-altered version of the situation. To his surprise, she offered to join him for the press conference. He took her up on the offer–she had been there, by coincidence, when he had been hijacked by the press the morning of Carl's death. She had been a calming presence, and the interview had gone extremely well. So she was next to him now, dressed perfectly for the part, as he walked to the podium.

It was time for the show.

"GRI family, friends, and members of the press—thank you for coming on such short notice," Rudy began. "And for the few of you that may not know her, let me introduce my wife, Victoria Dersch. I have a short announcement, and then I will take a few questions."

Rudy paused, looking briefly to Victoria before continuing.

"Today began with plans for a world-changing, celebratory announcement—one that would impact every man, woman and child on this planet. Unfortunately, that celebration has turned to tragedy. Earlier today, we lost several members of our GRI family."

In short order, Rudy recounted the explosion at Hanssen Scientific, and the likely loss of Professor Hanssen and his entire scientific team. He paused again, and Victoria put a hand to his shoulder. He gave her a somber nod.

"What makes this especially tragic," Rudy continued, "Is what I hold here in my hand." Rudy lifted a stack of papers from the podium, waving them in the direction of the cameras.

"A discovery made by Professor Hanssen, barely twenty-four hours ago. His team christened it the *mother lode*—a near-perfect asteroid from the depths of the asteroid belt. Early estimates put its value at over *one-quadrillion* dollars."

The buzz in the room was palpable; they had purposefully held back news of the asteroid, even from the GRI staff and media in attendance. First and foremost, it was to avoid the chance of a leak; but also, for the authentic reaction that now spread like wildfire across the room. The plan had worked to perfection; Rudy put the papers back down on the podium as he waited for the din to subside.

Time to set the hook.

"I wish we could celebrate this discovery in the way it so richly deserves. Professor Hanssen should be standing here with me. Instead, we have an unspeakable emptiness. And several unanswered questions. How does a lab full of computers explode into a raging inferno? And just hours after what may be the most valuable discovery in modern history?"

Rudy paused again, letting the implications float in the air. The low murmurings from the crowd continued as he leaned forward and gripped the podium, trading his somber look for a hardened scowl.

"We don't have the answers to these questions. Yet. But I can promise you this—we will do everything in our power to ensure that justice is served. We have already provided the data we have to the appropriate law enforcement authorities. And we will cooperate fully in the ongoing investigation—until those responsible for this heinous act are apprehended, and held accountable. *Nothing* is more important to us than our GRI family. And that includes a quadrillion-dollar asteroid."

Rudy paused again, for effect. The room was silent.

"I have time for a few questions—though please understand, this is an ongoing investigation."

As planned, the first question came from a GRI media correspondent at the front of the room—shouted at a pitch and a pace that overwhelmed the others trying to be heard.

"What leads you to believe this was more than just an accident? Have the authorities confirmed that the explosion was deliberate?"

"No," Rudy said. "As I described earlier, the explosion occurred just a few hours ago. Fire-bots are on the scene, but no definitive determination of the cause has yet been made."

Let me say this, though," Rudy continued. "That was a GRI-funded facility. We are intimately familiar with the equipment on site. And with the personnel. There is absolutely no reason, given the work being done, for a combustible substance of any kind to be at that location. And Professor Hanssen was a careful, deliberate man. He would never have allowed it.

"Yes, the woman in the blue scarf." Rudy selected a tall woman in the front row, just as they had orchestrated.

"Exactly when and how did you learn about the existence of this asteroid?"

Rudy nodded, flipping through a few pages of notes before answering. Best not to look *too* scripted.

"Late yesterday afternoon, Professor Hanssen notified us of his discovery, through his liaison here at GRI, Rolland Hughes. Rolland is a senior executive in our Space business. The data initially came to one of our Vice Presidents in Research and Development, Lester White. And I want to take a moment here to thank both of them for bringing it directly to my attention.

"With a discovery of this magnitude, we immediately launched two probes to stake our claim, as per the international protocols for asteroid ownership. Both are scheduled to arrive well inside the sixty-day deadline.

"I can only speculate that someone hoped we didn't yet have the data. That they could keep the discovery under wraps, and claim the asteroid for themselves. But again, that's conjecture on my part. The authorities will conduct a full investigation, and they will have all the resources of GRI at their disposal."

Another reporter jumped into the fray.

"Do you know how many people were in the building? Were there any others besides the Hanssen Scientific staff?" Rudy shook his head, collecting his notes back into a single stack.

"That's a question for the authorities on site. I can tell you that Hanssen Scientific employed a total of three staff–Professor Hanssen along with two others. Our attempts to contact those three have thus far been unsuccessful."

Rudy raised his hand, glancing again at Victoria.

"That's all I have time for, I'm afraid. We will provide additional information as soon as we have it. Our press office has additional data on the asteroid for those that may be interested. Thank you."

Rudy led Victoria from the podium, escorting her out the boardroom door, through the lobby, and outside to Bond, who was waiting at the curb. They slid into the back seat; Bond already had the instructions to take them home.

"Well done," Victoria said, placing a hand on his knee. "But bittersweet. I'm so sorry about Professor Hanssen and the others. Had you ever met him?"

"No. But Rolland told me he was a stand-up guy. Very loyal to us–and to his team."

"Maybe you should name that asteroid after him."

Rudy smiled, putting his hand on top of hers.

Maybe we should.

Before he could respond to Victoria's suggestion, a chirp came from his net-phone, alerting him to a new message. The sound was becoming all-too-familiar; it was from the Consortium.

"Go ahead," Victoria said. "I'm sure it's important."

Rudy shifted slightly in his seat, using his left hand to squeeze Victoria's knee, as his other hand activated the net-phone's secure channel. He accessed the message; the words flashed on the screen, disappearing almost as soon as he finished reading them:

Hanssen and Durand alive.
Pax in pursuit.
Plans unchanged.

"Everything okay?" Victoria had put her own hand on top of his.

"Just an update on Hanssen," Rudy said. "Still no body. So they haven't officially declared anyone dead yet."

Rudy turned to look out the window, caught in the tangle of his own thoughts. He was fully committed now; he would need the full resources of GRI. Not just for Iran, but to deal with Jonas Hanssen. And the Durand woman. They were loose ends, to be sure, but nothing he couldn't handle.

Whether he could continue to handle Victoria, however, remained to be seen.

Acknowledgments

After twenty-five-plus years in the offices and boardrooms of corporate America, I thought I had seen it all. But worse, I was beginning to feel like I knew it all. So I decided to write a book. Boy, has that straightened me out.

It's an incredible thing, the transition from an executive and management consultant whom others seek out for advice, to possibly the least knowledgeable writer on the planet. Perhaps other debut authors have felt the same way. But something happens when you let go of *teaching mode*, and enter the world of *learning mode*. It's liberating, to know nothing! For me, it was a magical journey of self discovery.

So not surprisingly, my first novel required an army of supporters. My journey began with a Kickstarter project, launched to raise money for research and publishing costs. In truth, it was also a test to see whether anyone actually believed I could write fiction. Turns out, a few people did. I'd like to particularly thank Karen & Fred Ford, Peg & Mike Long, Diane & Jeff Hamilton, Mala Kustermann, and of course, Bill Purdy, for their early and unwavering support.

I've lost track of the revision count for this first volume of the Dark Matters saga. Jennifer Ford, Scott Dow, and Eric Spiegel were early manuscript readers, providing invaluable comments on plot, character development, and writing style. I was also fortunate to find Patrick LoBrutto, who agreed to edit the entire manuscript with me. His client list reads like a who's-who of bestselling authors–but I doubt many of them monopolized six months of his time like I did. Kudos as well to Tamara Cribley of The Deliberate Page, who provided final interior edits and formatting. And what a cover! Thanks to Fiona Jayde Media for the incredible art work.

Last but not least, an enormous *thank you* to my family, and in particular my wife, Melissa. She allowed me the time it took to make this dream a reality. For that, I'm forever grateful.

About the Author

Michael Dow spent over twenty-five years in corporate America, with a business career that has run the gamut from consultant to CEO. He has worked in companies ranging from start-up to more than one billion dollars in revenues, and in locations from Washington DC to Saudi Arabia. Dark Matters is his first work of fiction (though competitors have accused him of writing fiction for years). He currently lives in Traverse City, Michigan, with his wife and two teenage daughters.

Have a thought, question, or feedback? Mike would love to hear from you! Reach him at mike@darkmattersbook.com.

If you want to be the first to know when the next Dark Matters book will be released, please join the email subscriber list.

No spam, never sold, never shared. Ever. I promise.

www.darkmattersbook.com/email-list